The Devil's Magus

By

Marius Creed

MAPLE
PUBLISHERS

The Devil's Magus

Author: Marius Creed

Copyright © 2025 Marius Creed

The right of Marius Creed to be identified as author of this work has been asserted by the author in accordance with section 77 and 78 of the Copyright, Designs and Patents Act 1988.

First Published in 2025

ISBN 978-1-83538-787-0 (Paperback)
 978-1-83538-788-7 (Hardback)
 978-1-83538-789-4 (E-Book)

Book Cover and Layout by:
 White Magic Studios
 www.whitemagicstudios.co.uk

Published by:
 Maple Publishers
 Fairbourne Drive, Atterbury,
 Milton Keynes,
 MK10 9RG, UK
 www.maplepublishers.com

A CIP catalogue record for this title is available from the British Library.

CONTENTS

Foreword

My fascination with horror began in adolescence – a time when the imagination is fertile ground for dark wonders. As a teenager, I was thoroughly and deliciously terrified by the novels of *Dennis Wheatley*, the chilling pages of Dracula by Bram Stoker, and the macabre tales of *Edgar Allan Poe* and *H. P. Lovecraft*. These stories etched themselves into my psyche and kindled a lasting love for the supernatural and the arcane.

As the years passed, that early spark grew into a deeper, more complex admiration for the horror genre and its many voices. I was drawn to the nightmarish visions of *Stephen King* and *Clive Barker*, the creeping dread spun by *James Herbert* and the darkly whimsical imagination of *Neil Gaiman*. Alongside them stood the mythic grandeur of *J. R. R. Tolkien* and *Ursula K. Le Guin*, and the intricate, brutal realms of *George R. R. Martin*. My bookshelves swelled, too, with the speculative dreams of science fiction masters: *Robert Heinlein, Isaac Asimov, Ray Bradbury, Philip K. Dick,* and *Kurt Vonnegut*.

It was in the late 1990s, while living and working in the United States, that the idea for *The Devil's Magus* first took shape. My intent was simple – though daunting – to craft a modern homage to the storytelling spirit of Dennis Wheatley, whose influence still lingered like incense in the corners of my imagination. Yet, like many creative pursuits, the novel moved at a glacial pace. Demands of career and life conspired to keep it unfinished. Part I was completed in the early 2000s before being shelved once again.

Only in 2010, after retiring and returning home to the UK, did the idea begin to call to me once more. But even then, time slipped away – until, in the strange stillness of the Covid-19 lockdown, I found the quiet I needed to return to the work in earnest. Part II came to life in those cloistered months, and by 2023, the final act was complete. What followed was an equally lengthy labour: the editing, refining, and reworking of the manuscript – shaping it into a story worthy of the genre that first captured my imagination.

Now, after decades of intermittent effort, I offer **The Devil's Magus** to the world. It is a novel born of many influences and eras, a tribute to the books and authors who made me a lifelong reader and, eventually, a writer.

I can only hope that readers find in its pages a glimmer of the magic, mystery, and menace that once thrilled me – and that I have, in some small way, done justice to the legacy of Dennis Wheatley.

Marius Creed
June 2025

Part One
Blood Oath

Virginia – 27 March, 1:55 AM

A split second later, the windows above their heads exploded with a deafening roar, showering them in a lethal cascade of jagged glass. The night erupted into chaos as freezing, hurricane-force winds tore through the air, shrieking like a banshee and slashing at their exposed skin. Instinctively, they threw their arms up, shielding their faces, their cries drowned by the fury of the storm. Mark lunged for Sam, pulling her into his arms as shards sliced through the air around them. With desperate strength, he dragged her down the steps, away from the tempest emanating from the shattered porch, and toward the lake's edge.

The unholy wind howled above their heads, a malevolent force that seemed intent on their annihilation. Sam sobbed uncontrollably; her screams lost in the maelstrom. Mark wept openly, his tears mingling with the blood trickling from a gash on his cheek. He clutched Sam tighter, his every movement driven by sheer survival instinct. Together, they stumbled and fell, their bodies battered by the relentless assault of nature's wrath.

And then, as abruptly as it had begun, the wind subsided. The silence that followed was eerie, as though the earth itself held its breath in the wake of the chaos. Mark led Sam to a weathered bench overlooking the now placid, moonlit water. They collapsed onto it, their breaths ragged and their bodies still trembling from the ordeal. The distant, low hum of the generator provided the only sound, a faint reminder of normalcy in a world that had suddenly turned upside down.

Mark turned to Sam, his heart shattering at the sight of her tear-streaked face, her eyes glazed and unseeing. Blood streaked her pale skin, the crimson stark against the moonlight. Rage erupted within him, a white-hot wrath that burned through his veins. His hands clenched into fists as he stared into the void, his voice a raw, guttural growl. "Worsley," he spat, the name a venomous curse. "He's behind this. All of it. That monster... he's evil incarnate."

He trembled with fury, his body shaking as he fought to contain the maelstrom of emotions threatening to consume him. "He must be stopped," Mark hissed, his voice trembling with conviction. "No prison, no punishment is enough for what he's done. He must die. I will find a way. I swear it. I'll kill him."

His words pierced the haze clouding Sam's mind. She turned to him, her tearful eyes locking onto his. For a moment, she simply stared, her expression unreadable. Then, slowly, she shifted her gaze back to the lodge, its darkened silhouette ominous against the night sky. Sam shuddered, her body wracked by a fresh wave of sobs. "Yes," she whispered, her voice barely audible but laced with a chilling resolve. Her tears continued to fall, but her face hardened, a flicker of unrelenting determination glinting in her eyes. "And I want to be there when it happens." Her voice steadied, cold and deliberate. "We have to end him. Together."

Chapter 1

A Quiet Storm

Norfolk, Virginia – 24 March, 3:15 PM local
Mark glanced at his watch and dismissed his small oceanography tutor group. "See you next week," he said, his voice carrying a practiced warmth. "And enjoy your weekend field trip." He received the predictable ribald responses and chuckled. "Don't get seasick!"

He watched them shuffle out, their laughter trailing down the hall. The forecast was not terrible, but he did not envy them. Even with spring approaching, the converted coaster they would be using for sediment research would be damp and bone-jarringly cold. Mark shivered just thinking about its incessant rolling – a torment he had endured during his own student days.

Then, without warning, a brutal, searing pain knifed through his chest. Mark staggered, gripping the desk as the room tilted around him. It was not just pain – it was something alive, writhing beneath his skin like molten wires tightening around his ribs. His breath hitched. Then, as suddenly as it struck, it was gone. Vanished. But the echo of it – something dark, something wrong – remained.

"How did you do that?"

Mark turned sharply to see Donna Purdy leaning in the doorway, her sharp brown eyes glinting with curiosity. "Do what?" he asked, masking his surprise with forced nonchalance.

"The pencil," she replied, stepping inside. "It spun by itself."

Mark followed her gaze to his desk. A single pencil lay there, still faintly rotating. A shiver trickled down his spine. "Oh, that? Just a trick I've been practicing." He waved it off, suddenly self-conscious. "Didn't realize I had an audience."

Her lips curved into a slow smile, teasing. "So, not only a renowned oceanographer but a magician too. Tell me, Mr. Benedict, what other secrets are you hiding?"

Mark shrugged, brushing off her playful tone, but Donna was not done. She stepped closer, her voice dropping into a conspiratorial whisper. "Do it again. I'll figure out how it's done."

He hesitated, unsure if her fascination was genuine. Donna was not his best student, but she was far from dull. Her allure was not merely her beauty; she knew how to wield her charm. She exuded confidence with her flowing blonde hair and impeccably tailored clothes. Mark had long been aware of her suggestive glances.

"Donna," he began carefully, "what do you really want?"

She tilted her head, her smile deepening. "Help with understanding the Ekman spiral. And maybe dinner? My roommate's out. I will get Chinese, you bring wine. We can mix business with pleasure."

Mark sighed, the weight of her insinuation heavy in the air. "I'm afraid I have plans tonight. Besides, relationships with students must remain professional, you know that."

Her disappointment was brief, replaced by a sly smirk. "Your loss," she said, tossing her hair as she left. But Mark could not shake the unease her offer left behind. Something about Donna always felt like playing with fire.

Well, the tutorial did not go too badly, he thought as he rose and arranged the chairs beneath the whiteboard. Mark moved to the window and looked over the campus of ODU. Old Dominion lacked the traditional setting of his alma mater, William and Mary, but it was a strangely agreeable environment. Unspectacular but comfortable.

Glancing down, he spotted Donna striding toward the car park, four hopeful males in tow. Doubtless, she would salvage her evening to her entire satisfaction.

He returned to his desk, methodically clearing away his papers and collecting the assignments for weekend marking. There was little excitement in his life right now. In general, he was content. He enjoyed his work, loved his beach condominium on the bay, and the occasional recreational fishing that relaxed him. Twenty-seven years old and still single, Mark understood why he was an obvious target.

Slim, blue-eyed, sandy-haired, of medium height and somewhat shy, he thought he was rather ordinary. Yet he had been told he possessed boyish good looks and that his natural reticence added an air of mystery that made him attractive. However, despite many opportunities, there were no women in his life at present, and he was not looking for any.

Mark had never been good at meeting women. He hated the 'meat market' feel of nightclubs and singles bars – the music always too loud for conversation, the social manoeuvring unnatural. He could never find the clever opening lines that they seemed to expect. He was just plain uncomfortable with it. He preferred meeting women through common interests or by chance, and even then, he was too shy to initiate anything. There had been a couple of brief encounters last year, where the women had taken the lead, but they had either proved unsatisfactory or simply faded.

Even allowing for his relative youth, he suspected he might never marry. The problem was simple – but tragic. He was still in love with his brother's wife.

A fresh wave of molten agony surged through him. Mark sucked in a breath, gripping the desk hard enough to whiten his knuckles. The sensation slithered away, leaving him rattled, breathless. His eyes fell on the pencil. Without thinking, he reached out and flicked it.

It spun. More than it should have. More than was natural.

He grabbed his bag and headed out. His medical appointment would not wait. But something told him – something deep in his bones – that his body was not the only thing about to change.

Chapter 2
Memories

V*irginia Beach – 24 March, 3.55 PM local*
Sam felt the tension in her shoulders begin to dissipate as she left the bookstore, the familiar bell above the door jingling faintly behind her. She waved to her colleague, Meg, who called out, "Bye, Sam! Have a nice weekend."

"What weekend? I'm working both afternoons!" she replied with a smile, raising her hand in farewell.

Financially sound, Samantha Benedict had only taken the job to help take her mind off her failing marriage and was mildly surprised when she found she really enjoyed the rather mundane work. Prior to dropping out of college she was a student of English Literature. She particularly liked the open, roomy and friendly environment of *Barnes and Noble*. The store was large enough to be termed a warehouse, but it managed to maintain a personal touch that welcomed the wide-ranging community that crossed its threshold. The cozy interior was her refuge, its polished wooden shelves and soft green carpets, a world apart from her failing marriage. The smell of fresh coffee from the in-store *Starbucks* mingled with the faint aroma of new books, creating a comforting cocoon. It wasn't much, but it was enough to distract her – at least temporarily – from the gnawing ache of loneliness.

Sliding into her car, Sam leaned her head back for a moment, letting out a long sigh. The day had been a steady stream of customers – some chatty, some curt – but she didn't mind. She liked the rhythm of it, the way the familiar environment of the bookstore steadied her in a life that felt anything but stable.

As she navigated the early rush-hour traffic along Virginia Beach Boulevard, her mind drifted to James. Their marriage had begun with such promise, a whirlwind of shared dreams and stolen kisses, but somewhere along the way, it had all unravelled. She had replayed the arguments in her mind a thousand times, searching for the moment things had gone irreparably wrong. Was it her fault? Or had James always been destined to drift away?

She thought back to the circumstances in which they had met. It had started at college with Mark, James' brother. Studying English Literature at William and Mary, Sam met Mark Benedict, a math major while out jogging. She had asked him the time, bemoaned the fact that she was going to be late for class, and he had joined her on the run back. They subsequently crossed paths on campus occasionally and progressed to a gradual friendship.

Mark was initially very shy, but she had worked hard to put him at ease and an effortless rapport had soon developed between them. They became inseparable as best friends but nothing romantic ever blossomed. Mark never tried to push it, and Sam would not have allowed it at that time anyway as she had a steady boyfriend back home.

It was not long before Sam became aware of the strange talents of the Benedict brothers, which would ultimately affect their lives forever. It had started when she locked her keys in her car while out with Mark. They had been to the movies to see '*The Witches of Eastwick*' chosen because the John Updike novel was part of one of her assignments that term. She smiled inwardly as she recalled the event.

"Well? Come on. Give it to me. What did you think?" Sam had pestered him as they left the theatre.

"No. You go first," he'd said, being non-committal as usual.

"I really enjoyed it. I didn't expect the book to translate easily to the screen, but they did a good job. The acting was great. Jack Nicholson's a trip; he cracks me up," she said happily.

"That wasn't acting – that was Jack Nicholson playing Jack Nicholson like he always does," Mark teased, "but he certainly had fun with the part. Personally, I'm more into Michelle Pfeiffer, though Cher looks incredible for her age too."

"In your dreams, buddy," she had laughed, "but the girls did do a good job as the sexually repressed females. John Updike isn't exactly known for his sympathetic portrayal of women."

They had reached her car, and she began searching for the keys. She fumbled in her purse for a few seconds when he noticed and pointed out that the keys were still in the ignition. "Damn Sam, you no-mind!" she had scolded herself, "This is the third time I've locked the keys in the car. Jeez! What an idiot! Let's walk over to *Java Joe's* for a coffee, and I'll call *Triple A*.

"Wait, let me try."

That was when she witnessed his bizarre talent for the first time. Mark had used his special gift to unlock the car without a key. He had then opened the door and extracted the keys. Sam remembered being both impressed and confused.

"How did you do that?"

"I don't really know how I do it – I just do it."

"Oh, come on; what do you mean by that?"

"It's hard to explain; in this case I visualised my arm, like a third invisible arm, passing through the car door and then I unlocked it with my unseen hand. I must concentrate, focus on what I want to touch physically and then do it."

"Give me a break! You're just teasing me," she had said. "It's probably something you learned from a car thief! Let's go get a cup of coffee anyway and you can explain more."

"Make sure you lock the car with the key this time."

They had crossed the street to *Java Joe's*. She remembered haranguing him to explain the trick while he insisted that there was no trick involved. He gave another demonstration. First looking around to ensure they were not being observed, he had placed a quarter on the Formica surface and then moved it around the table without touching it.

"Wow!" she had said, "You're good! I bet you have a magnet or something." She had looked under the table.

He had then taken an empty water glass from a neighbouring table, turned it over the quarter, and then flipped the coin. By then she was totally puzzled. Finally, she had removed her ring and put it under the glass, removing the quarter. He had flipped the ring over too and she had looked at him uneasily.

"Can you touch me so I can feel it?" she had asked.

He nodded and a few moments later she had felt an unsettling pressing sensation on the tip of her nose.

Sam recalled jerking away. "Whoa! That's creepy; I don't like it."

"Don't worry, I rarely use my gift unless there are practical reasons for it, like the car. Even I find it unnerving. I don't really understand it – I suppose I inherited it."

"Who from?"

"I think it comes from my mother's side of the family. My brother, Jim, jokes that our maternal ancestors were witches and warlocks in England!"

"That's rich – were they from Eastwick?" she laughed, "Does Jim have the ability too?"

"Most definitely! Much more advanced too. His gift is much, much stronger than mine. I can only move very small things that are within reach. His powers are amazing; there must be limits I suppose, but I don't know what they are. I do know that in recent years he never wanted to talk about them; neither did he want to use them."

The coffees arrived and she remembered that Mark had purposely changed the subject. It would not be long before she met his brother.

Sam pulled into her driveway. She sat in the car for a moment, staring at the house that had once been her sanctuary. The memories were everywhere – dinners on the patio, James' laughter reverberating in the hallways. But now the house felt empty, its walls echoing with silence.

Her thoughts turned to the time she first met James. Dear Mark had introduced her to the big brother that she had heard so much about. She fondly remembered James' first words, despite thinking them a little pompous at the time.

"Hello," he had said, "Actually, I prefer James; only Mark is allowed to call me Jim."

They had had a great weekend, all three of them and she had seen immediately why Mark idolised his brother. James was personable and self-confident without any trace of arrogance. Sam was smitten and after James left, she had really missed him. She was delighted when he returned a mere two weeks later and she fell for him hook, line and sinker. It was a whirlwind romance, resulting in a quick engagement and culminating in marriage less than a year later.

Gathering her things, Sam stepped inside. She paused in the entryway, her gaze lingering on a framed photo of her and James from happier times. She traced the edge of the frame with her finger, her heart heavy with regret.

If only she'd fought harder to save what they'd built. But deep down, Sam knew it wasn't just James she missed. It was the version of herself she'd been when she was with him – hopeful, vibrant, and unafraid. Now, she felt like a shadow of that woman, searching for a way back to the light.

Chapter 3

Dark Secrets

outheast England – 24 March, 8:45 PM local
The rain was relentless, soaking Nick to the bone as he trudged down the estate's dark driveway. Shadows from the skeletal trees loomed menacingly, and each step seemed to echo into the silent void.

"What the hell am I doing here?" he muttered under his breath. He knew, of course, he had explained it to Paula less than two hours ago.

"Oh Nick, do you have to go?" she sulked as he had left their bed.

"Yeah. It's a thousand quid for what can be three hours work at most. I can't afford not to go!"

"I wish you'd work regular hours like everyone else." She had sighed and rolled over onto her back, stretching her arms behind her head so that the nipples on her ample breasts pointed upwards invitingly. She knew his weaknesses. "Come on, surely you can spare ten more minutes?"

He had resisted the temptation, following his brain rather than the stirring in his loins. "Listen," he had said, fondly, "You stay right where you are. I'll be back in three or four hours, and then we can bonk to your heart's content, all right?"

So, here he was, soaked to the skin, on a dark, wet and chilly night, walking along the forbidding driveway of some country estate near Amersham. There were better ways to spend a Friday night for sure. Winter seemed longer than usual this year and most of the trees were late in budding. His strange and taciturn employer, Mr. James Benedict, had to recover something from the house that was of vital importance to him, and Nick was there as his minder. James stumbled beside him, clearly struggling with illness. He clutched his chest, his face pale and slick with sweat.

"Not much farther," James gasped, his voice strained.

Nick glanced at him uneasily. "You sure you're up for this? You look like you need a hospital."

James shook his head, his lips a thin, determined line. "This… has to be done tonight."

James was presumably expecting some sort of aggression, but that did not worry Nick, who was adept at handling himself in most situations. He glanced again at his companion who was suffering badly from some illness that caused him to groan and double up in pain every few minutes. James looked like he was perspiring with the effort, an extreme case of shingles, he had explained earlier, refusing to elaborate further, but he looked like he needed medical attention. It was slowing them down significantly; the ten-minute walk from where they had left the car was turning into something approaching twenty minutes. Nick felt he would be later than he thought, going back to Paula.

James groaned again and stopped. "Not much further," he gasped, "let me rest a minute."

Nick's mind returned to the cozy warmth of his Northwood flat and to Paula, snug in his bed. She was the latest in a string of relationships since he had left military life some two years before. Nick was a wanderer, a free spirit, still not quite ready to settle down to the constraints and responsibilities of married life. He had been a Physical Training Instructor in the Navy and was a tall, powerfully built, good-looking man, who never had any problems finding women who were interested in him, but once they started looking for some kind of commitment he would gently withdraw. Paula, a nurse, was different, though. She seemed content with his comings and goings and never seriously tried to control or manipulate him. They had been together three months now and things were good. Maybe she would be the one.

"Let's go," James said, interrupting the mood.

They continued in silence, the only sound was of their own footfalls and the thick, damp, night air muffled these.

Earlier, when they had arrived at the closed entrance to the estate, James had told him to wait in the car while he dealt with it. Leaving the headlights on to provide illumination, Nick had watched him approach the large, ornate wrought iron gates and push against them. They seemed to be locked, but after staring at the latch for a few seconds, James pushed again, and the right-hand gate moved slightly. Nick had slid out of the driver's seat to help, as Benedict was clearly in no condition for physical effort and pushed the gate wide enough for them to squeeze through. They were evidently powered gates, not intended to be opened by hand.

"Perhaps there's a release mechanism somewhere." Nick had ventured, but James was in no mood to search for it.

"Leave the car," he had said, "It's a ten-minute walk at most."

Nick had returned to the car to switch off the lights and lock it. Inevitably, it had started raining as they began the walk along the barely discernible driveway to Sir Giles Worsley's house and neither of them was suitably dressed. The eerie silence was pervading. All noise was somehow smothered by the saturated atmosphere and even the rain made no sound as it landed on the tarmac surface. The invisible trees on either side of them were still, and any water dripping from their leaf-shorn limbs was lost in the soundless night. Nick shivered and turned his collar up.

James knew he could not last much longer. The pain in his chest and trunk were unbearable. Using even his massive powers of concentration, he was only able to partially block the agonizing affliction. At least his companion had the sense to remain quiet. Nicholas Harper had come highly recommended from a small Watford agency that specialized in personal security, with not too many questions asked. He was a big man, but would he be able to handle Giles' German giant? Perhaps, but not the unearthly guardian Giles had left inside the inner chamber.

Another wave of pain, like thousands of red-hot needles, burned at his torso. He could not stifle his cry of anguish and fell to his knees. He pushed away Nick's offered hand as his mind rebuilt the barriers he had erected against the torment. He got up wearily and continued. They were almost there; at least the rain had stopped.

James was pragmatic, he knew his chances of surviving the wrath of Giles Worsley were minimal, but they were not nil and if tonight went according to plan, his outlook might improve significantly. Total freedom from Worsley's influence would enable him to rebuild his life and, perhaps, his marriage to Sam. What a fool he had been to lose her. So infatuated with the purpose, dreams and philosophies of Worsley and flattered by his attentions, he had been blind to the warning signs and threats to his four-year-old marriage. He deeply regretted that he had succumbed to the temptations of achieving vast powers and wished he could hold her now and tell her how sorry he was and how he wanted to make amends. She had returned to their native Virginia almost six months ago and he had heard nothing from her during the last two. After her final, desperate and fruitless plea for him to come home, she had stopped returning his calls and letters. How could he have been so unseeing? Well, he might get a second chance after tonight.

The stark outline of the house loomed out of the darkness. James stopped and summoned his reserves of strength, dipping deep into the dark recesses of his mind to block the pain for just a few more minutes. The building with its raised pillared entrance and majestic front wings, was, by day, very attractive with the soft amber hues of its Cotswold stone construction, but now it looked black, ominous and menacing.

"What now?" Nick asked.

"We knock at the door."

Nick could feel the adrenalin leaking into his veins. What action was about to start? Well, he would find out soon enough. They climbed the steps to the imposing doors. James looked a bit better now that they had arrived. He was tall and probably athletic when he was healthy. Nick watched as his employer coolly tugged on the old-fashioned door pull and a faint ringing could be heard penetrating the depths of the house. Silence returned.

"Don't think anyone's home." Nick said after a few seconds. He pushed the door, which was rock solid. "We won't be getting in this way."

"Oh, Worsley's definitely away but someone or something will be home." James murmured. "Anyway, I can open it."

Nick wondered what he had meant by 'something' and started getting an uncomfortable feeling in his gut. Then James placed his hands on the door and stood motionless for a few seconds. There was a sound of a latch lifting and the door swung open.

In front of them was a large, dimly lit hallway, with thickly piled oriental rugs partially covering a light marble floor. On their right, a wide staircase rose majestically, curving to a galleried first floor. A huge, impressive, but dimmed, crystal chandelier hung from the high ceiling. The walls were clad with intricately carved, dark wood panelling interspersed with occasional wall lamps on ornate sconces. James entered, closely followed by Nick who, heart now pumping vigorously, quickly took in his surroundings. They were alone.

James made straight for the staircase. He was coping with his shingles problem, but it was costing him dearly and he could only manage the stairs one at a time. The wall panels to the right contained a series of shadowy recesses, each permitting nightmarish glimpses of a strange, ugly, gargoyle-like figure carved from what could have been stone or wood. Nick was reluctant to reach in and find out; the whole place was giving him the creeps. They reached the top of the stairs.

Facing them was the same carved panelling with more ominous denizens in the small shoulder-height, dark alcoves. On their immediate right was a wide corridor giving access to the bedrooms of one of the two main wings of the house. To their left, the landing with its ornate wrought-iron balustrade overlooking the hall below extended to the opposite wall, which contained the entrance to the other wing. Wide strips of plush crimson carpet covered polished wooden floors on both the landing and the corridors.

James turned left and shuffled towards the west wing. Nick glanced over the balustrade, down onto the hall below. Still no sign of anyone, but the hairs at the back of his neck were bristling. The tension was high, the atmosphere thick and Nick was not comfortable; the persistent bad feeling that something nasty was about to happen would not go away. James looked nervous also. The corridor they were about to enter, looked to have hollows and doorways capable of human concealment, which did nothing to quell Nick's fears.

Suddenly, from out of the shadows within the first doorway on the right, a giant figure materialised. At six foot four inches, Nick Harper was tall, but the big man now barring their way, towered over him by a good five or six inches.

"That's Hans-Jurgen Moeller, one of Worsley's personal bodyguards," James explained, seemingly unsurprised by his appearance. "He won't say anything intelligible because he damaged his trachea in an unfortunate encounter with a cut-throat razor; so, there is not much point in talking to him. We do need him removed, however."

Nick removed his jacket, handed it to James and approached the huge adversary warily. "Out of the way then, old son." Nick said, purposely ignoring Jame's advice on conversation. He did not need a verbal reply, but talking made him more comfortable. The German, his massive arms folded, stood his ground, looking passive but supremely confident. Nick placed a firm hand on Moeller's arm and immediately regretted it. With surprising speed, Moeller unleashed a short punch to Nick's body, knocking the wind out of him, before lifting and throwing him into the galleried upper hallway.

Nick, lying on his back, gasped with pain. The bastard might have cracked one of his ribs, by the feel of it. He pulled himself to his feet and once more approached the German. Moeller left his sentry's position at the door and moved into the upper hall. This time Nick kept his distance, and they circled each other cautiously. Suddenly Nick darted in and caught the German with two quick and powerful punches to the head before retreating. Moeller grimaced, shook his head and came forward. Two more rapid exchanges went Nick's way until Moeller, realising he was being outboxed, rushed inside and grabbed him, slamming him hard against the wooden panelling of the wall.

Nick found himself locked in a terrifyingly strong bear hug, his arms, pinned to his sides, unable to counteract the enormous force that was squeezing him to death. Nick roared with pain as two more ribs popped, and he brought his knee up hard into the giant's crotch. The German grunted, and Nick gained a brief respite from the crushing force, enough to pull one hand free and thumb-jab him in his right eye. Moeller staggered back, wheezing, distressed sounds coming from his ruined larynx, thankfully releasing Nick from the deathly embrace. Nick stumbled and then quickly pulled himself upright to face the German who he now knew to be too strong for him.

Moeller, one eye closed, leaking pink tears, came for him again. A wicked looking knife appeared in his right hand. Nick reacted immediately, moving sideways but fractionally too late, the knife slammed into the flesh on his left side. The German stepped back grinning. Warm liquid was trickling down the inside of Nick's shirt as Moeller approached again and he desperately searched for some weapon to protect himself. He reached into one of the recesses, his fingers closing around one of the figures which was icy cold to the touch and surprisingly heavy. Moeller approached.

Then, inexplicably, Moeller stopped and looked down at his knife. A moment later it flew out of the German's grasp and across the hall to the top of the stairs. The German glanced fearfully at James, allowing Nick sufficient time to lift the figure and smash it against his foe's head. Moeller jerked backwards and Nick, following up, hit him with the figure again, sending him crashing against the balustrade separating them from the hall below. The giant swayed slowly, red blood gushing into his good eye and down his face, and then some unseen force lifted and pushed him over the balcony. There was a sickening thud as Moeller's heavy body hit the floor below. Nick, his left hand pressing against the wound in his side, moved forward slowly and looked down at the prostrate, motionless body.

"Go to him!" Benedict interrupted. "He has a key attached to a cord round his neck. Retrieve it and return quickly; I need to tend to your injuries as best I can.

Nick headed wearily for the stairs, stooping to pick up the knife. His chest hurt, his side stung, and he wanted out of there as soon as possible. He had earned his money tonight, all right, he thought ruefully. Nick reached the lower hall and approached the still figure. Moeller was lying face up on the marble floor, one arm sprawled across his unbreathing chest and blood was trickling from his nose and mouth. He looked dead but Nick was taking no chances.

He prodded him with his foot and, getting no reaction, with knife at the ready, he leaned over, loosened the tie round Moeller's neck and undid his shirt. He grimaced at the sight of the surgical scars around his adam's apple and reached under the shirt to search for the key. Suddenly the German's arm slipped off his chest. Nick managed to stifle the cry in his throat as a fresh surge of adrenalin flooded his blood stream. His pulse soaring, Nick lingered no longer. He located the cord, severed it with the knife, retrieved the key and headed back up the stairs to rejoin James.

James Benedict stepped through the doorway into Giles Worsley's bedchamber. The needles threatening to lance through his upper body were still being held at bay, but the effort was considerable, and there was still one major and dangerous obstacle to overcome. Nick had handled himself well even though James had needed to come to his aid. James was still carrying his jacket, and he dropped it on a chair as they moved through the lavishly furnished bedroom with an impressive antique four-poster bed and into the large bathroom.

They located a first aid kit, and James managed a temporary repair to Nick's punctured side and strapped his damaged ribs. Nick was uncomplaining and, mercifully, the knife-wound was not a bad injury, but it would require stitches later; he made a mental note to give him a large bonus if they survived the rest of the night.

"Listen to me," James said. "You have done all I expected of you, so far tonight and done it well enough to earn an additional bonus, but the next phase is significantly more dangerous in a way that is beyond your experience or understanding."

He could see the uncertainty in Nick's face but carried on. "There is a concealed chamber, known only to Worsley and very few of his close associates, which he uses to perform certain rituals and to store his most prized possessions and secrets. It is here where I expect to find the object I need."

He paused for a few more seconds and then went on. "Worsley is an expert in the occult, in matters paranormal or supernatural. He considers himself to be a master magician and is highly skilled in ritual magic popularly known as the Black Arts. Let me assure you that he has real magical powers, which he has used, and still uses, indiscriminately against his enemies. And, believe me, you're powerless against this magic so you must follow my instructions implicitly." He paused, looking directly at Nick, "I can see the disbelief in your eyes. I know you have difficulty accepting this but please humour me, or your life will be in grave danger."

"Okay, It's your show. Tell me what I have to do."

James could see the continued incredulity in Nick's eyes but continued regardless. "This inner chamber, as I said, contains Worsley's implements and ritual secrets, his 'tools of the trade'. They are contained in a wooden chest that is locked by the key you now possess. The need for a lock is questionable for the chest has an extremely deadly guardian; no earthly sentinel like the late unlamented Moeller, but a powerful supernatural entity or demon, conjured up by Worsley and compelled to be his sentinel and guard his treasures. This being is difficult to control but is constrained, while in our earthly plane, to remain in a magic circle, a pentagram in this case, from which it cannot escape. Unfortunately, the chest is within the pentagram also." James paused, "Are you following all of this?" he asked.

"Sure," said Nick, attempting, not too successfully, to conceal his scepticism.

"Well, whatever you think, if you value your life, you must listen to my every word. I also have some skills in these matters, and they may provide some protection, but I cannot vanquish this demon in my current state. With luck it will be absent initially, but once you enter the pentagram and disturb the chest it will most certainly appear. Our objective is to get in and out as quickly as possible." James paused and concentrated on pushing back the pain that was threatening to come to the fore, once more.

After a few seconds, he continued. "For added security the chest is anchored and bound to the altar by one of Worsley's magic spells. With time I could probably break the spell, but I do not have that luxury, so you will have to open it with the key and take the objects that are inside. You can leave any books and papers but take any obvious figurines, wood or other solid objects. Just take them all and get out of the pentagram as fast as you can."

"If you don't mind me asking, what will you be doing?" Nick inquired.

"Don't worry, I'll be close to you. I've a more important role than you realise; I'll be attempting to prevent Worsley's evil watchdog from killing us both. Besides you're not stealing anything that really belongs to Giles Worsley. Once you are out of the Pentagram, I shall select what belongs to me and leave the rest behind." James looked questioningly at Nick who nodded acceptance.

"One more thing," James added, "when the demon appears, avoid looking directly at it, for it is powerfully hypnotic and can take many forms to trick you. If in dire danger, or if I instruct you, step out of the pentagram. You may hear me chanting strange words; these are names of power in ritual magic which may help me slow down the demon long enough for you to get clear."

"All right, let's get on with it," Harper said impatiently.

James moved to a mirrored wall and reaching up, touched one of the metal fixings. Nick did not hear a sound, but slowly part of the wall opened inwards, revealing a shadowy dark chamber, which the light from the bathroom failed to illuminate. Motioning Nick to follow, James stepped inside.

Chapter 4
Reflections of Brotherhood

*N*orfolk, Virginia – *24 March 4:30 PM local*

Mark pulled out of the Lafayette Medical Center and heard, via his Satnav, that his usual two route options back to Virginia Beach were both clogged by rush hour accidents. He opted to take another route hoping every other driver wasn't doing the same. The doctor had been uncertain about the causes of the pain even though Mark had had another attack while in his office. He eventually decided it could be the beginning of Herpes Zoster, or shingles to use its common and more socially acceptable name. If confirmed, the pain was likely to get worse, but his symptoms were not typical. He had no rash, although that might appear later, and the pains affected the whole of his upper torso rather than one side or the other. Assuming the diagnosis was correct, he'd been given a prescription for anti-viral medication that might help.

Mark's thoughts inevitably drifted to his brother, Jim. The familiar pang of unease flared again, sharper than before – a sensation that had been shadowing him for some days. It wasn't just the shingle-like pains that tightened across his chest and back, though they were troubling enough – it was a deeper, almost primal instinct. Something was wrong. Jim was in trouble.

Mark had tried calling his brother's home in England several times, but the line always rang hollow – a reminder of the miles and silences between them. Jim was never home. His absence gnawed at Mark, urging him to act. Perhaps he should reach out to Jim's friend and employer, Sir Giles Worsley. It wasn't something Mark wanted to do – it felt like an admission that his concerns were more than just paranoia. But could he live with himself if he ignored the signs?

For as long as he could remember, Jim had been his anchor, his protector, the one person in the world who made him feel secure. Despite the three years separating them, theirs was a bond as close as if they had been twins. No petty squabbles, no simmering sibling rivalries, just an unwavering connection, a kind of shorthand in their hearts that allowed them to understand each other without words.

Yet, for all their closeness, they were undeniably different. Mark, with his slighter frame and shy demeanour, often felt like the shadow to Jim's sunlight. His light blonde hair and blue eyes only underscored the contrast with Jim's rich brown hair and piercing brown gaze. Where Mark was quiet and introspective, Jim was magnetic and self-assured. He moved through the world with the ease of someone who knew he belonged, leaving admiration – and occasionally envy – in his wake.

Mark had never envied him, though. How could he, when Jim's success never cast a shadow over him but, instead, lit the way forward? Jim had been more than a brother after their father's death from cancer when Mark was just ten years old. He had stepped into a role no boy should have to shoulder, becoming a protector, a guide, and, in many ways, a surrogate father. It wasn't just Jim's physical presence that had comforted him during those lonely, grieving years – it was his unwavering belief in Mark's potential, even when Mark doubted it himself.

Now, that bond felt stretched thin across the miles, the silence an unrelenting burden. Mark's chest tightened as Ward's Corner faded behind him. He couldn't shake the sense that something had shifted – something irrevocable. The thought sent a chill coursing through him.

He resolved to call Sir Giles. Whatever it took, he would find his brother. Because losing Jim wasn't just unthinkable – it was unimaginable.

Mark had never known his mother, an Englishwoman with a grace and warmth often spoken of in reverence by those who remembered her. She had died from toxaemia complications shortly after bringing him into the world, leaving a void that no one – not even her devoted husband – could fill. Frederick Benedict, a man of imposing stature and quiet resolve, had been utterly undone by the loss of his beloved Sarah. Her absence became a haunting presence, casting a long shadow over the family.

Frederick had sent his two sons to a private boarding school in northern Virginia when Mark was just seven years old. Mark had never quite forgiven him for this decision. The early years at school were a bitter trial, marked by homesickness that seemed to deepen with each passing day. Though he eventually learned to tolerate the austere routines and rigid expectations, he never truly embraced them. Jim's presence, however, had been his saving grace.

Jim, with his natural charisma and quiet strength, commanded respect wherever he went. Even the biggest and brashest boys at the school dared not cross him. Mark knew he owed his peace to Jim's protection; it wasn't just physical – it was the kind of unshakable loyalty that sent an unspoken message to anyone who might have thought of targeting Mark. Even after Jim graduated and moved on, his influence lingered like an unbroken spell, shielding Mark through the power of memory and reputation.

Apart from Jim, the only other person who truly filled the void of parental love was Nan, their English maternal grandmother. Nan, with her sharp wit and heart softened by years of loss and resilience, became the boys' anchor. She had endured her own share of sorrow – losing her first husband to the Second World War and later, her beloved daughter. Life's trials had made her both tender and unyielding. She found love again with an American and moved to the States, taking along her daughter, Mark's mother, from her first marriage.

Cutting across some side streets, Mark left the snarling traffic behind, the sound of engines fading into a low hum. His thoughts wandered back to those days of youth; summers spent at the sprawling family estate in Charlottesville. The house had been a sanctuary of sorts, a place where echoes of his mother's laughter seemed to linger in the quiet corners, though he'd only ever heard it in stories.

When their father passed away, Nan, once again widowed, had stepped into the role of caregiver with a brisk determination. She refused to entertain Mark's desperate pleas to leave boarding school, brushing them aside with the resolute practicality that defined her.

"Boarding school is the norm for the children of the well-to-do in Britain," she would say, her tone firm but not unkind. "And though you might not think so now, it's very good for you. As well as your academic studies, you'll learn discipline, independence, and how to cope with life's little disappointments in a dignified manner. Qualities, I might add, sadly lacking in most American children."

Mark hadn't believed her then, and he wasn't entirely sure he believed her now. The discipline and independence Nan had championed felt like hollow platitudes to a young boy yearning for the warmth and constancy of a true home. Yet, as he navigated the familiar streets, he couldn't entirely dismiss her words. The strength she had instilled in him – though veiled by years of resentment – had undeniably shaped him. Whether it was for better or worse, he wasn't sure. What he did know was that he carried her legacy within him, alongside the persistent ache of her absence.

That absence became stark and unrelenting during his final year of high school, when Nan passed away peacefully in her sleep following a stroke. It was a quiet ending to a life that had been anything but. Her passing left a chasm in Mark's life that even time had struggled to fill. For a boy who had already lost so much, this final departure felt cruelly inevitable, yet it was no less shattering. With Nan gone, he entered adulthood with only his brother, Jim, to guide him.

Jim had always been a force of nature, and in the wake of Nan's death, his role in Mark's life deepened. It was Jim who first noticed and nurtured Mark's fledgling telekinetic ability – a discovery that, for a time, gave Mark a sense of wonder and purpose amidst the grief. Jim's powers were awe-inspiring, his control over objects seemingly effortless. He could lift heavy items with the same ease he might lift a feather, moving them through the air with precision and grace, even at considerable distances. Mark couldn't help but marvel at his brother's gift, though he often doubted whether he could ever match it.

Jim, ever patient, tried to teach him. Mark's early attempts were frustratingly fruitless, his concentration faltering under the weight of expectation. But Jim never gave up on him, and eventually, with dogged determination, Mark found he could weakly influence small objects nearby. Pens, pencils, coins – things that were insignificant to the world yet monumental to him – began to shift and roll under his focused gaze. The pride he felt the first time he made a pencil tremble on its edge was almost overwhelming, but the sense of accomplishment was fleeting. Despite Jim's encouragement, Mark's abilities remained modest, his influence confined to minor movements of lightweight items.

Yet even those small triumphs were enough to remind him of his connection to his brother – a shared thread of the extraordinary in an otherwise ordinary life. Jim's mastery highlighted Mark's limitations, but it never became a source of jealousy. If anything, it deepened Mark's gratitude for the bond they shared, one forged in love, resilience, and the unspoken understanding of what it meant to endure loss.

When Nan passed in 1990, it was more than just her presence that was lost. The family home, that grand estate in Charlottesville where summers had felt eternal, was sold. It was an inevitable decision, but one that carried a profound sense of finality. Mark used his share of the estate to buy outright, a condominium a practical move that gave him a foothold in the adult world. But no matter how comfortable his new home became, it could never replace the sprawling warmth of the house that had held the echoes of his childhood.

Mark's thoughts drifted back to the present, his gaze settling on the small, unassuming houses that lined the street. It struck him that it had been almost a year since he'd last taken this route home. The memory of his last journey was vivid: the abundance of azaleas, their brilliant blooms casting a vibrant glow across the otherwise modest front yards, had made the scene feel almost celebratory. Now, only a few early varieties dared to bloom, their fragile petals a promise of the riot of colour that would burst forth in a few weeks' time.

His chest twinged again, the familiar pain intruding on his reverie. The discomfort had accompanied him throughout the journey, coming in sporadic bursts that jostled his thoughts. Was it duller now, or was he merely growing accustomed to it? He pushed the sensation aside, letting his mind slip backward once more, skipping over the years to land on the vibrant days of college – and on Sam.

College had been a revelation for Mark. In stark contrast to his earlier years of stifling routines and dormitories, it had been a time of discovery, of freedom, and of friendships that felt boundless. And then there was Sam. Sweet, effervescent Sam.

She wasn't the kind of woman who would turn heads in a crowded room, but to Mark, she was radiant. At five feet six, with a trim, athletic figure and wavy, chestnut-brown hair, Sam's beauty lay in the details. Her blue-grey eyes, flecked with green, sparkled with mischief and warmth. When she laughed – a sound that came easily and often – it was as though the world itself brightened, her joy spreading like wildfire. She dressed casually, wore little makeup, and moved through life with an effortless ease that Mark found utterly captivating.

Sam was everything he wasn't: gregarious, endlessly optimistic, and disarmingly carefree. She embraced life with both arms, her enthusiasm contagious even when it teetered on recklessness. True, her exuberance sometimes led to a certain irresponsibility or flakiness, but she had a way of softening even the harshest criticism with a single, irresistible smile. Everyone loved Sam, it was impossible not to. Her warmth wasn't selective; she extended it to everyone she met, and Mark often wondered how it was that he had been lucky enough to capture a place in her orbit.

Their friendship blossomed quickly, an inseparable bond forming between them that Mark cherished deeply – and painfully. God, how he adored her. But for all the joy Sam brought into his life, she also brought heartache. She had a boyfriend, a steady presence in her life since high school, though Mark had never met him. She didn't talk about the boyfriend much, as though he were an afterthought, but Mark knew better than to mistake her silence for indifference. He'd convinced himself that Sam preferred to keep their relationship safely in the realm of friendship, and he respected that boundary – mostly because he had no idea how to cross it without risking everything.

Still, there were moments. Glances held a second too long, laughter shared in ways that felt like secrets, touches that lingered just enough to make his heart ache. He wished he could summon the courage to tell her what he felt, to lay his heart bare and risk whatever might come. But he didn't. Instead, he lived in the quiet hope that someday, things might change.

And then, one day, they did – or so he thought. Sam mentioned, almost in passing, that she and her boyfriend had broken up. Mark's chest had tightened with a sudden, desperate hope, a tiny ember of possibility flaring to life. But by the time he could gather the nerve to act, it was too late.

Sam had already fallen. Head over heels, with no warning or hesitation. For Jim.

Mark forced a smile when she told him, though the words cut through him like a knife. It was Jim. Of course, it had to be Jim. His brother – charming, magnetic, always the centre of attention. How could anyone resist him? Mark tried to ignore the sharp ache in his chest, telling himself that Sam's happiness was all that mattered. He smiled, he nodded, but inside, his world was quietly unravelling.

It had been almost instantaneous – love at first sight. Jim had visited for the weekend and met Sam. From the moment they were introduced, Jim was his usual self – effortlessly dashing, endlessly witty, and utterly captivating. The three of them had spent the weekend laughing and talking, but by the end, Mark saw it. The way Sam's eyes lit up when Jim spoke, the way her laughter seemed brighter when he was around. She was falling for him – hard.

The following week, her conversations drifted to Jim every chance she got. By then, Mark knew. He'd already lost her, though he never really had her to begin with. Two weeks later, Jim returned, this time unmistakably for Sam. Mark was included in their plans, but it was painfully clear – Jim and Sam had become a unit. Within a year, Jim had swept her off her feet, and they were married.

Yet, strangely, Mark couldn't bring himself to resent his brother. He couldn't hate Jim for falling in love with her. How could he? Jim had even apologized, sensing Mark's quiet heartbreak. Despite the gnawing ache in his chest, Mark took solace in their happiness. Sam was part of the family now, and that meant she would still be a part of his life, even if not in the way he had once dreamed.

Still, he couldn't stop wondering if Sam had known how he felt. He often replayed the moment from her wedding reception – their goodbye. He had meant for it to be a simple, friendly kiss, but as their lips touched, it lingered. For a fleeting moment, something passed between them. Her eyes, shimmering with a hint of sadness, stayed locked on him as the car pulled away, leaving Mark standing alone with his unspoken words.

Another dull wave of pain assaulted his chest for a moment, disturbing his musings. Mark found himself on Shore Drive – he would be home in five minutes.

Chapter 5

Love and Loss

Virginia Beach – 24 March 5:30 PM local

Sam set the oven to preheat and sank into a chair at the breakfast table. A steaming cup of herbal tea sat cradled in her hands, its warmth, a small comfort against the growing chill in her heart. In the background, CNN Headline News droned on, its voices filling the silence of the house, a house that felt far too big now that she was alone.

Her gaze drifted out the window, her thoughts snagging on the bittersweet irony of her surroundings. The elegance of Middle Plantation was undeniable, a reflection of the love and care she'd poured into creating this home. And yet, the sprawling emptiness seemed to mock her. Moving to a smaller place made sense, but some part of her clung to this space, holding on to the fragile hope that James might see sense and come back to her.

She took a deep breath, letting the tea's aroma anchor her. But the past was insistent, pulling her back to the moment she'd first met James. Mark had been so excited to introduce her to his older brother, the man he admired so deeply. James had walked into her life with an air of quiet confidence, a man who seemed to belong to a world slightly out of reach. Again, she recalled his first words.

"Hello," he'd said, extending his hand with an almost regal composure. "Actually, I prefer James; only Mark is allowed to call me Jim."

At the time, she'd found his formality a little pompous, but the weekend that followed softened her view. James's charm wasn't overbearing; it was effortless. He radiated self-assurance, yet he never came across as arrogant. It was clear why Mark idolized him, and Sam quickly understood why she couldn't resist him. When James left that weekend, a void had opened, one she hadn't anticipated. She missed him deeply. So, when he returned just two weeks later, her heart had already begun its quiet surrender.

It was a whirlwind romance – heady, intoxicating, and all-consuming. By the time they were engaged, she was utterly captivated, swept away by the promise of a perfect life. Mark, to her surprise, gave his blessing without hesitation. She'd always sensed something unspoken in Mark's quiet affection, a shadow of what might have been if life had unfolded differently. But he never voiced it, never made a move, and she'd convinced herself it was for the best. She had loved Mark – still did, in a way – but James was the sun she'd revolved around.

Their early days together were a dream come true. Sam, a suburban girl from Reston, found herself immersed in a world she'd only ever glimpsed in movies. James's success was dazzling – a Harvard graduate turned self-made millionaire before thirty. His financial software had catapulted him into wealth, and he'd used it to build a life of sophistication and adventure. Together, they travelled to Europe, revelled in the richness of culture, and planned for a future brimming with promise. Her mother had adored James, seeing him as the perfect son-in-law, a man who brought security and charm in equal measure.

But perfection, she'd learned, could be a fragile veneer. Everything began to change when Sir Giles Worsley entered their lives. Sam remembered the first time she met him – a man of undeniable power and presence. His tailored suits, his commanding voice, his enigmatic aura – it was easy to see why James had fallen under his spell. But the more time James spent with Worsley, the further he drifted from her. At first, it was subtle – weekend trips, late nights immersed in cryptic texts Worsley had sent him. Then it became all-encompassing. He was consumed by strange rituals, secret meetings, and an obsession with mysticism that made her feel like a stranger in her own marriage.

Her pleas to reconnect fell on deaf ears. Plans for children were postponed indefinitely. The intimacy they'd once shared dissolved into a mechanical routine, and every attempt to bridge the gap between them was met with evasion. She'd wondered if there was someone else. He did seem besotted with the enigmatic Fiona Barnes, the only female member of Worsley's inner circle. Though not unattractive, she was almost twice his age, and Sam had dismissed the thought as ridiculous. Sam's desperation grew until, finally, she'd made the painful decision to leave.

Returning to the States had felt like both a defeat and a lifeline. Mark tried to mediate, offering a bridge between them, but the tension between their worlds was too great. James's calls went unanswered. Her mother, ever loyal to James, disapproved, urging her to reconcile. But Sam couldn't go back, not when her heart was breaking in a thousand different ways.

Now, as she stared out the window of a house that no longer felt like home, the ache of those memories pressed heavy against her. She rose, putting the leftovers of last night's casserole into the oven, her movements slow and deliberate. Life went on, she told herself, even if it felt like something vital had been left behind.

Chapter 6
Masks and Malice

London – 24 March 9:30 PM local

Sir Giles Worsley's senses prickled with unease. Seated in the opulent dining room of 10 Downing Street, he savoured the warmth of a post-prandial XO Cognac, its rich bouquet lingering as he contemplated the Prime Minister's mundane small talk. But then he felt it – a subtle yet undeniable intrusion. A breach of the sanctity of his Amersham estate. He closed his eyes briefly, focusing. It could only be James Benedict. No one else would dare challenge Flauros, let alone survive. A ripple of annoyance crossed his otherwise composed face. Moeller must have failed. Benedict would pay for his audacity, of that Worsley was certain, but for now, he needed an excuse to extricate himself from the Prime Minister's dinner party.

The Prime Minister droned on, speaking to Nigel Goodison, a guest who embodied mediocrity yet basked in the fleeting glory of having two thrillers on the bestseller list. Goodison's self-importance was rivalled only by his lack of originality. His wife, Heather, seated beside Worsley, was a stark contrast. Attractive and sharp-witted, she radiated an easy charm that had captivated Worsley throughout the evening. Her hazel eyes glimmered with mischief, and her glances hinted at unspoken invitations. Under ordinary circumstances, Worsley would have indulged himself – there was an undeniable pleasure in seducing the wives of pompous fools. But tonight was no ordinary night.

Heather Goodison had enjoyed the attention of Sir Giles, and she had detected an interest that held a promise of further excitement to come. He was a commandingly handsome man, and he exuded a heady mix of ruthlessness, elegance and refinement. Long but not too long, silver-grey hair swept back from a lightly wrinkled brow; pale, cold, penetrating steel-grey eyes, strangely hypnotic, sat comfortably separated by the wide bridge of a large, slightly hawkish nose; a strong, square jaw and thin lips. Her heart fluttered like a schoolgirl, twenty-five years her junior, as he leaned towards her conspiratorially.

Sir Giles, his touch on her hand calculated, his voice a velvet whisper; "My dear, your nose is bleeding."

Heather, her hand tingling at his touch, froze as his words penetrated. She raised a delicate hand to her face, her confusion palpable. When she pulled it back, her fingertips were stained crimson. "Oh my God!" she gasped, her voice trembling as rivulets of blood began cascading down her face, soaking into the neckline of her elegant evening gown.

Nigel Goodison turned, his initial irritation giving way to a pale-faced alarm. The sight of his wife's condition seemed to render him immobile; his discomfort tinged with embarrassment rather than concern.

"Quick man! The cloakroom!" Worsley commanded, his voice cutting through the stunned silence like a whip. He guided Heather to her feet, his demeanour exuding both authority and calm. "Pinch your nose hard," he instructed, his hand steady against her back as they hurried from the dining room.

The Prime Minister joined the effort, galvanizing the room into action. Guests exchanged uneasy glances but remained rooted in their seats, unsure of how to react. Heather stumbled slightly, her breathing shallow as she pinched her nose, the metallic taste of blood pooling in her throat. They reached the cloakroom just as a violent choking cough sprayed blood across the pristine tiles – and over Nigel.

"Heather! For God's sake, control yourself!" Nigel snapped; his tone drenched in irritation rather than sympathy.

Worsley turned sharply, his steel-grey eyes narrowing in contempt. The force of his glare silenced Nigel instantly. Gently, he guided Heather to the washbasin, where she retched, her sobs muffled by the flood of blood and shame.

The Prime Minister hovered nearby, his brow furrowed in concern. "This is extraordinary. I've never seen a nosebleed this severe. Shall I call for a doctor?"

Worsley shook his head, his hand firm on the back of Heather's neck. "Wait. I believe it's stopping," he said with practiced calm, though his mind was already elsewhere. His focus remained outwardly on Heather, but the undercurrent of rage toward Benedict simmered just beneath the surface.

Heather's sobs quieted, and she dared to lower her hand. To her relief, the bleeding seemed to have subsided. Still trembling, she clung to the edge of the basin, her face pale and streaked with blood and tears.

"May I?" Worsley asked, his voice softening as he reached for a towel.

The Prime Minister nodded. Worsley dampened the towel, his movements precise and almost tender as he cleaned Heather's face. His touch was deceptively gentle, a stark contrast to the storm brewing within him.

Once Heather was settled, Worsley addressed the Prime Minister. "I'll take them to their hotel. My car is nearby; I'll call my chauffeur."

The Prime Minister hesitated but eventually nodded, apologizing for the disruption. "You're too kind, Giles. I'm sorry the evening has ended this way."

"Think nothing of it," Worsley replied smoothly, though his tight-lipped smile betrayed his impatience. "I needed to leave shortly, regardless."

Twenty minutes later, Sir Giles reclined in the leather seat of his Rolls Royce, his countenance dark as the car sped toward Amersham. He had deposited the miserable Goodisons at The Dorchester, barely sparing a thought for Heather's humiliation. She had served her purpose, providing a convenient reason to leave.

His thoughts shifted to James Benedict. The boy had once shown such promise – a raw talent unmatched in generations. But his potential had been squandered, undone by moral hesitation and a fragile psyche shaped by a suffocating Christian upbringing. Worsley cursed his own impatience. It was a crying shame; he would have made a most worthy successor, but it was too late now. He had failed to last the course, and he knew too much.

Sir Giles realised his error in hurrying the boy; Benedict had learned the skills so readily and quickly but had required a lot more shaping and manipulation than he had been given. He had ascended so quickly to the grade of Adeptus Major, much faster than anyone in living memory, but the warning signs were there when he had moral difficulties with the sex rites that he had to complete to reach his current rank. Sir Giles could and should have managed him via deep hypnosis, but in his impatience to proceed, he had neglected to do so. The ritual human sacrifice in his consequent development had been just too much for him and proved to be the final straw.

Yet, before that unravelling, before Benedict's conscience got the better of him, Worsley had been proud – genuinely proud – of the man he was moulding. He had seen in Benedict something more than just another adept seeking power; he had seen his protégé, his chosen heir. Unlike the snivelling, power-hungry sycophants who clung to his coattails, Benedict had intelligence, ambition, and, for a time, loyalty. He had listened, learned, adapted. He had been the only one to truly appreciate the deeper intricacies of what they studied. Where others saw the ritual, James had seen meaning. Where others sought personal gain, James had sought knowledge. That was why Worsley had invested so much in him.

And he had made James a rich man. It amused him to remember how sceptical James had been at first when Worsley had demonstrated necromancy – not to raise the dead, but to consult them. The spirits that answered him had no need for gold, no concern for the material wealth of mortals, and yet they saw what men could not. The tides of fortune, the rise and fall of economies, the paths of empires were all laid bare to those who dared to look beyond the veil. With their guidance, James's investments had tripled within months. Worsley had orchestrated it all, whispering hints, steering him toward prosperity. He had never entertained the idea of exploiting James; no, he had looked upon him as a future equal, a brother in the Great Work, someone who would one day surpass even his own influence.

But in the end, James had disappointed him. Worsley let out a slow breath, his fingers gripping the arm of his chair. It was not just the betrayal that stung, but the waste. Had he been patient, had he guided him with a firmer hand, James could have been standing beside him, not against him.

He closed his eyes, a thin smile playing at his lips as he considered his options. Benedict's betrayal demanded a swift, decisive response. A simple assassination lacked elegance. No, Benedict deserved something more… poetic. Something that would break not just his body, but his soul. Worsley relished the thought, his anticipation sharpening as he prepared for the battle ahead. Tonight, the boy's rebellion would end, and Sir Giles Worsley would remind the world why he was to be feared.

Chapter 7
A Demon's Wrath

Southeast England – 24 March, 9:35 PM local

Nick's breath caught in his throat as his eyes adjusted to the oppressive gloom of the inner chamber. The dim electric lights cast an eerie glow on the dark marble floor, their flickering shadows seeming to pulse in time with his racing heart. The chamber exuded an ancient menace, its coldness seeping into his bones. Strange golden symbols – stars, circles, a large pentagram and arcane sigils – covered the floor, drawing his unwilling gaze toward the centre, where a small stone altar stood like a sentinel of dread. Atop it sat a carved wooden box, its edges adorned with intricately sinister designs.

The walls were shrouded in black, flocked with grotesque patterns that seemed to twist and shift under the dim light. They reminded him of some forgotten mausoleum or a place where dark gods were worshipped. Every surface seemed to whisper, taunting him with secrets not meant to be uncovered. The air was thick with a nauseating chill that clung to his skin, and his jacket, discarded earlier, now felt like a lifeline he desperately wished for.

"The guardian is absent," James said, his voice strained but commanding. "We have a moment's start. But as soon as you step into the circle, it will come. Be quick. Go!"

Nick's body moved before his mind could register the words. He darted forward, his footsteps echoing ominously in the otherwise silent chamber. The golden symbols seemed to hum as he stepped into the circle, his pulse pounding in rhythm with their unholy resonance. He reached the altar, his hands trembling as he tried to lift the box, but it was immovable, as if fused to the stone.

"Stop fumbling!" Benedict hissed from the shadows. "Open it with the key – now!"

Nick's hands shook as he unlocked the box. Inside was a collection of papers and a small, brown cloth bag. His fingers brushed against its contents

– a figure, crudely carved and sharp-edged, wrapped in razor wire. The sensation was enough to make his skin crawl.

"That's it!" Benedict's voice rose in alarm. "Get out now! It's coming!"

The atmosphere shifted violently. The air became ice-cold, and a sickly, sulfuric stench enveloped him. Nick's every instinct screamed at him to run, but his legs felt rooted to the spot. A smoky mist began coalescing on his left, bringing with it an overwhelming wave of dread. He clutched the bag and turned toward Benedict, but his path was blocked by the mist, which now twisted into a vaguely humanoid form.

"I'm scared, Nick," a familiar voice whimpered. "Please help me."

Nick froze. "Paula?" he whispered, his breath visible in the frigid air.

"Don't be a fool!" Benedict's voice was raw with urgency. "It's not her! Get out before it's too late!"

The mist solidified further, revealing a figure cloaked in a tattered hood. Its face – or the void where a face should have been – seemed to draw all light and warmth into it. A ghastly green glow emanated from the figure's core, and as Nick stared, the void transformed. Hideous, festering features emerged: eyes burning like molten coals, crimson flames licking at its gaping nostrils and suppurating sores. Its grotesque mouth stretched impossibly wide, as if consuming the very air.

Nick was paralyzed, trapped between terror and disbelief. His limbs refused to obey him as the demon's aura of despair crushed his will. From behind, he vaguely heard James chanting, his voice rising in a desperate litany of power:

"I command thee, demon. Depart this place in the names of YOD HE VAU HE, ADONAI, METATRON – "

The demon's guttural roar drowned out Benedict's words, and Nick finally wrenched himself free of its paralyzing grip. He turned and stumbled toward James, thrusting the bag into his hands. But as James retrieved the wax figure inside, his fingers slipped on the razor wire, slicing his skin. The wire seemed alive, tightening around the effigy as though feeding on his agony.

A monstrous laugh reverberated through the chamber as Nick's terror peaked. His lungs burned as the air thickened with smoke and sulfur. He grasped James , dragging him toward the door, but their path was blocked.

Moeller stood in the doorway, his massive frame silhouetted against the dim light.

"You were dead!" Nick shouted, disbelief mingling with horror.

Before he could react, Moeller's powerful arm swung, striking him with brutal force. The impact sent Nick reeling backward, crashing into the altar and collapsing into the circle. The golden symbols ignited in a blinding inferno of light, and the demon descended upon him with unrestrained fury.

Benedict's voice broke as he watched helplessly from the edge of the circle. "No! Nick!"

The demon transformed into a black fog, alive with fiery veins of red. It enveloped Nick, tearing at his flesh with invisible claws. Nick's screams were blood-curdling as the fog stripped away skin and muscle, leaving raw, exposed tissue. Shreds of his clothing disintegrated as the demon invaded every orifice, its fiery tendrils entering his mouth, nose, and eyes. The chamber echoed with his final, agonized shriek before he was reduced to a lifeless, charred husk.

James recoiled, his face ashen as the demon turned its eyeless gaze toward him. But he had no time to mourn or falter. Summoning the last reserves of his strength, he focused on the wax figure. Each knot of razor wire resisted his mental commands, but slowly, agonisingly, they began to unravel.

The demon howled in frustration, its form flickering violently as Benedict's efforts weakened its hold. At last, the wires fell away, and with them, the unbearable pain that had wracked his body for days. Renewed and resolute, Benedict rose, his gaze locking onto Moeller, frozen in fear, who still blocked the doorway.

Benedict stepped forward, his confidence radiating like a shield. With a flick of his mind, he cast Moeller into the circle. The German's hoarse scream was cut short as Flauros pounced on him, its cackle ringing out in a triumph of unspeakable horror.

Without a backward glance, James strode into the light of the bathroom. As the door closed behind him, muffling the guttural sounds of Moeller's torment, he walked away, with cold determination, pausing only to retrieve Nick Harper's jacket, which contained the car keys. He left behind the chamber and its horrors forever.

Chapter 8

Unease

Virginia Beach – 24 March 5:50 PM local

Mark sat on his deck, an ice-cold Corona in hand, the faint buzz of activity around Chesapeake Bay providing a soothing backdrop to his restless thoughts. The air was crisp, cooler than he would have liked, but not enough to drive him indoors. U2's *The Joshua Tree* played softly from the speakers, its melodies weaving into the ambient sound of distant waves and the occasional call of seabirds.

The sun still hung above the horizon, its golden light bathing the scene in a soft glow. Across the bay, the lights of the Bay Bridge Tunnel were already visible, stretching toward the Eastern Shore. Even at this hour, the gaps where the tunnels dipped below the surface could be discerned, and the far-off high-rise section of the bridge shimmered faintly in the evening haze.

Mark took a sip of his beer, its coolness refreshing against the dry edge of his throat. The view from his condo's rear deck was one of his favourite things about living here. The beach, sparsely populated now, was a constant source of fascination. Joggers moved steadily along the shoreline; their figures silhouetted against the glinting waves. A solitary fisherman cast his line, the arc of the rod catching the light as he worked. Even in quieter moments like this, the bay felt alive – a living, breathing entity that Mark had come to appreciate deeply.

The vista was one of his greatest comforts. From the deck of his condo, the beach unfolded like a canvas of endless activity. In the summer, the scene transformed into a vivid tapestry of life – children laughing as they built sandcastles that the waves would inevitably reclaim, couples strolling hand in hand, and throngs of people sunbathing on bright towels and chairs. Windsurfers carved the waves while sailboats and fishing vessels crisscrossed the horizon. Above, gulls circled and cried, their sharp calls cutting through the air, while pelicans glided low over the water, their awkward frames somehow elegant in flight.

Mark sighed, leaning back into his chair. He let his eyes drift, watching the distant pod of dolphins breaching the surface, their movements playful and free. Yet, the peaceful scene failed to quiet the gnawing anxiety building within him. It wasn't just unease; it was a bone-deep certainty that something was wrong. The feeling had taken root days ago, and no matter how he tried to reason it away, it clung to him, heavy and oppressive.

His mind kept circling back to his brother. James. There was something amiss – he knew it. The last time they'd spoken, a good while ago now, James had seemed distracted, his usual commanding presence tinged with an edge of something Mark couldn't quite place. Fear? Frustration? He couldn't be sure, but now the silence was deafening. No calls, no emails, no signs of life. It wasn't like James to disappear, and Mark's recent fruitless attempts to reach him had only deepened his concern.

Unable to bear the weight of his thoughts, Mark picked up his phone and dialled Sam. She answered after a few rings, her voice warm and familiar, though tinged with surprise.

"Hi Sam, it's Mark. Have you heard from Jim at all?" His voice was tight, betraying his unease.

"No, Mark," she replied, her tone softening. "He hasn't left any messages or written for a couple of weeks at least. Why? Is there something wrong?"

Mark hesitated, his free hand gripping the arm of his chair. He didn't want to alarm her, but the words spilled out before he could stop them. "I've got a distinctly uneasy feeling that Jim is in trouble – I've tried calling his work, home, and mobile for a couple of days now, but I get no reply. I just can't shake this sense that something's wrong. Badly wrong."

Sam's voice was calm, though he could hear the faintest thread of concern beneath her reassurances. "He's probably just out somewhere," she said. "You know how he gets – maybe he's in that soundproof meditation room of his. Look, it's gone eleven PM in England now. Why don't you try again in the morning?"

Mark exhaled, the logic of her suggestion failing to ease his mind. "Okay," he said reluctantly.

Sam's tone softened further. "How are you anyway, Mark?"

He managed a faint smile, though she couldn't see it. They exchanged pleasantries for a few moments, their conversation light and familiar, a brief reprieve from his worries. As they said their goodbyes, she promised to meet him for lunch next week. He thanked her and hung up, but the unease lingered, wrapping around him like a heavy fog.

The night had deepened by the time he put down his empty bottle and stood. The distant lights of the bridge still shone, unwavering against the growing darkness. He lingered on the deck, staring out at the water, his thoughts an unrelenting spiral of worry and what-ifs. What if James was in danger? What if he needed help?

The wind picked up, carrying with it the salty tang of the sea and a faint chill that crept beneath his collar. Mark shivered, but it wasn't just the cold that made him uneasy. Somewhere out there, beyond the bridge and the waves, something was wrong. He could feel it as surely as the wind on his skin.

With a final glance at the horizon, he turned and stepped back into the warmth of his home, his mind already racing with plans for what he would do if James didn't respond by morning.

Chapter 9
Desperate Escape

Heathrow Airport – 25 March 2:00 AM local
James sat heavily on the edge of the Sheraton Hotel bed, the weight of the night pressing down on him. He wore the heavy, slightly oversized hotel bathrobe, its fabric scratching faintly against his skin. His clothes, spattered with the remnants of his ordeal, were being express cleaned, though he doubted even industrial detergents could fully cleanse them or the stench of fear and desperation that clung to him. He had nothing else – no luggage, no belongings – just the toiletries pack the concierge had handed over with a strained smile.

Thank God he had taken his passport with him. Without it, escape would have been impossible. Now, as the clock ticked past 2:00 AM, he felt the full extent of his exhaustion – physical, mental, and something deeper, a spiritual weariness that made even the act of breathing feel like a struggle. His hands throbbed beneath their patchwork of band-aids, each cut from the razor wire a vivid reminder of how close he had come to losing everything.

James leaned back against the headboard, his eyes drifting toward the window. Beyond the thick curtains lay the dark expanse of Heathrow, its runways glowing faintly in the distance like veins of light pulsing through the city's lifeblood. He had driven here in a haze, barely aware of the journey, his mind occupied with the image of Harper's final moments. The screams, the fire, the inhuman laughter – it was all burned into his memory, a nightmare he couldn't escape even when awake.

He hadn't dared return to his apartment. That would have been suicide. Sir Giles would come for him – it was not a matter of if but when. James knew the man's methods too well to believe he would opt for anything as mundane as a hitman. No, Worsley would want a spectacle. A reckoning. His vengeance would be supernatural, grotesque, and as intricate as the rituals he commanded. James shuddered at the thought.

To buy himself time, he'd reserved a business-class ticket on United Airlines' morning flight to Washington Dulles. The night concierge had been helpful, even managing not to flinch at the sight of James's battered hands. The credit card he used to pay for the ticket, however, was a double-edged sword. It had been a necessary risk, but he knew it wouldn't take long for Worsley's network of spies to trace him here. Every action felt like a gamble, every decision a precarious step on a fraying tightrope.

A sip of Perrier offered little comfort as he considered his next move. Fleeing to America was just the beginning; he needed a place to lie low, somewhere even Worsley's long reach couldn't penetrate immediately. The hunting lodge in the Blue Ridge Mountains came to mind – a property he had purchased secretly years ago, intending to turn it into a surprise retreat for Sam. The project had stalled when they moved to England, but the lodge remained his one true refuge. Remote, unassuming, and maintained just enough to be habitable. It was the only place he could think of that might offer him the chance to regroup and fortify himself against the storm heading his way.

He had called Sam earlier, careful to keep his voice calm despite the turmoil roiling beneath. She had agreed to arrange for Mark to meet him at Dulles. What she didn't know was that Mark would be driving him directly to the lodge. There was no time to explain everything – no way to make her understand the gravity of what he faced without pulling her into the crosshairs as well. James had given her a list of supplies for Mark to bring, practical items, mostly, but each chosen with meticulous care, as though his life depended on them. Because it did.

The hotel room felt stifling, despite the chill seeping through the walls. James rose, walked to the door, and double-locked it, securing the chain for good measure. He moved to the desk and sat down, his hands trembling slightly as he picked up the hotel stationery. On one sheet, he wrote a letter to Sam, sealing it in an envelope. He poured into it what he couldn't say over the phone – his fears, his regrets, his hope that she might forgive him if the worst happened. It was a farewell, though he refused to acknowledge it as such.

On another sheet, he drafted instructions to his financial agent, ordering the liquidation of several investments. The proceeds would be transferred to one of Sam's accounts. He also arranged a large compensatory payment to Nick Harper's Security firm. He didn't want to think about why he was making these arrangements – only that it was necessary.

By the time he returned to bed, his body ached with the weight of everything he had done, and everything still left to do. He lay down, his head sinking into the pillow as exhaustion finally overtook him. Sleep, when it came, was restless. His dreams were haunted by flames and shadowy figures, the spectre of Worsley's wrath looming over him like a storm cloud.

When he awoke, the faint light of dawn would signal the start of another race against time, another desperate effort to stay one step ahead of the inevitable. But for now, he drifted into the uneasy space between consciousness and oblivion, each breath a quiet act of defiance against the darkness closing in around him.

Chapter 10

Emotional Reflections and Bonds

Virginia Beach – 24 March 8.45 PM

Mark guided his Jeep Cherokee along the familiar stretch of Great Neck Road, the rhythmic hum of the tires a faint backdrop to his swirling thoughts. Sam's call had come only minutes ago, her voice tight with concern and laced with an undercurrent of fear she hadn't tried to mask. It had only confirmed what he already felt in his bones – something was wrong, deeply wrong, with Jim. Mark had packed an overnight bag in record time and was now on his way to Sam's house, the tension in his chest easing slightly with every mile but refusing to dissipate entirely.

The psychic force that had been pushing down on him for days had eased somewhat, and even the nerve-wracking shingles-like attacks had subsided. But this reprieve only made him more uneasy. It felt like the calm before a storm, a sinister pause before something worse. Jim needed him – of that much, Mark was certain. But why, or how things had spiralled so far out of control, was still a mystery.

The quiet drive gave him too much space to think. He couldn't help but let his mind wander to Jim's history, particularly the one unforgettable incident that had both solidified their bond and driven a wedge of unease between them. Mark had always known Jim was extraordinary. The telekinetic powers, the confidence that bordered on arrogance, the unshakeable aura of control – it had all been a source of admiration and, at times, envy. But there had been moments when those powers revealed a darker side, a glimpse of something far more dangerous.

That day, during summer holidays at home, when they were kids, was burned into his memory with painful clarity. Mark was eleven, Jim fourteen, and they had been fooling around in his brother's room, flipping through contraband Playboy magazines, Jim had somehow acquired.

51

Jim said conspiratorially and mischievously with adolescent bravado, "Beth will be here in a moment to clean my room. I bet I can get her to show us her tits."

"Get out of here! Never in a million years!" Mark replied. He had not believed Jim would carry out his boast, but he'd seemed determined to try.

"Watch and learn little brother. She may not go for it with you here though, so you'll have to hide."

"But then I'll miss all the fun," Mark ventured with a little more audacity than he felt because, secretly, he was nervous and did not want to get into trouble if Beth reported them to Nan.

"No, you won't because you will be watching from up there." James pointed to the wide ventilation grill above the closet doors.

Together they quickly cleared the space on the shelf above the hanging rail and James helped Mark up onto the shelf. When Mark had arranged himself to get the best vantage point, Jim had closed the door. It was a bit uncomfortable, but he had a pretty good view of the room.

Beth Polanski was one of the cleaning ladies that Nan employed, and Mark thought her very pretty. Nowadays, he would have noticed that she wore too much make-up and provocative clothing that cheapened her, but back then she was like a goddess to them. Most of Nan's employees were street girls who had been arrested and were doing probation or otherwise trying to turn their lives around. Nan felt she was rescuing them by giving them employment and keeping them off the streets. Most did not like the mundane work, and they rarely stayed longer than a few weeks.

A few moments later, Beth, who had been tidying and cleaning Mark's room, knocked on the door.

"Master James, are you still in bed, you lazy boy?" she called.

Jim quickly hid the glossies in a bedside drawer. "I'm getting up now; you can come in."

Jim pulled back the covers and sat on the edge of the bed in his boxer shorts, as Beth entered and walked into the room. She had short, dark, curly hair and was very trim with large breasts that were restrained that day by a denim shirt that she'd knotted at the waist.

"I've got some money," Jim said, standing up.

Beth looked at him up and down. "Do you mean what I think you mean, you wicked boy?" she said noting the obvious erection under his boxers. Jim nodded. Beth went back to the door and locked it. She smiled and said, "You've got nerve, I'll give you that, and don't think I don't know about your dirty magazines." She paused and continued, "Maybe it's time you saw the real thing. Have you seen a naked girl before?"

Jim nodded but didn't say anything. He had lost his normal air of confidence.

"Have you ever had sex?" she taunted.

"Yeah, loads of times," he boasted. He was not very convincing, and Mark knew Jim was fibbing. "But I only want to see your tits."

"Bad boy! How much have you got?"

"There's thirty-five dollars in that vase."

"Thirty-five bucks?" She walked over to the vase on the dresser and removed the money, counting it before pocketing it in her shorts. She smiled again "You can have a lot more than tits for that, lover boy." She undid her shirt, pulled it off before unhooking her bra and slipping out of that too. She stood topless for a moment and then pulled down her shorts and panties. She stepped out of them and stood there stark naked, in the proud pose of someone confident with her body.

Mark remembered having to crane his neck to see everything that Beth was showing, and he remembered his reaction to seeing her magnificent breasts exposed, the dark nipples and large brown aureoles and then that completely forbidden place, the bushy black mound of hair between her legs. He was not sure about Jim, but, apart from magazines, he had never seen a naked woman before; his heart had been pounding so hard, he was certain that he would be heard and discovered.

"Well, come on, I haven't got all day. Take your shorts off!" Beth said, a touch impatiently.

This was unexpected and Jim had looked nervous and embarrassed. This was not quite what he had planned. Things had moved too fast; all he'd expected was for her to flash her boobs and go. Matters had gotten out of hand, and he had lost control of the situation, something he was not used to.

"Here, let me help you." Beth stepped towards him and quickly pulled down his shorts to reveal his upright penis standing out from a bed of dark hair. "My, what a big boy you are." Sensing his nervousness, Beth took Jim's right arm and placed his hand gently on her left breast. She slowly caressed his penis and pulled it against her pubic hair. Softly, she said, "Let's get into the bed; it will be more comfortable."

Without warning, Jim ejaculated, and Beth laughed. "My, you're eager!"

Jim, red-faced, quickly pulled up his shorts and turned away from her. Mark could see tears welling in his eyes. "Don't laugh at me!" he said in a choked voice.

Beth's voice became gentler, "Look honey, don't be upset; I didn't mean to hurt your feelings. What just happened is perfectly natural. There is nothing to be ashamed of, nothing at all; I have seen many grown men do the same." She approached him and put her hand on his shoulder. "We can still do it if you want," she said sympathetically.

"Get away from me!" he shouted. An invisible force suddenly lifted Beth off her feet and hurled her backwards across the room where she collided heavily with the door and wall. Beth struggled to her feet, bruised and shaken.

"What did you just do? How did you do that?" she asked, her voice wavering.

"Just get dressed and get out!" Jim had recovered himself but was still petulant in his anger.

She hurriedly put on her shirt and shorts without bothering with the underwear. She hastily picked up her bra and panties and unlocked the door. As she opened it Jim used his power again to throw her out and along the hall. She burst into tears. "Stop it! Please. Please stop," she pleaded, sobbing. Mark heard her hurrying away down the hall.

Mark, shocked by what he had seen, remembered emerging from his hiding place when Jim opened the closet doors. Jim had put his finger on his lips, warning him not to say anything. He opened the French windows, and Mark had followed him out onto the small balcony that overlooked the courtyard and swimming pool below.

"I'm not finished yet," Jim had muttered, cruelly.

Beth appeared, still clutching her underwear. She glanced up at them on the balcony nervously and hurried towards the servant's quarters beyond the pool. Suddenly she was lifted upwards and thrown sideways into the pool.

"Stop it, please," she screamed as she surfaced. She pulled herself out of the pool and lay there crying, a bedraggled, pitiful and terrified figure.

"Please Jim, stop; she's had enough, leave her alone." Mark had pleaded.

Beth had eventually got up and lurched sobbing to her quarters. He recollected they had stood looking at the pool in silence, a floating bra and two crumpled, saturated five-dollar bills serving as a reminder of the whole shocking event. Beth was never seen again. Later Nan had questioned them about what had happened. She had taken Jim to her room to speak to him privately, but Mark never learned the outcome; Jim would not discuss it. Mark never saw him use his powers so dramatically again.

Mark's heart still ached at the memory. What started as a juvenile attempt at mischief had spiralled into something neither of them could have anticipated. That was the day Mark learned two things: Jim's powers could be as terrifying as they were remarkable, and his brother could wield them in ways that left scars – not just on others, but on himself.

Mark shook off the haunting memory as Sam's neighbourhood loomed ahead, its sprawling homes and tree-lined streets a stark contrast to the turmoil raging in his thoughts. Middle Plantation was as picturesque as ever, with its stately colonial homes and carefully manicured lawns.

He parked in the driveway and entered through the backyard, where the winter-covered pool and tidy deck reflected Sam's meticulous nature. She stepped out of the kitchen to greet him, her face a mixture of relief and worry. Without a word, Mark pulled her into a hug, holding her tightly as if to reassure them both.

"Oh, Mark," she murmured against his chest. "You were right. You should have heard his voice… something's terribly wrong."

Mark stroked her hair gently, trying to calm her. "We shouldn't jump to conclusions," he said softly. "Let's get some rest tonight and head out early in the morning. We'll meet him at Dulles and figure this out together."

Sam pulled back slightly, her eyes shimmering with unshed tears. "James told me not to come. He was adamant. But I won't stay behind. I can't. Whatever's happening, I need to be there."

Mark hesitated. He hadn't known that Jim wanted him to come alone, but he also knew Sam well enough to recognize when her mind was set. "We'll figure it out," he said, sidestepping an argument he knew he wouldn't win.

Inside, over mugs of hot chocolate, they pieced together the details of Jim's cryptic call. Sam's recounting of his odd instructions and unusual shopping list only deepened Mark's unease, but he forced himself to focus on the here and now.

When the tension became too much, he changed the subject. "Remember that Jimmy Buffett concert at Walnut Creek?" he asked, a small smile tugging at the corners of his mouth.

Sam laughed, a warm, fleeting sound. "How could I forget? We were drenched in that storm!"

Mark chuckled. "And drunk."

"You were drunk," she corrected, arching an eyebrow. "I was the designated driver, as usual."

He shook his head, feigning indignation. "You make me sound like some kind of reckless fool. I was celebrating life, that's all."

"Uh-huh. Is that what you call belting out 'Margaritaville' at the top of your lungs while standing on the hood of my car?" Sam teased, crossing her arms with mock sternness.

Mark laughed, the sound deep and genuine. "I maintain that was a moment of pure artistic expression. Besides, you were laughing too."

She leaned back, her smile softening into something wistful. "I was. I remember thinking… I hadn't seen you that happy in a long time."

A quiet pause stretched between them. The warmth of their shared past flickered like an ember caught in the cold wind of the present. Mark's gaze dropped to the table, fingers tracing idle patterns against the wood. "Things were easier then," he murmured.

Sam sighed, studying him for a moment. "Yeah. They were." Her voice was gentle, but tinged with something deeper – regret, perhaps, or longing.

Mark met her eyes again, something unreadable in his expression. "Do you ever miss it?"

Sam hesitated, her fingers tightening slightly around her glass. "Of course, I do. But missing something doesn't mean we can go back."

"I know," he admitted, his voice low. "Doesn't stop me from wanting to sometimes."

They traded memories, the laughter easing some of the tension that had gripped the evening. For a moment, it felt like old times – before the complications, before the separations. Before life took them down different roads.

But the moment passed, and the weight of the present settled over them again. Sam glanced away first, as if afraid lingering too long in the past might make it harder to let go.

Mark exhaled and reached for his drink, his smile smaller now, more subdued. "Still," he said, voice lighter, "if you ever need a drunken rendition of 'Margaritaville' again, you know where to find me."

Sam smirked, shaking her head. "I think I'll keep that in mind."

As Sam stood to prepare for bed, she said, "Breakfast at 7:30?"

Mark nodded, watching her walk to the stairs. "Sounds good. Goodnight, Sam."

"Goodnight," she replied, pausing briefly at the top of the stairs. "And Mark… thanks for being here."

He lingered in the guest room doorway, watching her disappear into the master bedroom. The door clicked shut behind her, leaving him alone with his thoughts. For a moment, he allowed himself to wonder about the life they might have shared if things had been different. But guilt quickly replaced the thought, and his mind returned to Jim. Whatever storm his brother was facing, Mark would be there to help weather it.

He closed the door and prepared for the long day ahead of them tomorrow.

Chapter 11
Shocking Revelations

Washington Dulles – 25 March, 2:55 PM
Sam stared out at the blur of vehicles streaking past as they drove down the highway toward Dulles, the rhythmic hum of the tires against the road filling the silence between them. The rain had tapered off into a fine mist, turning the windshield into a mosaic of droplets that Mark's wipers swept away in steady intervals. The road ahead was grey, but the approaching airport signs heralded that they were getting nearer.

She glanced sideways at Mark, who had his hands firm on the wheel, gaze locked on the road with quiet focus. He had always been like this – steady, thoughtful, carrying more weight than he ever let on. She had learned to read the small signs: the slight furrow in his brow, the way his fingers tensed around the steering wheel when he was lost in thought. Time had changed them both, but some things remained the same.

For all their differences, they had always been able to navigate each other's moods with ease. Mark, with his quiet intensity, always thinking a step ahead, but never quite able to let go of the past. Sam pushing forward, even when part of her longed to stop and take stock of what had been left behind. They had their own ways of dealing with the weight of memory – his was introspection, hers was movement.

She adjusted herself in her seat, hugging her arms around herself as she exhaled softly. The prospect of seeing James again stirred something uneasy in her, a tangle of anticipation and apprehension. It had been too long. Too many unanswered questions, too much left unsaid. She wondered if Mark felt it too but knew better than to ask. He would keep his thoughts to himself until they were forced into the open, as he always did.

The airport Arrivals exit loomed ahead, and Mark flicked on the turn signal. "Almost there," he murmured, as if breaking the silence would somehow make the moment less weighted. Sam nodded, watching the terminal signs flash by as they followed the curve toward Arrivals. Whatever came next, they would face it together.

Mark and Sam waited in the crowded Arrivals area, their eyes scanning the steady stream of travellers emerging from customs. When James finally appeared, he looked nothing like the confident, self-assured man they remembered. His face was pale and lined, his shoulders stooped under an invisible weight. His once-pristine appearance was marred by exhaustion and despair. Sam's breath caught, and tears welled up in her eyes.

"Jeez, Jim, you look like shit!" Mark said, his voice forced into a casual tone to break the heavy silence.

James's eyes snapped to Sam, and for a moment, Mark regretted the words. James's fury was immediate and raw but not directed at him. "I told you not to come!" he barked, his voice low but tense. "Now I've got three of us to worry about."

Sam stammered, "I – James, I couldn't not come."

James cut her off with a sigh, his anger melting into something softer. "I'm not happy about this, but…" He paused, his expression shifting into something more vulnerable. "I can't deny it's good to see you – both of you." His voice softened further. "Come here."

Sam stepped into his arms, and James held her tightly, the embrace lingering longer than usual. When he finally pulled away, he turned to Mark and clasped his hand before pulling him into a quick hug.

"You're looking good, little brother," James said, his voice carrying a flicker of his old self.

"I can't return the compliment," Mark replied gently, his eyes studying James's lined face and bandaged hands.

Sam's voice broke in, trembling. "My God, James, what on earth has happened to you?"

James's gaze darted around the bustling terminal, and he shook his head. "Not here," he murmured. "I'll explain everything in the car."

They followed Mark to the Jeep, James deflecting questions with curt responses. When Mark remarked on James's lack of luggage, James dismissed it with a terse, "I'll explain soon."

Inside the Jeep, the atmosphere was thick with tension as James buckled himself into the back seat. He exhaled heavily, his hands shaking slightly.

"You need to trust me," he said, his voice low but steady. "We can't go back to Virginia Beach – not yet. Take the road toward Washington and head for Interstate 66. We're going west, into the Blue Ridge."

Mark frowned but complied, pulling out of the airport. The cityscape soon gave way to open roads as James remained silent, his fingers fidgeting with the bottle of water he'd brought. Finally, he broke the silence. "Last night, I killed a man. A good man."

Sam gasped, her hand flying to her mouth. "What? James, what are you saying?"

James raised a hand, "I didn't kill him with my own hands, but I led him into a situation where something, something unspeakable, took his life."

Mark glanced at him through the rearview mirror. "You're going to have to explain that."

"I will," James said, his voice heavy. "But first, you need to understand how I got here." He shifted uncomfortably in his seat, his gaze distant. "I was seduced by power – by promises of wealth and influence. Sir Giles Worsley saw my potential immediately. He took me under his wing and showed me... things I couldn't have imagined. He introduced me to the occult, to the forces beneath the surface of what we call reality."

Sam turned to face him, her expression unreadable. "James, this all sounds ..."

"Crazy? I know," he interrupted, "But it's the truth. I swear to you, I've seen things – done things – that defy explanation. Under Worsley's guidance, I became what some might call a sorcerer. A warlock. But I never saw myself that way."

He hesitated, gauging their reactions. Both stared at him, incredulous but silent. "Worsley himself is a master of the Black Arts," James continued. "He's crossed the Abyss, a level of existence that separates mere mortals from... something more. He is a Magus, and his power makes mine look insignificant. He can summon demons – control them. And right now, he's hunting me."

Mark exchanged a glance with Sam. "Why is he hunting you, Jim?"

"Let me provide you more background first. I know this is a lot to assimilate and it all seems unbelievable but at least humour me until I'm finished. I really have learned many things from Worsley. And you both know

I'm not an evil person. In the beginning I was strongly encouraged by Worsley to study the Qabalah, which is a set of esoteric teachings on mysticism, rooted in Judaism, that aids understanding of the concepts of man, the universe and God, the attainment of spiritual realisation. It is these teachings that most interest occultists like Worsley, as they see them as a path to enlightenment and, more importantly, to gaining enormous power. Qabalists believe that in the beginning all that existed was God and nothing else. Then God sent out an emanation of himself, a bright light if you will, which then produced a succession of emanations called sephirah, each possessing less of the divine light than the one before it. There were ten sephirah in all and collectively they make up the sephiroth."

Mark glanced in the rearview mirror. "You're losing me already, Jim. What does this have to do with... whatever you're running from?"

"Just bear with me, okay? This is important." He leaned forward slightly, his tone softening. "Think of the universe as nine concentric spheres, with the innermost one containing Earth. Qabalists believe that a spirit, created by God, descends through these spheres, picking up characteristics like wisdom, courage, and love – like layers or skins – before finally becoming flesh on Earth."

Sam turned in her seat, her expression sceptical but curious. "And when people die?" she asked.

"The soul sheds those layers as it ascends back through the spheres toward God," James explained. "But here's the catch – Qabalists don't believe devoutness is the key to returning to God. It's knowledge. Knowledge helps the soul ascend. Each sphere is guarded by angels, and only those with the right knowledge or passwords can pass."

Sam frowned, her voice uncertain. "That's... quite a system."

"It is," James admitted. "And it's not without risks. There are forces – dark, sinister ones – in the lower spheres that can trap ignorant or careless souls." He paused to take a sip from his water bottle, glancing at their incredulous faces. "You probably think I've lost it."

"Maybe," Mark said, "But keep going."

James hesitated before continuing. "Qabalists also believe that death isn't necessary for a soul to ascend the *sephiroth*. A soul can climb the spheres while still in the body. That's what Worsley can do. That's what he was teaching me to do."

Sam's mouth fell open. "James, are you saying…?"

"I was part of a secret magical order," James interrupted. "All those hours I spent meditating in my study – those weren't just for relaxation. They were training. Training to ascend the spheres. But it's not something just anyone can do. Most of Worsley's initiates never even make it to the first grade – *Neophyte*."

"Neophyte?" Mark asked.

James nodded. "The ranks, or grades, reflect how many *sephirah* someone has ascended. Those who don't make the grade remain probationers, doing whatever Worsley asks of them. He also leads a coven for rituals, though most of them aren't part of the order."

Sam crossed her arms. "And you were part of this… cult?"

"Yes," James admitted, his voice heavy. "I reached the rank of *Adeptus Major*, which means I ascended five spheres. My powers grew stronger than you could ever imagine. But the climb is dangerous. Evil forces block each stage. Overcoming them requires… sacrifices."

Mark's knuckles whitened on the steering wheel. "Sacrifices? What kind of sacrifices?"

James looked away, his voice dropping to a near whisper. "It started small. Animals. Then… it escalated."

Sam gasped, her hand covering her mouth. "James, no."

"I didn't know," James said quickly. "When I saw the child, I thought it was symbolic. But then… Worsley killed it. A baby." He stopped, unable to continue as tears filled his eyes.

The disbelief and shock in the car were deafening. Finally, Mark spoke, his voice tight. "Why, Jim? Why would you even get involved with something like this?"

"I've asked myself that question a thousand times. The truth is, Worsley is a master manipulator. He used his powers – and his charm – to draw me in. He promised me wealth, power, influence. And he delivered. My investments tripled under his guidance. He made me feel special, like I was destined for greatness. But it was all a lie. I was blinded by his charisma. He directed me to take the left-hand occult path which I later realised was more immoral as it rejects all religious authority and societal taboos."

Sam reached out, her voice soft. "Why didn't you leave earlier?"

"I tried," James said bitterly. "When I refused to go further – when I rejected his darker rituals – he turned on me. He used magic to bind me to his will. I was in constant physical pain - excruciating pain. He crafted a spell using a wax effigy with my hair and nail clippings, wrapping it in razor wire. Every knot was enchanted to tighten, and the agony was unbearable."

Mark now realised the cause of his own shingle-like pains, sympathetic sharing of his brother's agony. Did sticking pins in wax dolls really work? Surely not. Perhaps Jim had become susceptible to the suggestion of such a spell from Worsley. Yet they had both felt the pain. How could that be if the pain was not real? Mark did not know what to think.

Mark's face darkened. "And now he's hunting you?"

James nodded. "He won't stop until I'm dead – or worse. That's why we're heading to the lodge. I need time to prepare, to defend myself."

The Jeep fell silent again, the weight of James's words settled over them like a dark cloud, belying the blue sky that was just starting to break through the grey. Sam finally spoke, her voice shaking. "What do we do?"

"For now, just trust me," James said, his tone pleading. "Let me handle this. And pray it's enough."

"What happens now?" she asked softly.

"We carry on heading to the lodge," James said firmly. "I must prepare. Worsley will send something after me – something evil and deadly. But I'll be ready."

Mark's thoughts were a chaotic swirl as he drove. Black magic? Murderous demons? It sounded like something out of a horror novel, not reality. The events James described were appalling and defied belief. How could any of it be true? Mark shook his head, trying to process everything. Was this the ultimate proof of his brother's descent into madness? Or were these terrifying revelations the product of a disturbed imagination? He couldn't decide, but one thing was clear: James, the man he had always admired for his confidence and strength, was now consumed by fear – fear of Giles Worsley.

"Jim," Mark said finally, breaking the tense silence. "I've seen what you're capable of – your powers. Couldn't you use them against him?"

James's voice rose sharply. "My powers are strong, Mark. Stronger than you've ever seen. But even then, they're nothing compared to his!" He sighed, frustration evident in his tone. "Haven't you been listening? Worsley is virtually omnipotent. He can control people with a look. He can make you bleed with a touch. And Flauros – his demon – makes him invincible."

Mark's grip on the wheel tightened as James continued, his words spilling out in a desperate torrent.

"Flauros isn't just a demon. He's a devil – a force of unimaginable power. He killed Harper in a way I can barely describe, and he'll do the same to me. Worsley uses him as a shield, making himself invulnerable to any attack, physical or psychic. Bullets, weapons, telekinetic forces – none of it can touch him. Flauros absorbs it all. Incinerates it. Even if I caught Worsley alone, without his demon, I might have a sliver of hope – but it would still be a long shot. He's simply too powerful."

Mark swallowed hard. The fear in James's voice was palpable, and it made Mark's own stomach churn. His brother, the unshakable pillar of their family, was rattled to his core.

James took a deep breath and leaned back in his seat. "This is why we couldn't go home, Mark. Worsley will send something after me tonight or tomorrow, and I need time to prepare. He'll find me eventually – that much is certain. But if I'm ready, I might stand a chance."

"What kind of preparations are we talking about?" Mark asked warily.

"I've been fasting since yesterday," James explained, his voice taking on a clinical tone. "Only water. No impurities. It's essential for psychic clarity and strength during an attack. Lack of food and sleep heighten psychic powers. But I need further supplies – specialised items. I'm assuming you have brought the horseshoes with you as I requested. We'll stop in Harrisonburg. You and Sam can grab enough groceries for the weekend while I pick up what I need. Pay with cash to leave no trace. I'll also need some clothes, depending on what you've packed."

Sam, who had been silent, finally spoke. "Where exactly are we going?"

"An old hunting lodge in the Blue Ridge, near Avon," James said. His voice softened slightly as he added, "I bought it a couple of years ago. I'd planned to fix it up as a family retreat – a surprise for you, Sam. England put those plans on hold," James continued. "It's run-down, but I've been paying a local agency to maintain it. It's isolated, which is exactly what we need. When the attack comes, I don't want anyone else to get hurt."

Mark followed James's directions to the exit for Harrisonburg, pulling into a small shopping district. They split up to save time. While Mark and Sam gathered groceries and cleaning supplies, James wandered off to a local shop specializing in homeopathic and esoteric items.

As they stood in the checkout line, ready to pay with cash as James had advised, Sam turned to Mark. "What do you make of all this?"

Mark hesitated before replying. "Honestly? I don't know, Sam. I can't believe any of these wild stories about demons and black magic. I've never seen James like this. He's terrified of this Worsley guy, and that's not like him. I think he's had some kind of breakdown."

Sam's voice wavered. "How are we supposed to help him? He needs medical attention – professional help. We must get him assessed as soon as possible."

"I agree. But let's humour him for now. Let him play out this… this imaginary war with demons tonight. Maybe by morning, he'll have calmed down enough to listen to reason."

Sam sighed, her reluctance clear. "I hope you're right. I really do."

James returned to the Jeep about fifteen minutes later, one bag loaded with an assortment of herbs, powders, spices, and oils: the other containing some clanking pewter containers. He set the items down carefully, their oddity unspoken but tangible in the charged silence. Neither Mark nor Sam commented, though their exchanged glances betrayed mutual uncertainty. Without a word, they resumed their journey.

The Jeep sped along I-81, the highway stretching into the horizon as they passed through Staunton and Roanoke before taking I-64 toward Richmond. The mood in the car was tense but subdued, the occasional navigation instruction from James punctuating an otherwise wordless drive.

"Take the exit here," James finally said, his voice breaking the quiet. A short while later, he added, "Slow down – this next turn is sharp." Mark adjusted the Jeep's speed as they navigated a precarious hairpin descent, the road snaking through dense trees before opening into a scenic valley.

The descent revealed a quaint, rustic landscape. They crossed a small bridge spanning a creek, the water below reflecting the fading light of dusk.

"Turn right just before the Exxon Gas Station," James instructed. Mark followed the directions without question, the road narrowing as they passed farmland and meadows dotted with grazing livestock.

Soon, the surroundings began to change. The meadows gave way to dense forested foothills, the trees growing taller and closer together as they approached the Blue Ridge Mountains. The Jeep's tires crunched over gravel as the road began a gradual climb from a wooded valley.

James gazed out the window, a wistful expression softening his weary features. "I love this place," he said quietly, more to himself than to anyone else. The deciduous trees were still bare, but evergreens like pine, hemlock, and spruce provided splashes of vibrant green. His thoughts wandered to autumn, his favourite season in the Blue Ridge. He pictured the fiery reds of dogwood and black gum, the golden yellows of tulip trees, and the deep oranges of sassafras. It was nature's final, glorious act before winter's hush. *Will I live to see it again?* he wondered grimly, his resolve tightening.

"We're almost there," James announced as they passed a sign for *Rattlesnake Trail*, the nearby parking area marked by a wooden post. A few moments later, he added, "Fork right up ahead."

Mark squinted at the barely visible dirt track veering off the main road. "You're sure about this?" he asked, his voice tinged with doubt.

"Positive," James replied firmly. The Jeep bumped along the narrow, stony path, the uneven terrain making Mark silently grateful for the vehicle's off-road capabilities. After a short climb, they reached a clearing that opened into a small basin.

Before them lay a group of wooden structures nestled against the slope of a hill. The centrepiece was a large log cabin, flanked by two smaller barn-shaped outbuildings. The cluster of buildings overlooked a tranquil lake, its surface shimmering faintly in the fading light. A grassy meadow sloped gently down from the cabin to the water's edge. The lake was framed by a mix of evergreen trees and the faint outline of a dam could be seen at the far end.

The dam, overgrown with vegetation and small trees, seemed to blend seamlessly with the landscape. James gestured toward it. "The lake's man-made," he explained. "The dam was built years ago to harness a mountain stream, which still supplies the water."

Mark parked the Jeep near the cabin, taking in the serene yet isolated surroundings. "It's beautiful," he admitted, his voice subdued.

James nodded. "I wish I could have shown you this place under better circumstances," he said, turning to Sam.

"It is idyllic," she agreed, though her tone was uneasy. She forced a small smile. "Maybe one day we can use it the way you originally planned."

James smiled back. "Maybe," he said softly. *If I survive the night,* he added silently.

Shadows lengthened as the sun dipped below the horizon, the surrounding forest growing darker with each passing minute. James retrieved a set of keys from a hidden spot under the porch and climbed the steps. "I need to start the generator," he said over his shoulder before disappearing toward one of the outbuildings.

Sam and Mark unpacked the Jeep, carrying bags of groceries and supplies onto the porch. The rustic chairs there creaked as they sank into them, waiting for James's return. The faint hum of the generator starting up echoed through the still evening air, followed by the sound of James's footsteps on the gravel path.

He rejoined them, climbing the steps with the weariness of a man carrying the weight of the world. Without a word, he unlocked the cabin door and stepped inside, flipping a light switch. The warm glow illuminated the cozy interior, casting long shadows across the worn wooden floors and the simple, functional furniture.

Mark and Sam followed him in, their apprehension unmistakable. Whatever lay ahead, they were here now – together – and the night was only just beginning.

Chapter 12
Demonic Preparations

Southeast England – 25 March, 11:00 PM local

Sir Giles Worsley rose gracefully from the meditation mat, his red silk bathrobe draping around him like a cloak of authority. A thin smile played on his lips, one that radiated both satisfaction and malice. The confrontation was mere hours away now, and he savoured the anticipation. He would ensure that Benedict's death was not only inevitable but excruciating. There would be no mercy, no reprieve – only pain and ruin.

The room around him was sparse yet imposing, its stone walls adorned with intricate tapestries depicting mythic beasts and esoteric symbols. In the dim light, the chamber exuded an almost tangible weight, an oppressive atmosphere that seemed to vibrate with latent power. On the low altar before him lay an array of tools – a dagger with a hilt inlaid with obsidian, a golden chalice etched with sigils, and a stack of parchment marked with meticulous diagrams.

Sir Giles stretched, his movements deliberate and calculated. Every fibre of his being radiated control, the kind born of decades of mastery over both himself and the forces he commanded. This control was critical now. He had fasted, purified himself, and meditated with unwavering focus. The hours spent on the astral planes had been fruitful. With the aid of Benedict's personal belongings – a lock of hair, a discarded cufflink – he had located his former protégé. Finding him again would be child's play.

Yet, beneath his practiced composure, Giles seethed with rage. When he had returned to his estate the previous night and found the aftermath of Benedict's intrusion, he had been livid. The sight of Moeller's mutilated corpse, a testament to Flauros's failure, had pushed him over the edge. His fury had been so intense that he'd spent hours punishing the demon, bending its essence to his will, tormenting it until its cries reverberated across planes. Only when he was certain of its submission had he taken the creature back into himself, its volatile energy fueling his preparations for the coming battle.

He strode into the inner chamber, the heart of his domain. This room, hidden from all but his most trusted acolytes, was both sanctuary and battlefield. The air here felt heavier, imbued with the residue of countless rituals. In the centre of the chamber lay the pentagram, meticulously drawn with powdered silver and enclosed within a circle of protective glyphs. Tonight, it would serve as the gateway for a summoning unlike any other.

Flauros would not be enough this time. The demon had already failed with Benedict, and Sir Giles was not one to repeat mistakes. No, tonight he would call upon Abaddon – the destroyer, a devil of such magnitude that even the most skilled summoners hesitated to invoke it. The challenge of controlling Abaddon was immense, its volatile nature infamous among practitioners. But Giles relished the risk. Benedict could not survive such an assault. Even the faintest hope of resistance would be snuffed out in the face of Abaddon's wrath.

Still, Giles was not blind to the dangers. Should Benedict somehow evade the attack – or worse, repel it – Abaddon's fury would inevitably turn on its summoner. That was where Fiona came in. She would be his failsafe, his insurance against the unlikely. Her presence reassured him, though it stirred an uncomfortable pang of guilt. Fiona had been a loyal disciple for years, her devotion unwavering. She had given him everything, sacrificing her independence, her dignity, and, perhaps most tragically, her potential.

Fiona had risen to the rank of Adeptus Minor, a significant achievement but far below what Giles had once hoped for her. Despite her relentless effort, she lacked the brilliance required to ascend further. It had been a bitter disappointment, but she remained invaluable in other ways. She ran his covens, orchestrating rituals at his Cornwall estate with precision. Her specialty, ritual sex magic, was unparalleled – her mastery of the craft both an asset and a pleasure. Tonight, however, her role would be purely pragmatic. If Abaddon turned on him, Fiona would be the one to absorb the consequences.

Giles suppressed a sigh as he adjusted the tools on the altar. Fiona's limitations were a source of frustration, but they paled in comparison to the bitterness he felt toward Benedict. The boy had been a prodigy, a once-in-a-lifetime talent with boundless potential. Together, they could have ascended to Ipsissimus, achieving a level of power and enlightenment that defied comprehension. They could have bent reality to their will, reshaping the world in their image. But Benedict's moral scruples – those archaic, self-righteous shackles – had ruined everything.

"Damn him," Giles muttered, his voice low and venomous. Then his lips curled into a smile, cold and sharp. "And damn him I shall."

The anticipation thrummed within him like a second heartbeat. This was more than vengeance. It was a reclamation of control, a reaffirmation of his dominance over all who dared to defy him. As he began inscribing the final runes on the parchment, the room seemed to darken, the shadows deepening in response to his intent.

Tonight, Benedict would face the full heft of Sir Giles Worsley's wrath. And Giles would savour every moment of it.

Chapter 13

Desperate Defences

*B**lue Ridge – 26 March 12:05 AM local time*
James worked with a quiet intensity, the final touches to the pentagram consuming his full focus. Earlier, the three of them had cleared the centre of the main living area, moving what little furniture the lodge possessed. The space was bare now, save for the intricate geometric design that had taken hours to construct. The lodge itself, though once envisioned as a retreat, now served as a psychic fortress – a battlefield for the confrontation James was certain lay ahead.

The former hunting lodge was a spacious two-story log cabin, rustic but sturdy. Upstairs, a galleried landing overlooked the expansive ground floor, which featured an open-plan layout. There were also two bedrooms and a bathroom. The open plan area downstairs had been sparsely furnished: a stained leather sofa and three mismatched chairs sat atop worn Indian rugs that had seen better days. A large open fireplace dominated one wall, its soot-streaked stones standing testament to years of use. To the rear, a modest kitchen and dining area offered functionality over charm, while a back door led to a small porch overlooking the wooded slopes. The staircase opposite the fireplace climbed to the landing above, its creaks betraying the lodge's age.

Mark and Sam had agreed, reluctantly, to humour James, assisting in the preparations for his supposed battle against Worsley's dark forces. Their scepticism was evident in their every movement, but they said nothing. James, for his part, was exacting in his demands. Every detail had to be perfect. Dust and impurities, he had explained, could serve as conduits for malevolent forces, potentially compromising the magic circle he was creating.

They had cleared away the rugs and meagre furniture to create a large open space, then armed with cleaning supplies, the trio scrubbed the floor until it gleamed. Afterwards, with Mark's help, James began constructing the pentagram. Using chalk, string, a tape measure, and a protractor – items Sam had fetched from home – he approached the task with meticulous precision.

"Mark, hold the string here," James instructed, indicating the centre of the cleared floor. Mark obeyed, watching as James measured exactly seven feet outward and marked the edge of a circle. He moved with the deliberate care of a surgeon, marking precise angles and drawing radial lines from the centre point. Seventy-two degrees. Another seventy-two. Five evenly spaced marks formed the foundation of the star, and James carefully connected them, lines intersecting to create the five-pointed figure.

Sam, meanwhile, had lit a small fire in the hearth, its curling flames casting long shadows across the room. Though James had insisted she and Mark wouldn't stay in the lodge that night, Sam had busied herself upstairs, preparing the bedrooms in quiet defiance. Sitting on one of the beds, she tried to process everything. James's stories of child sacrifices haunted her. They were too grotesque to be true – or were they? She had pressed him earlier, demanding to know how Worsley could possibly orchestrate such atrocities. James's answer had chilled her to the core: Worsley's minions preyed on vulnerable women, desperate and drug-addicted, convincing them to deliver their babies for supposed adoptions. The horror of it was unbearable, and Sam had blocked the thought from her mind, retreating to the landing to watch James working below.

"Mark, fill a pitcher with water from the kitchen," James called. "Let it run for a few minutes first. I want it as pure as possible."

Mark did as instructed, while James continued setting up. He laid out the supplies they had gathered in Harrisonburg: five pewter vases, a matching bowl, white candles, and the freshly forged horseshoes he had asked them to bring. When Mark returned with the water, James murmured a series of unintelligible words over it, his hands tracing intricate symbols in the air.

"Just charging it," he said, his tone distracted but confident.

The charged water filled the vases, which James placed carefully in the valleys of the pentagram. The candles followed, one at each point of the star, their flames casting a faint glow as James "charged" the horseshoes and positioned them behind each candle with their open ends pointing outward. Finally, he arranged bundles of herbs beyond each vase, their earthy aroma mingling with the faint metallic tang of the horseshoes.

Sam leaned against the railing of the landing, watching it all with a mixture of unease and pity. She marvelled at James's precision but felt an overwhelming sadness for the man he had become. Once strong and admired, he now seemed fragile, a shadow of his former self. *How had Worsley damaged him so deeply?* she wondered. *Could James ever recover?*

James straightened, his shoulders heavy with weariness. "Sam, Mark, come here," he called, his voice resolute.

The two joined him, their expressions guarded. James met their eyes, his own filled with a mix of determination and resignation. "My defences are ready," he said. "I've done everything I can. The rest is out of my hands."

He paused, the weight of his words hanging in the air. "Worsley knows I'm here. I felt his presence on the astral plane moments ago. He'll send something – soon. Whatever it is, it will be directed at me. This room will be the battleground. You two must leave. It's the only way I can ensure your safety."

Mark started to protest, but James silenced him with a raised hand. "You can't stay here, not even outside. Go down to the parking area near Rattlesnake Trail. Wait until dawn. If you hear or see anything, do not come back. No matter what."

Sam and Mark nodded reluctantly. The finality in James's tone left no room for argument.

"Sam," James added softly, "wait on the porch for a moment. I need a word with Mark."

Mark watched as Sam stepped outside, her reluctance clear. Turning back to James, he felt a pang of unease. "What is it?"

James hesitated, then spoke with quiet urgency. "Mark, my chances of surviving this are slim. If I don't make it, promise me two things. First, don't go after Worsley. He's too powerful. Revenge would only destroy you and Sam. Second… take care of her. You've always loved her, and I know she cares for you too. Be there for her."

Mark swallowed hard. "Jim don't talk like this. You're going to make it."

James shook his head. "Just promise me."

Mark nodded, his voice tight. "I promise."

The brothers embraced briefly before James sent him to fetch Sam. She returned, tears streaming down her face, and the couple shared a final embrace and kiss. Watching them, Mark felt a confusing mix of emotions – love, guilt, and a desperate need to protect them both.

As James began lighting the candles and chanting, Mark stopped and looked back at Jim, through the glazed panel of the door but he was busy lighting the candles at each cardinal point of the pentagram. After that he dropped some herbs, liquids and powders into the pewter bowl, which he set down near the centre of the pentagram and set light to the contents. Then, safe inside his astral stronghold, he turned to each of the points making strange gestures and signs and appeared to be chanting. He caught Mark's stare and forcibly gestured him and Sam to leave.

"Come Sam," Mark said gently, "We have to leave now." They took one last look at James who was now seated in the pentagram in some yoga-like pose, and then they turned away and descended the steps and made their way towards the jeep. The night stretched before them, dark and filled with uncertainty.

❖

Chapter 14:

The Summoning

*S*outheast England – 26 March 05:30 AM local

Sir Giles Worsley stood in the dimly lit ritual chamber, his white robes glowing faintly in the glimmering candlelight. The air was heavy with the scent of incense, a heady mixture of myrrh and dragon's blood, designed to draw the presence of higher forces. The atmosphere pulsed with latent energy, the kind that made the skin prickle and the hairs on the back of the neck stand on end. He breathed deeply, centring himself, every movement a calculated act of authority and focus.

Fiona Barnes stood nearby, watching him with rapt attention. She had arrived hours earlier, carrying the young goat kid in her arms like an offering to the gods. They had meditated together, their minds reaching out across the astral planes to pinpoint Benedict's location. It hadn't taken long – Benedict's defences, while intricate, were no match for their combined expertise. They had found him in a decrepit log cabin in western Virginia, labouring over a pentagram in a futile attempt to shield himself. Giles had allowed his presence to be known, a cruel taunt to torment Benedict with the knowledge of his impending doom. The memory of Benedict's panicked awareness brought a thin smile to Giles's lips as he prepared to summon Abaddon, the Destroyer.

"We'll celebrate with my finest burgundy once this is over," Giles said, his voice smooth and confident as he rose to his feet.

He glanced at Fiona, now positioned outside the protective circle. She stood tall and composed, her hazel eyes glowing with a mixture of admiration and anticipation. Fiona was a striking woman – slim, athletic, and regal in her bearing. Her short, dark hair framed a face marked by high cheekbones and a commanding presence. Although in her fifties, she looked fifteen years younger and was likely using low magic to maintain at least some of her youthfulness. She was not beautiful in the traditional sense, but her elegance and charisma were undeniable. Dark eyebrows over widely separated hazel eyes, high cheekbones, a straight, rather narrow nose and a large mouth with lips that were a shade too thin, all combined to form a highly attractive outcome. She was a fine specimen of womanhood and unbridled in bed.

Giles appreciated her loyalty, though he regarded her more as a tool than a partner. Tonight, she would serve as both his medium and his safeguard – a role she accepted with unwavering devotion.

Fiona's heart raced as she watched Giles. He had donned white robes for the summoning as recommended in the grimoires for tonight's work. She had great esteem for power and there were none more powerful than Giles. A king among men, his aquiline features – sharp and severe – exuded command and magnetism. She adored him, though she knew her feelings would never be returned. Still, the prospect of being instrumental in this night's ritual filled her with pride, and she allowed herself a flicker of hope that success might kindle Giles's carnal desires.

The chamber was a meticulous study in ritual precision. A pentagram inscribed with powdered silver dominated the centre of the room, surrounded by a circle of protective glyphs drawn in black ink. Candles burned at each cardinal point, their flames steady despite the oppressive air. At the altar, carved from dark stone, lay the goat kid, its bleating subdued by a gentle spell. Channels etched into the altar would guide the sacrificial blood into a silver chalice set in a hollow below – a design, centuries old, perfected for summoning entities of the highest order.

Giles moved to the altar, the ritual sword in hand. The blade, imbued with his own energy, glinted ominously as he raised it above his head. His voice resonated through the chamber, commanding and unyielding.

"I conjure thee, O Spirit Abaddon, by the most glorious names: Adonai, Elohim, Elohe, Zebaoth, Elion, Tetragrammaton! By Baralmensis, Baldachiensis, and Apolorosedes, I command thee to come forth and do my bidding. Thou art conjured by the name of Heliorem. Come to me, speak to me visibly, and fulfil my desire without deceit. Adonai Saday commands thee!"

Fiona, lying prostrate outside the circle, felt a surge of energy as the incantation rose in force and volume. Her thin gown clung to her body, and her breathing quickened. The power emanating from Giles was intoxicating, and she surrendered herself to it, slipping into a hypnotic trance. Her hands clutched the personal items of Benedict – a photograph, hair, and nail clippings – her role as the medium to direct Abaddon's wrath now imminent.

Giles repeated the invocation twice more, each iteration intensifying the energy in the room. The temperature dropped sharply, and a palpable darkness settled over them. He moved with purpose to the altar, positioning the sword above the goat.

"I slay thee in the name and to the honour of Abaddon," he declared, his voice steady.

With a single stroke, he severed the goat's head, lifting it high as blood spilled down the altar's grooves into the chalice below. "O great and powerful Abaddon may this sacrifice be pleasing to thee. Do as I command, and greater offerings shall follow."

A foul stench filled the chamber as the air thickened. Fiona's body tensed, her excitement mingling with fear. The demon was coming.

The room grew icy, and an ear-splitting roar shattered the silence. Abaddon materialized within the pentagram, its monstrous form towering over Giles. The demon's crowned head, grotesquely human yet hideous, sat upon a thorax resembling that of an enormous insect. Powerful, clawed appendages sprouted from its torso, and its lower body ended in muscular, cloven-hoofed legs. A scorpion's tail curled menacingly behind it, its pulsating body shifting through shades of red, green, and brown.

"Hail, Abaddon! Hail, O Lord of the Locusts!" Giles proclaimed, unwavering despite the demon's furious shrieks. "Thee I invoke to destroy the soul of Benedict. Take this servant as your guide and return only when your work is done."

The demon roared once more before dissolving into a cloud of smoke that slithered toward Fiona. It coiled around her, seeping into her body. She shuddered violently as the possession completed, her face serene despite the turmoil within.

Giles exhaled slowly, his confidence unshaken. The summoning had gone flawlessly, and Abaddon was now unleashed upon his enemy. While the exit ritual would pose its own dangers, Giles was certain of his control. If Benedict somehow survived, Fiona would pay the price – but Giles was willing to accept that loss.

He considered rising on the astral plane to gleefully witness the destruction, but that would be dangerous and foolhardy; he could not risk Abaddon catching him outside his body. For now, he waited, his heart filled with cold satisfaction. Benedict's destruction was all but assured.

Chapter 15
An Unearthly Battle

*B*lue Ridge – 26 March 12:45 AM local

Mark stopped the Cherokee on the rising track just before the crest where they had first seen the lodge. "It's no good Sam, I can't leave him there alone and just wait in some remote spot until dawn. I'm going back to wait outside in case he needs help."

"I agree Mark," Sam replied in a low voice that was still choked from her farewell to Jim. "He must not know though, so let's leave the jeep here and walk back."

Inside the lodge, James sat cross-legged within the pentagram, his breathing steady and deliberate despite the rising dread in his chest. The candles around him flickered violently as the temperature in the room plummeted. Frost began to form along the edges of the windows and the wooden beams of the lodge creaked under the strain of the unnatural cold.

The noise came first – a deafening swarm of locusts that appeared out of nowhere, filling the room with a living, writhing storm. Their bodies clattered against the walls and ceiling, their collective hum reverberating through the lodge like the wail of a thousand tortured souls. James's heart sank. He knew immediately what was coming: Abaddon, the Destroyer, King of the Locust Demons. Worsley had summoned one of the highest-order entities, risking everything to ensure James's annihilation.

James began to chant, his voice rising above the din. He called upon the Names of Power, invoking the divine forces he hoped would keep the demon at bay. But even as he spoke, he knew the futility of it. This was no ordinary adversary. This was death incarnate.

Mark and Sam reached the porch of the lodge, the unholy sound emanating from within growing louder with every step. The windows glowed faintly with a sickly, pulsating light. They pressed their faces to the glass, and what they saw froze them in place.

The interior of the lodge was a nightmare. Swarms of locusts filled the air, their writhing bodies swirling in a vortex around the pentagram. James sat in its centre, his face pale but resolute, his voice unwavering as he chanted. But the swarm seemed to press against the invisible barrier of the circle, testing it, pushing it to its limits.

And then, just as suddenly as they had appeared, the locusts vanished. The silence that followed was even more terrifying.

"What the hell is going on?" Mark whispered, his voice trembling. "I'm going in."

Before Sam could protest, Mark opened the door and stepped inside. James's head snapped toward him, his eyes wide with fury and fear. "Get out, you fool!" he screamed, his voice reverberating unnaturally. A force lifted Mark and Sam from their feet, hurling them back onto the porch. The door slammed shut behind them, the lock clicking audibly.

Mark scrambled to his feet, pounding on the door. "Jim, open it! Let us in!" But the door wouldn't budge, and neither would the windows.

Inside, the room grew colder still. A smoky mist began to coalesce at the edges of the pentagram, twisting and writhing as it took shape. James's worst fears were realized as Abaddon materialized – a monstrous figure that defied comprehension. Its crowned, humanoid head sat atop an insectoid thorax, its massive wings humming with malevolent energy. Clawed appendages jutted from its torso, and its scorpion-like tail lashed the air with a venomous gleam. The creature's body pulsated with shifting colors – blood-red, sickly green, and decayed brown.

James continued chanting, his voice steady despite the terror coursing through him. "Leave me, O Lord Abaddon! I command thee to depart!" He invoked the Names of Power, his words resonating with desperate authority.

Abaddon roared, the sound shaking the very foundations of the lodge. But then, to James's astonishment, it stopped. Its form shimmered and shifted, shrinking and softening until it resembled a young woman with a kind, gentle face. Her voice, melodic and soothing, filled the room.

"James Benedict," she said, her tone almost maternal. "I mean you no harm. I have been summoned by a lesser warlock, one who lacks the power to control me. But I am bound to fulfil his command. There is, however, a way for us both to escape this fate."

James stared, his mind racing. Was this deception, or could it be true?

"Leave your earthly body," the figure continued. "Come with me to face the one who summoned me. I will destroy him for his arrogance, and you shall return to your body, free and unharmed."

James hesitated. The offer was too good to be true, and he knew the risks. Leaving the pentagram would strip him of all protection. But what if it was sincere? What if this was his chance to end it all and return to Sam?

Outside, Mark and Sam circled the lodge, searching for a way in. Sam spotted an open window on the second floor. "There!" she cried. Mark fetched a ladder, his hands shaking as he set it against the wall.

Inside, James made his decision. "Alright," he said. "I'll go with you."

"A sensible choice, human!" The girl who was Abaddon replied, the words denying its own human form.

James took a meditative position breathing slowly and rhythmically and, with the experience of someone who has risen on the astral planes many times, he slipped easily into a sleep-like state. His astral body appeared beside him and moved towards the edge of the pentagram. James took only one step out of the pentagram when Abaddon roared with bestial glee as it instantaneously transformed back into its true diabolical form and moved to grab him. However, James, had been anticipating the trick, and was too quick, returning to his body in a flash. The demon raged, furious with itself for displaying its hand a fraction too soon.

"Prepare to die, human!" It roared.

Outside, Mark steadied the ladder against the lodge, the rough wood creaking faintly under his weight as he tried to pry open the second-story window. The cold air seemed to grow sharper with every passing moment, the eerie silence around them pressing against his nerves like an unwelcome touch.

"Damn it," he muttered, his breath fogging the night air. "It's stuck. I can't get it open."

Below him, Sam called out, her voice tense with urgency. "We're wasting time, Mark. Let me try — I can fit through the gap."

Reluctantly, Mark descended, gripping the sides of the ladder tightly. Sam took his place, her smaller frame more suited for the task. She climbed swiftly, her determination intense. As she reached the window, she began to wriggle through the narrow opening, the rough wood scraping against her jacket.

"I can make it," she panted, squeezing herself inch by inch. "I have to."

Inside the lodge, James was intoning the words of power with as much resonance as he could muster while Abaddon cursed and raged. The clamour was horrific, and James could hardly hear himself above the din. The house started vibrating and the candles started shaking and spluttering. James knew that if even part of his protective circle was breached, it was over. He renewed his incantations with increased vigour in a desperate attempt to keep the pentagram secure.

On the landing, Sam's voice rang out, her shock clear. "James! What on earth is happening?"

James's heart plummeted. He looked up, his chanting faltering, and saw Sam silhouetted in the doorway to the gallery above. Her wide eyes locked onto his, her expression a mix of confusion and horror.

"No, Sam!" he screamed, his voice cracking. "Get out! Run now!"

But it was too late. Abaddon moved faster than anything mortal, its massive claws slicing through the air as it lunged for her. The demon's laughter was a guttural, inhuman sound, filled with malice and delight. Sam's scream echoed through the lodge as its claws closed around her.

"No!" James cried, abandoning the circle to save her. He reached out with his powers, slowing her fall as Abaddon hurled her from the gallery. She landed heavily in his arms, knocking him backward. The impact drove the air from his lungs, and he gasped, his vision spinning.

The demon loomed over them, its towering form radiating malevolence. James scrambled to shield her, his arms wrapping around her trembling frame as if sheer will power could protect her from the unthinkable horror bearing down on them.

"I love you," he whispered, his voice broken.

Sam's lips twisted into a cruel smile. Her face contorted, transforming into the grotesque visage of a crone. Before his eyes, she dissolved into mist, leaving him holding nothing but air.

James froze, the realization crashing over him. "No," he murmured, shaking his head. "No, no, no…"

Abaddon roared with triumphant glee, its claws closing around him. James screamed, the sound ripped from his very soul as the demon's talons tore into his flesh.

Outside, Sam and Mark reached the porch just in time to hear James's agonized scream. It pierced the night, a sound so raw and primal that it brought them to their knees. Mark clutched his head, screaming at the unbearable pain as he felt Jim's agony. Then suddenly it was gone.

"Mark, come on!" Sam urged, pulling him to his feet. Together, they ran to the windows, their eyes frantically scanning the chaos within.

The sight inside was a vision of pure nightmare. Abaddon, a creature of nightmarish proportions, was tearing James apart. Its claws shredded flesh and clothing with merciless precision, its scorpion tail stabbing repeatedly into his writhing body. Blood sprayed across the room, painting the walls in crimson streaks. The candles flickered madly, their light casting grotesque shadows that danced in time with the carnage.

James's body was lifted into the air by some unseen force, his limbs limp and lifeless. The demon flew in tight circles around him, slashing and raking with its claws, its laughter a chilling mockery of human joy. With one final, brutal swipe, it tore open his abdomen. His entrails spilled to the floor, a sickening heap that only added to the macabre tableau.

Mark and Sam watched in frozen horror as James's broken body began to spin, faster and faster, until it became a blur. Blood, flesh, and bone sprayed outward in a grotesque spiral, splattering every surface. Then, with a sickening crack, his body exploded, leaving nothing but a mist of blood and a spray of viscera in its wake.

The demon turned its monstrous head toward the windows, its glowing eyes locking onto Mark and Sam. It let out a howl of pure evil, the sound vibrating through the glass before it began to dissolve. Its form shrank into a pulsating orb of smoke, the malevolent energy radiating outward in waves.

Mark's instincts screamed a warning. "Get down!" he yelled, tackling Sam to the floor just as the orb expanded outward, engulfing the lodge in a burst of supernatural force.

A split second later, the windows above their heads exploded with a deafening roar, showering them in a lethal cascade of jagged glass. The night erupted into chaos as freezing, hurricane-force winds tore through the air, shrieking like a banshee and slashing at their exposed skin. Instinctively, they threw their arms up, shielding their faces, their cries drowned by the fury of the storm. Mark lunged for Sam, pulling her into his arms as shards sliced through the air around them. With desperate strength, he dragged her down the steps, away from the tempest emanating from the shattered porch towards the lake's edge.

The unholy wind howled above their heads, a malevolent force that seemed intent on their annihilation. Sam sobbed uncontrollably; her screams lost in the maelstrom. Mark wept openly, his tears mingling with blood trickling from a gash on his cheek. He clutched her tighter, his every movement driven by sheer survival instinct. Together, they stumbled and fell, their bodies battered by the relentless assault of nature's wrath.

And then, as abruptly as it had begun, the wind subsided. The silence that followed was eerie, as though the earth itself held its breath in the wake of the chaos. Mark led Sam to a weathered bench overlooking the now placid, moonlit water. They collapsed onto it, trembling, their breaths ragged and their bodies still trembling from the ordeal. The distant, low hum of the generator provided the only sound, a faint reminder of normalcy in a world that had suddenly turned upside down.

Mark turned to Sam, his heart shattering at the sight of her tear-streaked face, her eyes glazed and unseeing. Blood streaked her pale skin, the crimson stark against the moonlight. Rage erupted within him, a white-hot wrath that burned through his veins. His hands clenched into fists as he stared into the void, his voice a raw, guttural growl. "Worsley," he spat, the name a venomous curse. "He's behind this. All of it. That monster… he's evil incarnate."

He trembled with fury, his body shaking as he fought to contain the maelstrom of emotions threatening to consume him. "He must be stopped," Mark hissed, his voice trembling with conviction. "No prison, no punishment is enough for what he's done. He must die. I'll find a way. I swear it. I'll kill him."

His words pierced the haze clouding Sam's mind. She turned to him, her bloodshot eyes locking onto his. For a moment, she simply stared, her expression unreadable. Then, slowly, she shifted her gaze back to the lodge in the distance, its darkened silhouette ominous against the night sky. Sam shuddered, her body wracked by a fresh wave of sobs.

"Yes," she whispered, her voice barely audible but laced with a chilling resolve. Her tears continued to fall, but her face hardened, a flicker of unrelenting determination glinting in her eyes. "And I want to be there when it happens." Her voice was steadied, cold and deliberate. "We have to end him. Together."

⋯⊷⊶◀❖▶⊷⊶⋯

Chapter 16
Sinful Satisfaction

Southeast England – 26 March 6:45 AM local

The morning light crept through the edges of the heavy curtains, casting a soft glow over the opulent bedroom. Sir Giles and Fiona lay entwined in the luxurious embrace of his large, four-poster bed, their bare skin glowing with the heat of a night consumed by fervent passion. Giles reached over to the ornate bedside table, refilling their wine glasses with a flourish. He handed one to Fiona, their fingers brushing in a silent acknowledgment of shared triumph.

"To the night's work," he toasted, his voice resonating with fulfilment.

Earlier, Abaddon had emerged, its essence pulsating through Fiona's form before materializing fully, its immense power palpable even in its departure. Giles had performed the formal dismissal ritual; his every word laced with precision and authority. To his relief, the demon had left willingly, appeased and eager to return to its own dark pursuits. Benedict was no more, his life consumed by the will of the entity they had summoned.

Fiona's exhilaration was uncontainable. Her eyes sparkled with an unearthly fervour as she recounted her experience, her voice tinged with awe and a faint trace of lingering darkness.

"Oh, Giles, what a thrill it was," she began, her tone breathless. "I became Abaddon. I could feel its strength coursing through me – the fury, the cunning, the unyielding power. I was unstoppable, omnipotent. When Benedict resisted, it only heightened the pleasure. I liked James, truly, but at that moment, his destruction was ecstasy. I felt Abaddon's wrath as though it were my own, and when we tore him apart… the rush was indescribable, like a storm of pure elation. Your control over such a force is nothing short of miraculous. You are a master beyond compare."

Giles listened intently, a mixture of pride and envy showing in his eyes. He pressed for details, eager to savour every facet of the event he had orchestrated yet missed firsthand. A short while later, they had indulged themselves with food and drink in celebration of the night's work and before long they were also hungrily feasting on each other in his bedroom with a vigour that was worthy of a Beltane Sabbat.

"That he needed eradication is unfortunate," Giles mused later, swirling his wine thoughtfully. "His potential was immense – likely irreplaceable. Yet, his moral rigidity blinded him. He could never progress beyond his puritanical code. When he overcame my spell and evaded Flauros, killing Moeller in the process, I knew he had become a liability."

Fiona leaned closer, her face a mix of curiosity and caution. "Aren't you worried about the aftermath? Investigations? James wasn't just anyone – his absence will raise questions."

Giles waved a dismissive hand, his confidence unwavering. "Supernatural executions leave no trace that mortals can comprehend. He'll likely be reported missing. I may even initiate the inquiry myself to maintain appearances."

Fiona nodded, her mind already calculating. "Have your secretary make the inquiries in a couple of days. It'll keep everything appropriately mundane."

"I doubt his limited family will suspect anything concrete," Giles added. "Even if they do, my influence runs deep. I have resources and allies to ensure no disruptions."

Their conversation shifted to upcoming events. Fiona's eyes gleamed as she spoke of the Beltane Sabbat and her plans for the next esbat.

"Giles," she said, her tone laced with a mix of entreaty and command, "could you make time for the next full moon? I'd like to grant gifts to the worthiest members of the coven."

Giles sighed, the mass of his commitments evident. With eight sabbats a year, his busy schedule precluded his presence at many of the esbats that Fiona also ran at Trevaunce Manor. It was only days ago that he was there for the Ostara sabbat. Trevaunce was his family seat, a country estate in East Cornwall, managed by Fiona. Despite the demands of his various businesses causing him to travel worldwide or work mainly in the London area, he loved visiting Trevaunce whenever he could. His powers were considerably enhanced there due to the energy that emanated from two ley lines that intersected at the old stone circle, the site of most of their rites.

The covens that Fiona ran were important events to further his powers and they enabled him to assess any prospective talent to recruit to his order.

Most followers were unsuitable to become adepts, but the esbats also provided a means to practice, pass on the ways of ritual magic and empower him for his next phase as Ipsissimus. Fiona assisted him when he attended and educated their disciples in several aspects of low magic.

"I'll be at Trevaunce for Walpurgis Night, of course. As for the esbat, I'll try. Mark me as tentative, and I'll confirm soon."

Their words lingered in the air, a testament to their shared ambition and darker desires. Drained of wine and spent from their exertions, they sank into the pillows, the satisfaction of their night's conquests lulling them into a deep, untroubled slumber that would last until midday.

Chapter 17

Cleansing Dark Shadows

Virginia – 26 March, 02:00 am

The grief still possessed them but there were no tears left. Mark washed the blood from his hands and face with water from the lake and using his handkerchief he bathed the blood from Sam's face also. They were remarkably unscathed from the glass that had exploded over them. Sam had a couple of small cuts on her head, which were hidden by her hair. Mark had two shallow scratches on his forehead and one cut on his right cheek, but none needed attention. Both had minor cuts and scratches on the backs of their hands.

Together, they walked back up the track to collect the jeep. After bringing it back and parking next to the lodge, Mark asked her if there was anything left inside that she could not replace or do without. Fortunately, Sam had taken her purse with her when she had left with Mark earlier; she could not have faced entering the place with what she knew to be inside. Mark said the only option was to burn the place to the ground. No one would believe what had happened so they could not report it. He explained that they must leave, return to Virginia Beach and later report James missing. They must not tell anyone that they had even been here.

Mark went to the generator room and picked up two containers of diesel fuel. He brought them back to the porch and then collected the spare container of gasoline from the jeep. Gritting his teeth, he entered the lodge. He tried not to look but it was unavoidable; there was blood and other bodily waste everywhere. Shredded pieces of flesh, shards of bone and torn bloody clothing were scattered throughout both upstairs and down; intestines and other organs lay on the floor and the sickly stench of death was pervasive. Nothing remained of Jim that was recognisable. Mark gagged while he splashed the diesel fuel all over the room. The log fire had long burned out and any smouldering embers had insufficient heat to ignite the diesel. He then took the much more flammable gasoline and scattered that too, this time ensuring he avoided the fireplace. He left the empty diesel containers in the room but returned the empty gas can to the jeep.

Telling Sam to wait in the car, Mark returned and wiped the lodge doorknob and window frames of any fingerprints although he felt sure the fire would burn everything. He tried to think where they had been and what they had touched, that was outside the lodge and then retraced his steps to the storage buildings, the ladder, the generator and the seat down by the lake and wiped them free of fingerprints as best as he could. He finally returned to the lodge door, lit a match and tossed it inside. The gasoline ignited with a small explosion and the fire quickly spread throughout the room. By the time he reached the jeep the lodge was ablaze. He started the Cherokee, and they left that ill-fated spot without looking back.

They retraced their route back to Avon, the jeep rolling steadily through the dark, empty roads. Signs to Richmond guided them forward, though the silence between them was as heavy as the events they had fled. Not a single vehicle had crossed their path. By the time they merged onto I-64 at Yancey Mills, the horizon was beginning to lighten with the first hints of dawn.

Apart from Sam voicing concern about the fire spreading to the woods, their journey had been conducted in near silence. Mark had reassured her, though his own doubts gnawed at him. "There's enough clearance around the lodge," he'd said. "The fire should burn itself out. Besides, there's barely any wind – it shouldn't spread." But he knew that even if the fire reached the woods, there was nothing they could do now.

They stopped for gas at an isolated station, paying in cash to avoid leaving a trail. The pump hummed as Mark filled the tank, the sound almost surreal in the quiet dawn. As they pulled back onto the highway, the tension between them began to crack under the weight of unspoken thoughts.

Sam finally broke the silence. "James was right all along," she said. "All that talk about demons and magic… it was true. And I never believed him. I thought he was delusional." She hesitated, her voice trembling. "I'll never forgive myself for doubting him when he needed us most."

Mark tightened his grip on the wheel. "I was the same, Sam. He knew we didn't believe him, but he didn't hold it against us. It's just… who would believe something like that? Even now, after seeing it, I still can't fully process what happened. It's incredible. But you're right – it was real. All of it.

Whatever the monsters or demons were, Jim's death wasn't random. Worsley orchestrated this. He killed Jim, and he must pay."

"I know, Mark," Sam said, her voice gaining strength. "I want him dead too. But how? How do we even begin?"

Mark hesitated, knowing this wasn't the time to plan but understanding her need to focus on anything but the nightmare they had just escaped. "We'll have to go to England," he said eventually. "I can take a leave of absence from ODU. Most of my tutorials are done, and the next few weeks are just revision for the exams at the end of April. If I must resign, I will, but I doubt it'll come to that."

"I'll quit my job," Sam responded without hesitation. "The sooner we leave, the better. We can stay at the Kensington apartment while we're there."

Mark nodded. "Agreed. But we need to be prepared. I'll need time to study this… whatever it is Jim was involved with. I have a colleague, Patrick Mulroney, who teaches anthropology at Maine University. He might be able to help or at least point me in the right direction."

"I understand," Sam said, though impatience tinged her voice. "But I don't want to waste time. This must be done."

"I feel the same, but we can't rush in blindly," Mark said. "We need to recover, get over the shock, and …"

"Mark," Sam interrupted, her tone steady but cold, "what happened isn't something I can get over. It's the reason I'm still standing. Of course, I'm grieving, but that grief is fueling me. I need to settle this."

Mark sighed and shifted gears – figuratively and literally. "We need to get our story straight, just in case. It's unlikely, but if someone saw the fire or noticed us on the way out, we must be ready. Hunters, hikers, anyone – there's a chance someone could've seen something."

"What if someone saw us at the airport?" Sam asked.

Mark frowned. "Unlikely anyone would give a detailed description, but we can't rule it out. Let's say I was at your place in Virginia Beach all weekend. Neighbours likely saw me arrive Friday night. We went out Saturday morning, had dinner out in the evening, and spent today walking in First Landing State Park. Does that work?"

Sam nodded, though uneasiness flickered in her eyes. "I hope we don't have to lie. It doesn't sit right with me."

Mark dropped the subject, sensing her discomfort. The car lapsed into silence again, but his mind couldn't escape the vivid memories of Jim's final moments. He could still feel the echo of the attack, the searing pain he had somehow shared. For Jim, it must have been excruciating, though mercifully brief. Yet, even now, Mark felt an odd sense of Jim's presence – as if he were still near, watching over them. He knew it was impossible, but the feeling lingered.

Beside him, Sam began to cry softly. Mark reached over, brushing her cheek with the back of his hand. The gesture was small, but it carried all the tenderness he couldn't yet put into words. She leaned into his touch for a moment before they both turned their eyes back to the road ahead.

The horizon was brightening, a cruel reminder that life outside their nightmare continued. Mark pressed down on the accelerator. They had to keep moving.

James watched them with a profound sadness, the weight of his death pressing heavily on his ethereal form. He was no longer tethered to his earthly body, and he knew his soul should now ascend through the spheres toward God. Yet, something held him back, an invisible chain binding him to the mortal plane.

He had left his physical form moments after Abaddon had taken him, his spirit slipping free in the chaos of the demon's rage. Abaddon, consumed by blind fury and destruction, hadn't noticed the premature departure. James had ascended quickly, moving far from the carnage below, his silver cord severing cleanly as his body succumbed. Though he could never return to the physical world, his heart resisted moving further from where he could still observe it. Perhaps it was unfinished business, or perhaps it was love – either way, his departure was not yet complete.

There was, at least, one small solace: Abaddon had not cast him into hell.

When the demon had gone, James returned to the scene, drawn to the grief and anger emanating from Sam and Mark. Their emotions were deep, almost tangible in his spectral state, but the bond he had shared with Mark was not enough to bridge the divide between the living and the dead. He reached out to them in vain, his frustration mounting with each failed attempt to make his presence known.

He could see their pain and the nascent fury that burned behind it, driving them toward a dangerous path. Their talk of vengeance troubled him deeply. The vendetta they envisioned was reckless, and he feared for their safety, knowing the enemies they faced would not be bound by mortal limitations. Even in death, his love for them compelled him to protect them, though he was unsure how.

James reflected on his limitations. He could not shield them from physical harm, no matter how fiercely he willed it. But perhaps he could aid them against the supernatural forces they might encounter. Those dark entities, existing in both their world and his, could pose an even greater threat than Worsley. If he could find a way to intervene – if his death could serve some purpose – he would grasp the chance without hesitation.

Still, the realm he now inhabited held its own perils. Shadows lurked in this liminal space, threats that could unravel him if he wasn't vigilant. Yet ironically, the skills he had learned under Worsley's tutelage, steeped in the very darkness he had fought against, now offered him the tools to survive. He could navigate this plane, ward off its dangers, and perhaps even manipulate its energies to influence the living world.

His mind was made up. James would not ascend – not yet. Whatever fate awaited him beyond, it could wait until his loved ones were safe. For now, he would remain close to Sam and Mark, their silent guardian in the shadows. If he could not stop them from pursuing their vengeance, he could at least watch over them, guiding them through the darkness ahead.

With this resolve, James felt a small flicker of peace amidst the turmoil. His death had been brutal, but his story wasn't over – not while he could still help those he loved.

Chapter 18
A Guardian's Resolve

irginia Beach – 29 March 10:00 AM local

V Mark methodically packed for his overnight trip to Maine University, his mind preoccupied with the burden of their mission. His flight out of Norfolk was scheduled for 2 p.m., connecting through LaGuardia to Bangor. Patrick, his trusted colleague at Orono, had insisted on meeting in person, brushing off phone discussions as insufficient for the complexity of the topic. Mark appreciated Pat's diligence; a face-to-face meeting would allow him to absorb the material fully and leave armed with books and reference papers that might guide him in the shadowy world he was stepping into.

Life since returning home had been a relentless whirlwind. Sam, resolute and focused, had thrown herself into preparations for their impending journey to England. She had quit her job without hesitation and was already crafting a meticulous plan of action. Playing the role of a distraught wife, she had contacted Worsley's office to inquire about Jim, her voice trembling with feigned concern. When Worsley's staff confirmed he hadn't been seen in days, she pressed them to involve the British police. Her performance had been flawless, though the effort clearly drained her. Yet, it was this relentless focus that kept her from succumbing to the horrors of the past few days.

Mark, on the other hand, had taken a more deliberate approach. He had secured unpaid leave from Old Dominion University, preparing a thorough handover for his temporary replacement. The revision plans and notes he left behind were immaculate – a stark contrast to the chaotic uncertainty consuming his personal life. Yet even as he tied up these loose ends, his thoughts remained locked on Worsley. The 'how' of his revenge remained elusive, but the 'why' burned brightly, fuelling his determination. This trip to Orono was the first step in preparing for what lay ahead. In just two days, he and Sam would board a flight to London, their path uncertain but their resolve unwavering.

Meanwhile, Sam sat in her study, compiling a "to-do" list with the precision of someone wielding purpose as armour. Her role as the grieving, devoted wife required her to see Worsley, a prospect she dreaded. Could she face him without betraying her loathing? Could she mask her fury and fear long enough to glean the information they needed? She would also need to locate and compensate the family of the security guard who had died – a painful but necessary task, one she hoped James's diary or computer in England might help her navigate.

Mark had been protective, worrying constantly about her state of mind. But Sam had discovered reserves of strength she hadn't known she possessed. Her resolve had crystallised in the wake of tragedy. Gone was the carefree woman who had drifted through life, content to adapt to its whims. The events of the past few days had burned away that naivety, leaving someone hardened by purpose. Her aim was clear: Worsley must die.

She leaned back in her chair, forcing herself to banish the torrent of emotions threatening to overwhelm her. Her mind drifted to James's final conversations, replaying his words like a puzzle she needed to solve. He had painted Worsley as untouchable, a master of dark forces, his power bolstered by an impenetrable network of human and supernatural resources. Even James, for all his strength and knowledge, had warned them against seeking vengeance. Yet here they were, preparing for a confrontation that seemed both inevitable and impossible.

What did she know of Worsley? He was charismatic, elegant, and ruthless – a dangerous blend of allure and menace. Beneath his refined exterior lay something odious and evil, a man unafraid to kill and adept at manipulating forces Sam had once dismissed as fantasy. His mastery of dark magic, his role as a Grand Master in Fiona Barnes's Cornwall coven, and his rumoured invulnerability painted a chilling picture. The mention of Flauros shielding him from bullets seemed particularly insurmountable. Coupled with his wealth and vast network capable of tracking enemies, using tools to monitor the use of bank accounts, credit cards and mobile phones, Worsley seemed an impossible foe.

Sam clenched her fists. It all felt so hopeless. But as despair threatened to take hold, she reminded herself that answers wouldn't come here. England held the key – answers, resources, and perhaps a sliver of hope in this seemingly impossible battle.

James wandered the first astral plane, his thoughts tethered to the mortal world as he periodically checked on Sam and Mark. Their sleep was troubled, shadows of their grief and fear manifesting in their dreams. Using what he remembered of low magic, James attempted to ease their rest, weaving faint threads of calm into their subconscious. Whether his efforts bore fruit, he couldn't be sure, but the act itself gave him purpose in his spectral state.

Occasionally, he ventured further, his incorporeal presence skimming the periphery of Worsley's sphere of influence. James observed Worsley and his staff from a careful distance, taking great pains to avoid detection. The risk was ever-present, but his vigilance brought a small comfort: Worsley, it seemed, was not actively hunting Sam and Mark. Not yet.

Still, James felt the pull of urgency. He had tried, without success, to locate a genuine sensitive – a medium or spiritual conduit – who might serve as a bridge to communicate with Sam and Mark. His frustration grew with each fruitless attempt. The astral plane was not devoid of other travellers, but most were novice dreamers, their consciousnesses barely aware of their surroundings. Dubbed the "sleep plane," this realm often featured souls whose night-time wanderings mirrored their earthly habits. He encountered individuals still dressed in their pyjamas or, amusingly, entirely naked – proof of their inexperience. James chuckled wryly, imagining their embarrassment when they discovered their ability to manifest clothing or change their forms with a thought. That awakening, literal and metaphorical, would send them hurtling back to their physical bodies.

Amid these untrained wanderers, James occasionally experienced more profound encounters. Twice, he stumbled upon confused, newly departed souls, their perplexity real in the shimmering ether. He guided them gently toward the next phase of their journey, his understanding of this plane's rules aiding their transition. On one occasion, he found a soul under attack by a malevolent entity, its twisted energy clawing at the hapless spirit. James intervened, his resolve steeled by a deep well of compassion. The confrontation was swift but decisive; he purged the dark force, restoring peace to the victim.

For his own safety, James altered his appearance, reshaping his spectral form to avoid recognition. Even a hint of familiarity in this interim zone could invite dangers he was not yet prepared to face. Despite his caution, there was one encounter he could not avoid. The archangel Uriel appeared, radiant and imposing, his presence both awe-inspiring and unnerving.

"Why have you not begun your journey toward the Lord?" Uriel's voice resonated, cutting through the ether with divine authority.

James met the archangel's gaze, his spirit steady despite the weight of the inquiry. "My stay here is temporary," he explained. "I remain to watch over souls in danger, those I hold dear. When they are safe, I will move on."

Uriel considered his response, his expression inscrutable. "Your reason is just, but the pull of the higher planes will grow stronger with time. You will not be able to resist indefinitely."

James nodded, already aware of this truth. He felt the subtle tug even now, an almost magnetic pull urging him upward. At best, he estimated he had a month before the call became irresistible. A month to help Sam and Mark, to shield them from dangers both seen and unseen.

His understanding of the planes gave him an edge. During his training under Worsley, James had achieved access to the third plane and caught fleeting glimpses of the fourth. Each plane held its own rules, its own mysteries, and ascending required exponentially greater power. The seven planes of existence represented a journey both spiritual and transcendent, but for now, James's path lay firmly in the sleep plane. Here, he could act as a guardian, a silent watcher over his loved ones. Yet his search for a sensitive channel remained critical; without a way to directly communicate with Sam and Mark, his influence was limited.

Despite the obstacles, James was resolute. His time in this realm was finite, but while he remained, he would do everything in his power to protect them.

Chapter 19

Occult Secrets

Orono, Bangor – 30 March 09:00 AM

Pat arrived promptly at eight to pick Mark up from the hotel, his reliable demeanour a comforting contrast to the chaos Mark had been navigating. The drive to the university campus was filled with polite conversation and the kind of catching up that skims over heavier subjects. Mark had shared only what he dared, carefully omitting the grisly details of Jim's death. Officially, Jim was missing, and that was the story Mark intended to keep. What he needed from Pat was clear: a foundational understanding of the ritualistic and esoteric practices that had consumed Jim, particularly black magic and its darker implications.

As they reached Pat's office, the smell of fresh coffee greeted them. Books and reference materials were already scattered across the table, their spines a mix of old leather and modern binding. Pat had come prepared. After pouring coffee for both, the two settled into chairs, the air between them shifting to a more serious tone.

Mark placed a small voice recorder on the table. "Do you mind? I'd like to record this for later – Sam needs to hear it too."

Pat nodded. "Of course. Let's get started."

The recorder's red light blinked steadily as Pat began, his voice taking on the practiced cadence of a seasoned academic. "Most scholars agree that the primary driving force behind black magic is the unrelenting hunger for power. It's a theme as old as time itself. Consider the biblical story of the Garden of Eden – Adam and Eve are tempted by the serpent, who promises that eating from the Tree of Knowledge will make them 'as gods'. Power through forbidden knowledge: it's the cornerstone of black magic."

Mark leaned forward, his attention rapt as Pat continued. "Traditional Christian teachings often portray black magic as invoking demons or even Satan himself, with power drawn directly from the Dark One. While that's more aligned with Satanism, there's another perspective: that black magicians control demons solely for their purposes, independent of any allegiance to a deity or devil. Many magicians believe that humanity and divinity are intrinsically linked, and that with the right knowledge, humans can achieve godhood. This is especially true among practitioners influenced by the Kabbalah."

Pat paused, taking a sip of coffee. "Magical principles operate on imitation, mimicry, and analogy. A foundational belief is expressed in the phrase, 'as above, so below.' It reflects the idea that the macrocosm – the universe – is mirrored in the microcosm, the individual, and vice versa. That's why black magic is often called the 'Left Hand Path.' Traditionally, in many cultures, the left side is associated with evil."

Mark's pen hovered over his notebook, though he relied primarily on the recorder to capture everything. Pat rose and began writing on a nearby whiteboard. "Now, let's delve into the Kabbalah, or QBLH in its original Hebrew. The term means 'that which is received' or 'oral tradition.' It emphasises that this knowledge was historically passed down orally."

The whiteboard soon displayed several spellings: *Kabbalah, Kabala, Cabala, Qabalah.*

"These variations are largely due to different linguistic interpretations. In general, Kabbalah or Kabala with a 'K' refers to the Hebrew tradition. Cabala with a 'C' usually signifies a Christian interpretation, while Qabalah with a 'Q' is associated with Hermetic and Golden Dawn traditions, which I will come to later. From what you've described, I suspect your brother – and likely Worsley – were entrenched in the latter school."

Pat's voice took on a reverent tone. "The Kabbalah is deeply rooted in the mystical aspects of Judaism. It explores the paradox of an infinite, unknowable God creating a finite, mortal universe. It seeks to unravel the relationship between the divine and the human, the purpose of existence, and the nature of reality itself. While its spiritual focus is profound, modern occultists like your brother see it differently – as a roadmap to personal power."

Mark absorbed the information, the threads of his brother's obsession becoming clearer yet darker. The implications of what Jim had delved into – and what Worsley was still immersed in – felt both overwhelming and insidious. He glanced at the recorder, its blinking red light capturing the words that might eventually guide him and Sam to answers they desperately needed.

"But what are these Sephiroth that James mentioned?" Mark asked.

Patrick returned to his seat. "Kabbalists believe that, in the beginning, there was nothing but God – a limitless, infinite presence. From this divine void, God emanated an aspect of Himself into the nothingness, a process that resulted in a sequence of ten emanations. Each of these emanations, or sephirah – the singular form of sephiroth – contained progressively less of God's divine essence. Together, these emanations are referred to as the 'Splendid Lights of the Sephiroth' and are understood to be facets of God's identity and the structure of the universe itself."

"These sephiroth are not just abstract concepts; they form a bridge between the divine and the mortal. They are the pathway for humanity to ascend toward God and for God's influence to reach the human soul."

Mark nodded, slowly processing the weight of this explanation.

Patrick continued, gesturing as he spoke. "The universe, in Kabbalistic belief, is made up of nine concentric spheres, each encapsulating the one within it. The outermost sphere is God's domain. Beneath that lies the sphere of the stars, followed by seven more spheres representing the planets, with the innermost sphere belonging to the moon. At the very centre lies Earth. The Kabbalists believe that the human soul descends through these spheres from God into a mortal body, where it becomes trapped. Upon death, the soul attempts to ascend back through the spheres to reunite with God.

"But this journey is fraught with peril. Each sphere is guarded by bands of angels who try to turn the soul back. Worse still, the space between Earth and the moon is said to be teeming with demonic entities eager to ensnare souls. For the Kabbalist, knowledge – rather than piety or a sin-free life – is the key to navigating this dangerous path. More significantly, Kabbalists believe this journey isn't limited to death. It can be undertaken while still alive, which is likely what your brother, Worsley, and his like were studying to achieve."

Mark's brow furrowed as he pieced this together with Jim's past conversations. "That aligns with what Jim told me before," he admitted.

Patrick returned to the whiteboard. "The ranks and grades you mentioned on the phone likely refer to degrees of initiation in certain magical orders. Based on what you've described, it seems likely that Worsley models his practices on the **A∴A∴**, a magical order whose name is marked by the three triangular dots after each 'A'. The initials probably stand for *Astrum*

Argentium – 'Silver Star' in Latin – or possibly *Arcanum Arcanorum*, meaning 'Secret of Secrets.' Both names reference traditions rooted in the teachings of Aleister Crowley, a prominent and controversial occultist from the early 20th century.

"Crowley formed the A∴A∴ after leaving the Hermetic Order of the Golden Dawn, another highly influential magical society of the late 19th century. The Golden Dawn was a very real and significant order that had far-reaching effects, even on mysticism today and it had some very eminent members of society at that time. Their membership included the famous poet William Butler Yeats and the notable authors Algernon Blackwood and Arthur Machen and probably several others well known at the time, who wanted their association with the order kept secret. The Golden Dawn had strong ties to Freemasonry and Rosicrucianism but eventually dissolved due to infighting and political disputes. Despite this, its impact on modern mysticism remains profound, influencing traditions such as Wicca and Thelema."

"Thelema?" Mark asked, the unfamiliar term catching his attention.

Patrick smiled faintly. "Thelema is essentially a spiritual philosophy or religion founded by Crowley. Its core text, *The Book of the Law*, advocates for individuals to discover and fulfil their 'True Will' – a concept akin to one's innermost purpose or destiny. From what you've described, it's likely that your brother and Worsley were involved in rituals inspired by these teachings."

Patrick gestured to a pile of books on his desk. "Crowley carried much of the Golden Dawn's structure into the A∴A∴, including its system of ranks and initiations. Members worked in isolation, interacting only with their immediate superiors and subordinates. The founders believed this approach would avoid the egotistical conflicts that plagued the Golden Dawn. It's possible Worsley is either a member of such an order or has created his own, following similar principles."

Mark leaned forward, the impact of this revelation sinking in. "But Jim also mentioned covens. If the A∴A∴ doesn't practice group rituals, what were the coven meetings about?"

Patrick's smile turned wry. "Ah, covens. They are an entirely separate matter. A black magician could very well be a member of an order like the A∴A∴ while simultaneously running independent covens for their own purposes. Witchcraft and Wicca intersect with some of these traditions but are distinct subjects. I can loan you some books on this, but the essence is that covens are typically more communal and ritualistic than solitary orders like the A∴A∴."

He drew a breath, then added, "Let's pivot to the ranking structures you asked about. That may clarify how these systems of power and initiation work."

Patrick paused, flipping through one of the large reference books on his desk. After a moment, he looked up. "Ah, here we are. Bear with me as I read some of this; Thelema isn't my specialty."

Mark leaned back, preparing to take it all in.

"The A∴A∴ is structured into eleven grades, divided into a preparatory stage and three initiatory orders. The first stage, 'Student,' focuses on acquiring general knowledge of various systems of spiritual attainment. At the end of this phase, the student takes an open-book exam and undergoes a brief ritual before advancing to 'Probationer'."

Patrick glanced at Mark, who nodded, encouraging him to continue.

"The Probationer's task is to prove their ability to undertake the 'Great Work.' In this context, the Great Work – also known as *Magnum Opus* – refers to the path of spiritual evolution and self-realization. Specifically, in Thelema, it involves achieving 'Knowledge and Conversation of the Holy Guardian Angel' and discovering one's 'True Will.' Medieval alchemists used the same term to describe turning base metals into gold, but in Thelema it's more about spiritual transformation."

Mark interjected, "So the Great Work is about self-discovery?"

"Precisely," Patrick replied. "The Probationer practices self-reflection and records their progress for a year before advancing to the next grade, 'Neophyte.' These early stages are deliberately lengthy, filtering out those who lack true commitment."

Patrick stood, placing a chart on an easel. It depicted the Kabbalistic Tree of Life. "Neophyte corresponds to *Malkuth,* the base of the Tree of Life. It's the first true initiation, symbolizing spiritual planting. The goal here is to gain control over oneself and begin mastering the astral planes."

Mark's curiosity deepened. "Astral planes? Do you believe in those?"

Patrick smiled. "Whether I believe in them or not, isn't the point. Many do, and they act as if they're real. The astral planes are said to be levels of existence, each with its own rules. But let's keep going."

He resumed reading. "Next is 'Zelator,' focusing on yoga practices like *Asana* and *Pranayama.* This stage emphasizes energy-building exercises. From there, advancement continues through *Practicus, Philosophus,* and *Dominus Liminis,* each focusing on intellectual growth, moral discipline, and preparation for higher spiritual work. Philosophus even includes defying personal fears and morality to transcend one's sense of self."

Patrick paused, glancing at Mark. "Some of these stages likely involve sexual or sacrificial rites. It's speculative, but plausible given the secrecy of these orders."

Mark shifted uncomfortably, but Patrick continued, "Next comes 'Adeptus Minor,' a significant milestone in the Order of the Rose Cross. This level focuses on mastering the Holy Guardian Angel's guidance and contributing to the order's goals. Beyond this are *Adeptus Major* and *Adeptus Exemptus,* requiring leadership and significant magical prowess."

Mark's mind was reaching overload, but he recalled that Jim had reached the stage of Adeptus Major.

Patrick's tone became graver. "To advance further, one must cross the Abyss – a perilous spiritual trial. The Abyss is guarded by Choronzon, a demon representing chaos and ego. Success means becoming a 'Magister Templi,' achieving profound understanding and shedding all personal limitations."

Mark sat up straighter, recalling Jim's mention of Worsley crossing the Abyss.

"The final two grades," Patrick concluded, "are 'Magus,' representing mastery over creation and wisdom, and 'Ipsissimus,' the pinnacle of attainment. The Ipsissimus is believed to live in perfect harmony with the universe, beyond human limitations."

Patrick closed the book. "That's the structure. It's a lot, I know. Want me to photocopy the essentials for you?"

Mark exhaled deeply. "Yes, please. That was a great deal to assimilate. Now coffee is required. Definitely some more coffee."

James had quietly observed much of Patrick's detailed explanation, acknowledging that his interpretation of Worsley's order was mostly accurate. Still, he couldn't help but question why Mark needed to delve so deeply into the structure of these esoteric ranks and rituals. It was not going to help him.

Now fully aware of Worsley's true nature, James was astounded that someone so corrupt could have reached the third order of the Silver Star. The trials of crossing the Abyss, especially facing the demon Choronzon, demanded profound humility and self-awareness – qualities Worsley clearly lacked. Yet somehow, he had either managed to deceive Choronzon or found some loophole, which only made him more dangerous. James wrestled with the enigma: how could Worsley claim the powers of a Magus, an entity supposedly defined by balanced wisdom and divine insight, while remaining so consumed by ego and malice?

The thought was chilling. If Worsley was truly striving for the ultimate rank of Ipsissimus – complete harmony with the universe – his unchecked ambition and growing power could make him unstoppable. James's frustration deepened as he realized how far beyond Mark and Sam's reach Worsley was. Any attempt to confront him would almost certainly end in their destruction.

"If only I could tell them," James thought bitterly. "Convince them to let this go."

But he knew the futility of such hopes. Mark and Sam were resolute, their grief and anger blinding them to the insurmountable danger ahead. With a heavy sigh, James drifted away, burdened by his inability to intervene.

◈

Part Two
Stalking the Fiend

Chapter 20
The Hunt Begins

Abingdon Grove, London W8 – 2 April 1030 AM

The taxi pulled up in front of the red-brick Edwardian building, its grandeur softened by the morning light. Sam and Mark stepped out, their luggage thudding onto the pavement as they took in the imposing structure. The building's façade was an elegant mix of stone mouldings and bay windows, framed by marble-capped brick pillars. Six marble steps led up to a grand set of arched double doors, a fitting entrance to what James and Sam had once called home.

Their flight from Heathrow had landed less than two hours ago, and though weary from the overnight journey, the weight of their mission ground deeply on them. Mark glanced at Sam, her face unreadable as she gazed at the building. He knew her composure was fragile, a delicate veneer over the pain of returning to a place steeped in memories of James.

The doorman greeted them, his warm smile breaking the tension. "Mrs. Benedict! It's been far too long."

"Charlie!" Sam exclaimed, the warmth in her voice genuine. "It's wonderful to see you again."

Charlie's eyes flicked to Mark. "And Mr. Benedict?"

Sam's expression faltered for a moment before she gestured toward her companion. "This is James's brother, Mark."

Mark extended a hand. "Good to meet you, Charlie."

Charlie shook it firmly. "A pleasure, sir. I've called the lift for you." He deftly helped with the luggage, ushering them toward the old-fashioned wrought-iron elevator.

"Wow," Mark remarked, running a hand over the intricate metalwork. "I didn't think elevators like this still existed."

"They're rare, but this one's been lovingly maintained," Charlie said, opening the doors. As they stepped inside, Mark marvelled at the concertina-style gates, the whole contraption moving upward with a steady hum after Charlie secured the outer door.

The lift creaked to a halt on the fourth floor, revealing a marble-tiled hallway with soaring ceilings. Each floor hosted only two apartments, lending an air of exclusivity. Sam produced a set of keys and unlocked the door to 4A, hesitating for a moment before stepping inside.

Mark watched as she paused in the entryway, her hand gripping the door frame. "Are you alright?"

Sam nodded. "It's just… strange being here again."

Mark gave her space as she ventured in. For Sam, the apartment was a time capsule of her life with James, the echoes of his laughter lingering faintly beneath the city's muffled hum. She walked through the rooms slowly, bypassing the door to James's study and pausing at the threshold of the master bedroom.

"I'm fine," she said softly, turning back to Mark. "Would you mind taking the master bedroom? I don't think I can sleep there."

"Of course," Mark replied without hesitation. While Sam made for the kitchen, he set the luggage in their respective rooms before taking a quick tour of the apartment. The living room was a masterpiece of taste and tradition, with its marble fireplace, Persian rug, and large, leather Chesterfield sofa with matching chairs. A grand mirror in a gilded frame presided over the room, flanked by gold-coloured sconces. Every detail spoke of care and precision, from the antique furnishings to the parquet floors that gleamed beneath his steps.

Mark stopped to admire a large rosewood wheel barometer in the hallway, its mother-of-pearl inlay catching the light. "This is beautiful," he murmured as Sam joined him.

"It was one of James's favourite finds," she said, her voice tinged with both pride and sadness. "He loved antique wooden boxes too, as you can see." Sam gestured towards the living room and indicated a fine inlaid rosewood writing slope on the hall table. "We poured so much love into this place. It feels like a sanctuary, even now."

Mark nodded. "You've created something extraordinary here. An oasis in the chaos of London."

Sam smiled faintly, glancing around the apartment. The dim lighting cast warm shadows on the bookshelves. "It is, but unfortunately, we don't have time to enjoy it. We need to focus on what comes next."

Mark gestured to the living room. "Let's sit down and talk. We need to figure out how to do this."

Sam went to get the coffees. After returning she sat down. Her countenance was resolute, but there was something else beneath it – a flicker of exhaustion, of grief held at bay by sheer willpower. "Mark, we need to start by understanding Worsley's movements. His schedule, his patterns – everything."

"I agree. But confronting him directly feels impossible with what we know so far. He's dangerous, Sam. James told us so, several times and Pat also made that clear."

"Then we outsmart him. We don't attack directly – we find his vulnerabilities. Everyone has them."

Mark sighed, leaning back. "You're right. Maybe we start by using James's connections. His study here might hold something useful."

"And Fiona Barnes," Sam added, her voice steady but tinged with uncertainty, "she's close to Worsley. If we can find a way to approach her…"

"That's risky. But I agree, if anyone knows his weaknesses, it's likely to be her."

Sam's expression wavered for a fraction of a second. "I can't let him get away with what he's done, Mark. Not to James. Not to anyone." Her voice was quieter now, but no less determined.

Mark reached across the table, gripping her hand. His touch was warm, grounding, and for a moment, the tension in Sam's shoulders eased. "We'll do this together. No matter how long it takes or what it costs, we'll find a way."

She swallowed, nodding, her grip tightening around his. In that moment, their shared resolve was more than just necessity – it was a silent promise, a pact forged in grief, in love, in the unwavering pursuit of justice. Whatever lay ahead, they would face it together.

As Mark and Sam moved through the apartment, unpacking their luggage and settling in, James observed them from the astral plane. His was an existence both liberating and maddening. He could see them clearly, sense the tension in the room, the unspoken words between them, but he could not reach them. No sound he made could be heard; no gesture could be noticed. He was a ghost, lingering just beyond the veil of their awareness, no matter how much he tried.

His frustration burned within him. He wanted to warn them; to tell them they were in far more danger than they could possibly comprehend. Worsley was relentless. The forces he commanded would not hesitate to rip through flesh and soul alike. And yet here they were, stubbornly putting themselves directly in harm's way. Mark, ever the pragmatic one, was already strategising. And Sam – God, Sam – her worry was painted across her every move. If only he could make them see, make them understand.

His eyes lingered on Sam longer than he meant to, memories of happy times came flooding back. Despite being dead to her world, he still loved her. That truth was undeniable. It ran through him like a deep, slow current, a part of his being he could never shake. Seeing her like this – so close, yet so impossibly out of reach – was a cruel torment. But ashamedly, what gnawed at him even more was the way she and Mark gravitated toward each other. It was subtle, just the smallest things: the way their bodies aligned when they stood together, the flicker of concern in Mark's eyes when Sam spoke, the hesitant but growing warmth between them.

James clenched his fists, though there was no physical body for him to exert the tension through. It should have hurt, watching them. It should have made him resentful, despite him asking Mark to look after her when they were at the lodge. And yet, to his own surprise, it did not. Mark was a good man. More than that, he was steadfast, kind, and exactly the kind of person Sam needed. James had dragged her into a world she should never have been part of, burdened her with nightmares she should never have known. She deserved someone who could offer her peace, stability. And even though it stung, he understood now that he so foolishly quit that role when he came under Worsley's spell.

He allowed himself a small, bitter smile. Approval came somewhat reluctantly, but it was there, nonetheless. He had lost his war with Worsley and now he needed to make sure they would not lose theirs. Then he could take comfort in the knowledge that Sam wouldn't be left alone. That Mark would be there.

⊶⊷◀❖▶⊶⊷

Chapter 21
Seeking Help

Northwood, Northwest London – 3 April 10.30 AM

Mark and Sam had taken the Tube to Northwood where they were to be met by a car. James' files and address book had yielded a wealth of information, and they were heading for the security agency that had been used to provide Nick Harper.

The conference room at Vigilant Alert Security exuded professionalism and discretion, its minimalist décor emphasizing functionality over style. Colonel Bill Turner, the retired officer heading the agency, sat at the head of the table. Sam and Mark sat opposite him, their looks serious as they laid out their case.

"Colonel Turner," Sam began, her tone steady but earnest, "thank you for meeting with us. My husband, James Benedict, used your agency in the past. He trusted your expertise, and now we're here because we need your help."

Turner nodded, his demeanour calm but attentive. "I appreciate your trust, Mrs. Benedict. From what you've mentioned in our initial contact, this sounds like an unusual and dangerous situation. Why don't we start with what you're facing?"

Mark leaned forward, his voice cutting through the room with quiet intensity. "We're dealing with a man named Sir Giles Worsley. He's not just dangerous; he's methodical, connected, and, quite frankly, ruthless. James was investigating him, uncovering things Worsley would kill to keep hidden. And he did. James is dead because of this man, and so is Nick Harper whom you had assigned to protect James."

Turner's jaw tightened. "I'm sorry for your loss, Mrs. Benedict. We only knew that Nick had died when James told us and provided payment – £20,000. There were no details and no official reports of fatalities. We have had to report Nick as missing."

Mark interrupted. "Nick unfortunately suffered an unspeakable death at Worsley's hands, and we are sorry for that. I'm afraid that all evidence of that will have been destroyed."

Turner's eyes sharpened. "And you believe Worsley is still a threat to you?"

Sam nodded. "Absolutely. He has resources beyond what most of us can comprehend – connections in high places, people who do his bidding without question. He's manipulative and capable of unspeakable acts. We need to protect ourselves."

Mark added, "And not just protect us. We want to stop him. Whatever Worsley is planning, it's bigger than us. If we don't act, others will die."

Turner steepled his fingers, considering their words. "Worsley sounds like the kind of man who operates in the shadows, wielding both power and fear. If you're planning to go after him, you need to be prepared for the long haul – and to play smart. Do you have any idea how you'll approach this?"

"We're still piecing it together," Mark admitted. "But we know the locations where he operates – his estate at Trevaunce Manor in Cornwall, for one. It's where he conducts his… rituals. We still need to gather intelligence, identify his weaknesses."

Sam interjected, her voice firm. "That's where you come in, Colonel. We need guidance and protection – someone skilled enough to handle whatever Worsley throws at us."

Turner leaned back, nodding. "We can provide that. I have a man in mind – a retired Royal Marine, Dougal Finlayson. He's one of the best. He'll protect you, and he has experience with high-risk operations."

Mark glanced at Sam, then back at Turner. "We also need tools – things that won't leave a trail. Untraceable credit cards, burner phones. Worsley's reach is vast, and he'll track us if we aren't careful."

"Consider it done," Turner replied. "But let me be clear: this isn't just about having the right tools. Worsley sounds like a predator who thrives on control. To counter him, you need information and strategy. Going in blind will only get you killed."

"We're not going in blind. We've been going through James's files, his notes. He left us a roadmap. It's incomplete, but it's a start."

Sam added, her tone softening but losing none of its determination, "James believed in this, Colonel. He believed Worsley had to be stopped. We owe it to him – and to ourselves – to see this through."

Turner regarded them for a long moment, his sharp eyes assessing their resolve. "You're walking a dangerous path. Worsley won't go down easily, and there's no guarantee you'll come out unscathed. But I respect your determination. I will join you later today, and we'll provide the tools you need to stay off the grid. I'll also have my team investigate Worsley; see what additional intelligence we can gather."

Sam and Mark exchanged a glance, their shared resolve clear. Sam extended her hand. "Thank you, Colonel. We won't waste this chance."

"You realise that this could all prove very expensive."

"That will not be a problem, Colonel. We can pay you a substantial deposit, up front."

"Thank you. I will give you an account number that will not lead to us if Worsley is already monitoring you. Dougal will explain all later."

Turner shook her hand firmly, then Mark's. "Stay sharp, both of you. And trust Dougal – he'll have your back. It sounds like you're going up against a monster, but with the right preparation, even monsters can fall."

As they left the office, the weight of their mission pressed heavily on them, but so too did the strength of their resolve. They were no longer alone in this fight. And that made a big difference.

James had borne witness to every moment, an invisible observer powerless to intervene. He recognized the professionalism and skill of Turner's organization, which was why he had used them before. Yet, his spirit churned with unease. Competence alone would not be enough to confront Worsley – a man whose cunning, resources, and malevolence far surpassed ordinary comprehension. The odds against Sam and Mark were staggering, and the thought of them stepping into the lion's den without a full grasp of the peril gnawed at him. They were playing a game with stakes they couldn't fully grasp, and the potential consequences left James grappling with an overwhelming sense of helplessness.

Every moment spent lingering in this plane intensified his frustration. The connection he yearned for – a voice, a vessel, someone who could serve as his conduit to the living – remained maddeningly elusive. How could he guide them, warn them, protect them, when he was little more than a whisper lost in the void? Their resolve, though admirable, could lead them straight into disaster. Desperation surged within him, a fraught plea unspoken, he had to find someone, anyone, through whom he could communicate. The clock was ticking, and with each passing moment, the danger to Sam and Mark grew more imminent. His failure to act felt like a betrayal of everything he had stood for in life – and now in death.

Chapter 22

A Stranger in the Night

arpenders Park, Northwest London – 3 April 6.30 PM
Paula Reynolds sat alone on her worn sofa, a cup of untouched tea cooling on the table in front of her. The rain tapped gently against the window, its rhythmic sound a stark contrast to the storm of grief swirling within her. Nick Harper was gone. The reality still hadn't fully settled; it felt like a cruel joke, an absurd nightmare from which she couldn't wake.

Nick had been her anchor, the first man who truly saw her for who she was – beyond the shadows of her past. His best friend, Doogie – Dougal Finlayson – had once confided that Nick was smitten, and for Paula, that word had carried the promise of something permanent, something real. She had dared to hope for a future with him, one filled with warmth and stability, a stark departure from the chaotic life she had known. But now, those dreams lay in tatters, leaving her adrift.

She wiped at her eyes with the sleeve of her jumper, staring at the rain-streaked glass. "Why, Nick?" she whispered to the emptiness. "Why did it have to be you?"

Her thoughts wandered back to her childhood, a time that felt more like a half-remembered bad dream than a life lived. Paula's mother, Flora, had been a single parent with a penchant for chaos. Flora had wanted a son, naming her imagined boy "Paul" long before she discovered she was having a daughter. When Paula was born, it was as though she was a disappointment from her first breath.

Flora fancied herself a white witch, a practitioner of Wicca and a self-proclaimed conjurer of potions and spells. She'd hawk her so-called magic remedies to gullible strangers, dabble in fortune-telling, and pose as a medium with shaky psychic abilities at best. Most saw her for the fraud she was, and Paula's childhood became a never-ending series of moves – one town to the next, one failed scheme after another.

Her mother's lifestyle meant constant upheaval. There were always new "marks" for Flora's grifts, and worse, a parade of unsuitable boyfriends who often doubled as enablers for her drug habit. Paula learned early how to disappear into the background, a skill born of necessity in a home that teetered between neglect and outright danger.

When Paula was ten, social services finally intervened. Flora's drug use had spiralled, and one particularly volatile boyfriend had made it clear Paula wasn't safe. She was placed in foster care, bouncing between homes that, for the most part, were kind and stable. Still, the scars of her early years clung to her.

At fourteen, Paula received the news that Flora had overdosed. The grief was strange, muted by the knowledge that her mother had always been more of a burden than a comfort. Yet, she mourned – not just for Flora but for the mother she had never truly had.

Despite her rocky beginnings, Paula had managed to carve out a semblance of a normal life. She did well in school, driven by a need to prove she was more than the sum of her past. Nursing had been a natural choice – caring for others came easily to someone who had spent much of her life caring for herself. Now, she worked at Watford General Hospital, a job she loved, though it didn't come close to filling the void Nick had left behind.

Paula reached for her tea, now cold, and grimaced. She set it back down, unable to muster the energy to make a fresh cup. Instead, her thoughts returned to Nick and the fragile happiness they had shared. His sudden death felt like a cruel twist of fate, a reminder that life's small joys could be ripped away in an instant.

She thought of Doogie. He had been a rock in Nick's life and had tried to be the same for her in the wake of Nick's presumed death. She appreciated his support but couldn't help wondering if he was just as lost as she was. They had both been blindsided by the news, and now, they were left to pick up the pieces of a puzzle that no longer fit.

Paula stood and walked to the window, pressing her hand against the cold glass. The rain blurred the streetlights outside, their glow diffused into soft orbs that seemed to float in the darkness.

She whispered to the night, "I'll keep going, Nick. I don't know how, but I'll find a way. For you." And for the first time in days, she allowed herself to cry – not just for Nick, but for all the losses she had carried alone for so long.

Later when the rain stopped, the house was quiet except for the soft ticking of the wall clock. Paula Reynolds sat curled up on her sofa, her legs tucked beneath her, staring blankly at the cooling cup of tea on the table in front of her. The day had been long, her thoughts consumed by the lingering ache of Nick's absence. She had replayed his voice in her mind so many times that it now felt like a phantom echo in the stillness of her home.

A chill rippled through the air, raising goosebumps along her arms. She sat up, her senses sharpening. Something was different. The familiar comfort of her home suddenly felt… invaded.

When she turned, she saw him. A man stood near the window, his form faintly translucent, shimmering like a mirage. She became aware that he might be an astral traveller who was probably asleep at home somewhere, dreaming of his adventure. From a child, Paula had seen what she assumed were ghosts until her mother explained about astral travellers. She saw them only occasionally over the years mainly at night. On one occasion at hospital, she had seen one departing, a patient who had just died, rising and disappearing through the ceiling. Such apparitions were invisible to anyone else present, and she soon learned to ignore them. Mentioning them to friends and colleagues had only created awkwardness, suspicions and weird comments.

"Who are you and what are you doing in my house?"

The figure stepped forward, his movements deliberate but unthreatening. "You can see me! Thank Goodness! My name is James Benedict," he said softly. "I mean you no harm."

"Why are you here?"

"It's hard to explain… I'm essentially dead," James replied, his tone sombre. "I don't belong to your world anymore. But I came here because I need help, your help."

She stared at him, a little bewildered, she had never actually conversed with one before. It wasn't even a proper conversation. She was speaking to him, but his replies were registering silently in her head. "This is some kind of joke, right? You're dreaming, maybe? This is very strange and unsettling for me."

"It's neither a joke nor a dream," James said gently. "I know this is hard to believe, but I came here to check on you. Now I find you have a rare gift, Paula, and you can help me prevent others from dying."

Paula's lips parted, a protest forming on her tongue, but she stopped herself. "But why me?" she asked, her voice trembling. "What do you actually want from me?"

James hesitated, his form flickering slightly. "I need you to help me stop a man named Sir Giles Worsley. He's a powerful and dangerous individual, someone I was once foolish enough to follow. I thought I understood him, thought he could offer answers I'd been searching for. But he's far more dangerous than I ever imagined."

"Dangerous how?" Paula asked, her voice growing firmer as her curiosity began to overtake her fear.

"He's not just a criminal or a manipulator," James explained. "Worsley deals in dark magic, the kind of power that corrupts everything it touches. He uses people, destroys lives, all in the pursuit of his twisted goals. He killed me. And he killed Nick."

Paula's stomach tightened at the mention of Nick. Her suspicion flared anew. "What do you mean, he killed Nick? How do you even know about Nick?"

James's expression was painful. "Because Nick was helping me. He was loyal, brave, and good – qualities that are an anathema to Worsley. Nick died because of me, because I underestimated what Worsley was capable of."

Paula felt tears prick at her eyes, anger bubbling beneath her grief. "So why are you here now? What can you possibly do about it if you're dead?"

"I'm here because I can't rest until Worsley is stopped," James said earnestly. "And I need someone in the living world to act as my voice. Someone who can help me protect the people Worsley is targeting now."

Paula crossed her arms, her scepticism returning. "And you think that's me?"

"Yes," James said simply. "You can see me, hear me. That makes you very rare. And I can guide you, help you connect with two people who are fighting to stop Worsley – my wife, Sam, and my brother, Mark. They're in danger, Paula. They need someone they can trust, someone who can bridge the gap between me and them."

Paula frowned, her mind reeling. "So, what? You want me to just call these people and tell them I'm your messenger? They'll think I'm insane."

"They won't," James assured her. "They've already arranged for someone to protect them – a man named Dougal Finlayson, who I believe you know. He'll understand, and he can vouch for you. Through him, you can reach Sam and Mark."

Paula looked away, her thoughts tangling with doubt and fear. *Doogie? Was Doogie also involved?* "And what happens if I say no?"

James's voice softened, a quiet desperation creeping into his tone. "Then Worsley will keep growing stronger. Sam, Mark and possibly Finlayson will face him alone, and they'll die. And their deaths will be on me, just like Nick's. Please, Paula. I know I have no right to ask this of you, but you're my only hope."

The strain of his words settled heavily on her shoulders. After a long silence, she met his gaze, her expression resolute. "Alright," she said quietly. "I'll help. But only because Nick deserves justice. And so do you."

James's form brightened, his relief almost palpable. "Thank you, Paula. You have no idea what this means."

Paula raised her hand to stop him. "Don't thank me yet. If we're going to do this, you owe me answers. About Nick, about Worsley – everything."

"You'll have them," James promised. "For now, focus on getting to Sam and Mark. And Paula… thank you."

As James's form began to fade, Paula sank back onto the sofa, her mind a whirlwind of thoughts. She had no idea what she'd just agreed to, but one thing was clear – her life was embarking on a very different chapter.

James was excited. For the first time since his death, someone could truly see him, hear him. Not just glimpses of his form but actual conversation, real understanding. Delight surged through him, an almost euphoric relief. He was no longer alone in this spectral void. He had a conduit, a voice in the physical world.

She had been wary at first, sceptical, but she listened. And, more importantly, she believed. James had explained everything – Worsley, the dark forces at play, the danger Mark and Sam were in. And Paula, with her rare gift, had agreed to help him.

With her aid, he could guide them. He could warn them of what was coming. He could do more than just watch helplessly from the other side. His role wasn't over yet.

The pull of the spheres was ever-present, an insidious force calling him deeper into the beyond, but James knew now that he could resist it. For a little while longer, at least. As long as Mark and Sam needed him, as long as there was a battle still to be fought, he would remain. He was not done. Not yet.

Chapter 23
The Weight of a Meeting

Abingdon Grove, West London – 4 April, 9:00 AM

The apartment was quiet except for the gentle buzz of activity as Mark and Sam went about their morning routines. The previous day had been a whirlwind – a blur of meetings, security preparations, and emotionally charged decisions. Now, as the sunlight filtered through the tall windows, the burden of what lay ahead began to hang over them.

Sam sat at the kitchen table, drinking her tea. Across from her, Mark was scrolling through his phone. "I can't believe we agreed to meet Worsley," Mark muttered, breaking the silence.

Sam looked up, her expression both weary and resolute. "We didn't have a choice. If we're going to find out what happened to James, we need to confront him. Even if the thought of it makes my stomach churn."

"Yeah, but the man is a walking red flag. Everything we've learned and already knew about him screams 'stay away'."

"Tell me something I don't know," Sam replied. "If he's already reported James missing, he's trying to control the narrative. We need to stay ahead of him."

"True. And at least we're not going in blind. Dougal will likely have us wired up like secret agents."

Sam managed a faint smile. "You mean like bumbling secret agents. I stumbled over the foot stool containing one of his hidden cameras this morning. He must have had a laugh when he saw it on the feed."

Mark chuckled, the sound easing some of the tension in the room. "Maybe he did, but he's too professional to admit it."

Dougal's arrival the day before had brought a strange mixture of reassurance and unease. The retired Royal Marine commando had served in the legendary Special Boats Unit, the elite special forces unit of the Royal Navy. He efficiently transformed the apartment into a fortress of discreet surveillance. Cameras now monitored every corner, inside and out, while tiny microphones ensured that he could keep track of them no matter where they were. The credit cards and burner phones he'd provided gave them a sense of security, though the aliases printed on them felt oddly surreal.

"He is a bit reserved, but that may be shyness. He's thorough," Sam said, "I just hope it's enough. Worsley's not the kind of person you underestimate."

Mark leaned back in his chair. "At least we've got a team now. Dougal's here, and we've got that meeting with Nick Harper's girlfriend tonight. Maybe she'll have something useful for us."

Sam's face softened. "I hope so. Losing Nick must have been devastating for her. I can't imagine what she's going through."

"Yeah, it's a lot for anyone to deal with, let alone someone who didn't even know what Nick was really involved in."

"We should focus on what we can control right now. Did you finish filling out the police forms about James?"

Mark groaned. "I did, but it felt weird. Reporting him missing when we know exactly what happened… it's hard to wrap my head around. I'll drop them off this morning."

"I know," Sam said softly. "But it has to be done. At least now the police are involved, even if it's just for show."

"Alright, what's next on the agenda? Besides figuring out how not to have a panic attack during tomorrow's meeting with Worsley."

Sam smiled faintly, her eyes betraying her own anxiety. "We prepare. Go over what we're going to say, what we're not going to say. And try not to think about the fact that we're walking into the lion's den."

Mark raised his mug in a mock toast. "Here's to walking into the lion's den."

Sam laughed softly, shaking her head. "You're impossible."

"True," Mark said, grinning. "But at least I'm consistent."

The light-hearted moment lingered, a brief reprieve from the heaviness of their mission. But as they returned to their tasks, the burden of the coming days settled back over them.

Chapter 24
Plans and Ghostly Guidance

Abingdon Grove – 4 April, 6:30 PM

The evening had arrived, and the apartment was quiet again, with Mark and Sam, both steeling themselves for tomorrow's meeting with Worsley and the unknown revelations that might come from Nick's grieving girlfriend shortly. Despite the overwhelming odds, they clung to the fortitude that had brought them this far – a determination to see justice done, no matter the cost.

The knock at the door came a few minutes later. Sam opened it to find Paula standing there, her face serious but composed. Behind her, Dougal, who had met Paula outside, stepped out of the shadows, giving Sam a nod before following Paula inside.

"Thanks for coming," Sam said, stepping aside to let them in.

Paula glanced around the room, her gaze resting briefly on Mark before she took a deep breath. "I need you to keep an open mind about what I'm about to say. It's… a little unconventional."

Mark exchanged a sceptical glance with Sam. "Unconventional? Nothing can surprise us, considering what we're already dealing with."

Paula nodded. "Fair. But I'm sure this is going to sound even stranger. James is here."

Mark froze. "Here? What do you mean *here*?"

"I mean he's in the room with us," Paula said calmly. "You can't see him, but I can. He's been communicating with me, and he wants to help. He also wants you to stop what you're planning."

Sam's lips parted in shock, while Mark let out a disbelieving laugh. "Come on. You can't expect us to believe that."

Dougal leaning casually against the wall. "Let her finish, laddie. We're already in deep with all sorts of madness. This might not be the craziest thing."

Paula continued, "We both knew you'd doubt me, so ask him something only he would know. Childhood memories, private moments – whatever it takes to convince you."

Mark leaned forward, his scepticism softening into curiosity. "Alright. James and I used to sneak out as kids to raid old Mr. Grainger's apple tree. One time we got caught. What did Grainger say when he confronted us?"

Paula paused, her eyes unfocused as though listening. Then she smiled faintly. "He said, 'If you boys spent half as much energy studying as you do thieving, you'd be geniuses.'"

Mark's jaw dropped, his voice barely a whisper. "That's… that's exactly what he said."

Sam folded her arms, her tone cautious. "Fine. If he's here, what did James say to me the night he proposed?"

After a pause, Paula's smile widened. "He said, 'I can't promise you a perfect life, but I can promise you every moment will matter.' And he had a red rose in his hand."

Sam's breath hitched, her eyes glistening. "That's… true. Exactly true."

Satisfied but shaken, Mark sat back in his chair. "Alright, I believe you. But if he's here, why doesn't he just show himself?"

"Because I'm the only one who can see or hear him," Paula explained. "I've got an unusual ability, let's say. But he's made it clear – he wants you to abandon this mission. He says it's suicidal."

Sam straightened, her resolve hardening. "That's not going to happen. If anything, the danger makes it more important. Worsley needs to be stopped. That said, it is good to know that James hasn't been cast into hell for the rest of eternity."

Mark said, "Yes, but why is he not rising through the spheres to God?"

James via Paula, explained that he was staying to ensure that they gave up their quest to confront Worsley, which was a fight they could never win.

Sam reiterated, "It is imperative that Worsley is stopped! There is no scenario that will prevent me from doing that."

Mark nodded. "He's already taken James and Nick. How many more people does he get to destroy before someone fights back?"

Paula hesitated, then relayed James's response. "He's angry. Frustrated. He says you're underestimating Worsley's power and his ability to manipulate people. That meeting with him tomorrow? He thinks it's a trap."

Dougal chimed in. "That could be right. But traps work both ways. If we know what to expect, we can counter it."

James's frustration seemed to intensify, and Paula's voice reflected his tone. "He says you don't understand what you're up against. Worsley can control minds, bend people to his will without them even realizing it."

"Then tell James to teach us how to resist it," Sam said firmly. "If we're walking into a trap, we need every advantage we can get."

Paula sighed, nodding as though hearing an unseen argument. "He says fine. He'll help, but he still thinks you're making a mistake."

Dougal cleared his throat, his tone shifting to business. "While we're strategizing, there's something else. My agency has intel on Fiona Barnes. She's in town, staying at her Chelsea pad for a couple of nights. She's connected to Worsley, right?"

Sam nodded. "She's his protégé, one of his inner circle."

Dougal continued. "There's also a May Day Eve Sabbat at Trevaunce Manor in Cornwall. If Worsley's going to show up anywhere, it's likely there. And there's a chance he'll attend one of Fiona's esbats before then. We'll need more intel to confirm."

Paula frowned thoughtfully. "If Fiona's in town, maybe I can get close to her. She's involved in this… world, right? If I can gain her trust, I might get invited to an esbat and find out more."

"That's risky," Mark said.

"So is everything else we're doing," Paula shot back. "But it's worth a shot."

Sam sighed. "It's a lot to process. We're walking into a storm, and it feels like we're making it up as we go."

Dougal grinned. "Isn't that how the best plans start?"

Sam chuckled despite herself. "Maybe. Let's sleep on it and figure out the next steps in the morning."

As they began to wind down, Dougal added, "One thing's for sure – we'll need disguises if we're crashing a Sabbat. I'm thinking cloaks, maybe some fake horns and a tail. What do you think, Mark?"

Mark grinned. "Sounds good, as long as I don't have to chant anything. My Latin's almost non-existent."

The light-hearted banter lingered as they began clearing up, the burden of their mission still present but momentarily eased. They weren't just a group of individuals anymore – they were a team, bound by a shared determination to face whatever lay ahead.

Dougal moved to the chair in the study and leaned back, staring at the ceiling for a long moment. He had volunteered for this mission the second he learned it had ties to Nick's death. No hesitation. No second-guessing. Avenging Nick was all that mattered.

He and Nick had been inseparable once, bonded by their shared naval backgrounds. Dougal had served as a Royal Marine, tough as nails, while Nick had been a club-swinger – a Physical Training Instructor who took an almost sadistic delight in pushing recruits past their limits. Their friendship had been built in the barracks, solidified over years of service, late-night socialising, the odd barfight, and a mutual understanding of what it meant to live by discipline and loyalty. Nick had been like a brother.

Then Paula had entered Nick's life, and things had changed. At first, Dougal had been wary – not of Paula herself, but of what she represented. Nick had always been the independent one, never tied down. But Paula had done what no one else ever had – she'd softened him. In a good way. And Dougal hadn't resented her for it. She was good for Nick, and deep down, he'd known Nick had finally found something worth holding onto.

Now Nick was gone, and Dougal was here, hunting down the people responsible for his death. The whole damn thing was surreal. He was supposed to be dealing with threats he could see – men with guns, enemies with faces. But instead, they were communicating with a ghost named James, unravelling an occult nightmare that made his military training feel like child's play.

This wasn't his world. Magic, demons, spirits – it was all so far out of his comfort zone that he sometimes wondered if he'd lost his grip on reality. But one thing kept him grounded – his mission. He wasn't just here for vengeance. He was here to protect the people who had been dragged into this madness. Mark and Sam, who had suffered more than anyone should. And most of all, Paula.

He couldn't let her go through this alone. Not after what she had already lost. Protecting her wasn't just about keeping a promise to Nick – it was about making sure she didn't end up broken like the rest of them.

With a deep breath, Dougal sat forward, rolling his shoulders. There was no turning back now. Whatever this mission demanded, whatever horrors lay ahead, he would face them head-on. For Nick. For Paula. For all of them.

Chapter 25

Dance with the Devil

Canary Wharf, London – 5 April, 11:00 AM
The elevator doors slid open with a soft chime, revealing the sleek, modern interior of Sir Giles Worsley's office suite. The air was cool, and the subtle scent of polished wood and expensive cologne hung in the air. Mark and Sam stepped out, their footsteps muffled by the plush carpeting. They exchanged a glance, silently reaffirming their resolve.

Worsley's assistant, a poised young woman with an air of quiet efficiency, escorted them to his office. The space was as imposing as its occupant – floor to ceiling windows offered a panoramic view of the Thames, and every piece of furniture seemed deliberately chosen to convey power and sophistication.

"Ah, Mr. Benedict, Mrs. Benedict," Worsley greeted them warmly as he rose from behind his mahogany desk. His voice was smooth, cultured, and disarming. He gestured to two chairs in front of the desk. "Please, sit. It's a pleasure to meet you Mr. Benedict and to see you again Mrs. Benedict, though I wish it were under different circumstances."

Mark and Sam took their seats, careful to keep their gazes low, as James had warned them. Mark focused on Worsley's silk tie – a deep burgundy with subtle patterns – and Sam kept her eyes on the edge of the desk.

"We appreciate you seeing us, Sir Giles," Sam said, her tone polite but cool. "We're very worried about James."

"Of course, of course," Worsley replied, his expression shifting to one of practiced concern. "James is a valued colleague and a dear friend. His sudden disappearance has been most troubling. I've been doing everything in my power to assist the authorities."

Mark's jaw tightened. He knew better than to take Worsley's words at face value, but he forced a calm tone. "Do you have any idea where he might be? Or why he left so suddenly?"

Worsley sighed, leaning back in his chair with an air of thoughtfulness. "James has always been… enigmatic. Brilliant, but prone to bouts of introspection. It's possible he needed time away. A change of scenery, perhaps."

"Time away?" Sam echoed, her voice sharpening. "James wouldn't just vanish without telling us. And he wouldn't abandon his work."

"Ah, his work," Worsley said with a faint smile. "He was deeply committed, though I sometimes wondered if he pushed himself too hard. Stress can lead people to act in unpredictable ways."

Mark leaned forward slightly. "What exactly was he working on before he disappeared?"

Worsley's smile faltered for a fraction of a second, so brief it could have been imagined. "He was exploring some very niche topics – esoteric studies, ancient rituals. His brilliance often led him down unconventional paths."

"Unconventional?" Sam pressed, her tone laced with scepticism.

Worsley chuckled lightly, the sound as smooth as silk. "Nothing dangerous, I assure you. Though I admit, James had a fascination with the arcane that occasionally bordered on obsession. It's possible he stumbled upon something that compelled him to investigate further – perhaps overseas."

Sam clenched her fists in her lap, her nails digging into her palms. She forced herself to take a calming breath before replying. "James wouldn't just leave without a word. And if he had a reason, he would have told us."

Worsley leaned forward, his gaze intense despite their avoidance of his eyes. "I understand your concern, Mrs. Benedict. Truly, I do. But human behaviour is complex. Sometimes, even those closest to us keep secrets."

Mark sensed Sam falter, her posture stiffening as though caught in an invisible net. Without hesitation, he leaned over and touched her arm. "Sam, remember the conversation we had with the police?" he said, his voice calm but pointed.

Sam blinked, her tension easing as she nodded. "Yes, of course. We've informed the authorities, Sir Giles. If you hear anything, please let them or us know immediately."

Worsley smiled faintly, his composure unshaken. "Naturally. If I learn anything, you'll be the first to know. And if I may, should you discover anything, I hope you'll extend me the same courtesy."

Mark gave a noncommittal nod. "Of course. We all want James back safely."

Worsley rose, signalling the end of the meeting. "Thank you for coming. I'll continue to do everything in my power to assist in finding James. I do hope we can resolve this mystery soon."

Mark and Sam stood, each fighting the urge to lash out or confront the man they knew was responsible for James's death. Instead, they forced polite smiles and exchanged pleasantries before leaving the office.

As the office door clicked shut behind Mark and Sam, Sir Giles Worsley allowed his practiced mask of concern to fade into something colder, sharper – a predator's calculating stare. He turned to the window, gazing down at the river, his fingers tapping lightly on the polished surface of his desk.

Mark and Sam had played their parts well, but he had seen the flickers of loathing behind their polite facades, the barely concealed hatred simmering beneath their words. They had actively avoided his gaze. They knew. Or at least, they suspected. A faint smirk tugged at his lips. How delightfully naive they were to believe they could stand against him. Yet, their resolve intrigued him, a rare display of courage – or foolishness. For now, he would let them move unimpeded. The game was far more entertaining when his opponents believed they had the upper hand. But if they dared cross a line, Worsley mused, his amusement would swiftly turn to action. And he was very, very good at ending games.

As the elevator doors closed, Sam exhaled sharply, her hands trembling. "I hate him. Every word, every look – it's all a lie."

"We'll make him pay, Sam. But we need to be smart. Let's regroup with Dougal and figure out our next move."

James dared not observe the meeting with Worsley. The man's perception extended beyond mortal sight, and despite James's efforts to cloak himself in layers of astral disguise, Worsley would have sensed him. It was a risk too great to take. James knew that even in death, he was not beyond Worsley's reach.

As far as Worsley was concerned, James had been cast into hell by Abaddon himself. It was imperative that it remained that way. If Worsley so much as suspected that James still had influence over the living, that he was still guiding Mark and Sam, their danger would multiply tenfold.

James longed to intervene, to pull them away from their reckless pursuit, to urge them to abandon their quest before it was too late. But he knew that was not possible. Not now. Mark and Sam had passed the point of no return.

His only option was to remain unseen, to stay one step ahead of Worsley and his cabal of powerful adepts. The shadows between realms were his only refuge, and he would use them to his advantage. For now, silence was his greatest weapon. But if Worsley ever learned the truth… James feared there would be no hiding from him then.

Chapter 26

A Chill in the Air

Abingdon Grove, London – 5 April, 6:30 PM
The living room was alive with the quiet energy of planning. Mark, Sam, Paula, and Dougal sat around the coffee table, with papers and maps spread out between them. James's presence lingered unseen, but Paula occasionally tilted her head as though listening to his input.

"Fiona's in Chelsea," Dougal began, his voice steady and professional. "She's at her flat now, but I've got surveillance set up. If she moves, we'll know."

Mark leaned back. "The question is, how do we approach her without tipping her off? If she suspects anything, it's game over."

"That's where Paula comes in," Sam said, glancing at her new friend. "If we can get her to connect with Fiona naturally, it won't look suspicious. And James…" She hesitated, then smiled faintly. "James can give her a little nudge."

Paula nodded, her manner resolute. "I can do it. If Fiona senses something unusual, she'll be more likely to listen to me. Especially if I mention seeing an astral figure and James can provide that."

"She's likely a manipulator," Mark said bluntly. "Be careful what you say and how much you reveal. We can't afford to make her suspicious or give her anything she can use against us."

"I know," Paula replied. "But we need to establish trust first. I'll keep it vague, just enough to pique her interest."

Dougal's phone buzzed, and he glanced at the screen. "She's on the move. Looks like she's heading to a restaurant nearby. I'll follow her and let you know the location."

Paula stood, smoothing her blouse. "I'll head to the area now. James and I can be ready when you give us the green light."

"Be careful," Sam said, her voice tinged with concern.

"I will," Paula promised.

Chelsea, London – 5 April, 7:15 PM

Paula stepped out of the cab, her heels clicking softly against the pavement. She glanced around, spotting Doogie who had left a couple of minutes earlier, leaning casually in a shop doorway. He gave her a small nod.

"She's inside," he murmured, tilting his head toward the cozy, upscale restaurant. "Table by the window. Order something light and wait for James to do his thing."

Paula smiled. "Thanks, Doogie. Keep an eye on things."

Inside, the restaurant was warm and inviting, the soft hum of conversation and clinking glasses creating a relaxed atmosphere. Fortunately, there were a couple of empty tables. Paula handed the waiter her coat and took a seat at a small table near Fiona's and ordered a glass of wine and a starter. She resisted the urge to look directly at Fiona, instead focusing on her menu and waiting for James to act.

A subtle chill swept through the air. Fiona, seated at her table, frowned, her hand instinctively drawing her shawl closer. She shivered slightly and glanced around, brows knitting as if registering something just beyond ordinary perception.

From her place nearby, Paula noticed the shift. It was her cue. She leaned forward just enough to bridge the distance, her tone light, almost playful.

"Pardon me for interrupting, but did you feel that just now? Like a cold breeze… indoors?"

Fiona's gaze snapped to her. Her smile remained polite, but her eyes narrowed slightly, assessing. "I did," she said carefully. "It was very brief, but yes – odd. Almost like… someone walked past."

Paula offered a faint, knowing smile. "It happens to me from time to time. I suppose I'm sensitive to these things. My mother was a practitioner of Wicca – a white witch, some would say. Maybe I inherited something."

There was a pause.

Fiona looked at her more closely, the polite mask slipping just enough to betray deeper interest. She didn't respond right away, instead lifting her glass and taking a slow sip, eyes lingering on Paula above the rim.

Paula resisted the urge to fill the silence. She'd dropped the bait; now she needed Fiona to take it willingly. Best not to appear too eager. Inside, her heart beat a little faster. This was progress.

Eventually, Fiona set down her glass and tilted her head slightly. "Your mother practised? That's... unusual. Most people grow up with superstition and little else."

Paula shrugged gently. "She kept to herself mostly. It wasn't a religion for her, more a way of being. I was never really involved. I suppose I watched from the edges."

"Still," Fiona said, her voice quieter now, "those things leave a mark – in the best sense. Sometimes sensitivity skips a generation. Sometimes it lands where it's needed."

That caught Paula's attention. A vague phrase, but heavy with implication. She kept her tone light.

"I'm not sure I'd go that far," she said. "But now and then, I do get feelings... or see things I can't explain. A flicker of movement, the sensation of being watched when no one's there. Nothing too dramatic."

Fiona smiled faintly. "The best kinds never are."

She looked away for a moment, eyes scanning the room as if reassessing her surroundings through a different lens. Then, casually:

"I've always been curious about such sensitivities. My circle occasionally explores intuitive work. There's a poetic symmetry to it – the unseen brushing up against the ordinary."

Paula's pulse quickened. She recognised the shift – the conversation was tilting. Fiona had begun to probe in earnest.

"I've always liked the poetry of it," Paula said gently. "Though some of the things I've sensed didn't feel poetic at all. Sometimes they feel... cold. Watching. Unsettled."

Fiona leaned forward slightly, her posture still elegant, still composed – but now entirely focused. "That's very interesting. It's rare to meet someone who admits such things aloud."

"I don't talk about it often," Paula admitted. "People either laugh or lean too close."

Fiona chuckled softly. "And which am I doing?"

Paula smiled. "Still deciding."

There was a pause, the kind that lingers not from discomfort, but mutual consideration. Inside, Paula felt the tension of the game – she wanted in but couldn't show it. Fiona was reeling her closer, but only if she played this just right.

Fiona eased back into her seat. "Some friends and I gather now and then. Discreetly. We call it an esbat, though the names don't matter. A full moon in Cornwall can be quite an experience."

Paula tilted her head, her expression intrigued but cautious. "That sounds fascinating. Though Cornwall's a bit of a journey, isn't it?"

"When you see the place, you realise it is well worth the travel time. I have transport," Fiona said smoothly. "I could give you a lift. If you're ever inclined."

Paula nodded slowly, allowing a hint of curiosity to surface – just enough. "I might be," she said. "Depending on the moon."

Fiona's smile returned, soft and approving. "Then perhaps we should speak again. I'll be across the road at Vitor's Wine Bar tomorrow night, around seven-thirty. Come if you feel like continuing the conversation."

"I just might," Paula replied, letting the words hang with a hint of ambiguity.

He hovered near their table, tethered not by gravity but by will – and worry.

From where he drifted, half-seen and wholly intangible, James could observe without being observed. The living world shimmered like heat-haze through his vision, sound and sensation muffled, yet still present. This wasn't the true astral plane, not quite – more a liminal overlap, a no-man's land where he could watch... and wait.

Fiona's aura pulsed darkly. Subtle, elegant, calculated – much like the woman herself. Her composure was practiced, but James had known her long enough to catch the flickers: a stiffening of the jaw, the way her fingers paused around her wineglass when Paula mentioned her mother's Wicca. She was intrigued. More than that – she was measuring.

Good. That meant Paula was getting under her skin. She had done well. But this – this performance she was giving – he hadn't anticipated just how good she'd be. The way she leaned in, offering just enough of the truth to be disarming without triggering suspicion, was impressive.

Still, she was walking a knife's edge.

Fiona would not trust easily. She rarely had – even before Worsley twisted her deeper into his circle.

James floated closer, drawn to Paula. She was calm, but he could feel the subtle current of nerves in her body, the stiff set of her shoulders, the careful control of her expressions. She wanted the invitation – needed it, to get closer to Worsley's inner sanctum – but she was wise enough not to seem eager.

He wished he could touch her, just once. Brush her hand. Whisper encouragement. But interference on this side was dangerous. Even now, his presence might be noticed if he lingered too long. The more he concentrated, the more the air around them chilled – and Fiona had felt it.

Her eyes flickered once, glancing over her shoulder. She sensed something, but not clearly.

Not yet.

He couldn't afford to be seen by Fiona. Not now. Not like this.

Still, he hovered, unseen and aching. Watching Paula risking everything to infiltrate Worsley's web made him burn with guilt. She shouldn't have to do this. None of them should. And yet, if they didn't, who would?

Fiona's voice dropped again, softer now – the invitation given.

James felt a surge of relief. Paula's smile was perfect – warm, curious, unhurried. Fiona believed it. Or at least, she wanted to.

He drifted back, the thread of his will growing thin. His time here was limited. Staying too long frayed the soul. But before he faded, he sent a whisper of thought through the thinning veil, hoping – praying – it might reach her.

Careful, Paula. She's more dangerous than she seems.

Then, with a sigh that echoed only in the realm of spirits, James was gone.

As Paula stepped away from the table and out into the crisp night air, she exhaled slowly, letting her performance settle behind her eyes like the closing scene of a carefully rehearsed play. Her pulse was steady now, but only just.

She crossed the street, heels tapping softly against the pavement, Fiona's invitation still echoing in her mind. Vitor's Wine Bar. Seven-thirty. She'd done it.

And yet… something tugged at her.

She slowed, glancing instinctively over her shoulder. No one followed, yet the air seemed different – denser. A chill slid down the nape of her neck, feather-light but certain, like fingers brushing her skin.

The breeze stirred her hair. Then, from somewhere just beyond hearing, something stirred the air. A thought. A whisper. Not a sound, exactly – more a presence.

"Okay, James," she murmured under her breath. "Message received."

Abingdon Grove, London – 9:30 PM

Paula returned to the apartment with Doogie and James, her expression a mix of satisfaction and apprehension. Sam and Mark were waiting anxiously, and they both stood as she entered.

"How'd it go?" Sam asked.

"Better than expected. We talked about Wicca, and she's invited me to an esbat in Cornwall. She's interested in me – thinks I could be a potential initiate."

Mark raised an eyebrow. "That's… a little unsettling."

"It's progress," Paula said firmly. "And it gives us a way in. James has said that there is no way that Worsley will miss the Beltane Sabbat at the end of the month, and maybe he'll attend the Esbat too."

Dougal chuckled. "Let's just hope you're not too convincing, or she'll have you chanting spells before you know it."

Paula laughed. "I'll cross that bridge when I get to it Doogie. For now, we've got an opening. Let's use it."

Despite his levity, Dougal was concerned for Paula. She was composed, pragmatic as ever, but there was something beneath the surface – a load she carried with every breath, every glance. He had known grief intimately, seen it harden men, make them reckless, make them cold. Paula wasn't either of those things, but there was a fire in her now that hadn't been there before. It was the same fire he had seen in Nick Harper.

Dougal felt it too. The desire to avenge his death was a consuming force. But Paula – she was the one standing on the precipice. He wanted to protect her, shield her from the inevitable fallout of the war they were waging. And yet, even as he recognized her pain, he was realizing something else, something far more troubling – he himself was beginning to feel something for her.

It was too soon. Too raw. Too tangled in the grief they both carried. Now was not the time for such thoughts, not when Paula needed a friend, an ally, someone who wouldn't complicate things further. He pushed it down, deep where it couldn't cloud his judgment. She needed support, not another burden. And he would be damned if he let anything happen to her. For Nick's sake. For his own.

James lingered in the Astral plane, watching as the evening unfolded. Paula had done well – better than he had dared to hope. Fiona was intrigued by her, drawn in by Paula's subtle charm and the carefully woven hints of mysticism. It wasn't easy to win the attention of an adept, particularly one as cautious as Fiona, yet Paula had managed it effortlessly. He had felt the moment when Fiona's interest shifted from polite conversation to genuine curiosity. That was the moment Paula had her.

He had kept his distance, cautious yet fascinated. Though Fiona possessed power, she had only barely registered his presence, merely sensing a passing chill. That was an advantage. It meant he could observe her without fear of discovery, something that would prove invaluable in the days to come. Worsley was beyond his reach – his power too great, his senses too keen. But Fiona? She was different. She was formidable, yes, but she wasn't Worsley. And that meant James had a way in.

This was a long game and tonight had been an important step forward. Paula had positioned herself well, and James would be there, in the shadows, unseen yet watchful. There was still much to learn, but now, for the first time in a long while, James felt the faintest glimmer of hope. They had a chance.

Chapter 27
A Fragile Alibi

Abingdon Grove, London 6 April – 9:00 AM
The apartment buzzed with activity. Mark sat at the dining table, laptop open as he sifted through property listings in Cornwall. His brow furrowed as he scrolled through options near Trevaunce Manor, their proximity and anonymity paramount. Across the room, Sam paced, her phone glued to her ear as she confirmed the latest financial transfer to the untraceable account set up by Colonel Taylor's security firm. As soon as she put the phone down, it rang again. She took the call slipping into the hall.

Paula, a rare day off work, was seated on the couch, glancing over the documents detailing her new identity as Paula Jennings. She felt a strange detachment as she examined the driver's license, the bank statements, and the lease agreement for a modest flat in Bushey. Her life as she knew it was slowly being erased, a precaution against the watchful eyes of Worsley and Fiona.

Dougal leaned against the doorframe, arms crossed, watching the room with quiet intensity. "We've done all we can for now," he said, his voice calm. "Paula, you're set for tonight. Stick to the plan – earn Fiona's trust without giving too much away. Above all, be careful."

Paula nodded. "I'll be careful. James can always provide me with any guidance he feels necessary. The sooner I gain access to her circle, the better chance we have of learning what they're planning."

Mark looked up from his laptop. "And if she suspects anything, walk away. We can't afford to lose the progress we've made."

Sam ended her call and joined them, her air grim. "That's the least of our worries. The police are coming this afternoon. They want to ask more questions."

Mark's gaze sharpened. "About what?"

"James," Sam replied. "And the property in Virginia. It seems they've linked him to the fire."

The room fell silent. Paula glanced between them, a flicker of unease in her eyes. "Do they suspect foul play?"

"Seems likely," Sam said. "They're coordinating with the Avon police. Apparently, someone saw a Jeep Cherokee near the property shortly before the time of the fire."

Mark exhaled slowly. "We stick to the story. We know nothing about the property, and we haven't heard from James. They'll want DNA samples probably. We'll have to comply, but it won't tie back to the fire."

Sam nodded, though her hands fidgeted at her sides. "Let's hope that's true."

Abingdon Grove, London 6 April – 1:30 PM

The doorbell rang, its sharp chime cutting through the tense quiet of the apartment. Sam smoothed her hair and glanced at Mark, who gave her a reassuring nod before opening the door. Dougal and Paula moved to another room and closed the door.

Detective Inspector Brian Stevens and Detective Sergeant Ed Hughes stepped inside, their professional smiles polite but inquisitive. Stevens was a man in his fifties, his face lined with years of experience. Hughes, younger and sharp-eyed, carried a notepad ready to record every detail.

"Thank you for seeing us," Stevens began as they sat in the living room. "We won't take up too much of your time. This is a follow-up regarding James Benedict."

Sam folded her hands in her lap, her expression carefully neutral. "Of course. Anything to help find him. Would you like tea or coffee?"

Stevens declined the offer. "We've been in contact with the Avon police in Virginia regarding a suspicious fire at a property owned by your husband. Initial investigations suggest it was arson. We understand James flew into Washington Dulles Airport a few hours before the fire. Do you know anything about this?"

Mark feigned surprise, glancing at Sam before responding. "We had no idea. Jim never mentioned a property in Virginia, let alone a trip. This is the first we're hearing of it."

Hughes jotted down notes, his pen scratching softly against the page. "Do you know why James might have gone there? Business, perhaps? Or a personal matter?"

Sam shook her head. "James was… private about certain things. He didn't always share the details of his work, but under normal circumstances he would certainly have informed me that he was coming to America. I was at home then."

Stevens leaned forward slightly, his tone probing but not accusatory. "The Avon Fire Department is conducting a forensic investigation. They're analysing the ruins for DNA evidence. There's also a witness who claims to have seen a Jeep Cherokee near the property around the time of the fire."

Mark's stomach tightened, but he kept his tone light. "A Jeep Cherokee? A common vehicle, so that could be anyone. Besides, Jim would have had to hire a car. Do they have anything more concrete?"

"Not yet," Stevens admitted. "It seems likely that someone would have met him at the airport – there is no record of him renting a car. No-one remembers seeing him after arrival, but it's early days. If you think of anything that could help us understand why James was there, please let us know."

Sam hesitated, her gaze dropping momentarily. "Of course. We just want him back safely."

"There's one more thing," Hughes interjected. "Would you both be willing to provide DNA samples? It's standard procedure to help identify remains if necessary. It will only take about 5 minutes."

Mark felt Sam stiffen beside him. He placed a steadying hand on her arm and nodded. "Of course. Anything to help."

As the door closed behind the detectives, Sam exhaled shakily, returned to the living room and sank onto the couch. "That was… a little close for comfort."

Mark sat beside her. "We did fine. They don't have anything solid, and we gave them nothing to work with."

Sam shook her head. "But if they find James's DNA…"

"They won't, the fire will have destroyed everything. But even if they do, it won't lead back to us."

Sam was unsure.

Paula had not been present, hiding in another room, but she had eavesdropped. She joined them, her face pale but determined. "They seem suspicious. They might not have any evidence, but they are certainly looking for it."

Dougal, who had also remained hidden during the interview but watching and listening via the security system, finally spoke. "Then we make sure they find nothing. You're under scrutiny now, so be careful. Every move you make must be above suspicion."

Sam met Mark's gaze. "We can't stop now. Not with Worsley and Fiona out there. We'll handle the police, but we must keep going."

Mark nodded. "We will. One step at a time. Now let's think about Paula's meeting with Fiona tonight. It is imperative that that goes well."

Chapter 28
Shadows and Secrets

Chelsea, London 6 April – 7:30 PM

The warm glow of Vitor's Wine Bar spilled out onto the pavement, its Iberian charm welcoming and unpretentious. Inside, the low hum of conversation mixed with the faint strains of music, while the flicker of candlelight danced across the richly textured walls. Paula stepped inside, her senses momentarily soothed by the cozy ambience. She took a seat at the bar and ordered a glass of Vinho Verde.

Doogie had assured her he was nearby, keeping watch from the shadows, but Paula still felt a ripple of unease. James's warnings played in her mind: Be cautious. Don't drink too much. Watch your words. She carried her false identity with her, a reminder of the risks involved in her mission. At least he would be watching.

At the bar, Paula noticed a tall man loitering across the street, his movements deliberately casual. He leaned against a lamppost, his face obscured by the brim of his hat. She wondered why he was there. Was he suspicious or was she being paranoid? Dismissing her thoughts she sipped her wine.

Outside, Dougal spotted him too, his years of training honing his instincts. With practiced subtlety, he shifted his position to keep the man in sight while remaining inconspicuous.

Fiona arrived fifteen minutes later, her apology as charming as her tailored suit. "Paula, darling, I'm so sorry for the delay. The traffic in Chelsea is an absolute nightmare."

Paula smiled, pushing aside her unease. "No problem. I've been enjoying the atmosphere here. It's lovely."

Fiona waved to the bartender and ordered a whole bottle of Vinho Verde along with a small selection of tapas. "You have excellent taste. This wine is divine, and the pulpo here is to die for."

As the wine flowed, so did the conversation. Fiona leaned in, her gaze steady but warm. "So, have you given any more thought to my invitation for the esbat next week?"

Paula swirled her glass, feigning indecision. "I'm curious, but I don't know much about these gatherings. What's their purpose?"

Fiona's face lit up, her enthusiasm infectious. "Oh, they're beautiful ceremonies – celebrations of the Moon Goddess on the nights of the full and new moons. They're about connecting with nature, harnessing energy, and embracing our inner self. They are wonderfully empowering experiences."

Paula nodded, hiding her scepticism. She recalled James's warnings about Fiona's esbats containing darker practices than the Wiccan ones. Still, Fiona's charm was difficult to resist. "It sounds fascinating. What about the Sabbats you mentioned last time?"

"Ah," Fiona said, her voice lowering conspiratorially. "They are much bigger occasions. The Sabbats are a whole level grander – festivals tied to the sun's cycles. There are eight each year, celebrating everything from the return of spring to the harvest. Beltane, though – " She leaned closer, her eyes gleaming. "Beltane is particularly special. It's held on Walpurgis Night at the end of this month. There's fire, passion, and so much energy. A very powerful warlock will be attending this year's celebration. It will be unmissable. You simply must come."

Paula smiled faintly, her mind racing. Fiona's excitement was genuine, but Paula knew the truth. James had described the bacchanalian excesses and sinister rituals of these gatherings. Yet she kept her tone light. "Mm – I'll think about it. It sounds… extraordinary."

"That is an understatement! Let's go back to my place for some more wine and we'll talk some more."

Fiona's flat was as tastefully decorated as Paula had imagined – elegant furniture, soft lighting, and artful splashes of colour. But as Paula glanced around, her eyes held the more eccentric touches: a ceremonial dagger mounted on the wall, a silver snake swallowing its own tail, an ouroboros, Fiona called it. A silver chalice on a marble pedestal caught her gaze, and an intricately carved wooden mask that seemed to watch her.

Fiona poured them drinks, red wine this time, glinting like rubies in the firelight. Paula took a sip, savouring the bold flavour, but soon felt an unfamiliar warmth spreading through her body. Her thoughts grew hazy, and a heady mix of arousal and confusion clouded her mind. She heard James speaking in her head. *Be careful. She's drugged you.*

Fiona moved closer, her touch light but insistent. "You're so beautiful, Paula," she murmured, her voice low and intoxicating. Paula's protests melted away, her defences dulled by whatever Fiona had slipped into her drink. She let Fiona undress her slowly and sensually.

The night blurred into a whirl of erotic sensations – Fiona's lips, her probing tongue, carnal lust, the softness of the bed, the flicker of candlelight and alcoholic haze. Paula's emotions swung wildly between desire and guilt, her thoughts fragmented but persistent: Nick... James... *What am I doing?*

When Paula finally stirred, panic jolted her awake. "I need to go," she said abruptly, her voice thick with anxiety. "I have missed the last train," she said, registering the time.

"Stay the night." Fiona suggested.

"I can't, I have work in the morning."

"Of course, darling. I'll call a cab – don't worry, it will be pre-paid – I have an account with a local firm. But we really must meet again soon. Here is my personal number; call me and we can travel to Cornwall together on Thursday."

Outside, Dougal watched as the cab arrived. His stomach tightened when he recognised the driver – it was the same man he had spotted earlier. Quickly, he made a call, summoning a colleague in an unmarked car.

As the cab pulled away, Dougal noted the direction and when his driver arrived a minute later, they set off hoping to catch sight of it. Suddenly Dougal spotted it. They began tailing it their movements cautious but determined. Twice, they lost the vehicle in the maze of London's streets, and traffic lights, but each time, Dougal's instincts led them back on track. When the cab finally stopped outside Paula's flat in Bushey that he'd arranged for her, Dougal watched with relief as she exited safely and entered her apartment.

"Stay with the cab," he instructed his colleague. "I need to know if this is Fiona's doing or Worsley's. Either way, we'll find out."

Fiona stretched and purred. The night had gone well. Paula would attend her esbat, she was sure of it. She'd cursorily checked the contents of

Paula's handbag and was satisfied that there was nothing suspicious about her. She would probably call off the surveillance she'd arranged unless the cab driver reported anything out of the ordinary.

No, she was ideal and ripe for manipulation. She was attractive, sensuous and with her psychic talents, would make a most welcome addition to her list of initiates at Trevaunce Manor. She may be even trainable to become one of Giles' Neophytes. Fiona was sure he would welcome her. Yes, a good night's work, she thought smugly.

Paula sat on her bed, her head in her hands. The night's events replayed in her mind, each memory laced with regret. Her sexual encounter with Fiona, her first ever with a woman, had left her conflicted – a mix of guilt for betraying Nick's memory and loathing for the woman tied to his death.

But there was another feeling, one that gnawed at her, a spark of guilty connection to Fiona's charm and passion. Paula hated herself for it. She whispered into the empty room, "I must not let this happen again."

"Paula." James's voice drifted into her consciousness, soft and familiar, but tinged with concern. She felt his presence before she saw him, a faint shimmer in the air that coalesced into the spectral outline of the man she had come to depend on.

She stiffened, her shoulders tightening. "You saw? Of course you did. I heard your warning, but it was too late."

"I saw enough." His voice felt gentle in her mind, but there was no judgment in it, only understanding. "And I know what you're feeling. Guilt is a heavy burden, Paula, but you didn't betray Nick."

She let out a shuddering breath. "It feels like I did. It feels like I let myself be drawn in, even knowing who she is, what she's done."

James sighed, stepping closer though he remained insubstantial, his presence hovering at the edge of her perception. "You did what was necessary. This connection with Fiona – it's invaluable. She's drawn to you, and that gives us a chance to learn more, to get closer to Worsley's inner circle. That's the mission."

Paula shook her head. "I know that, but it doesn't make it easier. It felt real, James. I felt something, even though I despise her. And that terrifies me."

James was silent for a moment, his face unreadable. Then he said, "Attraction is complicated. So are emotions. The mind and the heart don't always move in the same direction. But listen to me – whatever happened tonight, whatever you felt, it doesn't define you. You're not betraying Nick by doing what you must to bring Worsley down. You're honouring him."

Her throat tightened. "And if I lose myself in this? If I become… like them?"

James crouched before her, his eyes searching hers. "You won't. Because you're not. Because you have an inner strength. Because you have us – me, Dougal, Mark, Sam. And because you still remember who you are."

Paula swallowed hard, nodding slowly. The ache in her chest didn't lessen, but James's words anchored her, grounding her frayed emotions.

"Get some rest," James murmured. "You'll need your strength. Fiona won't stop at this. She's drawn you in, and she'll test you further. But we'll be ready."

Paula let out a long breath, exhaustion seeping into her bones. She pulled the blanket over her lap and cast one last glance at James. "Thank you."

His form flickered, his presence beginning to fade. "Always." Then he was gone, leaving Paula alone in the dim light of her room, her thoughts still tangled, but her resolve a little stronger.

Chapter 29

Circles of Caution

Abingdon Grove, London – 7 April, 10:00 AM
The morning light filtered through the living room window, casting a soft glow over the table. Paula sat with her hands wrapped around her cup, her expression a mix of exhaustion and determination. Across from her, Sam leaned forward, her brow furrowed in concern, while Mark methodically scribbled notes in the margins of a map of Cornwall. Dougal, as usual, stood near the window, his posture relaxed but his gaze sharp, scanning the street outside for anything unusual.

Paula broke the silence, her voice steady but carefully measured. "I need to tell you about last night. You need to know exactly what we're dealing with. Fiona's charming, magnetic even, but there's something darker under the surface. She's skilled at reading people, at manipulating them, and she made it clear that she wants me to be a part of their world."

Mark put down his pen and gave her his full attention. "Go on. What happened?"

Paula recounted her evening with Fiona – the warm conviviality of the wine bar, the unsettling objects in her flat, her insistence that she belonged with the Order, the carefully woven temptation in her words, and the subtle yet undeniable way she tested Paula's loyalty. Paula also mentioned the drugged wine that dulled her senses causing her to sleep, leaving her vulnerable. She was sure that Fiona had been through her handbag so was thankful that the contents had been sanitised by Doogie's agency. But she carefully omitted the most personal details, the ones that would only complicate things further. Some truths, she decided, were better left unsaid.

She had already discussed it with James, and they had agreed – it was better this way. If Mark, Sam, or Dougal knew just how far Fiona had taken things, they would be even more fearful for her safety, and that was the last thing she needed. Sam, in particular, would worry herself sick, and Dougal might do something reckless. This wasn't about comfort or personal boundaries anymore; this was about strategy. If she was going to stay close to Fiona, gain her trust, and uncover the secrets of the Order, she had to accept that this might happen again. And when it did, she would have to grin and bear it. She wasn't naïve enough to think she could escape Fiona's attention now – if anything, she had been drawn deeper in. But the deeper she went, the more valuable the information she could bring back. That was what mattered.

When she finished, Sam's face was pale. "Paula, I'm so sorry you had to go through that. We should have prepared you better."

Paula shook her head. "It's not your fault. I knew the risks. I just didn't think… I didn't think she'd be so effective. But it wasn't all bad news. She trusts me enough to invite me to the esbat at Trevaunce Manor in three days, and she's giving me a lift. And she's hinted at the Beltane Sabbat at the end of the month."

Mark exhaled slowly. "That's a win, but it doesn't make what you went through any less awful. Are you okay?"

"No, but I'll survive, and the end justifies the means. Let's just call it taking one for the team."

Dougal, who had been silent, was angry, but his emotional determination to protect Paula was conflicting with the obvious value of her staying close to Fiona. "I'm sorry that you had to go through that, Paula, but we've got another concern. After last night, I spotted someone tailing Paula's cab. It wasn't Fiona, but it might have been someone connected to her or Worsley."

"Who was it?" Sam asked, her voice rising with alarm.

"Owner of a small cab company in Chelsea, near Fiona's flat. I'm assuming Fiona knew him and called him when arranging the taxi for Paula. We ran background checks – nothing overtly suspicious. Could be unrelated, but we can't assume that."

Mark frowned. "So, we may have eyes on us. That complicates things."

"Not necessarily," Dougal said. "It means we need to stay vigilant. I'll keep monitoring the situation, but for now, let's focus on what we can control."

Mark nodded, shifting the conversation. "Speaking of control, I've found us a place to stay near Trevaunce Manor – a converted farm building on Bodmin Moor. It's remote, secure, and close enough for recon without drawing attention. We can move in on Tuesday, giving us time to scout the area before Thursday's esbat."

"That's a solid plan, but what about Worsley?" Sam asked. "If he's there on Thursday, do we act?"

Paula shook her head. "James says no. He's adamant that we focus on gathering intel and wait until the Beltane Sabbat. We'll need more time to plan, and Thursday's esbat will give us a chance to observe the manor, Fiona, and any rituals. It's safer to wait and prepare."

Dougal nodded approvingly. "Agreed. A rushed attack is a dead man's plan. Use the esbat to learn their routines and weaknesses. Beltane's our best shot."

Sam sighed. "It feels like we're always waiting, always one step behind."

Mark placed a reassuring hand on her shoulder. "I get it, Sam. But if we're going to take Worsley down, we can't afford to make mistakes. Waiting isn't weakness – it's strategy."

A brief silence fell over the group, broken only by the soft clink of Paula's mug against the table. Finally, she looked up, her smile faint but genuine. "So, it's settled. We move to Bodmin Moor on Tuesday, gather intel during the esbat, and prepare for Beltane. Let's make sure all this waiting pays off."

Dougal grinned. "And let's hope Bodmin Moor doesn't come with ghosts. I hear the moors are crawling with them."

Paula chuckled softly. "At this point, Doogie, a ghost would probably feel quite normal."

The group shared a brief laugh, the tension in the room easing. But as the conversation turned to logistics and supplies, the burden of their mission remained, a shadow lingering over their plans.

Chapter 30

Shadows on the Moor

odmin Moor, Cornwall – 9 April, 10:30 AM

The wind swept across the rugged expanse of Bodmin Moor, carrying with it the faint scent of damp earth, moorland grass and heather. Dougal adjusted the strap of his pack, his sharp eyes scanning the twin security fences that marked the boundary of Trevaunce Manor Estate. The outer fence bristled with barbed wire, while the inner one was topped with vicious razor wire, a menacing barrier that screamed *Keep Out*. Every fifty metres or so, security cameras perched like watchful sentinels. They had no visible signs of movement or of being powered so he was unsure whether they were currently operational. He disregarded them for now.

Dougal had started his walk in Bodmin Moor with Mark and Sam, who'd wanted to stretch their legs. They had covered about a mile along a path that ran parallel to the fence, when Mark spotted a wooden signpost which read "To the Fogou". Sam had conveyed an interest and she and Mark had headed up that path which led away from the fence, agreeing to meet up with Dougal later at Carn View. Dougal continued alone looking for weaknesses in the security fence as well as areas that might serve as viewpoints for surveillance.

After another mile or so, he stepped back to survey the surrounding area and spotted a high rocky outcrop about a mile from the fence. Dougal consulted his ordnance survey map, confirming its designation as Hebdon Tor. It might provide an ideal vantage point for observing the estate, particularly the stone circle Paula had learned about from Fiona. If rituals were conducted there, as suspected, this spot would be crucial. There were further tors beyond Hebdon Tor which might also serve, but they would be even further away.

The climb to the top was laborious without an obvious path but rewarding. Dougal paused to catch his breath, taking in the sweeping view of the moorland. The landscape stretched out in a patchwork of rocky tors and plains with muted greens and browns, punctuated by patches of bracken and gorse. There were also incongruous clumps of wild rhododendrons, their early light mauve blooms softening the bleak landscape. Wild moorland ponies were dotted around in small groups along with sheep and cattle that farmers were permitted to graze on the public land. Dougal spotted cows resembling the Highland Cattle of his beloved homeland as well as a few Belted Galloways.

Returning to his mission, Dougal used his binoculars to see over the security fence revealing part of the manor house, several hundred metres beyond. Apart from glimpses of the roof, the majority of the house was obscured by woodland, save for one end. The open moorland to the left of the visible part of the house from his perspective, revealed a stone circle nestled in a shallow hollow. He studied the site carefully. Surely there could not be two stone circles on the estate. No… this had to be the place.

Satisfied with his findings, Dougal took out his flask of coffee and settled on a rock, letting the calm of the moment wash over him. His thoughts drifted to the journey the day before, a mix of tedium and amusement.

The drive from London had been uneventful until they hit the A303. There were just the three of them as Paula would be travelling down with Fiona the following evening. The sight of Stonehenge on one side of the road, had prompted a flurry of excitement from Mark and Sam, their faces pressed against the car windows like children on a school trip. Dougal chuckled at their enthusiasm but kept his focus on the road.

The A30 led them through Devon where they stopped in a village for lunch at a fifteenth century pub, again causing wonder for the Americans. Sam had enjoyed a baguette, but Mark had been less impressed by his burger. After a short stretch on the M5, they took the A30 south of Exeter. Forty minutes later they were in Cornwall, winding past the stark beauty of Bodmin Moor. A few miles before the town of Bodmin, they turned left on a narrow road, sign-posted Nansebyn.

Sam and Mark were bewildered by the narrow country lanes. Sam had said "I don't think I'd like driving on these roads."

"What happens if two cars meet head-on?" Mark had asked, his tone equal parts horror and fascination.

Dougal had grinned and teased. "You play chicken. Or hope the other driver's more patient than you and prepared to reverse." After a pause he had continued, "No, the lanes normally contain small passing areas where if you see another car coming you pull in and wait. Narrow lanes are the norm down here, but you soon get used to them."

Their accommodation, Carn View, was a converted barn situated about a mile from the small village, of Nansebyn. Sam and Mark had marvelled at its quaintness, their awe tinged with disbelief at its age. After unpacking, they had ventured to the Prince of Wales pub, where they were welcomed with warmth and good ale. It had been a rare moment of lightness amidst the tension of their mission.

Dougal finished his coffee and descended from Hebdon Tor, skirting the boggy areas, his boots compressing the sphagnum moss and spongy moorland grass. He skirted the fence, keeping to the barely noticeable narrow trails. After a couple of miles, he saw a figure approaching from the path ahead. He was a thick-set man, his gait heavy and deliberate. The man's eyes narrowed as he advanced.

"You're too close to the estate mate," the man growled, his voice low and threatening. "Turn back."

Dougal squared his shoulders. "I'm hiking on public land. Perfectly within my rights."

The man's lips twisted into a sneer. "Rights, huh? I'll show you who has rights, mate!"

Before Dougal could respond, the man lunged. Dougal sidestepped, his instincts kicking in. The first punch glanced off his shoulder, and Dougal retaliated with a sharp jab to the man's throat. The thug staggered back, choking violently, but reached for a gun in his side pocket. Dougal acted swiftly, kicking the weapon from his hand, sending it skittering across grass. He shoved him to the ground.

The man groaned, clutching his wrist, which now bent at an unnatural angle. "You're a dead man," he spat, his voice ragged. "You don't know who you're dealing with."

Dougal crouched, his voice cold. "I know enough. You know nothing." He searched the man, confiscating a large knife before rising. "Stay down if you know what's good for you."

The man muttered a curse but made no move to follow as Dougal disposed of the gun by throwing it high over the fence. He travelled back along the path, adrenaline coursing through his veins. He'd seen enough and headed back to Carn View.

Mark and Sam stood looking at the Fogou, after descending stone steps into a ditch which surrounded a mound. A stone entrance in the mound had a weathered slate sign that stood to one side, informing them that this was Polzen Fogou, an ancient underground passage dating back to the sixth or fifth century BC.

Sam let out a low whistle. "So let me get this straight – we're about to enter an almost three-thousand-year-old hole in the ground?"

Mark grinned, removing a flashlight from his backpack. "Exactly. I mean, when do we ever do anything safe and sensible?"

"Never," Sam muttered. "And that's what worries me."

They entered carefully, the air growing cooler with each step. The narrow passage swallowed them in darkness, save for the beam of Mark's flashlight flickering over the ancient stone walls. The craftsmanship was impressive – rough-hewn but solid, a testament to the ingenuity of Iron Age builders.

"I have to admit," Mark said, running a hand over the carefully fitted slabs, "this is seriously cool. Can you imagine building something like this with nothing but stone tools?"

Sam shivered as she looked around. "I can imagine them using it to hide from invading warriors, but I'd rather not think about what happened to the ones who didn't make it."

Mark turned to her with amusement. "That's the spirit. Full appreciation of history – with a side of horror."

They reached the end of the main passage, where a much smaller stone-framed opening led into a little chamber beyond.

"Think you can squeeze in?" Sam teased.

Mark gave the opening a long, sceptical look. "Sure, if I dislocate both shoulders and sacrifice my dignity."

"Dignity? When did you ever have that?"

Mark rolled his eyes. "Remind me why I brought you along again?"

"Because without me, you'd have wandered into a death trap at least five times by now."

Deciding against trying to contort himself through the small gap, Mark turned back, retracing his steps. That's when he spotted a side tunnel he hadn't noticed before, its entrance almost hidden from view. "Hey, check this out. It is designed so you can't see it coming in from the main entrance."

Sam followed him as he ducked inside, the passage curving sharply before opening up slightly. A faint, silvery light filtered through from the far end, where a hinged metal grill led to the outside world. They clambered through it carefully, emerging in the ditch on the other side of the mound, the exit invisible from the entrance.

Mark dusted off his jeans and looked back at the structure with newfound admiration. "You know, for people without modern engineering, they really knew what they were doing. A secret escape tunnel? Genius."

"Makes you wonder what else they were hiding," Sam said, brushing dirt from her hands. "Maybe treasure? A portal to another realm? A stash of ancient beer?"

Mark chuckled. "If it's beer, I'm definitely coming back. But seriously, this place is incredible. We need to learn more about it."

Sam nodded, gazing back at the entrance. "Agreed. But first, let's make sure we can actually get out of here without triggering some ancient curse."

Mark laughed. "You've been watching too many movies."

"And you haven't watched enough. Come on, let's go before we end up on some ghost-hunting documentary."

With one last look at the Fogou, they turned and made their way back, already eager to uncover more of its secret.

Carn View – 9 April, 6:30 PM

By the time Dougal reached Carn View, the afternoon sun was dipping low, casting long shadows across the barn's stone walls. Inside the charming rustic building, a freshly lit log fire providing a pleasing ambience, Sam and Mark were poring over maps, their faces lighting up when they saw him.

"You're back," Sam said, relief evident in her tone. "Find anything?"

Dougal grinned. "I discovered a rocky outcrop, Hebdon Tor, that's a perfect vantage point. And then I had a little chat with one of Worsley's goons."

Mark raised an eyebrow. "Chat?"

Dougal chuckled. "A brief altercation. He started it and let's just say he won't be bothering anyone anytime soon. How was the fogou?"

Mark replied, "Incredible, it was over two-and-a-half thousand years old."

"Amazing!" Sam interjected, "Those ancient peoples with presumably very primitive tools produced some incredible engineering. There was a passageway to a small storage area…"

"And a second cleverly concealed passage which led to another exit," said Mark, "you might be able to make use of that if hiding from more of Worsley's thugs."

"It's made me want to do some more research." Sam said.

Mark changed the subject. "Do you think your encounter with the goon will have any effects?"

"The estate will be wondering who the hell I am – that's for sure."

Sam ventured, "Well we now know for sure that the estate is patrolled. We must be careful. The fact that you injured him will send a signal to ramp up the security."

Despite the levity in his tone, Dougal's mind lingered on the guard's warning. *You don't know who you're dealing with*. Whether it was bravado or a genuine threat, Dougal knew one thing for certain – Worsley's shadow loomed large over everything.

✦

Chapter 31

Whispers of the Manor

Carn View, Cornwall, 9 April – 7:30 PM

The table at Carn View was scattered with maps, research papers, and empty mugs. Mark, Sam, and Dougal worked with quiet determination, each engrossed in their respective tasks. The old farm building offered them a rural charm, with its exposed beams and a crackling fire, but the air inside was tense with purpose.

Earlier, Sam had researched the fogou, purely as a personal interest item, after it had excited her yesterday. She had discovered that Polzen Fogou was the only one on Bodmin Moor in Cornwall. All others in Cornwall were much further west. She discovered that they are pronounced "foogoo" with an alternative spelling of fougou. Their purpose was unknown and open to debate, but popular theories included refuges, bolt holes or used for food storage due to the excellent ventilation they possess.

Sam sighed. "It's like James was always a couple of steps ahead of Worsley, but it still wasn't enough." Her voice softened, her grief barely contained. "We really need more of his advice… I have an increasing list of questions for him. I need Paula."

Dougal spoke up, glancing at his watch. "Well, she should be arriving at Trevaunce Manor about now. She'll contact us once she has settled in."

Mark put down a pen he'd been absently twirling. "I hope so." He paused briefly before continuing, "this telekinesis thing isn't working any better for me despite hours of practice; it's so infuriating. My powers are still as pathetic as they ever were. I can't see how it'll even help us in our goals anyway."

"Don't sweat it, laddie. We'll rely on the basics – strategy, vigilance, and, if necessary, a good old-fashioned fistfight. Speaking of which, I've got more kit arriving tomorrow."

"Kit?" Sam asked, raising a brow.

"Long-range rifles, night vision gear, small explosives and other specialised items. It's mainly precautionary, but If Worsley's got his goons patrolling, I'd rather be armed and see them before they see us."

"Just make sure Mark doesn't get his hands on any of it. He's likely to blow something up."

Dougal chuckled, "Noted. I'm feeling peckish; time to go down the pub. However, we need to be careful as Worsley may have eyes inside. Two Americans coming in two nights in a row could arouse curiosity."

"We could pretend to be Canadian holiday makers." Sam ventured.

"Not sure that would be much better. Let's play it by ear. Just don't be too loud or showy."

They agreed and Mark grabbed a flashlight for the return as they prepared for the 20-minute walk to the Prince of Wales. As they set off, their boots crunching on the gravel driveway, the cool evening breeze bit at their cheeks, but the fading light still revealed their picturesque surroundings that contrasted with the darkness they were shortly to face.

Trevaunce Manor, Cornwall – 7:45 PM

The Bentley glided to a stop at the grand entrance of Trevaunce Manor, its headlights illuminating the grey stone facade. Despite Paula's qualms after her previous encounter with Fiona, the chauffeur-driven journey in the grand vintage vehicle had been comfortable and relaxed. Fiona's easygoing charm and genial personality meant they quickly settled into light and humorous discussion, suitably abetted by the cocktail cabinet and Fortnum and Mason hamper.

The chauffeur opened Fiona's door and held it while she got out. Paula did not wait and got out on the other side. She walked round and joined Fiona heading for the steps that led to the large imposing double doors. "What about the luggage?"

"Don't worry about that. It will be brought to your room."

The house loomed like a silent sentinel, its ornate carvings and imposing turrets casting eerie shadows. The doors swung open to reveal a heavy-set man, perhaps of Middle Eastern ethnicity with hypnotic pale blue eyes and a hooked nose. He was dressed in livery that did not sit comfortably upon him.

"My Lady," he greeted Fiona deferentially, bowing slightly, before turning to Paula. His eyes locked briefly with her own, and she felt a shiver despite the warmth of her coat.

"Thank you, Abdul, this is my dear guest, Paula. Treat her well." Fiona turned to Paula, taking her arm. "Come. Let me show you my… well, it's Sir Giles' sanctuary, but as I manage the place for him and stay here a lot more than he does, I like to think of it as my own."

The grand entrance hall was a study in contrast. Plush crimson rugs muffled their steps, while the high vaulted ceiling soared above them, illuminated by a grand chandelier that glittered with hundreds of crystal droplets. The walls were lined with portraits of severe-faced ancestors whose eyes seemed to follow Paula as she moved. A massive stone fireplace dominated one wall, its hearth currently cold and empty, but above it hung an ornate mirror with a gilded frame shaped like intertwining serpents. Paula's reflection seemed faintly distorted, and she quickly looked away. A wide sweeping marble staircase on the right, led them up to a galleried landing.

"The Manor has been in Giles' family for generations," Fiona said with a smile, her voice warm but tinged with pride. "It's wonderful. Each wing has its own character, its own… energy."

She led Paula to the west wing, where the air grew noticeably cooler. The long corridor was lined with tapestries depicting scenes of feasts, hunts, and battles. The bedrooms here were spacious but sparsely furnished, each with a heavy four-poster bed and a single armoire. One room, however, caught Paula's attention. The bed was draped in black velvet, and above the headboard was an intricate carving of a horned figure surrounded by flames.

Fiona noticed her gaze. "This was one of Giles' ancestors rooms. He was a fascinating man – an occult scholar who travelled the world collecting rare artefacts." She gestured to a corner where a glass case held a collection of ritual knives, each with elaborate handles inlaid with precious stones.

Paula forced a smile, her unease growing. "It's… different, but very inspiring."

They moved to the east wing, where the decor was lighter, almost inviting. Fiona described it as the family's main living area, with sunny sitting rooms and a library filled with strangely titled, leather-bound volumes that exuded the comforting scent of old parchment. But even here, Paula spotted oddities: a globe with unfamiliar constellations, a chess set where the pieces were human figures frozen in expressions of terror, and a tapestry depicting a ritual beneath a blood-red moon. Outside, Fiona pointed to a door on the opposite side of the corridor and said, "That is your bedroom; you can see it later." They continued the tour.

Fiona's voice softened as they entered the northern wing. "This part of the manor is my favourite. It's where we draw our inspiration."

The corridor here was narrower, the walls painted a deep, shadowy red. Candles in wrought-iron sconces flickered, casting eerie shadows that seemed to move independently of the flames. They entered a large chamber that Fiona called the Ritual Room. The air was heavy with the scent of incense, and the walls were covered in arcane symbols that seemed to pulse faintly in the dim light.

A stone altar stood at the centre of the room, draped in black silk and surrounded by unlit candles. Above it, a mural depicted a dark winged figure descending from the heavens, its face obscured but its outstretched hands radiating power. Around the mural's edges were Latin phrases that Paula couldn't decipher.

Fiona's voice grew reverent. "This is where we conduct some of our most sacred ceremonies. It's a place of immense power, connected to the very energy of the land."

Paula suppressed a shiver. "It's… astonishing."

"You'll feel it soon enough."

"Is this where tomorrow's esbat will be held?"

"Oh no," Fiona laughed, that is a larger gathering and will be outside under the full moon which will be visible tomorrow night. We have an amazing ancient Stone Circle on the moor. There are ley lines there, providing enhanced power to our revelry.

Back downstairs in the entrance hall, Fiona led her to a door to the cellar. Stone steps were revealed which they descended. The air grew colder, and Paula's breath misted in the dim illumination. At the far end of the cellar was an ornate iron gate that led to a low, arched passage. Fiona gestured toward it. "Except for Abdul, it is forbidden for any of us to enter that gate unless Sir Giles is present. Beyond that is the Dark Chamber. It predates the Manor and is believed to have been used for ancient rituals. Some say it amplifies energy, while others believe it's a gateway of sorts."

Paula hesitated. "A gateway to what?"

Fiona's smile was enigmatic. "That depends on the one who opens it."

"What was that noise? It sounded a bit like a groan."

Fiona was dismissive, "Probably just the wind; this area often produces eerie sounds."

Paula was unsure. It sounded more like a human noise, someone in pain. They returned to the steps and up to the main hall, where Fiona guided Paula to a parlour filled with overstuffed armchairs and a roaring fire. A tray of tea and biscuits awaited them, though Paula noticed a decanter of dark red liquid on a side table.

"Tomorrow, you'll see Trevaunce in its full glory." Fiona said, pouring herself a glass of wine after Paula had declined. "It's an experience you'll never forget."

Paula nodded, her emotions a whirlwind of awe and unease. The Manor was both captivating and deeply unsettling, a place where beauty and menace intertwined seamlessly. She sipped her tea, feeling Fiona's gaze linger on her. Beneath the surface charm, Paula sensed a darkness that she couldn't yet fully comprehend. After a short while, they climbed the stairs and proceeded to the door Fiona had indicated as her bedroom earlier.

"This is your room. Rest well, darling, I shan't be joining you tonight." The door opened into a tastefully furnished guest room. Fiona kissed Paula lightly on the cheek. "We'll need all our energy for tomorrow's esbat."

Paula closed the door, relieved. Her baggage had been delivered to her room. A door on the opposite side of the bed led to an en suite with a claw-footed bathtub and separate shower. After a cursory inspection, she moved back to the comfortably large bedroom. The room was tastefully furnished in the regency style. There were two bedside tables, a coffee table and two easy chairs between the foot of the bed and the opposite wall where there were two chests of drawers separated by a heavily draped window. Past the entrance to the bathroom were two large armoires. *Very nice* she thought.

She retrieved her phone, switched off the lights and compiled a text summarising the day's events. She sent it to Doogie and turned the lights back on to find James standing by the bed.

"I was wondering when you'd turn up." She grinned.

"I've been watching you all day, careful to remain unseen. You have done well. Fiona likes you." James responded. "Be wary of Abdul. He's a low-level adept but has psychic powers. Though Fiona can't, Abdul would certainly sense my presence."

"This place gives me the creeps!" Paula said with a shiver. "Particularly the Ritual Room and the Dark Chamber in the cellar, but I didn't see that because the Gate was locked."

"Even Fiona dare not go there on her own. I have been in both areas in the past, and I would rather forget what I experienced. The Dark Chamber has a terrifyingly evil aura and is reserved for Worsley's worst diabolical rituals. There is also a dungeon beyond that gate, where Worsley often incarcerates people while he or Abdul punishes them, psychically."

"That sounds terrifying!" Paula shuddered.

"I should leave you to unpack and get ready for bed. I'll check on the others and then be back to watch over you tonight." James slowly faded away.

Prince of Wales, Nansebyn – 9:30 PM

Mark and Sam were settled into a corner table with Dougal, all having enjoyed hearty meals.

"That steak was better than I expected." Mark said, leaning back with satisfaction.

Dougal grinned. "That's because you're eating UK sirloin – not the same as your cut which is more akin to top rump over here. Our sirloin is the equivalent of your porterhouse."

Sam laughed. "Still divided by a common language." There had been quite a lot of friendly banter between the Americans and the Scot, but now it was time to return to more serious considerations. "I wonder how it is going with Paula?"

Dougal responded, "She said she would text when she got here. Nothing heard yet so either she's not arrived yet or she hasn't had an opportunity. I'm guessing all is ok, but probably quite stressful for her. She's a great lassie though and sure to come up with some useful information. I'm positive James will have his eye on her."

"You can be sure of that! James will be watching her like a hawk, but also with caution so as not to alert Fiona." Mark added.

The pub was alive with warmth and chatter, the air thick with the scent of ale and hot food. Laughter erupted from the next table, but the trio remained insulated, their mission far too serious to be swayed by the pub's conviviality. They were maintaining a low profile.

Dougal's eyes were drawn to a man nursing a pint at the bar. His dishevelled appearance and frequent glances toward the door set him apart from the other patrons. "That one's strange. He looks anxious about something. I bet he's got a story," Dougal muttered, nodding toward the man.

Mark followed Dougal's gaze. "Reckon it's worth asking?"

"Definitely. You stay here, we don't want to spook him" He rose, approached the man, and introduced himself. "Hi, Dougal Finlayson. Care for a pint and some company?"

The man hesitated, suspicious, but relented as Dougal signalled to the barman. "Arthur Parker," he said, shaking Dougal's hand. "I don't know what you want, but if it's about the Manor, leave it alone."

Dougal's interest piqued. "What do you know about Trevaunce Manor?"

Arthur lowered his voice, leaning in. "Enough to know it's cursed. Witchcraft gatherings, and other esoteric stuff. My girlfriend, Joan, went there for some of their coven ceremonies. After the third one she never came back."

Dougal's expression hardened. "When was that?"

"Middle of last month, it was celebrating the March equinox, I think, I can't remember the name"

"Did you tell the police?"

Arthur scoffed. "And say what? That she vanished after going to a magic ritual? They'd have laughed me off the premises."

"Whatever, you must have reported her missing?"

"Well, I didn't. I'm assuming that her employer has done by now, not that it will do any good. The owner of the Manor, Sir Giles Worsley, has the police in his pocket. In fact, most of the village is in his pocket. I tried questioning people driving up to the gate but was discouraged by the owner's heavies."

"Discouraged?"

Arthur pointed to a couple of bruises and marks on his face. "Beaten up!"

"I suppose you didn't report that to the police either?"

Parker shrugged. "What would be the point?"

"What did you mean that the Manor owner has most of village in his pocket?"

"To keep them sweet, he gives each house in the village £500 every Christmas. The landlord here might even be a member of the coven. He was the one who told Joan about it."

"What is it that you do?" Dougal asked.

"I'm a freelance reporter. I work mainly for a weekly Cornish rag. I tried to create a story about the Manor and Joan's mysterious disappearance. Though the editor seemed interested initially, he then dropped it. I'm thinking Worsley may have got to him too."

Their conversation was interrupted by the entrance of two large men. Arthur stiffened. "Those thugs work for Worsley. The shorter one was one of the ones who attacked me. They're the reason I don't ask too many questions."

The shorter of the two spotted Arthur and made a beeline for him. "Poking your nose in again, Parker?" He said threateningly.

Dougal stepped between them, his powerful frame commanding attention. "He's with me. Back off!"

The thug's sneer faltered. "This ain't none of your business."

"It is now," Dougal replied coldly. The two thugs exchanged glances, squaring for action, but Dougal's unflinching demeanour made them pause.

"Take your problem outside. We want no trouble in here." The landlord interrupted.

The larger man indicated the door to the other thug, and they left, muttering under their breath. "You haven't seen the last of us. Keep away from the Manor."

Dougal gazed after them. So much for keeping a low profile, he mused. The entire pub had witnessed what happened and the hum of conversation was only just returning. He turned to Arthur and said, "Let me introduce you to my friends."

Dougal returned to the booth with Arthur and presented him to Mark and Sam, adding "I think we should leave." To Arthur he said, "You should come with us. You're not safe here. We can continue our discussions at our lodgings."

Arthur nodded and all four left the pub.

Behind the bar, Ned Jago watched them go, rubbing his chin thoughtfully. He had been running the Prince of Wales for more than twenty years, and he knew when something wasn't right. This lot weren't just passing through – no, they had an agenda. They had spoken to Arthur Parker, and one of them had seen off a couple of the Manor's security men like it was nothing. That didn't happen often. Most folks in Nansebyn knew better than to cross Worsley's people.

He reached for the bar towel, wiping down the counter as he turned the situation over in his mind. Had Arthur invited them? Should he inform the Manor? They wouldn't like strangers poking around, asking the wrong kind of questions. But something about these people made him hesitate. They weren't just troublemakers. There was something else going on, something bigger. Maybe it was worth finding out more before he said anything. Something didn't ring right.

With a final glance at the door where they had left, Ned poured himself a whisky and took a slow sip. He had a feeling this was only the beginning.

Carn View, Cornwall – 10:15 PM

Arthur sat at the kitchen table, nursing a cup of coffee. Dougal recounted his conversation with Arthur at the bar for the others. Arthur confirmed the thugs were linked to Worsley's security team. "You must have seen the fence that surrounds the estate – you'd think it was a top-secret military compound. They increase the security team numbers when their meetings or ceremonies are taking place. They scare the local people and make sure no one gets near to the fence." Arthur said bitterly. "The police never do anything. But I can't stop. Joan's in there somewhere, and I won't give up."

Sam placed a comforting hand on his arm. "We won't either. Worsley's responsible for my husband's disappearance. We'll find Joan, and we'll stop him."

"You'll need to be careful." Arthur said. "The villagers can act as Worsley's ears. As I told Dougal, I'm pretty sure that the landlord of the pub is a member of the coven and others may be too."

Dougal nodded. "Arthur, your local knowledge will be invaluable. Stick with us, and we'll get to the bottom of this. But for now, tomorrow is the big day when I set up my surveillance spot on Hebdon Tor to view the night's events."

"Perhaps we should minimize our visits to the pub," Sam suggested.

"Yes," replied Dougal. "I could do a quick run to Bodmin after tomorrow, to get some groceries, if we are to eat here more often."

"Well, don't rely on me to do all the cooking," said Sam.

"I wouldn't dare do that." Mark said, "I've tasted your culinary skills! Perhaps we could eat out a bit further afield? Bodmin must have some nice eateries."

"There is also the cafe on the edge of the village, which might be a bit safer than the pub. I noticed a grill in the yard here, if we want steaks. Mark is a dab hand at cooking on the grill."

"I'd better get charcoal for the barbecue then," said Dougal.

The room fell into a companionable silence, the group united by their shared determination. Outside, the wind moaned, but inside, they were fortified by a growing sense of purpose.

Mark said "Well I think that's enough for tonight. Arthur, would you like a ride home? That's a cold wind out there and Dougal will drive you."

"No thanks. The walk will do me good and help clear my head."

"If you see any sign of Worsley's heavies, call the number I gave you and I'll be there at the rush." Dougal promised.

When Arthur had left, Dougal told the others that Paula had texted him about five minutes ago. He related the contents to them.

Chapter 32

The Stone Circle

*T*revaunce Manor, Cornwall – 10 April, 8:30 AM

Paula stirred from a restless sleep, her dreams haunted by fragmented images of masks, flickering candles, and whispers she couldn't quite understand. A soft knock at the door startled her fully awake. She sat up, pulling the heavy duvet closer.

"Come in," she called, her voice still groggy.

The door creaked open, revealing Abdul. He carried a gleaming silver tray, his movements precise and deliberate, his voice incongruously guttural. "Compliments of Lady Fiona, Madam. Please enjoy a light breakfast and then join her in the drawing room when you are ready."

Abdul's gaze was unreadable. He placed the tray on the table, the scent of freshly baked croissants and ripe fruit wafting through the room.

"Thank you, Abdul. Tell Fiona I'll be down in about forty-five minutes," Paula replied, avoiding his penetrating stare. She gave a small shudder as the door closed behind him.

Paula turned her attention to the tray. A porcelain teapot sat alongside a matching bone-china cup and saucer, small tea plate, milk jug and sugar bowl, a full silver toast rack, golden croissants, fresh butter, and an assortment of preserves. She took a deep breath, steadying herself. Before touching the food, she decided on a quick shower to shake off the unease lingering from her sleep.

Fiona was waiting for her, perched on a plush armchair in the drawing room, a vision of elegance as usual. The room was an exquisite mix of opulence and eccentricity: plush rugs with intricate patterns, heavy velvet drapes that muted the morning light, and a collection of peculiar artifacts displayed on polished mahogany tables. A gilded mirror over the fireplace reflected the scene, its frame carved with intertwined serpents and vines.

"Darling," Fiona said, "I hope you slept well."

Paula forced a smile. "Perfectly well, thank you," she lied.

Fiona gestured to the seat opposite her. "Sit. There are things we need to discuss."

Paula lowered herself into the armchair, her posture guarded but outwardly relaxed.

"At tonight's celebration, you will primarily be an observer," Fiona began. "You may partake in the revelry, of course, but I will ensure you are spared the rituals. As a novice, it's important to ease you into our ways gradually."

Paula nodded, her heart pounding. She was both relieved and unnerved by Fiona's words.

"However," Fiona continued, her gaze sharpening, "in the weeks leading up to Walpurgis Night, I would like to be your guide. There is much to learn, and I have high hopes for you. Are you interested?"

The question hung in the air, charged with expectation. Paula hesitated, her mind racing. She needed to get closer to Fiona, to learn more, but the significance of the offer felt suffocating.

"Yes, very interested. I'll need to arrange my life to accommodate this guidance. I'm owed considerable leave from work, so a couple of weeks shouldn't be a problem, but beyond that, I can't say."

Fiona smiled, a spark of triumph in her eyes. "Excellent! I will initiate you as a Probationer in our order. It's a modest first step, but it will prepare you for greater things. We will begin soon. For now, I want to show you the site of tonight's ritual – our very own Stone Circle."

"I'd love that."

"Good. Let's go. Afterward, I'll leave you to your own devices. I have much to do to prepare for tonight's gathering."

Paula returned to her room to change her shoes and get a jacket. She joined Fiona at a side entrance on the ground floor of the North Wing.

The journey to the circle took them through the garden, briefly along a winding path bordered by ancient oak trees until it opened to the moorland. The air was crisp, carrying the scent of earth and moss. Paula followed Fiona, pleased she had brought sensible shoes.

After a gently sloping climb they reached the crest, and in the centre of a shallow depression, the Stone Circle came into view. Paula gasped. It was breathtaking and eerie all at once. As they neared, she could see that the stones formed a near-perfect ring, their surfaces weathered and covered in lichen. She counted eighteen stones in all, sizes varying slightly but averaging about two metres in height and spaced about twelve metres apart.

At the centre stood an altar carved from what looked like black granite, its edges adorned with cryptic symbols and its top containing shallow channels presumably to collect sacrificial blood. Surrounding the stone circle were smaller cairns, their purpose unclear but undeniably significant.

"Isn't it magnificent?" Fiona said, her voice almost reverent.

Paula nodded. "It's… incredible. How old is it?"

"Maybe five thousand years" Fiona replied, excitedly. "True stone circles are rare. Many other structures wrongly described as stone circles are more likely ring cairns or burial mounds. Ours here is on private land belonging to the estate. The only other true stone circle in Cornwall is the "Merry Maidens" in a field between Newlyn and Land's End. The Altar in the centre is a much later addition by the Worsley family to facilitate their rituals. That is a mere two hundred years old." Taking a breath, she added, "The circle lies on the confluence of two ley lines. It somehow channels that energy. Tonight, under the full moon you'll most certainly feel it."

Paula's unease deepened. "And the rituals – what are they like?"

Fiona turned to her, a mysterious smile playing on her lips. "You'll see, I couldn't possibly do them justice, with mere words."

As they walked back, Paula's mind raced with questions, each one more troubling than the last. She couldn't shake the feeling that she was walking into something far darker than Fiona's warm demeanour suggested.

Arriving back at the house, Fiona said, "And now I must leave you. Feel free to roam anywhere on the estate or in the house but please don't try to enter any rooms that are locked."

"What about if I want to take a walk outside the estate, say into the village?"

"Nansebyn is about two miles from the main gates, but there is nothing much there except for the pub and a small shop and post office. Abdul could arrange a car and drive you if you like. You are my honoured guest remember?" Fiona smiled.

"Oh no, I like walking."

"If you prefer to walk, there is a side gate by the main gates at the end of the drive. It lets you out, but to get back in you will need to press the button on the small intercom panel and someone will buzz you in. Turning right along the road will take you to Nansebyn. Just make sure you are back by six pm at the latest. It is going to be a wonderful night."

Paula sat on the edge of the bed, staring out at the dense woods beyond her window. The room was quiet, but the stillness felt oppressive rather than peaceful. She had texted Doogie to tell him she was able to leave the estate and perhaps meet up with them. Doogie replied that he was tied up, but Mark and Sam would meet her in a car parking area that served local footpaths. It was clearly marked and about halfway between the house and the village. They decided to meet at about 2 pm.

How to pass the time between now and then? Her mind replayed last night's tour with Fiona, particularly the cellar and the faint groan she had heard, echoing through the walls like a trapped spirit's lament. She shuddered, unable to dismiss the sound or the unease it had stirred in her.

James's warnings surfaced in her thoughts. He had spoken of the Dark Chamber beneath the Manor, a place where Worsley conducted his most sinister rituals. But he had also mentioned something else – a dungeon beyond the locked gate. Could someone be trapped down there? The idea took hold, refusing to let go.

She rose slowly, wrapping her cardigan tightly around her and moved toward the door. The groan had been real – of that, she was now certain. And if someone was down there, she couldn't just ignore it. Grabbing her phone, she slipped into the hallway and down the main staircase, her heart pounding as she made her way toward the door that led to the cellar. It was not locked.

The stone staircase descended into darkness, each step colder than the last. She'd left the door open to provide some illumination. She was sure there had been dim lighting last night, but she couldn't find any means of turning it on. The air grew heavier, carrying the faint scent of damp earth and mildew. Paula switched on her phone's light, the beam cutting through the oppressive gloom. Shadows danced on the rough stone walls, creating shapes that made her skin crawl.

The cellar was a large space, the walls containing alcoves and side passages, but her attention was drawn to the iron gate at the end opposite the steps. It loomed like a portal to another world, its intricate wrought-iron design twisting into forms that resembled writhing figures. Paula's footsteps seemed magnified in the silence.

She reached the gate and gripped the cold iron bars, peering into the darkness beyond. The beam of her flashlight barely penetrated the void. She couldn't make out where the dungeon was, let alone the Dark Chamber. They must be further along the wide passageway.

"Hello?" she called, her voice trembling. "Is anyone there?"

Her words seemed to vanish into the abyss. She waited, her ears straining for a reply. The silence was suffocating.

"Please, if you can hear me, say something," she urged, her voice louder this time.

A faint shuffle echoed from somewhere deep within the darkness. Paula gasped, her grip tightening. "Are you hurt? Do you need help?"

A voice behind her shattered the silence. "You shouldn't be here!"

Paula spun around heart pounding, her light landing on Abdul. He stood mere feet away, his face as impassive as ever, but his eyes carried a warning. The shadows seemed to deepen around him, his presence exuding a quiet menace.

"You frightened me," Paula stammered, her voice shaking. "I… I thought I heard something in there."

Abdul's gaze flicked to the gate, then back to her, seemingly able to see in the dark. "The cellar is not a place for wandering, Madam. Lady Fiona would not approve."

Paula swallowed hard, his words sinking in. "I didn't mean any harm. I was just curious."

"Curiosity can be dangerous," Abdul said evenly. "Please, return upstairs."

The finality in his tone left no room for argument. Paula nodded, backing away from the gate. Abdul watched her climb the steps, his presence like a shadow at her back.

Joan lay curled in the damp straw of the dungeon floor, her body trembling uncontrollably. Three weeks. Three weeks of agony, three weeks of psychic torture that left her mind flayed open, exposed to the relentless probing of her captors. The iron shackles had bitten into her wrists and ankles, their cold weight a cruel mockery of her defiance.

She had resisted. She had not broken. Not yet. Protective spells woven deep into her mind had shielded the knowledge Worsley and his acolytes sought – Zarathustra's Grimoire, hidden within the sanctum of her former coven. But the barriers were weakening. Every session with Abdul left her raw, her thoughts scattering like brittle leaves in a storm. How much longer could she last before she slipped? Before the last shreds of her will crumbled.

Arthur had warned her. He had pleaded with her not to come to Trevaunce Manor, begged her to stay away from Worsley, Fiona and the coven. She should have listened. Oh, how she wished she had listened. She had ignored the fear in his eyes, the way his hands had trembled when he grasped hers, pleading with her to let it go. He had always been the pragmatic one, steady and rational, but beneath that exterior, she had seen the depth of his feelings for her – feelings she had only recently begun to reciprocate. They had been on the cusp of something real, something she had foolishly thought there would be time to explore. Now, trapped in this cold abyss, she longed for his arms around her, for the warmth of his voice reassuring her that she was safe. But Arthur was far away, and she was alone in the dark.

A voice had called out earlier, distant and uncertain – "Is anyone there?" Joan had heard it, but she had been too weak to respond. The words had echoed through the walls of her mind, tormenting her with the cruellest of ironies: help had been just beyond reach, but she could do nothing to grasp it.

The Esbat was tonight, so maybe she would be left in peace for one night. Abdul had promised her something special for tomorrow. A spirit. A powerful, ravenous entity drawn from the depths of the void, one that would strip her defences layer by layer, feasting on her pain, her memories. She was not sure she could endure it. She was not sure she would survive.

Tears welled in her eyes, but she forced them back. She would not give them the satisfaction. She would not surrender. But deep inside, beneath the layers of defiance, a terrible truth gnawed at her resolve.

She was already broken.

Paula found a way into one of the Manor's gardens, emerging into the crisp afternoon air, the sunlight washing over her like a balm. She breathed deeply, the contrast between the oppressive cellar and the tranquil gardens was vast. She wandered down a stone path lined with manicured hedges, camelias, azaleas and rhododendrons, some in bloom others budding.

The gardens were a masterpiece of design, with fountains bubbling softly, the daffodil and tulip beds shining, but apart from some early roses other flower beds were yet to present the magnificence summer would bring. A stone bench beneath a canopy of wisteria waiting to bloom, offered a perfect spot to sit and collect her thoughts. Paula sank onto the bench, closing her eyes.

Here, the world felt normal again – calm, serene, untouched by the dark energy that seemed to pulse through the walls of the manor. But even in this sanctuary, the memory of the cellar lingered. The locked gate, the groan, Abdul's ominous words – it all felt like pieces of a puzzle she wasn't sure she wanted to solve.

As she sat, Paula resolved to tread carefully. The manor held too many secrets, and every step deeper into its shadows seemed to tighten the grip of its unseen power. For now, the gardens were a refuge, a place to gather her strength for whatever lay ahead.

Chapter 33

A Moorland Reunion

Bodmin Moor Car Park – 10 April 2:10 PM
The tarmac car park with a half-dozen unoccupied cars, gazed out onto the wild expanse of Bodmin Moor, the barren beauty of the land bathed in the muted afternoon light. It had taken Paula a further twenty minutes to reach the rendezvous after reaching the gate, the brisk wind tugging at her coat as she spotted Mark and Sam waiting near the trailhead. Sam waved enthusiastically, her bright smile a contrast to the tension hanging over the group.

"Took you long enough," Mark teased, folding his arms as Paula approached. "What, did you stop for a cream tea on the way?"

"Very funny, have you seen that ridiculous OTT security fence? It took me a while to vault over that!" Paula replied with a chuckle.

Sam grinned, looping an arm through Paula's as they headed toward the footpath. "Well, you're here now, I assume James is here and I've got a million questions for him. So, let's get talking."

The footpath wound through patches of gorse and spongy moorland grass, the wind carrying a faint scent of earth and moss. Paula recounted her experiences at Trevaunce Manor, including the groan she'd heard in the cellar and Fiona's plans to induct her as a probationer.

Mark frowned. "The groan could be Joan Summers. Arthur Parker said she disappeared after one of these gatherings."

Paula had no knowledge of the names Mark had mentioned but decided not to interrupt him right now.

James, speaking through Paula, agreed with Mark. "It's possible, but if she's there, she'll be heavily guarded – both physically and psychically. Worsley would have layers of protection in place. I'll check it out when I am sure Abdul is not nearby."

Sam shivered, wrapping her scarf tighter. "This just keeps getting darker. Paula, are you okay with Fiona mentoring you? That's how it started for James."

"I'm nervous, but if I can continue gaining her trust, I'll be able to learn things no one else can. It's a risk, but one well worth taking."

Mark's brow furrowed. "Just make sure you're not getting in too deep. These people aren't playing games."

"That's rich coming from the guy who's practicing telekinesis in his spare time." Sam teased.

"At least it doesn't involve drinking blood or chanting rites in Latin."

Paula chuckled, "Speaking of rituals, Sam, what's your latest research on Beltane and Walpurgis Night?"

Sam lit up, her enthusiasm bubbling over. "It's fascinating – and a little terrifying. Beltane is a Gaelic festival marking the beginning of summer and is associated with fertility, renewal, and the strengthening of the connection between the human and spirit worlds. Bonfires are central to Beltane celebrations, symbolising purification, protection, and transformation. People and livestock would pass between fires for blessings and protection. Maypole dancing can be involved, a fertility ritual involving weaving ribbons around a central pole, representing the union of masculine and feminine energies." Sam paused for a breath. "Walpurgis Night is more rooted in European folklore, particularly in Germanic and Scandinavian traditions. It is associated with warding off evil spirits and witches. Both festivals share themes of fire, fertility, and the thinning of the veil between worlds, whatever that means. Beltane is more about life and renewal, while Walpurgis Night has darker connotations, linked to witchcraft and the supernatural. That's about it, but there must be a lot of stuff that doesn't even make it into the public domain."

Paula closed her eyes briefly, listening to James's input. "Worsley's rituals likely involve inversions of traditional Beltane practices. While Beltane celebrates fertility and renewal, Worsley would twist those symbols into something destructive – wanton debauchery, sacrifices, blood rituals, and summoning entities that thrive on chaos."

Mark interjected, his tone sceptical. "And tonight's esbat? Is it just a warm-up, or are we looking at something equally grim?"

James's response was grimly practical making Paula shudder as she recited, "Tonight's ritual will probably be less overtly violent than the Sabbat at the end of the month. Esbats are traditionally for worship of the Moon Goddess and carry out spell work, but Worsley's group won't stick to harmless practices whether he's there or not. Expect drug-induced bacchanalia, acts of hedonism, granting favours and potentially a summoning ritual. Animal sacrifice isn't off the table."

Sam groaned. "Great. So, it's a full moon party with a side of demonic horror. Sounds delightful."

"Maybe they'll hand out party favours. You know, horns and pitchforks." Mark said jokingly.

Paula laughed despite herself. "I could use a pitchfork to fend off Fiona. She's getting a bit too friendly."

Sam nudged her playfully. "Well, at least you're popular."

James answered a couple more questions as they began their return to the car park. He reminded them that Worsley's invulnerability was due to Flauros and the only chance of bringing him down necessitated his demonic familiar departing from him.

"A seemingly impossible scenario then?" said Mark.

"Flauros, Flauros come out, come out wherever you are." Sam chanted.

The group shared a brief laugh, but the gravity of their mission soon returned. Paula looked at her watch and sighed. "I'd better get back to the Manor. Fiona expects me back early to prepare for the esbat."

Mark placed a hand on her shoulder. "Be careful, Paula. If anything feels off, break away from what you are doing. Don't take unnecessary risks."

Paula nodded. "I won't. You two stay out of trouble, too."

As Paula left to walk back, Sam linked her arm through Mark's. "She's brave, isn't she?"

Mark nodded. "Brave, undoubtedly, but I can't help worrying about her. Fiona's charm is dangerous. It could be easy to lose perspective. I don't want Paula to suffer being drugged again."

Sam sighed. "We all must take risks. But for now, let's focus on what we can control – like figuring out how to get you to move a rock with your mind."

Mark chuckled, shaking his head. "If I do, it'll be because you annoyed me into it."

"Whatever works."

Their laughter carried on the wind, the flippancy a brief reprieve from the impending gloom.

James reflected on the conversation that had unfolded, frustration gnawing at him. The physical world, once so tangible and immediate, now felt distant and unreachable. He felt shackled. He could only watch, listen, and offer what little guidance he could through Paula. But it wasn't enough. Not nearly enough. They were walking a deadly tightrope.

The threads of fate were weaving tighter around them, pulling them toward something inescapable. Worsley's influence was growing, and with each passing day, the stakes became more dire. Mark was right about Fiona, she was cunning, her charm a potent weapon, and James knew how easily someone could fall under her spell. He had fallen and he had paid for it. And now, watching Paula walk the same treacherous path, he felt helpless to stop it.

His own entanglement with Worsley's world – the allure of knowledge, the temptation of power had been his undoing. He had thought himself in control, that he was playing the game, not being played. But he had been wrong and he'd paid for that arrogance with his life.

He had to believe Paula was more aware than he had been, that she would see the warning signs he had ignored. But there was no denying the danger. Worsley and his followers were predators, and Paula was walking willingly into their den to gather information, to avenge Nick and protect the others. She needed to be careful. They all did.

Then there was Mark. It was frustrating to watch him hesitate, to doubt. He wanted to shake him, to tell him to embrace his power before it was too late. The fight ahead would demand everything they had. And Mark needed to be ready.

James turned his attention to Sam. She was the sceptic, always questioning, always looking for the rational explanation. But she was also fierce and determined. If anyone could keep Mark grounded, it was her. And she would need to. He worried that Mark's doubts, his reluctance, would make him vulnerable.

A sense of urgency that was impossible to ignore, pressed down on James. Time was running out. The esbat was tonight, a sizeable hazard, of that there was no doubt, but the real threat lay in what was coming. Beltane and Walpurgis Night. The rituals leading up to it were merely preparation, a slow unravelling of the barriers between worlds. And if Worsley's ambitions were left unchecked, the consequences would be catastrophic.

He dare not go near the esbat tonight, he dare not risk detection. He would watch from afar and pray that Paula would be safe. But he had to do more. He had to find a way to break through, to use his abilities to help them more directly. Because if they weren't ready – and they were not yet – they had no chance at all. For now, all he could do was watch over them and pray.

Chapter 34
The Puppet Master

anary Wharf, London – 10 April, 4:30 PM
Sir Giles Worsley leaned back in his leather chair, the panoramic view of London's financial district stretching out before him. Late afternoon sunlight gleamed off the glass towers, bathing the room in a golden glow. He sipped a perfectly chilled glass of Montrachet, his expression one of smug satisfaction.

The day had been exemplary. He had just closed an investment deal so lucrative it would cement his reputation in financial circles for years. Simultaneously, he had orchestrated the bankruptcy of a long-standing rival, a man who had dared to challenge his dominance. Fool, Worsley thought with a sneer, swirling his wine. He should have known better.

His mind drifted to other triumphs. The investigation into James Benedict in America had reached a dead end. The police had hit an impasse, their resources stretched too thin and all evidence too weak. Worsley took delight in knowing that even in death, Benedict's name could still be manipulated like a pawn in his grand game.

His wife and brother, Sam and Mark Benedict, had gone quiet in recent days. A few scattered credit card transactions suggested they were still in London, but Worsley considered them little more than an afterthought. Still, caution was his mantra, and he made a mental note to place them under greater surveillance. Precautionary measures, he told himself. After all, he hadn't ascended to his position of power by underestimating even the smallest of threats.

His attention shifted to the report Fiona had sent earlier. One of his security team members had been injured in an altercation with an unknown hiker near Trevaunce Manor. His man was recovering, but the incident was a reminder that even in his sanctum, there were vulnerabilities.

Fiona's handling it, he mused. He trusted her – up to a point. Still, he had instructed her to double the patrols around the estate. Trevaunce Manor was more than just a retreat; it was a keystone in his plans. If anyone dared to trespass, they would pay the price.

Worsley set his glass down, his gaze fixed on the shimmering Thames. Although he had told Fiona he wouldn't attend her esbat in Cornwall that evening, he was reconsidering. It might be entertaining to put in a surprise appearance. More importantly, it would provide an opportunity to discuss the preparations for Walpurgis Night.

The Sabbat at the end of the month would be more than a spectacle; it would mark a defining moment in his life. Worsley's lips curved into a self-satisfied smile. The ritual would finalize his transition to the grade of Ipsissimus, the highest level of initiation in his arcane order. This elevation promised him ultimate power, the kind that would make him untouchable.

Invincible, he thought, savouring the word. The notion of becoming a figure above reproach, wielding influence over both the mundane and the mystical, was intoxicating. He imagined the looks of awe and fear on the faces of his peers. He would be a god among men, unassailable and omnipotent.

Pressing a button on his desk, Worsley summoned his secretary. She entered silently, her movements efficient and precise.

"Arrange the helo to take me to Trevaunce Manor," he said, "I'll depart at six. Tell my valet to pack an overnight bag and meet me at the helo pad. He will accompany me. And let Fiona know."

"Very good, Sir Giles," she replied, her voice betraying no emotion as she retreated.

Worsley leaned back again, a sense of triumph washing over him. The evening ahead promised a mix of amusement and indulgence. Fiona's gatherings always drew an eclectic crowd – politicians, artists, policemen, bank tellers, businessmen, and low-level occultists. Many were sycophants, desperate for a sliver of his attention, but they served their purpose.

He allowed himself a small chuckle. How predictable they all are, he thought. Clamouring for scraps while I feast on the whole table.

Despite his outward composure, a flicker of something darker stirred within him. His rituals had grown more extreme in recent years, the line between power and cruelty increasingly blurred. He relished the fear in others' eyes, the way they faltered when he spoke. It was proof of his superiority, a reminder of his rightful place above them all.

But power came with its challenges. His mind lingered briefly on the faces of Sam and Mark Benedict. Their low profile could mean they were regrouping, waiting for the right moment to strike.

Worsley's eyes narrowed. "Let them try," he muttered aloud. His voice echoed softly in the empty office, a promise to himself. "I'll destroy them, just as I have all the others."

The clock ticked closer to his departure time. Worsley rose from his chair, straightening his tie and adjusting his cuffs. The helicopter would soon whisk him away from the cold sterility of London's skyscrapers to the wild, untamed beauty of Cornwall. There, amidst the standing stones and the eager faces of his followers, he would bask in the glow of his triumphs.

Tonight's ceremony was merely a prelude. The true celebration, the ultimate ascension, awaited him at the end of the month. For now, he would enjoy the fruits of his labour, confident that his empire, his power, and his destiny were firmly in his grasp.

With a final glance at the skyline, Worsley strode from the room, his footsteps echoing with the confidence of a man who believed himself matchless.

❈◆❈

Chapter 35

Circe's Descent

Trevaunce Manor – 10 April, 7:30 PM

Paula stood at the edge of the grand drawing room, her face an effortless mask of admiration and curiosity. Inside, her stomach churned. Fiona was practically glowing with excitement, her exuberance spilling over as she detailed the changes to the evening's plans.

"He's landed, just left the helipad and will be here in a couple of minutes," Fiona said, her voice bright with anticipation. "Sir Giles Worsley himself! This will elevate the ceremony so much."

Paula nodded, her appearance carefully calibrated to project awe. "He sounds incredible," she said, her tone warm. Inside, she felt a cold knot of dread. "The man who murdered Nick and James. The one pulling all the strings. And now, I'm about to meet him."

Fiona swept across the room, her silk robe flowing, Paula following in her wake. "I was going to have Abdul act as High Priest subordinate to my High Priestess role tonight – he's an adept, after all – but with Giles here, it's only fitting he takes the Grand Master role with Abdul as his assistant. My role will now be subordinate to Giles. It's an honour, Paula, truly. To witness his leadership, his power." She paused and added, "And you're about to meet him! You're so privileged."

"I'm sure it will be unforgettable."

Fiona's energy bubbled over as she described tonight's ceremony. "The full moon is more than a symbol; it's an amplifier of power. We'll invoke one of the moon goddesses tonight – Selene, Tanith, Lady Astaroth, or perhaps, even Lilith herself. Any one of them brings something unique. Giles might even let us glimpse necromancy rites if his mood allows."

"That sounds... extraordinary. Necromancy? Do you mean... "

Fiona interrupted, "Yes, Sorcery that summons spirits of the dead to foretell the future providing us with... "

Fiona was silenced as the heavy oak doors of the drawing room swung open with theatrical precision and Sir Giles Worsley entered. His presence was magnetic, commanding attention without effort. Dressed in an impeccably tailored suit, his chiselled features carried an unsettling combination of refinement and cruelty.

"My dear Fiona," he said smoothly, striding across the room to kiss her hand. "How delightful to be here again."

Paula's pulse quickened. She watched Fiona preen under his gaze before turning to her. "Giles, this is Paula, the acolyte I told you about. I have high hopes for her."

Sir Giles turned his piercing gaze to Paula. "Ah, Paula," he said, taking her hand. "You are even more beautiful than Fiona had described."

The faintest smile played on his lips as he held her hand a moment longer than necessary. Paula felt a tingling sensation run along her arm, and she forced herself not to flinch. "It's an honour to meet you, Sir Giles," she said, infusing her voice with admiration. Inside, her thoughts screamed. This is the man who destroyed my world.

"The path Fiona is guiding you on is not for the faint-hearted," Worsley said, his voice low and rich. "But, if she believes you are capable, I'm sure you will succeed. I look forward to seeing your progress."

"Thank you." Paula replied, maintaining her composed exterior.

Worsley turned back to Fiona. "I must prepare. Tonight, will be exceptional." With that, he strode from the room, leaving an almost palpable silence in his wake.

Paula let out a soft exhale. "What an impressive man," she said, her tone light.

"Isn't he just?" Fiona replied, practically glowing. "I knew you'd feel it." She clapped her hands together. "Now, we must get ready. The guests will arrive soon, and there's so much to do."

Paula tilted her head, feigning curiosity. "What kind of people attend?"

"Oh, it's a fascinating mix," Fiona said breezily. "Locals, mostly. A banker, a doctor, a couple of farmers, a policeman, some businessmen, bored housewives, and a few amateur occultists. None of them are suitable for the order, of course. But they're useful in other ways. They'll be here to revel, indulge, and hope for favours from Giles."

"And what should I expect?" Paula asked, her voice steady.

Fiona's eyes gleamed. "The usual revelry – euphoric dancing, invocations, and perhaps a blessing from Giles. He might even grant a wish or two, depending on his mood. But don't let the coven's hedonism fool you. They have no idea of the true power at work tonight."

Fiona gestured toward the door. "Your robe is on your bed. Black velvet with gold astrological symbols. Wear nothing underneath and use the simple shoes provided. I'll come up and collect you in thirty minutes."

Paula nodded and excused herself, her calm demeanour belying the storm inside. Back in her room, she texted Doogie: *Worsley's here. Things have escalated. Proceed with caution.*

She glanced at the robe lying on the bed, its intricate patterns glinting faintly in the dim light. She stripped and with a deep breath, she stepped into the bathroom, turning on the shower to steady her nerves. As the hot water cascaded over her, she whispered to herself, "You can do this, Paula. Just a little longer."

Hebdon Tor – 10 April, 8:05 PM

Dougal lay flat on the damp grass just below the tor peak, his powerful binoculars trained on the stone circle in the distance. The preparations he'd observed were strange, but thorough. Whoever was responsible had poured what could have been blood, in a large precise circle around the altar, the liquid glinting a little under the emerging moonlight. Earlier he had built a large bonfire, yet unlit, halfway between the altar and the stone circle edge, using brushwood delivered in three large bundles by someone on an ATV. Along the path from the north side of the house, staves with torches had been planted, probably to be ignited when the ceremony was to start.

Dougal's phone buzzed softly. Paula's text flashed on the screen: *Worsley's here. Things have escalated. Proceed with caution.* His jaw tightened as he dialled the barn. The phone rang twice before Mark's voice, sharp with tension, answered.

"Dougal? What's going on?"

"I've got news," Dougal said evenly. "Worsley's here. He must have arrived by the helicopter I saw landing around 7:45."

"What?!" Mark's voice cracked with alarm. "Dougal says Worsley's shown up!" he repeated to Sam, putting the call on speaker.

Sam's response was immediate. "Worsley? At the house? We weren't expecting that. Does Paula know?"

"Yes. She just texted Dougal." Mark explained.

Dougal nodded reflexively, though they couldn't see him. "There's nothing we can do right now except wait. I'll keep observing from here."

Mark paced the length of the small living room. "This escalates the danger to Paula. I can't think. What can we do?"

"Nothing!" Dougal barked." Apart from Worsley's presence raising the danger stakes, nothing has really changed, we keep to the plan as affirmed by James."

"Dougal, are you sure there's nothing we can do?" Sam asked. "What if Paula's cover is blown?"

Dougal's voice came through the speaker, calm but firm. "There's no reason to think her cover is at risk. She's smart, and she knows how to play her part. We must trust her."

"But what if – " Mark began, only for Dougal to cut him off.

"Mark, listen to me," Dougal said sharply. "We can't storm in there or act impulsively. That's just not realistic. The best thing we can do is stick to the plan. Paula's not alone – James is watching over her. And I'm here, keeping an eye on everything."

Sam interjected. "It's not just her safety that worries me, Dougal. If Worsley suspects anything, she could become… collateral damage in whatever he's planning tonight."

Dougal sighed, his voice softening. "I get it, Sam. I do. But panicking won't help her. I'll monitor the situation, and the moment there's a sign she's in real danger, I'll act somehow. But for now, we wait."

Dougal signed off the call and lowered his phone, his gaze returning to the scene below. The first flickers of torchlight appeared on the path from the house as someone began lighting them. The ceremony must be imminent. Ensuring his night vision binoculars were handy, he felt the familiar tension in his chest, a mix of adrenaline and concern. *Hold steady, Finlayson*, he told himself. *They're counting on you.*

Mark collapsed onto the couch. "I hate this, Sam. Sitting here, knowing she's walking into danger and there's nothing we can do."

"I know. It's tearing me up too. But Dougal's right – we can't act recklessly. There is nothing we can do realistically. Worsley's unexpected presence is unfortunate, but Paula's purpose remains the same. Trust in her."

"What if we're wrong to do that? What if Worsley sees through her and… and she doesn't come back?"

"Then we'll make sure it wasn't in vain. But Mark, I believe in her. There's more power in Paula than you imagine. She's strong."

"I just wish I didn't feel so hopeless."

"You shouldn't," Sam said quietly. "We're here for her. And as long as we're here, we'll fight. For her, for James, for all of it."

Mark glanced at her. "You're annoyingly optimistic, you know that?"

Sam grinned. "You're just mad because I'm right."

Despite himself, Mark grinned. "Maybe. But I still think you're infuriatingly cheerful."

The shared laugh broke the tension.

Trevaunce Manor – 10 April, 8:45 PM

Fiona swept into Paula's room, her garb a breathtaking combination of elegance and menace. Paula was stunned and beguiled.

Fiona was wearing a flowing gown of midnight-black silk, the fabric shimmering faintly in the low candlelight as though alive with its own dark energy. The gown was form-fitting through the bodice, where intricate embroidery in crimson thread depicted occult symbols – pentagrams, crescent moons, and serpentine shapes winding upward toward her shoulders. The neckline exposed her collarbones and the delicate curve of her throat, where a polished obsidian pendant in the shape of an inverted pentacle rested.

Her long sleeves flared at the wrists, lined with deep crimson satin that flashed whenever she moved. Around her waist, a belt of interlinked silver crescents hung loosely, each segment engraved with ancient runes. From it dangled a ceremonial dagger, its hilt encrusted with garnets that gleamed like fresh drops of blood.

On her head, she wore a delicate circlet of twisted silver and gold, its design mimicking the curling horns of a goat. At its centre was a ruby shaped like an eye, catching the light and seeming to watch all who dared meet her gaze. Beneath the circlet, Fiona's hair tumbled in glossy waves, interwoven with thin chains of gold that tinkled softly when she moved.

Her feet were bare, stained faintly with what appeared to be red and black pigments, a ritualistic touch that seemed both symbolic and practical as she prepared to lead the group across the cold moorland.

Paula couldn't help but stare, her emotions a whirlwind of awe and dread. Fiona's presence was magnetic, her attire, not mere clothing, but a declaration of power and dominance. Paula forced herself to smile, feigning admiration. "You look… incredible. But how did you manage to dress so magnificently so quickly?"

Fiona smiled mysteriously, "Let's just say I had some mystic help. This is my High Priestess outfit for tonight. You'll soon understand its significance."

"Now for you," Fiona said, her voice smooth and approving. "Lift the cowl and let me see."

Paula did as instructed, pulling the cowl on top of her head, the shadow it cast adding an air of mystery.

"You look incredible," Fiona said.

"What should I expect when we join the others?"

Fiona's aspect softened as she explained. "Real names are never shared in our circle. Tonight, and from now on, you are Circe. The others will use names they've chosen, often those of demons or fallen angels. It's a tradition of anonymity and reverence for the darker forces we honour."

"What will they ask me?" Paula pressed, her voice betraying a hint of nerves.

"Nothing intrusive," Fiona reassured her. "They may ask for your chosen name, and there will be light-hearted conversations. Topics like politics, sports, hobbies – anything harmless. Just ensure nothing about your real identity slips out. Now, shall we?"

The main living room was alive with a strange energy, the gathered members draped in dark robes similar to the one that she wore. Some were carrying a variety of musical instruments; flutes, pan-pipes, tambourines and one man had a marching drum.

Fiona led Paula to the centre of the room, her commanding presence silencing the chatter. "This is Circe, our newest member. Treat her well; she is under my protection."

A wave of murmurs swept through the room, and one by one, the members approached, introducing themselves by their chosen names.

"Hi Circe, I'm Moloch," a tall man said.

"I'm Syrinx," added a woman, her mischievous eyes glancing to her Panpipes. "Welcome."

The names came in a dizzying array: Shiva, Set, Loki, Kali, Dagon. Paula smiled and nodded, committing what she could to memory while maintaining her composed façade.

The room buzzed with anticipation. Though there was no sign of Worsley, the air was thick with the expectation of his arrival. He weighed heavily on Paula's mind, though she kept her anxiety buried beneath a mask of calm.

The group filed out of the manor through the garden, their robes flowing in the faint breeze. As they proceeded, flaming torches lined the path, their dancing light casting long shadows over the open moorland. The sound of the group's footsteps mingled with the occasional murmur of conversation, creating a peculiar mix of solemnity and excitement.

At the head of the group was Abdul, his transformation startling even to Paula, who had grown accustomed to seeing him in livery. His sleeveless black tunic, rough and coarse like sackcloth, bore dark red sigils that seemed to pulsate in the torchlight. The tattoos spiralling up his arms were intricate and unsettling, their meaning unclear but plainly significant. The staff he carried, carved from blackened wood and topped with a ram's skull, added to his ominous presence. The shards of obsidian embedded in the skull's empty sockets seemed to absorb the light from the flaming torches, giving the impression of faint, watchful eyes.

Paula noticed Fiona's feet were still bare as they stepped onto the path. It struck her as strange, a deliberate shedding of footwear that contrasted with the rest of the group, who wore simple clogs or sliders. The ground beneath her own feet felt firm but cold, a constant reminder of the physical world she was stepping away from.

As they moved, Paula's gaze was drawn to the red glow in the distance. The wind carried faint chants, low and rhythmic, blending with the crackle of fire. The man with the drum began a slow march beat and the others with instruments followed suit beating their tambourines and playing mournful sounds on their flutes and pipes.

As the group crested the small rise, the circle came into full view. The bonfire at the stone circle loomed ahead, its light licking the night sky with tendrils of flame. The impressive stones, weathered and ancient, stood sentinel around the altar at the centre and the bonfire in between. The music began to rise to a wailing cacophony. Someone was using something that sounded like a discordant vuvuzela. Paula felt her pulse quicken as they descended the final stretch of the path into the shallow depression that contained their destination. Whatever lay ahead, she was committed now.

Chapter 36

The Esbat

Trevaunce Stone Circle – 10 April 9:15 PM

The air around the stone circle hummed with energy beneath the aura of the silvery full moon, Abdul stood by the altar his arms held aloft, rippling in time to the music. The bonfire to his left was roaring upward into the night sky. The coven members moved in unison, their dark gowns flowing like liquid shadows in the flickering light. Their faces were hidden behind masks gilded with occult designs, providing an eerie, otherworldly anonymity.

The group had dropped their instruments and shed their shoes on arrival but the music somehow continued, moving from harsh dissonance to melodious enchantment. The rhythm of drums was slow and deliberate at first, a heartbeat pulsing through the chill night air. The sound of pan pipes and flutes added to the supernatural rhythm winding like a serpent through the movement, twisting and shifting in ways that defied natural harmony. Voices rose softly, chanting ancient words in a way that seemed to wrap itself around Paula's mind like a silken thread.

Fiona stood beside Paula, her bare feet planted firmly on the cool ground, the edges of her robe swaying gently in the breeze. Her eyes, dark and intense, followed the movements of the dancers with a mixture of satisfaction and reverence.

"It's mesmerising, isn't it?" She said, her voice low but carrying easily over the music. "The energy they create is enhanced by the pure, unfiltered power of the circle. Can you feel it, Circe?"

Paula nodded, her mouth dry. She could feel it – the air itself seemed alive, charged with a strange, electric vitality. Her pulse quickened in time with the beat of the drums, and the firelight cast hypnotic patterns that danced across the ancient stones.

The chanting grew louder, more insistent, as the dancers' movements became wilder. Their circling steps quickened, and their arms rose high toward the full moon, their voices blending with the unnatural harmony of the flute. The music, alien and unearthly, seemed to bypass Paula's ears and resonate directly within her chest. Her head swam, and for a moment, the rest of the world faded away.

"Do you feel the call, Circe?" Fiona whispered, her voice like velvet. "The moon goddess pulls at us all. Don't resist it. Let it guide you."

Paula blinked, trying to focus, but her body betrayed her. She felt her feet moving of their own accord, carrying her forward, closer to the circle of dancers. She glanced at Fiona, who smiled knowingly and gestured for her to go. Paula hesitated for only a moment before discarding her footwear and stepping into the ring of bodies.

The music surged as Paula joined the circle, her movements tentative at first but soon aligning with the cadence. The drums seemed to dictate the beating of her heart, and the flute sang to something deep within her soul. She raised her arms as the others did, her fingers brushing the night air as she spun and stepped in time with the rest.

The fire flared higher, its light casting writhing shadows on the ancient stones. The dancers' robes swirled around them, creating an enthralling pattern of flowing fabric and flickering flames. Paula felt her body move with a freedom she hadn't known before, as though the music had unlocked something ancient within her.

Her breath came in shallow bursts, exhilaration and unease mingling in her chest. She should have been frightened – she knew the power in this circle was not to be trusted – but in this moment, she felt alive. More alive than she had in years. The doubts and fears she had carried with her seemed to dissolve in the heat of the fire and the intoxicating rhythm of the dance.

Fiona's voice rang out from the edge of the circle, commanding yet melodic. "Feel the power of the moon, my children! Let it flow through you, filling you with her grace and strength. Tonight, we are one with her divine light!"

The dancers' voices rose in response, a wordless cry of devotion that seemed to pierce the heavens. Paula's lips parted as if to join them, but no sound came. She felt caught between two worlds – the mortal one she had always known and the shadowy, seductive realm of the coven.

Fiona watched from her place outside the circle, her lips curving into a satisfied smile. "Beautiful," she murmured to herself. Paula – her Circe – was proving far more acquiescent than she had anticipated.

"Feel it, my darling," Fiona whispered under her breath. "Let it consume you."

For Fiona, the dance was not merely ritual; it was a test. The power of the esbat was intoxicating, yes, but also revealing. It peeled away the layers of pretence, exposing the true nature of those who embraced it. And tonight, it would lay bare who Circe truly was.

The rhythm of the drums reached a fevered pitch, the chanting voices blending into an overwhelming cacophony. Paula spun with the dancers, her senses flooded by the primeval energy coursing through the circle. She felt the heat from the fire on her face, the vibrations of the chants resonating deep in her chest. Then, without warning, it stopped.

The music ceased in an instant, leaving a vacuum of sound so profound it felt like the earth itself held its breath. The silence was deep, a stark contrast to the chaos that had preceded it. The flames of the bonfire leaped higher, burning white-hot for a moment before dimming to a faint, eerie blue.

Paula froze mid-step, her breath catching in her throat. She felt it before she saw it – a shift in the air, a burden that pressed down on the circle like an invisible hand. A faint, shimmering aura appeared near the altar, a swirling distortion that grew brighter and more defined with each passing second. Gasps rippled through the crowd as the figure began to take shape.

The aura solidified into the unmistakable form of Sir Giles Worsley. His appearance was both ethereal and terrifying, as though he were both part of this world and something far beyond it. He wore a deep crimson robe, its fabric seemingly alive, rippling in a wind that didn't touch the others. Intricate gold symbols traced the edges of the robe, glowing faintly in the dim light. A bishop's mitre of intertwined iron and gold adorned his head, the ruby at its centre casting a blood-red gleam that seemed to pierce through the darkness.

Worsley's feet hovered inches above the ground as his body levitated, slowly ascending until he stood atop the altar. The air crackled with energy, a faint hum filling the silence as if the atmosphere itself recognized his presence.

Cries erupted from the crowd, breaking the stunned stillness. "Master!" "Lord!" "Hail the Grand Master!" Their voices were filled with awe, fear, and reverence, a chorus of devotion that sent chills down Paula's spine.

She stood motionless, her heart pounding. The figure before her was the man she had been hardened to despise, the orchestrator of so much destruction. Yet, as he stood there, larger than life and exuding a presence that seemed to command the elements themselves, Paula could not deny the power he radiated. It was magnetic, suffocating, and utterly terrifying.

Worsley raised his arms, his movements deliberate and regal. The cries of the crowd subsided into a reverent hush, the silence now broken only by the crackling of the blue-tinged flames.

"My children," he began, his voice deep and resonant, carrying across the circle without effort. "Tonight, under the gaze of the Moon Goddess, we gather to honour her light, her wisdom, and her power." Paula was enraptured, unaware that Fiona had moved to her side.

His piercing eyes scanned the crowd, lingering briefly on each masked figure as though he could see beyond their disguises. "You have come here not as individuals, but as one – a collective bound by purpose, ambition, and devotion. Together, we harness the energy of this sacred place, and together, we shall rise."

The crowd murmured their assent, their faces turned upward like plants seeking the sun. Paula felt Fiona's hand brush her arm, a subtle gesture of approval as they stood side by side.

Worsley continued, his tone growing sharper, more commanding. "But power is not given freely. It is earned through sacrifice, through will, and through understanding the depths of one's own desires. Tonight, I will grant favours to those who dare to step forward and claim them."

His words hung in the air, heavy with implication. The crowd stirred, some shifting nervously, others visibly eager. Paula's pulse quickened, her mind racing. What kind of favours? At what cost? She noticed that Abdul stood by the altar with a large wooden box by his side.

The tension in the circle was extreme, the throng poised between anticipation and dread. The fire flared brighter, its blue glow intensifying as the throng held its collective breath.

Fiona leaned toward Paula, her voice low and triumphant. "And so, it begins."

The circle was hushed, the firelight casting flickering shadows on the faces of the coven as Sir Giles Worsley raised his arms. His crimson robe shimmered in the unnatural glow of the flames, the gold symbols embroidered on its surface seeming to writhe like living things. The light of the bonfire shifted, turning an eerie green, bathing the stones and the crowd in a sickly, pulsating glow.

Paula – Circe – stood frozen at the edge of the circle. Her heart still pounding as Worsley's voice boomed across the gathering, resonant and commanding. "Tonight, under the gaze of the Moon Goddess, we summon not only her light but the force of her shadows. Bear witness as I call upon the one who is my familiar, who bridges the realms of man and spirit."

The air grew heavier, settling on Paula like lead. She struggled to breathe as Worsley's voice rose in an incantation, the ancient words harsh and grating, twisting in her ears. An emerald aura enveloped Worsley still standing on the Altar swirling like a mist until part of it coalesced into a humanoid form. A hooded figure emerged, to stand in front of Worsley, its frame stooped and grotesquely small, like a misshapen dwarf. *Flauros!*

Flauros, stood on the Altar at Worsley's feet, its head bowed beneath the deep cowl of its robe. When it lifted its head, Paula caught a glimpse of its face, and her stomach churned. Its features were distorted, its eyes glowing with a malevolent light, its jagged teeth bared in a twisted grin. The aura pulsed around them, tendrils of green light linking the demon to Worsley. Hatred burned inside of Paula. This monstrosity had killed Nick!

The crowd recoiled instinctively, gasps and murmurs rippling through the group. The presence of Flauros filled the air with an oppressive dread, its very existence an insult to nature. Paula's legs felt weak, but she forced herself to stand firm, her mask of composure betraying none of her anger and terror.

Worsley's lips curled into a smile, his voice smooth and mocking. "Do not fear, my children. Flauros serves me, and through me, it serves you. Worsley's gaze swept across the circle once more. "Step forward, if you dare," he said, his voice a challenge. "And let the moon bear witness to your courage. Come, and let your desires be known."

After a pause, an older man, judging by his stooped frame, his mask depicting a snarling wolf, stepped forward hesitantly. "Master, I… I am losing my sight. I have advanced macular degeneration, and the doctors say they can do nothing. I beg for your intervention."

Worsley studied him for a moment, his countenance unreadable.

"Remove your mask!"

Then he turned to Flauros, gesturing silently. The demon stepped closer to the man, raising a clawed hand. The green aura surrounding it brightened, and with a flick of its wrist, a tendril of the energy shot forward, entering the man's eyes as a wisp of glowing smoke.

The man cried out, his hands flying to his face as the glowing smoke faded. For a moment, he stood still, trembling. Then he gasped, tears streaming down his face. "I can see!" he shouted. "I can see everything! Thank you, Master. Thank you!"

The crowd erupted in murmurs of awe, their fear momentarily replaced by reverence. Worsley raised a hand, silencing them. "The gift of sight is not freely given," he said coldly. "Use it wisely, or it will be taken from you."

Next, a woman stepped forward, her voice trembling. "Master, I have terminal cancer, a uterine sarcoma which is too advanced for the doctors to treat. Please, I beg for your intervention and mercy."

Worsley's eyes gleamed with dark satisfaction. "Mercy is mine to bestow, lift and open your robe." he said. "Flauros, attend to her."

The demon approached her, its movements slow and deliberate. It extended a hand, and once again, the green smoke emerged, this time enveloping her sexual organs and abdomen before entering her body. The woman shuddered, clutching her stomach. After a minute the smoke emerged from between her legs and returned to Flauros.

"Your cancer is cured," Worsley said, his tone final, "your doctors will find it gone."

Tears streamed down her face as she knelt. "Thank you, Master."

A younger man, his mask depicting a coiled serpent, asked for power to seduce and dominate those he desired. Worsley smiled faintly, "Flauros is not needed for this. Abdul, the black candle." Abdul took the candle from his box and handed it to the man. Worsley continued, "Light this in their presence," he instructed. "Their will shall bend to yours.

The next petitioner was an obese young woman, her huge frame barely covered by her oversized robe. She stepped forward hesitantly, her voice barely audible. "Master, I…, I wish to lose weight and be beautiful again, but I crave food continuously. It is an addiction. I have tried to diet, but I am too weak. Please, I beg you for help."

Worsley's expression darkened. "Weakness disgusts me. You have the power to cure yourself, yet you come to me? You are unworthy of my intervention."

The woman fell to her knees, sobbing. "Please, I'll do anything. Just help me."

Worsley's hand shot out, and the green aura around him flared angrily. "You will do nothing, for you are nothing. You are unworthy of this coven. Leave us and never return. You are fortunate I am in a merciful mood, or your punishment would be far greater."

The woman scrambled away, her cries echoing into the darkness. The crowd remained silent, the influence of Worsley's wrath hanging heavy in the air.

One by one, others stepped forward, each presenting their desires. Not all required Flauros. Worsley's gifts ranged from tokens of wealth to tools of manipulation. A woman requested influence over her rivals, and Worsley handed her a silver amulet, its surface etched with runes.

"This will give you their secrets," he said. "But be warned knowledge comes with a price."

Another asked for punishment on the men who had raped her and was given a charm to beguile them and a poison to kill them.

Paula stood at Fiona's side, her face a mask of detached curiosity. Inside, however, her thoughts churned with unease. The favours Worsley granted were not gifts – they were traps, each one tethering the recipient further into his web. She felt the weight of his gaze as he turned toward the remaining members of the circle.

"And you, Circe?" he said, his voice cutting through the silence like a blade. "Have you no desires to lay before the altar?"

Paula's breath caught, her mind racing. She felt Fiona's eyes on her, expectant and encouraging. "I…" she began, her voice steady despite the turmoil within. "I am honoured to observe tonight, Master. I seek only to learn."

Worsley studied her for a moment, his air unreadable. Then, he smiled – a slow, knowing smile that sent a chill down her spine. "Wisely spoken," he said. "The hunger for knowledge is the most potent desire of all."

As the last supplicant approached, Worsley raised his hand, silencing the murmurs of the crowd. The flames of the bonfire surged higher, casting grotesque shadows on the ancient stones. He knelt before the altar, his voice trembling as he spoke.

"Master, I seek vengeance. The man who destroyed my family walks free. I ask for the power to make him suffer."

Worsley's eyes gleamed with dark delight. "Ah, vengeance. The purest of all emotions." Abdul reached into his wooden box and retrieved a small dagger, its blade blackened as though forged in fire. He handed it to Worsley. "This blade," Worsley said, holding it aloft, "will deliver your justice. But remember, the blood it spills binds you to its curse."

The appellant took the dagger with reverent hands, his head bowed. "I accept the price, Master."

The crowd erupted in cries of devotion, their voices rising in unison. "Hail Lord! Hail the Grand Master!"

Worsley turned back to the circle, his voice commanding. "You have seen my power. You have felt my mercy. Now, shed your pretences and embrace the freedom I offer. Cast off your robes and submit to the energy of the Moon Goddess."

The emerald aura surrounding Worsley and Flauros expanded, spreading outward to envelop the entire circle. The air thickened with a strange, heady scent – an intoxicating blend of musk and floral sweetness that stirred a primal hunger within the coven. Cries of ecstasy and abandon rose as members discarded their robes and masks, their inhibitions dissolving in the pheromone-laden atmosphere.

Paula, naked, felt the lust, the pull, her body moving almost against her will as the music resumed, its rhythm pounding like a heartbeat. Around her, bodies intertwined, the coven descending into a frenzy of decadent release. She tried to resist, her mind screaming for control, but the aura's influence was overwhelming. A man grabbed her arm, pulling her roughly into the fray. His hands roaming with abandon, and Paula struggled against the hedonistic desire that was assailing her. Before she could succumb, Fiona appeared, her voice sharp and commanding.

"Leave her! She is mine."

The man froze, his eyes wide with terror, and quickly released Paula, backing away without a word. Fiona pulled Paula close, her expression a mix of anger and possession. "Stay by my side," she said, her tone leaving no room for argument. "You're not ready for this."

Paula groaned, her body trembling with both fear and desire as she clung to Fiona, the chaos of the circle raging around them.

Minutes later, Worsley's voice rang out, deep and resonant, rising above the chaos. "Enough!" he commanded, and the circle stilled as though struck by an unseen force. The music stopped abruptly, and the frenzied movements of the coven ceased. One by one, they turned to face him, the sweat on their bare bodies cooling in the night air, their faces masks of awe and fear.

"Tonight," Worsley began, his voice carrying with unnatural clarity, "we have opened the gates of desire, torn down the walls of inhibition, and surrendered ourselves to the power of the Moon Goddess. But this is only the beginning."

He stepped forward, his aura blazing brighter, illuminating the circle in an eerie green light. His gaze swept over the crowd, his eyes like twin flames that seemed to pierce into the souls of those before him.

"Tonight, we call upon Lilith," he declared, his voice filled with a dark reverence. "The Mother of Night, the First Woman, the Queen of Demons. She who defied the heavens and claimed her own destiny."

The name itself seemed to vibrate in the air, carrying with it an unspoken impact. Some in the crowd gasped, their looks wavering between awe and trepidation. Others dropped to their knees, their heads bowed in submission.

Worsley stepped back, standing atop the altar as if it were a throne. He raised his hands high, his robe flowing like liquid fire around him. "Lilith!" he called, his voice echoing across the moor. "We summon you to this sacred circle. We offer you the energy of this gathering, the power of our desires, the strength of our devotion."

He gestured toward the bonfire, which roared to life, its flames shifting from blue to a deep, blood-red hue. The stones of the circle seemed to vibrate, a low hum filling the air as the energy within the gathering reached a crescendo.

"I summon you by the power of your names: Lilith, Layil, Ardat-Lili, Laylah.

Mother of Sin, reveal to me your true form, speak truth and answer truly. Grant me the knowledge and wisdom of the Night."

"Come to us, Queen of Shadows!" Worsley cried, his voice now laced with an almost ecstatic fervour. "Bless us with your presence, your wisdom, your wrath!"

The green aura surrounding Worsley flared outward, expanding to encompass the entire circle. The coven gasped as the light passed over them, its touch sending shivers down their spines. Paula clutched Fiona's arm, her heart pounding as she felt the energy press against her skin like a living thing.

Fiona leaned in close, her voice low and reverent. "This is what it means to stand in the presence of true power," she whispered. "Watch closely, Circe. You are witnessing history."

The air grew heavier, the bonfire's flames twisting into shapes that defied logic – serpents, wings, and shadowy figures that writhed and danced. A low, grating sound filled the circle, not from any human throat but from the very earth itself. The crowd trembled, some collapsing to their knees, their hands pressed to the ground as if seeking stability in the face of the overwhelming force.

Paula felt her vision blur, her senses overwhelmed by the intensity of the moment. The name of Lilith hung in the air, a constant chant whispered by every voice in the circle, rising and falling like waves against a shore.

Worsley stood at the centre of it all, his head tilted back, his arms raised. The green and red lights intertwined around him, casting his shadow impossibly large against the stones. His face was a mask of triumph as he roared, "She comes!"

The air crackled with energy as Worsley's final cry echoed across the moor. The chanting ceased, replaced by an unnatural silence so profound it seemed to smother all sound. Even the wind had stilled, the world holding its breath as the green and red lights swirling around the altar reached a fevered intensity.

The bonfire surged upward in an unnatural column of flame, its hue shifting to a deep, pulsating black edged with crimson. From the heart of the fire, a shape began to emerge – a figure both radiant and terrible, stepping forward as if the fire itself had given birth to her.

She stood before the altar, tall and commanding, her presence overwhelming. Her form was that of a woman, but her beauty was unearthly, her features both perfect and unsettling. Her skin gleamed like polished marble, smooth and luminous, yet it seemed to shimmer with an undertone of shadow, as though darkness itself clung to her. Her hair cascaded down her back in waves of deep black, flecked with sparks of crimson that danced like embers, defying gravity as they flowed around her.

Her eyes were the most striking of all – piercing and unearthly, glowing with a light that shifted between fiery red and brilliant green. They held both the allure of an eternal lover and the menace of a predator, locking onto anyone who dared meet her gaze. Her lips, full and blood-red, curled into a faint smile that was both seductive and cruel.

She was draped in robes of shadow and flame, the fabric moving as though alive, caressing her body and swirling at her feet. Wings unfurled from her back – massive and feathered, but black as the void, their edges tipped with a faint, iridescent shimmer. Each movement she made was graceful and deliberate, her presence commanding absolute attention.

The coven fell to their knees as one, their naked bodies trembling. Some covered their faces, unable to bear the sight of her; others gazed up in awe, tears streaming down their cheeks as they whispered her name. The oppressive energy in the air seemed to coil around them, pressing down with a load that was almost unbearable.

Paula knelt among them, her heart pounding in her chest. She couldn't tear her eyes away from the figure before her, even as her instincts screamed at her to look away. She felt both drawn to Lilith's terrible beauty and terrified by the power radiating from her.

Worsley, standing at the altar, bowed his head deeply. "Great Queen of the Night, Mother of Shadows, we welcome you. We are your servants, your children. Command us."

Lilith's voice was unlike anything Paula had ever heard. It was soft yet resonant, melodic yet edged with a sinister undertone that made her skin slither. When she spoke, her words seemed to bypass the ears and sink directly into the mind, each syllable laced with both promise and peril.

"My children," Lilith said, her gaze sweeping across the gathered coven. "You have summoned me with your devotion, your desire, your surrender to the forces that bind and unbind this world."

Her eyes settled on Worsley, and her smile deepened. "You, my faithful servant, have done well. The energy you have gathered here feeds my power. You shall be rewarded."

Worsley straightened, pride radiating from him, though there was a flicker of nervousness in his eyes as she continued. "But remember, power is not without cost. You walk a path that demands everything, and should you falter…" She let the words hang, her smile turning cold. Worsley bowed again, murmuring, "I live only to serve you, Great Queen."

Lilith turned her attention to Fiona, her look softening slightly. "Ah, my High Priestess," she said, her voice a purr. "You have nurtured this circle well. Your devotion pleases me."

Fiona's face lit with a mix of reverence and pride. "Your presence is our highest honour, my Queen. Guide us as you see fit."

Lilith stepped closer to Fiona, reaching out to touch her cheek with fingers that glowed faintly. Fiona gasped, her eyes fluttering closed as a shiver ran through her body. "You shall lead them into the shadows of truth," Lilith said, her voice low. "Continue as you have, and greater power will be yours."

Lilith's gaze swept over the rest of the coven, her eyes narrowing. "But know this, all of you," she said, her voice hardening. "To summon me is to invoke not only my favour but my wrath. Betray me, and you will taste the abyss. Serve me, and you will find rewards beyond your imagination."

Her words were a double-edged sword, leaving the coven trembling. Some murmured vows of loyalty, others wept openly. Paula felt the influence of Lilith's gaze pass over her, and for a brief, horrifying moment, she thought the goddess saw through her, into the deepest corners of her soul.

Then Lilith spoke again, her voice slicing through the noise like a blade. "You girl," she said, her glowing eyes locking onto Paula. "Come to me."

The world seemed to stop. Paula froze, her breath catching in her throat. Every gaze in the circle turned to her, and the bulk of their attention pushed down like a physical force. Her legs felt like lead, but Fiona gave her a gentle nudge, her expression unreadable.

"Go," Fiona whispered. "You cannot deny her. She has chosen you."

Paula's heart pounded as she stepped forward, each movement slow and deliberate. Her instincts screamed at her to run, but her body betrayed her, compelled by the authority in Lilith's voice. As she neared the altar, she felt the heat of the green and crimson aura surrounding the goddess, an energy that seemed to seep into her very bones.

Lilith's eyes never left her, their piercing glow holding Paula captive. "What is your name?" the goddess asked, her voice carrying an undercurrent of both command and curiosity.

Paula hesitated for a heartbeat, her mind racing. "Circe," she replied, her voice barely more than a whisper.

Lilith smiled – a smile that was both approving and unsettling. She reached out and took Paula's trembling hand. The touch sent a jolt through Paula's body, like lightning coursing through her veins. Lilith turned her hand over, examining it as though searching for something hidden beneath the skin.

She moved closer, her gaze sweeping over Paula's form with a deliberate intensity. Her movements were slow, almost predatory, as she circled Paula, her wings brushing the air with a faint, rhythmic sound. Lilith's presence was overwhelming, her beauty and terror magnified in this moment of singular attention.

Finally, Lilith stopped, her eyes narrowing as she looked back at Worsley. "This one is special," she declared, her voice resonating with finality. "She carries a light and a shadow I have not seen in centuries."

Worsley's face lit with triumph, though a flicker of something darker – jealousy or fear – crossed his features. "Great Queen," he said, bowing low. "She is yours to command."

Lilith turned back to Paula, her mien unreadable. The goddess leaned in, her lips brushing close to Paula's ear as she whispered something inaudible. The heat of her presence, the mass of her gaze – it was too much. Paula's vision blurred, her knees buckled, and the world tilted around her.

The last thing she saw before the darkness took her was Lilith's faint, knowing smile.

Part Three
Sacrificial Fire

Chapter 37

Aftermath

*T*revaunce Manor – 11 April 8:15 AM

Paula woke with a start, the sheets tangled around her legs and her heart pounding. Her breath came in shallow gasps as fragmented memories from the night before rushed back. Lilith's face, terrible and beautiful, loomed in her mind. Her voice echoed faintly, though the words were elusive. Paula pressed a hand to her chest, trying to steady herself.

"I know what you are up to!"

The whispered words chilled her to the bone. Had she imagined them? Or had Lilith truly seen through her façade?

Paula squeezed her eyes shut, her thoughts racing. *I've blown it. They know. I've let everyone down.*

She opened her eyes again, scanning the room. It was her bedroom in Trevaunce Manor, familiar yet suddenly oppressive. The door creaked open, and Fiona stepped inside, her smile radiant and unexpectedly warm.

"My dear, you're awake at last," Fiona said, her tone a mix of concern and delight.

Paula pushed herself up on the pillows, her body still trembling. "What… happened to me?"

Fiona moved closer, sitting gracefully on the edge of the bed. "Oh, my darling, you were wonderful. The energy you channelled was extraordinary, but it all got too much for you. You fainted. We couldn't wake you and had to carry you back here."

Paula's mind raced. *She believes I fainted from the ritual… not from fear.* Relief washed over her, though she kept her expression neutral. "I'm sorry," she murmured. "Did I ruin the ceremony?"

Fiona laughed softly, brushing the concern away with a wave of her hand. "Not at all! The ceremony was practically over when it happened. And, my dear, you should know – Lilith favoured you. She declared you special. Do you have any idea how rare that is?"

Paula's stomach churned. "Special?" she echoed, trying to sound awed. "What does that mean?"

"It means that Sir Giles wants you in our order as soon as possible. You're blessed, Paula. To have Lilith herself choose you…" Fiona trailed off, her gaze filled with a reverence that made Paula shiver.

"Is Sir Giles still here?" Paula asked. "Will I get to see him?"

"Unfortunately, no," Fiona said with a hint of disappointment. "He had to return to London early this morning. But we'll begin your training tomorrow. You have a special destiny ahead of you."

Paula nodded slowly. "I remember Lilith calling me and taking my hand… and then nothing. It's all a blur."

"She whispered something to you. Do you recall what she said? Was that why you fainted?"

Paula's mind raced for a plausible answer. "No… apart from asking my name, I don't remember her saying anything directly to me. Her gaze, though – it felt like she was looking into my soul. That's the last thing I remember."

Fiona's smile widened. "That sounds about right. A goddess's gaze is not something easily withstood. Still, it was a great honour for our coven that she chose you. You should be proud."

Paula forced a smile. "I suppose I am."

Fiona rose gracefully. "I'll leave you to rest. The day is yours. There's a breakfast buffet in the drawing room until 10:30, or I can have a tray brought to you."

"That won't be necessary," Paula said. "I'll come down after a shower."

"Wonderful, Enjoy your day, my dear. Tomorrow, your training begins."

As soon as Fiona left, Paula grabbed her phone and texted Doogie. *I need to meet with the others today. Urgent.*

She barely had time to set the phone down before James appeared, his spectral form materializing at the edge of the room. His face was a mask of concern.

"You look terrible," he said, his voice soft but urgent.

"Thanks," Paula replied dryly. "Last night wasn't exactly a walk in the park."

James moved closer, his eyes searching hers. "I could only observe from afar. I dared not let them see me – too many adepts and demons. So, what happened? I felt the surges of energy, but mostly it seemed like chaos. I lost track of you."

Paula recounted the events, her voice steady despite the tremor in her hands. She told him about the ceremony, Lilith's terrible beauty, and the moment when the goddess called her forward. "Lilith took my hand, James," Paula said, her voice dropping, "she said I was special, but she looked at me like she knew everything. She whispered something – I know what you are up to."

James's face darkened. "And then?"

Paula shook her head. "I don't remember. Fiona said I fainted, and they carried me back here."

James's jaw tightened. "If Lilith knows and has labelled you as special, Paula, this changes everything. Worsley will start watching you more closely and want to keep you in his sights. You'll need to be careful – more than careful."

"Do you think she really knows? Or was it just... some test?"

"I honestly don't know, but we must assume the worst. You'll need to tread carefully with Fiona and Worsley. Keep your cover intact, no matter what."

Paula sighed, her exhaustion seeping into her voice. "I feel like I'm walking on a knife's edge, James. One wrong move..."

"You're stronger than you know. Last night proved that. But we need to regroup – get everyone on the same page. This isn't just about you anymore. Whatever Worsley and his coven are planning, it may be bigger than we realised."

Paula met his eyes, her resolve hardening. "Then we'd better make sure we're ready."

Carn View – 11 April 8:15 AM

Dougal sat at the kitchen table, his fingers curled around a mug of coffee. His face was pale, his expression tight with a mixture of exhaustion and dread. Across from him, Mark and Sam sat motionless, their gazes locked on Dougal as he recounted the events of the previous night.

"It was diabolical," Dougal said. "I watched it all yesterday and through the night until it finally ended. Even from two miles out, it was… something I'll never forget." He paused, "The night vision binoculars helped, but the firelight and whatever aura they were summoning occasionally flooded them. I kept switching between those and the regular binoculars because the moonlight, fire and the demonic glow lit up the area well."

"What did you see, Dougal? What exactly happened?" Sam probed.

Dougal took a deep breath, his voice lowering as though the weight of the words themselves was too much. "I saw incredible things. Things I'd never have believed if I hadn't seen them with my own eyes. Mysterious dancing… weird music that seemed to carry across the moor, even at that distance. And then…" His voice faltered.

"What?" Mark pressed. "What else?"

Dougal's hand trembled slightly as he set down his mug. "Demons. I saw demons appear. One of them stood beside Worsley, and… " He hesitated, as if saying the words would make them more real. "Worsley levitated. He was standing there, commanding them. It wasn't some trick or illusion, Mark. It was real."

Sam gasped. "Demons? Are you sure?"

Dougal nodded grimly. "Absolutely sure. And Paula…." He swallowed hard. "She was part of it. She joined the dancing. They were all wearing the same black robes, so it was hard to distinguish her from the others at first. But then they all stripped naked… and there was an orgy."

Mark stiffened. "An orgy? Was Paula – did she…?"

"I don't think so. Fiona intervened. It looked like one of the men was about to… well, force her, but Fiona stopped him. I can't be certain from the distance, but I'm reasonably sure she protected Paula."

"But why? Why would Fiona protect her from what was part of the ceremony?"

Dougal shook his head. "I don't know Sam. Maybe Paula's special to her, or maybe she had other plans. But that's not the worst of it."

"What do you mean?"

"Toward the end, Paula, still naked, approached a female demon. She went right up to it. The demon seemed to embrace her and then she just collapsed. Fell straight to the grass."

Sam let out a small cry, and Mark's chair scraped loudly against the floor as he shot to his feet. "Collapsed? What happened then?"

Dougal's voice cracked. "They carried her off. I don't know if she was unconscious or…" He hesitated, his voice dropping to a whisper. "She might be dead."

"No," Sam said, her voice shaking. "No, she can't be. Paula's strong. She – she wouldn't – "

"We should have stopped her. We should have found a way to get her out of there."

Dougal's phone buzzed loudly on the table, cutting through the tension. He snatched it up, his heart pounding in his chest as he read the message. Relief washed over his face, and he let out a breath he hadn't realized he was holding.

"She's alive," he said, holding up the phone. "It's a text from Paula. She wants to see us urgently."

Sam burst into tears, half-laughing, half-sobbing. "Thank God."

"What does she want to talk about? Did she say anything else?" Mark asked

Dougal quickly typed a response. *What time? Where?* A moment later, Paula's reply came: *11 AM. Same place as last time.*

"She's meeting us at 11," Dougal said. "Same spot as before."

Mark sat back down. "Thank God she's okay. But what the hell happened last night? What did they do to her?"

Dougal set his phone on the table. "We'll find out soon enough. But whatever it is, it's clear that last night wasn't just a ritual. It was something much darker. And Paula's at the centre of it."

Sam wiped her eyes, her voice trembling but resolute. "We'll get her through this. Whatever it takes."

Mark nodded. "Yeah. Whatever it takes."

Trevaunce Manor – 11 April 09:15 AM

Paula pushed a forkful of scrambled eggs across her plate, her appetite non-existent as Fiona chatted brightly about the plans for the day. The dining room's tall windows let in the morning sun, but its warmth did little to thaw the cold knot in Paula's stomach.

"So, my darling Circe," Fiona said, her tone laced with affection. "What are your plans for today?"

Paula looked up, forcing a faint smile. "I thought I'd take a walk. Stretch my legs, maybe head toward the village."

Fiona's manner shifted, her smile becoming slightly more guarded. "That sounds delightful, but now that you've been favoured by Lilith, Sir Giles has insisted on precautions. For your safety, of course."

"Precautions?" Paula asked, her heart skipping a beat.

Fiona nodded, taking a delicate sip of tea. "A member of our security team will keep an eye on you whenever you're off the estate. Don't worry – they'll remain unobtrusive. You might not even notice them. It's just to ensure no harm comes to you."

"That's… considerate," she said, despite the alarm bells ringing in her head. "I hadn't realized Sir Giles was so protective."

Fiona smiled. "You're special now, Paula, as I always knew you were. That means avoidance of risk. But you can trust us to take care of you."

Paula shut the bedroom door behind her, her mind racing. Fiona's revelation about the surveillance threw her plans into chaos. *I need to write everything down but how can I pass the papers to Dougal if someone's watching me?* She grabbed her phone and typed out a quick text to Dougal: *Forget the meet. Surveillance ordered. Unobtrusive, but it's there. I'll write everything down. Need a safe drop-off method.*

The response came a few minutes later: *We'll use the café just outside of Nansebyn, on the road out that leads to the A30. Get a coffee and snack to blend in. I'll position Sam there. Conduct the drop in the restroom. Quick and Easy.*

Paula let out a shaky breath, her heart still pounding. She sat at the desk, pulling out a blank sheet of paper. Every detail she could recall from the esbat – the ritual, the demon Flauros, the orgy, Lilith's appearance, the aura, Worsley's demeanour and actions – flowed from her pen. She added James's observations: Lilith's potential amusement, her possible disdain for Worsley, and the possibility that she is waiting to see if I succeed. By the time she finished, her hand ached, she'd managed to get everything down on a single sheet of paper using both sides. The paper was filled with cramped, hurried writing. She folded it, placed it in an envelope and slipped it into her jacket pocket.

The Walk to Nansebyn – 11 April 10:45 AM

The walk to the café was brisk, Paula's thoughts a jumble of tension and determination. She kept her pace steady, her eyes darting occasionally to see if she could spot her "shadow." She saw no one, but the menace of unseen eyes followed her like a spectre. She'd passed the car park leading to the rendezvous point they had used previously. It was a pity they'd not been able to use it this time.

She entered the village passing a pretty row of grey-stone terraced cottages. She came to the road that was marked to the A30, The Prince of Wales pub was just beyond it, but she turned right and followed the road. Round the next bend was the café, amusingly named "The Miners' Diner". She assumed that was to reflect the history of the tin mining that had been once associated with the area. There were half a dozen cars in the parking area.

The café was surprisingly lively when she entered, the clinking of plates and soft hum of conversation providing a welcome cover for her nerves. She ordered a black coffee and a flapjack at the counter and scanned the room, her gaze landing briefly on Sam, who sat at a corner table. Sam didn't acknowledge her, keeping her head down as she flipped through a small notebook.

Paula carried her coffee and snack to an empty table near the restrooms and waited, her fingers brushing the envelope in her pocket. When Sam stood and walked casually toward the restrooms, Paula followed two minutes later, her heart pounding in her chest.

Sam was leaning against the sink, her expression calm but her eyes sharp. "Got it?"

Paula nodded, pulling the envelope from her jacket. "Everything's in here. What I saw, what James told me – everything about Lilith and Worsley."

"Any issues getting here?"

"None," Paula said. "But they're watching me. I couldn't see them, but I can feel it."

"What you must have gone through, you are so brave. I couldn't have done it. You did amazingly well," Sam said. "We'll go through this and get back to you. Stay sharp, Paula. You're walking a very fine line."

Paula hesitated, her voice trembling slightly. "If they find out…"

"They won't," Sam interrupted. "Just keep your cover intact."

"You be careful too. If anything happens to any of you, I'd never forgive… "

"Stop! We're all in this together. We've got your back. Now, you use the john, while I head out. Then finish your coffee before heading back."

Carn View – 4:30 pm

Sam, Mark, and Dougal gathered in the dimly lit living room, the paper they'd read lying on the coffee table between them. The atmosphere was thick with tension. Mark and Sam had read and reread her notes earlier, but Dougal had only returned fifteen minutes ago. He had only just read through Paula's notes, his look was dark.

"What a terrible thing to endure!" Sam said.

Dougal leaned back. "So, Lilith might be waiting to expose Paula? Or worse, she could be toying with Worsley himself? According to James, demons aren't exactly known for their loyalty."

Mark frowned. "It's like we're caught between two storms – Worsley and Lilith. Either one could destroy her if they choose."

"Or…" Sam said, "Lilith could be playing a deeper game. She might want Paula to succeed, just to throw it in Worsley's face. Demons don't like being summoned, especially by arrogant sorcerers who think they can control them."

Dougal grunted. "If that's the case, Paula's in even more danger if he realises that. Worsley won't tolerate a threat to his authority – not from Paula, not from anyone."

"We can't just sit here and analyse this to death. We need to act somehow."

"And do what Mark?" Dougal shot back. "Storm Trevaunce Manor? That'll get us all killed."

"Enough, both of you. Paula's relying on us to stay calm and think this through. We need a plan, but it must be smart."

"James has said countless times that Worsley is invincible while he is protected by Flauros. Our plans should include ideas for getting Flauros to leave him." Mark ventured.

"How the hell can we do that?" Sam said.

"Ask James, when we get the chance."

The room fell silent, the burden of their predicament pushing heavily on them all.

Finally, Mark spoke. "Whatever happens, we not letting her go through this alone."

"Agreed. We'll fight for her or with her. Whatever it takes."

"Whatever it takes." Sam echoed.

Chapter 38
Training Begins

Trevaunce Manor – 12 April 9:05 AM

Paula's footsteps echoed softly against the polished stone floor as she walked toward the library in the East Wing. Her palms were damp, and a nervous energy coursed through her. Today marked the beginning of her training, and while she had steeled herself for this moment, the enormity of it loomed large in her mind. The library, at least, wasn't one of the sinister rooms she had dreaded. Its wide windows let in shafts of golden light, forming a warm glow over the rows of ancient, leather-bound books.

She hesitated at the door, clutching her hands together as her thoughts churned. *Six months! I'm supposed to survive six months of this! No way! We need to destroy Worsley and get the hell out of here!*

Her agreement to infiltrate Worsley's inner circle, to get close enough to learn his secrets and destroy him, felt heavier than ever. The syllabus Fiona had handed her the night before had been overwhelming – dense, intricate, and utterly foreign. She'd only agreed to this mission because of its necessity, and the promise of James's guidance was her only solace.

The thought of James brought a flicker of comfort. *He's been through this. He said he'd help. I just need to get through one day at a time.*

Fiona greeted her warmly as Paula entered, her smile as polished as the room itself. She was impeccably dressed as always, her demeanour poised and authoritative. "Good morning, Circe," she said, using Paula's chosen name within the order. Her tone was pleasant, but her eyes carried a sharpness that Paula couldn't ignore.

Paula returned the greeting, doing her best to mask her nerves. She glanced around the library, taking in the towering shelves and the large mahogany table where Fiona had set a single book.

"This is where it begins," Fiona said, gesturing to a leather-bound tome resting on the table. "Your training will introduce you to the core principles, symbols, and practices of Thelema. Much of it will be challenging, even disorienting at first. But with discipline and dedication, you'll find clarity."

Paula managed a nod, though her stomach tightened at the mention of challenges. Fiona stepped closer to the table, picking up the book.

"This," she said, her voice reverent, "is *Liber AL vel Legis*, the cornerstone of our teachings. Known more commonly as *The Book of the Law*, it contains the central tenets that guide us: 'Do what thou wilt shall be the whole of the Law,' and 'Love is the law, love under will.' These principles may sound simple, but they demand profound reflection."

Fiona handed the book to Paula. "This is yours to study," Fiona continued. "You'll begin with the first assignment: Interpret key verses from the text." She handed Paula a sheet with her assignment, listing the verses on it. "Write your thoughts – there are no right or wrong answers, only the process of understanding."

Paula forced a polite smile. "Thank you," she said, her voice steady despite the apprehension bubbling within her.

As Paula departed, Fiona lingered in the library, her thoughts still centred on the young woman. She had potential – real, untapped potential. There was something about her, an energy Fiona had rarely seen in initiates. It wasn't just intelligence or ambition, but something deeper, more primal. She had been chosen by Lilith herself at the esbat, and that alone marked her as special.

Fiona had watched the ritual unfold with growing excitement. As the circle was cast and the invocations spoken, she had sensed the shift in the air – the pulse of power as Lilith's presence filled the space. And when the goddess's attention fell upon Paula, Fiona knew it was no coincidence. Paula had been drawn into their world for a reason, and it was now Fiona's responsibility to ensure that she thrived within it.

She wanted to see Paula succeed, to flourish in the order. If guided correctly, she could become something remarkable. Perhaps even rise through the ranks to a position of real influence. Fiona imagined introducing her to the deeper mysteries, leading her into the labyrinth of power and knowledge that few ever glimpsed. The thought sent a thrill through her.

And then, of course, there was the more personal matter. Paula was intoxicating – her beauty, her spirit, the way she carried herself. That night in London had been a taste, but Fiona wanted more. She had seen the conflict in Paula's eyes, the mixture of guilt and attraction. It only made her more irresistible.

Perhaps tonight, she mused. A private visit, away from the constraints of ritual and expectation. Just the two of them. She would make Paula see that resistance was unnecessary – that surrender could be just as powerful as control.

With a slow smile, Fiona turned back to the table, her fingers idly tracing the leather cover of her own copy of *Liber AL vel Legis*. Yes, tonight could be very interesting indeed.

Paula sat cross-legged on her bed, the book open before her. The gilded lettering of *Liber AL vel Legis* shimmered in the soft light filtering through her window. Her initial attempts to read it had been disheartening – the dense language and cryptic phrasing felt more like riddles than revelations.

"You look like you're about to throw that book out the window," James's voice said lightly inside her head. Paula turned to see his spectral form leaning against the wall, his manner amused.

She glanced at him, exasperated. "It's not even close to making sense. I feel like I'm reading a language I don't recognise. The verses she has assigned for me to interpret, seem crazy."

James smiled faintly. "That's because you're not supposed to 'get it' on the first read. These texts are designed to unravel your assumptions and force you to think differently. Come over to the desk and let's break it down."

"What is Thelema? What is this 'Do what thou wilt shall be the whole of the Law,' thing? It sounds crazy, selfish."

"Calm down and relax." Jame said firmly. "You will come to understand soon. That core concept of Thelema is the idea that each person has a divine purpose, a calling or *True Will*, that goes beyond personal desires and societal expectations. Forget that for now and think on it later. Let us concentrate on Fiona's assignments."

Paula took a deep breath and nodded.

"Take this first one, *"every man and every woman is a star"*. This is deceptively simple," James said. "Think about stars. They burn brightly, but they also exist independently in the vast cosmos. The verse is about individuality and the divine spark within every person. How do you see that idea reflected in your own journey?"

Paula scribbled notes, her frustration easing slightly. "So, it's about realizing that everyone has their own path, but they're still connected in some way?"

James nodded. "Exactly. The stars are part of constellations, but each star shines on its own."

She turned to the next one. *"Who calls us Thelemites will do no wrong, if he looks but close into the word. For there are therein Three Grades, the Hermit, and the Lover, and the man of Earth.* She wants me to reflect on the concept of the Three Grades and how these roles might manifest in my own life or the lives of those around me"

"These represent stages of spiritual development," James explained. "The Man of Earth is the material, the everyday. The Lover is the one who connects deeply with others. The Hermit turns inward to seek ultimate truth. How do you see yourself fitting into these stages?"

Paula hesitated. "I guess... I'm between the Lover and the Hermit. Trying to connect while also hiding a part of myself."

"Good," James said. "Be honest in your interpretation. Fiona won't expect you to have definitive answers, only thoughtful ones."

James's assistance continued. Finally, they reached the last verse in the assignment. *"Compassion is the Vice of kings."*

Paula frowned at this verse. "This one feels... wrong. Like it's saying compassion is a weakness."

James's expression softened. "It challenges conventional morality. Strength and leadership, in this context, come from making hard decisions without letting emotions cloud judgment. It's not saying compassion is useless – it's saying it can't always take precedence."

Paula nodded reluctantly. "So, it's more about balance?"

"Exactly. Write what you feel. Fiona will want to see your struggle as much as your insight."

When James left, she felt happier. She could handle this with James's help. But she wanted to do more to help Mark, Sam and Dougal. She sent Dougal a text. *Had first session with Fiona. Went ok. Given homework. James helping me. I want to help you more. Please advise.*

She hit send and waited, her pulse quickening as the message delivered. Some moments later, her phone buzzed with Dougal's reply.

Good work. Can you provide information on the estate management? Staff numbers? Routines? anything useful? Same for the security organisation. Don't appear too interested just vaguely curious.

Paula frowned, her thoughts racing. The staff at Trevaunce Manor were enigmatic at best, and any attempt she'd made to engage with them had been met with silence or avoidance. The young women who cleaned the rooms and prepared meals would lower their eyes and scurry away the moment she tried to speak to them. *Had Abdul forbidden them to speak?* she wondered.

Maybe James could provide more information. She'd ask him when he came back.

She decided to take a casual walk through the manor, her steps unhurried as she observed her surroundings. She passed through the main corridor, where another young woman was polishing the ornate wooden panels. Paula paused, feigning interest in a painting on the wall.

"That's beautiful work," she said, her voice friendly. "Do you know who painted it?"

The girl stiffened, her hands gripping the cloth she held. Without looking up, she murmured something in broken English and quickly turned away.

Paula sighed, frustration bubbling beneath her calm exterior. *Who are these girls, and why are they afraid to talk?*

She decided to make her way toward the rear gardens, a walk to stretch her legs if asked. She wound her way round the house to the drive and headed towards the gate. She'd noticed Abdul peering out of a window at her, intimidating but she kept her pace steady and nonchalant, her eyes scanning for anything out of the ordinary.

As she neared the gate lodge, she could see two men standing by the gate as usual, their postures relaxed but their eyes alert. They had been there when she had taken her walks outside before. Not necessarily the same men but there all the same. They wore plain black jackets, trousers and boots, their demeanour unmistakably professional.

The lodge itself was an old stone building, partially obscured by ivy. She detected faint movement – but the curtains were mainly drawn closed, making it impossible to see inside.

Paula lingered by a flower bed, pretending to admire the blooms as she watched the men out of the corner of her eye. They seemed focused on the gate, occasionally speaking into their radios. She headed back.

She entered her bedroom to see that James had returned. She brought him up to date with all that had happened. With additional information from James, she had been able to construct some notes.

Staff: 6 - 8 young women, possibly more. Foreign, hesitant to engage. Maybe illegal immigrants. Or slaves? Abdul directs them.

Security: At least two men always at the gate, more inside the lodge. Several likely patrolling the estate's perimeter. Professional demeanour, likely armed.

Lodging: Staff appear to live in staff quarters in the basement of the East Wing. Security presumably based in the gate lodge.

Routines: Cleaning staff work silently, early mornings to late afternoons. Security focused on perimeter. Routine unknown.

She summarised the information in a text and sent it to Dougal. She sighed and opened the Book of the Law. A couple of minutes later her phone buzzed. *Great start! Focus on the lodge. Can you find out how many security shifts there are? Don't compromise yourself.*

She went back to her studies feeling like she was now a more useful member of the team.

Trevaunce Manor – 12 April, 11:30 pm

Paula awoke to the sensation of fingers lightly tracing her arm, the soft pressure sending an involuntary shiver through her. She stirred, her breath catching in her throat as she recognized the scent of sandalwood and jasmine – Fiona.

"You're beautiful when you sleep," Fiona murmured, her voice a velvet whisper against Paula's ear.

Paula tensed but didn't move away. She had expected this, had known it was inevitable. Still, the reality of Fiona's presence in her bed was something else entirely. A necessary evil, she reminded herself. To strengthen her position, to avoid suspicion.

Fiona's fingers trailed down her bare shoulder, her touch gentle but insistent. "You feel it, don't you?" she purred. "The pull between us. You don't have to fight it."

Paula swallowed hard, her mind warring with her body. She could say no. She could push Fiona away, find an excuse. But that would only make things more difficult. Worsley's inner circle would scrutinize her, question her commitment. And Fiona... Fiona would be disappointed.

She turned slightly, her eyes locking onto Fiona's in the dim candlelight. "I..."

Fiona placed a finger to Paula's lips. "Shush. Don't speak. Just feel. Let yourself enjoy what is meant to be."

Paula felt Fiona's lips brush against hers, soft and searching. A spark ignited low in her stomach, betraying her resolve. Guilt crashed into her like a wave – Nick, James, the mission – but her body responded despite it. She hated this, hated how easily Fiona's touch made her forget, even for a moment. James had told her Fiona's special talent was sexual rituals. She knew how to locate her pleasure centres.

Fiona deepened the kiss, her hands sliding over Paula's waist, her voice a seductive whisper. "Surrender isn't weakness, Circe. It's power. Let me show you."

Paula's resistance faltered. She had to do this. She had to make Fiona believe she was hers. And so, with a shuddering breath, she let go. But as Fiona claimed her, Paula couldn't escape the truth – the part of her that wanted this, that enjoyed the pleasure coursing through her. And that, more than anything, was what amplified her guilt the most.

Joan lay on the cold stone floor of the dungeon, the silence pressing down on her like a weight. The night of the esbat had granted her a brief respite, and for some reason, she had been left alone last night. But that mercy had passed. She knew what was coming, and this time, she would not survive it.

The chains at her wrists had long since cut into her skin, dried blood crusting over her raw wounds. Her body was weak, her mind frayed. The protective spells in her consciousness had held for weeks, but they had come at a cost. Every day, Abdul had stripped away another layer of her strength. Tonight, he had promised her something worse. A special entity. A being that would not merely break her but consume her.

A chill slithered through the dungeon air, and she knew it was here.

A shadow stretched across the far wall, shifting unnaturally, bending in ways no human form could. The air thickened, a presence pressing against her from all sides. A whisper, low and sibilant, filled the chamber, though the voice came from nowhere and everywhere at once.

"You are ready to be undone."

A freezing touch brushed her forehead, seeping into her skull, sinking into her thoughts. She gasped, her body convulsing as the entity pried into her mind, not with force, but with an unbearable, crawling patience. It did not rush. It savoured.

Tears streamed down her face, but no scream came. She had no voice left to scream. Her memories unravelled, piece by piece, siphoned from her soul. She saw flashes of her past – her childhood, the coven, Arthur's face, his voice telling her to stay away. She clung to that image, the last tether to her humanity. But the entity was relentless. Her vision darkened, her body convulsed once more, and then, silence.

The silver cord that tethered her to life trembled… then parted.

Her body fell limp. But her consciousness drifted, light, unburdened. She was rising, pulled toward a light that shimmered in the darkness. The pain was gone. The fear was gone. Only release remained.

Chapter 39

Secrets Buried, Truths Unearthed

Trevaunce Manor — 13 April 9:05 AM

Paula handed the now neatly written document to Fiona in the library, her palms slick with sweat. Fiona smiled at her knowingly and then flipped through the pages slowly, her expression unreadable. As she reached the end, her lips curved into a faint smile.

"You've done exceptionally well, Circe," Fiona said, her voice tinged with genuine surprise. "Your interpretations are nuanced, thoughtful. I see you've grappled with the verses honestly, which is rare for a probationer so new."

Paula blinked, caught off guard. "Thank you." she said quietly.

Fiona closed the notebook, her gaze sharpening. "This confirms what I suspected. You are special, Circe. Sir Giles will be pleased. I look forward to seeing how you develop. I have some problems to resolve today so it is free study time for you to further read *The Book of the Law*. Feel free to have some leisure time as well."

Paula left the library with a mix of relief and unease. She had wondered how Fiona would act after last night's encounter, but she was professional and businesslike.

James appeared in her room moments later, his smile triumphant. "She's impressed," he said. "And that's exactly what we needed."

"I just hope I can keep this up."

"You can," James said firmly. "As I have said before, you're capable of more than you imagine."

Paula hesitated for only a moment before speaking. "You saw last night, didn't you?"

James nodded, his air unreadable. "I was aware."

She exhaled slowly, pacing the room. "I can handle it. I have to. If I hesitate, if I show weakness, she'll sense it. And then all of this will have been for nothing."

James studied her, his spectral presence shimmering slightly in the dim light. "I won't lie, Paula. That took incredible strength and resolve. To hold your ground, to stay in control... I don't know many that could have done the same."

Paula crossed her arms, a bitter smile tugging at her lips. "It's not strength, James. It's necessity. I won't let them win, and if that means playing my part, then so be it. However, I'd like this to remain between you and me. I don't want to involve Sam, Mark or Dougal."

James inclined his head slightly, acknowledging her determination. "Are you sure you don't want the others to know?"

"Yes," Paula said quickly. "Not Mark, not Sam, and especially not Doogie. They wouldn't understand. They'd want to pull me out, and we can't afford that. It would then make my sacrifice meaningless."

James sighed but didn't argue. Instead, he gave her a look of quiet admiration. "You're tough, Paula."

She forced a laugh. "You keep saying that. Maybe one day I'll believe it."

James watched her for a moment longer, then nodded. "Just be careful. You're walking a fine line."

"I know," she whispered. "But for now, I'm still standing."

After a brief pause, she said, "Well, I have a relatively free day. Doogie has asked me to see if I can get more security information. For instance, the number of shifts they work and a better idea of personnel numbers and further information that may help. I am concerned that if I start hanging round the lodge, they may get suspicious."

"Leave it with me." James said. They won't see me unless Abdul turns up. I can get inside and observe and pick up whatever info I can.

"Great! I may go for another wander after reading another section of that riveting book!"

An hour later Paula was exploring the house again. She passed a couple of maids doing their chores, both avoided interacting with her. She found herself approaching the corridor to the Northern wing.

The sudden sound of voices made her pause. They were coming from the corridor – a heated exchange carried on the sharp tones of anger.

"You bloody fool!" Fiona's voice, furious and cutting, reverberated through the air. "You were supposed to scare her, torture her, bind her to your will – not kill her! Do you have any idea what you've done?"

Paula's breath caught in her throat. The icy tone in Fiona's voice was unlike anything she'd heard before. The response came in Abdul's low, croaky growl, unapologetic but tense.

"I'll throw her down the old well," he said. "It's very deep. She won't be found there."

Paula's hand flew to her mouth as she stifled a gasp. *Who are they talking about?* Her mind reeled, racing back to the groan she'd heard in the cellar days before. *Could it be related?* A sickening thought gripped her. *Joan Summers!*

She retraced her steps as quickly as she could without making a sound, fearful of discovery. If they suspected she had heard… it didn't bear thinking about. She returned to her room with adrenalin induced haste.

James was waiting for with a smile on his lips. "I've gathered the information Dougal wants! My God, what's up? You look like you've seen a ghost."

"James…" Paula began, her voice unsteady. Her words tumbling out in a rush. "They killed someone. Fiona was so angry and said it wasn't supposed to happen. Abdul mentioned the old well to dispose of the body."

"Paula! Calm down and give me the exact conversation as you heard it. It's important. Take a deep breath and tell me."

Paula recounted everything that was said.

James's face darkened. "If Abdul was supposed to bind someone, then it means they had wanted her alive – for a reason."

"But who was she?" Paula asked, her voice trembling. "Could it be Joan Summers?"

James nodded grimly. "Most likely. But if she merely broke the rules or posed a threat to the coven secrets, they would have likely killed her outright. No, she must have had information or something that they needed. Abdul's specialty is psychological and supernatural torment. He'd have summoned visitations, monsters that would have terrified her, all to shatter her mind, to make her compliant."

Paula shuddered. "That groan I heard in the cellar… could it have been her?"

"Very likely," James said. "Arthur mentioned Joan disappeared around the March Ostara Sabbat. If she was here since then… Paula, the terrible things she must have endured. It is a testament to her bravery that she held out for so long. I am annoyed I didn't check it out earlier, but Abdul is so often there that I dared not risk a visit."

"Why would they do this to her?" Paula whispered, tears pricking her eyes.

"As I said, she must have known something dangerous – something they couldn't risk getting out, or, more likely, something that they wanted." James replied. "But killing her was a mistake, so she obviously had not divulged whatever they or Worsley wanted. No wonder Fiona was livid."

"Do you think she's… at peace now?"

James hesitated before speaking softly. "I hope so. But Paula, this means the stakes are even higher for you. They obviously don't hesitate to destroy threats."

"Is there any way we can stop them getting rid of the body."

"I fear, knowing Abdul, that deed will already be done. The well is old and very deep. It has a protective cover to stop people falling into it. It's in the woodland to the south of the house."

"What about an anonymous tip off to the police?" Paula suggested.

"We could think about that. Unfortunately, Worsley has the local police in his pocket. Maybe Dougal's boss could help."

"Yes. Now we must let the others know."

"Let's pause and compile a lucid text for Dougal that tells all that has happened. I'll pass him the security information that I learned today later, once they have digested this shock."

Carn View – 13 April, 12:15 PM

The living room was unusually quiet after they had all read Paula's message on Dougal's phone. The atmosphere was heavy, the horror of what they were reading settling over them like a suffocating weight.

Mark was the first to speak, his voice low and angry. "They tortured her. They killed her. What kind of monsters are these people?" It was a rhetorical question. They were already well aware of the answer

"It's worse than that. They didn't just kill her – they broke her. If Paula's right, they destroyed her piece by piece, but they hadn't wanted to kill her. That was a mistake on Abdul's part."

Sam let out a shaky breath. "Joan Summers… Arthur's friend. How do we even tell him this? 'Hey, Arthur, your friend was tortured to death and dumped in a well'? It's unthinkable."

"We must tell him. He deserves to know."

Dougal shook his head. "Not yet Mark. Let's see if we can confirm the details first. If we tell Arthur now, and we're wrong – or worse, if we can't prove it – it'll destroy him for nothing."

"What if Paula's in danger?" Sam asked, "If they find out she knows…"

"She's playing it smart, she's careful, and she has James to guide her. We must assume she is ok."

Mark said angrily. "This isn't enough. These people are monsters. We seem to be just sitting here while they're torturing and killing people."

Dougal's gaze hardened. "We're not just sitting. We're planning steadily. And when we're ready, we'll strike. But we must be ready."

The room fell into a tense silence, the gravity of their situation hanging over them. Finally, Sam spoke, her voice quieter but resolute. "Whatever happens, we can't let Joan's death be for nothing. And we can't let it happen to Paula."

"Agreed. We'll make them pay. But for now, we stay the course, gather as much information as we can and continue to adapt and plan."

Trevaunce Manor – 13 April, 12:25 PM

Fiona paced the drawing room, her heeled shoes tapping against the polished wood floor in a sharp, rhythmic beat. Her hands clenched at her sides, and her expression was a tempest of rage and frustration. Abdul had gone too far, and the consequences of his recklessness now weighed heavily on her shoulders. The very thought of explaining this disaster to Sir Giles made her stomach churn.

She stopped abruptly, staring out the tall windows that overlooked the sprawling grounds of Trevaunce Manor. Her reflection in the glass mirrored the storm within her. *This wasn't supposed to happen.*

Joan Summers' name echoed in her mind, bringing with it a mix of annoyance and regret. She cast her thoughts back to the day Joan had joined the coven – a seemingly insignificant addition, yet one that had set this disastrous chain of events into motion.

Joan had arrived in Cornwall after her job transfer, seeking community and kinship. During her first meeting with Fiona, she'd been polite, unassuming, and utterly ordinary in her demeanour. Fiona had nearly dismissed her outright until Joan mentioned, almost offhandedly, that her previous coven in Lancashire possessed a handwritten grimoire attributed to Zarathustra.

Fiona's interest had been piqued instantly. *Zarathustra's Grimoire – how could something so rare and powerful have remained hidden all this time?* The possibilities were tantalising. Sir Giles Worsley had been equally ecstatic when Fiona informed him. His obsession with ancient texts and magical tomes was well known, and this grimoire promised to be a crown jewel that he craved for, for his collection.

Joan had been welcomed into the coven under the guise of fellowship, but Fiona's true intentions were clear. She had subtly worked to coax the grimoire's secrets from her, questioning her about its location and the identity of her former coven's leader. At first, Joan had seemed ignorant, brushing off the inquiries with vague answers. But as Fiona's methods became more pointed, Joan revealed that she was bound by an oath of secrecy, both mundane and magical.

Joan Summers had been a stubborn anomaly in Fiona's carefully managed plans. From the moment Fiona realised Joan had ties to an elusive Lancashire coven whose Grand Master owned *Zarathustra's Grimoire*, her value had been clear. But that value had come at a cost – a cost Fiona now regretted paying.

The young woman's refusal to divulge anything meaningful, even under the psychic assaults Fiona had unleashed, was infuriating. Joan's mind had been shielded by formidable wards, likely placed by her former coven, making subtle manipulation impossible. Fiona had escalated matters during the Ostara Sabbat, calling on Abdul's expertise.

Abdul's methods were far from gentle. As the coven's enforcer and a master of psychic torment, he specialised in breaking minds with brutal precision. Locked away in the cold, damp dungeon beneath Trevaunce Manor, Joan had endured horrors beyond imagination. Abdul had conjured unearthly serpents to slither through the cell, their glowing eyes burning into Joan's soul. Shadows had taken on menacing forms, whispering vile threats that would have echoed in her ears even when she covered them.

"Tell us," Abdul's voice would hiss in her mind, weaving fear and confusion into every syllable. The air around her had often grown icy, a suffocating ambience, falling down on her chest, leaving her gasping for breath. And yet, Joan's resolve had not broken – not completely.

Fiona had trusted Abdul to extract the grimoire's secrets without killing her. But when he'd reported her lifelessness on the cold stone dungeon floor, that morning, her anger had been immediate and absolute.

Trevaunce Manor – 13 April, 3:30 PM

Fiona sat rigidly in her study, the phone clutched tightly in her hand. On the other end of the line, Sir Giles Worsley's deep voice answered her call. She braced herself for what was coming.

"She's dead," Fiona said, her voice clipped. "Abdul killed her. We've lost Joan Summers – and with her, the best chance to learn the location of the grimoire."

A sharp silence stretched across the line before Worsley spoke, his tone low and dangerous. "How, exactly, did this happen?"

Fiona swallowed hard. "He pushed too far. His methods were... excessive. I had warned him to be cautious, but he ignored me. He thought he could break her quickly, but she was too strong. Her heart gave out."

Worsley let out a sharp exhale, the crackle of frustration audible even through the receiver. "You're telling me that because of Abdul's incompetence, we've lost a vital source? A lead we've spent weeks cultivating. Do you have any idea what you've cost me, Fiona?"

"It wasn't my doing!" Fiona snapped, the rare crack in her composure slipping through. "I gave clear instructions. Abdul overstepped."

"That doesn't absolve you of responsibility," Worsley said, his voice cold and cutting. "This was your operation. You should have kept a tighter leash on him."

Fiona gritted her teeth, forcing her voice to remain calm. "She was shielded, Giles. Whatever protections her coven placed on her mind, they were unlike anything I've encountered before. Even Abdul struggled to penetrate them."

Worsley's tone turned icy. "And now those secrets are gone – buried with her in whatever pit Abdul has undoubtedly tossed her into."

Fiona hesitated, her next words careful. "Abdul suggested the old well in the woodland of the estate. It's deep, hidden. The body won't be found."

Worsley laughed, but the sound was devoid of humour. "You think I care about hiding her body? The grimoire, Fiona. That's what mattered."

"I know," she said quietly. "But I now intend to find members of her old coven in Lancashire. I have already put my team onto it. If they…"

"If?" Worsley interrupted sharply. "I don't deal with 'ifs', Fiona. Those people will talk, or they will suffer the same fate as Joan. You see to it personally and make sure Abdul understands that his leash is now very, very short."

"Understood," Fiona said, her grip tightening on the phone.

There was a pause, and when Worsley spoke again, his voice was quieter but no less menacing. "And Fiona – if you can't control your people, I'll find someone who can."

The line went dead.

Fiona sat in silence, staring at the receiver in her hand. Her anger burned white-hot, but it was laced with an unsettling undercurrent of fear. Worsley's warning was not idle. If she failed again, she wouldn't just lose her position – she might lose her life.

The thought of confronting Abdul made her stomach churn, but she had no choice. The next time she saw him, she would make him pay for his failure, ensuring he understood the consequences of neglecting to follow her orders. But right now, Fiona was left with nothing but questions and the bitter taste of failure. She needed the location of the coven in Lancashire urgently. This was now an operation she needed to manage in person.

Chapter 40
An Opportunity

Trevaunce Manor – 14 April, 9:04 PM

"Good morning, Circe. How did your self-study go yesterday?" Fiona's tone was clipped, businesslike, though her smile remained firmly in place.

Paula, suppressing her nervous energy, mustered an enthusiastic response. "Very well, thank you. Once I got used to the writing style, I started to find it quite fascinating."

"Good," Fiona said, nodding as she reached for a folder on her desk. "You'll need that curiosity to keep moving forward."

Paula watched as Fiona opened the folder, revealing neatly typed documents and a couple of photocopies of ancient-looking texts. Fiona's expression grew serious as she handed them to Paula.

"I have some bad news," Fiona said, her tone light yet firm. "I'll need to leave for a few days to attend to some urgent matters. During that time, your progress will be self-directed. I've printed off several assignments and provided additional texts for you to study."

Paula took the folder. "Of course. What do you need me to focus on?"

Fiona leaned back slightly. "Your main task will be to learn the structure of the Qabalistic Tree of Life and its correspondence to Thelemic concepts. Explore each Sephiroth and their symbolic meanings. It's critical that you understand the interconnections. Additionally, feel free to take some leisure time. Just ensure that Abdul is informed of your movements."

Paula hesitated, pretending to consider something. Then, as casually as she could, she asked, "Would it be possible for me to go up to London for a couple of days? I need to sort out some things at home and work. Looking at the long-term training plan you've outlined, I need to rationalise how I'll balance this commitment with earning a living."

Fiona's expression turned thoughtful, her head tilting slightly as she studied Paula. "You don't need to concern yourself with that," Fiona said after a moment. "You'll be compensated generously. In fact, I'll pay you a salary that exceeds what you're earning now. If you wish, I can arrange for a nursing agency position nearby to help you keep your skills sharp."

"That's incredibly generous," Paula said, feigning wide-eyed gratitude. "Thank you so much. I'd love that, but I still need to go to London to finalize everything – resign from my current job and prepare my flat for long term vacancy."

Fiona tapped her manicured nails on the desk, considering. "That seems reasonable. I cannot spare you a car, but you can take the train from Bodmin Parkway to Paddington. Abdul will arrange a car to take you to the station whenever you decide to leave. I'll let him know."

"Thank you," Paula said, allowing a relieved smile to spread across her face. "I appreciate it."

Fiona nodded dismissively. "Good luck, Circe. And don't waste the time you've been given. We'll resume the training when I return."

Paula collected the materials and left the room, her heart racing. She could hardly believe what she'd just achieved.

Paula closed the bedroom door carefully behind her, her breath coming in shallow bursts. She sank onto the edge of her bed, clutching the folder tightly.

"I can't believe it," she whispered to herself.

"You're pulling it off beautifully," James's voice said from the corner. His spectral form appeared, leaning casually against the wall. "But Fiona's no fool. She'll have eyes on you the whole time."

"I know, but I'm confident Doogie will come up with a plan to evade anyone following me. This gives me a real chance to regroup with the others, face-to-face. We can finally plan without feeling like someone's breathing down our necks."

"And that's crucial. You're deep in the lion's den, Paula. If Fiona suspects even for a moment that you're up to something, you won't get another chance."

"I'll be careful. I'll make sure everything looks perfectly normal. The other bonus to this is that Fiona won't be visiting me for a few nights."

James perused the work sheets Fiona had given her. "These look straightforward. I can help you with these in London. We may need to offer one or two alternative interpretations or an incorrect one, merely to give Fiona something that she can correct and provide guidance.

"Of course. Now let me text Doogie."

Carn View – 14 April, 10:15 AM

The living room of Carn View was quiet, the weight of Paula's latest message consuming everyone. Dougal sat at the head of the table, his fingers drumming thoughtfully against the wood. Mark and Sam exchanged worried glances, the tension in the room palpable.

"This is indeed a good opportunity," Dougal said, breaking the silence, "I can make use of the extra resources we have in London. But we can't underestimate Fiona or her people. They'll almost certainly have someone shadowing her every move."

Mark leaned forward. "I agree, so how do we make sure she gets to us without drawing suspicion?"

"We use a decoy as bait; it's standard procedure in situations like this. I'll talk to the Colonel. We have good people in London. He'll find a woman that could act as a stand-in for Paula. They would have to be dressed the same way or exchange clothing somewhere hidden from observers. Someone who looks enough like her to draw attention and lead any tails away. That will take some arrangement"

Sam's eyebrows shot up. "A decoy? You really think that could work?"

"It's not guaranteed, but it is commonly used because it invariably works well. The idea is that her tail will follow the wrong person while Paula slips away to meet us. The key is making it look natural. The decoy doesn't even have to look exactly like Paula – just enough to create confusion if they're relying on visual identification."

"So how can we improve the odds of it succeeding?"

"You can't. That's my job. You and Sam will be at Abingdon Grove. We'll make the switch in a busy area," Dougal replied. "Somewhere with lots of people – like King's Cross or Leicester Square, maybe, but Colonel Bill will sort that out. And we need to keep the meeting short, sweet and to the point, no more than an hour, because the longer the tail is on the bait, the greater the chance of something going wrong. Once done Paula will come to you."

Sam tapped her fingers on the edge of the table. "Alright, let's assume it all goes to plan, how are we all getting to London?"

"I'll drive us, Paula will make her own way by train. We'll leave first thing tomorrow morning.

"Will we have time to stop at Stonehenge?" Sam asked, hopefully.

Dougal smiled. "Okay, but not for long as it is urgent for me to get up to Smoke to sort matters out with Colonel Bill. We will arrange to get together with Paula in Abingdon Grove the following day."

"Smoke?"

"Brit Slang for London."

Mark nodded slowly. "Alright, we've got the start of a plan. But this isn't just a logistics exercise, Dougal. Paula's putting herself on the line every day. How much more can we ask of her?"

Dougal's gaze softened slightly. "As much as she's prepared to give, Mark. We all know the risks she's taking, and she's made that choice. The best thing we can do is make sure her effort counts. I'll get the Colonel working on it right away."

Dougal left the room to call his boss.

The room fell into a brief silence before Sam spoke again, her voice hesitant. "This trip will allow us to create a presence in London for our watchers."

"Good point." Mark replied. "Maybe we can have a little fun. Have a couple of nice meals out. Somewhere that serves something better than pub grub."

"That would be nice."

Dougal returned. "All arranged. The Colonel is working on it. He will leave a package with instructions in Paula's flat. Now we need to think about Arthur's visit this evening."

Mark leaned back in his chair. "We tell him the truth. He deserves to know, even if it's hard to hear."

"Do we tell him everything, though?" Sam asked. "The details? Abdul dumping the body?"

Dougal's jaw tightened, and he looked down at the table for a moment before answering. "Now we are surer of the facts, we don't sugarcoat it, but we don't need to be graphic, either. Joan was a friend, not just to Arthur, but to the people she stood for. He deserves to know the brave fight she put up right until the end."

Sam's eyes glistened, sadly. "She was brave. Even after everything they put her through, it seems she didn't break."

Mark's voice was steady. "And we let Arthur know that her death wasn't in vain. What we've learned because of her, and the details from James over security arrangements… it's given us a fighting chance to get at Worsley."

Dougal sighed, his voice quieter now. "He's going to take it hard, very hard. But Arthur's tough. He's been in this fight longer than any of us. He'll know what to do."

The three of them sat in silence for a moment, the enormity of the evening ahead settling over them. Finally, Dougal stood, his demeanour resolute. "Right. We'll meet him tonight, then get ready for London tomorrow. I need to text Paula now and tell her to get up to Smoke tomorrow with a view to meeting the following day. Now I need to carry out more surveillance of the Manor and their security teams."

Trevaunce Manor – 14 April, 2:15 PM

Paula sat at her desk, staring out of the window. The bright sunlight seemed to mock her restlessness. Everything was arranged – Abdul had agreed to have a car take her to Bodmin Parkway in the morning in time to catch the 10:31 to Paddington. Dougal was coordinating a plan for her arrival in London. But the prospect of leaving, even briefly, filled her with a mix of relief, excitement and anxiety.

Her thoughts were elsewhere, though. James's presence felt muted as if even he was weighed down. Paula turned back to the "Tree of Life" on her desk but found it impossible to focus on the Sephiroth and the rising through the spheres. Her heart wasn't in it, and neither was James'.

"One day at a time," she whispered to herself, trying to push away the unease gnawing at her.

Carn View – 14 April, 6:45 PM

Arthur Parker sat in the corner of the small living room, his head in his hands. The normally stoic man looked aged beyond his years, his face drawn and pale. Mark, Sam, and Dougal sat nearby, the weight of the moment heavy in the room.

"I still can't believe it," Arthur said, his voice breaking. "Joan… gone. And the way they treated her…" His voice trailed off, and he clenched his fists tightly.

Mark leaned forward, "We're so sorry, Arthur. Joan didn't deserve this. She was brave – she held out against them. You should know that."

Arthur looked up, his eyes bloodshot. "Just over three months ago, we met in the pub. She was full of life and inquisitiveness. She'd recently transferred here for her job, but it wasn't just work she was looking for. She told me she'd been part of a coven in Lancashire. She wanted to find one here. I tried to warn her off, telling her that the goings on at the Manor were depraved and sinister, but she was adamant."

Dougal nodded slowly. "That's how they got to her. Trevaunce Manor offered her what she was searching for, and then they used it to trap her."

Arthur's jaw tightened, his grief giving way to fury. "She was my friend, we became close. She trusted me, and I let her walk straight into their hands. Worsley, Fiona, Abdul – they'll pay for what they did to her. I'll make them pay."

His voice rose with each word, and Sam reached out to touch his arm. "Arthur," she said gently, "we understand how you feel. Believe me, we do. But you can't do anything rash. If they even suspect you're onto them…"

"They won't suspect anything," Arthur interrupted sharply. "Because I won't give them the chance. I'll take care of it myself."

Dougal leaned forward, his voice firm but calm. "Arthur, listen to me. You can't go after them – not yet. We have no proof. If you act now, they'll bury any evidence before we can use it."

Arthur shook his head. "Proof? You want proof? She's in that well, Dougal. You know it, and I know it."

"And if we can confirm that," Dougal said, his eyes locking with Arthur's, "then we'll have something real. Something that can take them down. But we must be smart about this."

Arthur's hands trembled as he looked away, his voice barely above a whisper. "She deserved better."

The group fell silent for a long moment before Mark spoke. "Dougal's right. If we're going to do this, we need to know exactly what we're walking into. That means figuring out how to get onto the estate without being seen."

Sam nodded. "We've got Paula on the inside, but she's already taking huge risks. If we can get in ourselves, even briefly, we might be able to find the well and confirm Joan's…" She hesitated, her voice faltering. "Her remains."

Arthur clenched his fists, his voice hardening. "And what happens after that? You think Worsley will just let us stroll off his property?"

"No," Dougal said firmly. "That's why we'll need a plan for exfiltration too. It's not just about finding the well – it's about getting out safely and getting what we need to expose them. I'm gathering data about their routines. I'll find a way to get in and out."

Arthur looked at each of them, his grief mingling with determination. "I hope you do it quickly, I hate sitting here talking about plans while Joan's lying in that damned well. I wish I'd stopped her from joining them."

Mark shook his head. "None of this is your fault, Arthur. Joan made her choices, just like we've made ours. What matters now is making sure her death isn't in vain."

Dougal leaned back, his voice softer but no less serious. "We'll make sure they pay, Arthur. But we do it the right way – methodically, with proof they can't sweep under the rug. Are you with us?"

Arthur's eyes burned with rage, but he nodded slowly. "I'm with you. For Joan."

As the discussion wound down, the group sat in silence, the enormity of what lay ahead settling over them. Dougal poured each of them a drink, raising his glass.

"To Joan," he said quietly.

"To Joan," the others echoed, their voices heavy with grief and resolve.

Arthur stared into his glass, his knuckles white as he gripped it. *I'll make them pay,* he thought to himself. *No matter the cost.*

Chapter 41

City Schemes

Paula's Flat, Bushey – 16 April 09:15 AM

Paula stood at the window of her flat, watching the morning sun cast its warm glow across the street below. She cradled her coffee, savouring the rare sense of calm after her journey from Cornwall. Yesterday's train ride, winding through the rolling countryside and along the rugged Devon coastline, had been a welcome reprieve. For a few fleeting hours, she had felt like an ordinary person again, not a pawn caught in the treacherous games of Worsley and his followers.

Returning to the flat in Bushey yesterday evening, had brought reality crashing back. Inside, a neatly wrapped package awaited her. It contained a scarf, and a set of elegant but understated clothes, along with detailed instructions for her task today.

As she tied the scarf carefully in place, and viewed herself in the mirror, Paula muttered to the empty room, "Well, at least they have good taste."

"Flattery for your captors?" James's words in her head, as he materialized by the door.

"More like appreciating a rare moment of comfort. You don't get much of that at Trevaunce Manor."

"True enough, but don't get too comfortable. Today isn't just about meeting the others – it's also about hoping you're one step ahead of the unseen surveillance team."

"No need to remind me about that. First things first. Now to give my notice to Watford hospital."

Abingdon Grove, London – 16 April, 1:15 PM

Mark stood near the window of the living room, looking out at the quiet street below. The faint sound of bustling traffic filtered in from the distance, but his thoughts were miles away, replaying the events of the past twenty-four hours. He turned as Sam entered the room, carrying two mugs of coffee.

"Still brooding?" she teased, handing him a mug.

"Not brooding. Just… thinking."

Sam took a seat on the armrest of the couch, cradling her mug. "About yesterday?"

"Yes. It was good to step away for a bit. Stonehenge, the dinner last night… it felt like old times."

Sam smiled warmly. "It did. I've always wanted to visit Stonehenge, but yesterday, seeing it for real was awesome."

"Shame we couldn't walk among the stones."

"I know, but we were on a tight time schedule." Sam agreed. "Just being there, imagining the rituals and history tied to that place… it was incredible."

Mark chuckled. "Dinner was the real highlight for me, though. What was the place called?"

"The Wisteria," Sam supplied. "I haven't laughed that much in ages. The waiter was obsessed with the sticky toffee pudding."

"And he wasn't wrong," Mark added. "The chicken skewers were superb, too."

They both fell silent, their shared memories hanging between them.

Mark leaned back against the sofa, wanting to continue the mood. "Thinking back to better times, like when we were students, do you recall that road trip we took to the Outer Banks?"

Sam let out a sarcastic chuckle. "How could I forget? You insisted on taking the scenic route, and we ended up completely lost in some backwater settlement. Getting lost was a common occurrence for you!"

"Hey, in my defence, I was trying to be adventurous. Besides, if we hadn't gotten lost, we wouldn't have found that tiny seafood shack by the pier."

Sam sighed, a wistful smile touching her lips. "Best crab cakes I've ever had. And that old fisherman – what was his name?"

"Ray," Mark supplied. "He had so many teeth missing we called him 'Ray Gums'. He told us he'd been catching blue crabs there for over forty years. Swore up and down that the secret to a good crab cake was just the right amount of *Old Bay* seasoning and *a whole lotta love*."

Sam laughed. "And then he tried to set me up with his grandson."

Mark grinned. "Yeah, he took one look at me and decided I wasn't worthy. Said I had 'city boy' written all over me."

"Happy days."

"Yes, they were. Back in times when things felt… simple."

Sam's smile faltered slightly, her gaze drifting to the floor. "Yeah. Before all of this. Before things got complicated."

A comfortable silence stretched between them, the significance of their shared history settling in the room.

The doorbell interrupted the mood.

"That'll be Dougal."

Sam rose to get the door.

"Paula's just behind me," Dougal said as he entered.

"How did it go?"

"Smooth as silk."

A minute later, Paula arrived, wearing a blond wig and scarf.

"Wow you look different!"

"You made it," Sam said, relief evident in her tone.

Paula removed both scarf and coat and embraced each of them in turn. "It's good to see you all."

"Where did you make the change over?"

"In TK Maxx just down the road in Kensington High Street. We used one of the changing rooms. Sue gave me her wig, and we exchanged scarves and coats which were very different, but the shoes and slacks we were wearing were identical. She really did resemble me – good job Doogie. It obviously worked."

Dougal piped up, "Sue is now walking to St. James' Park via Kensington Gardens and Hyde Park, to make it last a reasonable amount of time. We have our own eyes on her."

Sam handed Paula and Dougal their coffees. "We haven't got a lot of time. Let's talk."

They gathered around the coffee table. Paula glanced at James, who stood near the window, his gaze fixed on the street below. She took a sip of her coffee before speaking.

"James says we need to discuss a way of getting to Worsley."

Paula looked at James, who turned toward her. She relayed his words, "As discussed before, a large part of his power comes from his demon familiar Flauros. While Worsley has Flauros within him, he is invulnerable. So, the question is, how can we catch him without Flauros? Bear in mind he is still extremely dangerous without him."

Dougal broke the silence. "If Flauros isn't within him, would a bullet kill him?"

Paula replied for James. "Yes." After a pause, she continued, "During certain rituals, especially when he's granting favours to his followers, the demon exits from Worsley. Usually not far enough to take away his invincibility, but occasionally, in the excitement maybe. That's your window."

Dougal leaned back, "So, we just need to be there during one of these rituals and get a clear shot. Simple."

"Simple?" Sam arched an eyebrow. "You must take a difficult shot from over 2 miles away. What's simple about that?"

"I can do it and would do it without hesitation, now that I've seen his evil with my own eyes. Don't worry about me, I'm good at my job."

Mark spoke. "Even if we pull it off, what happens afterwards? If Flauros is there. Won't it kill everyone else?"

Paula hesitated, looking back at James. "Unlikely James says, if Worsley is dead, his demon is free from captivity and can escape back to Hell. He doesn't think he'd hang around. It may be a risk we have to take. Breaking Worsley's hold on the coven is the first step. Without him, the structure falls apart."

Dougal nodded. "He's right. Worsley's the lynchpin. Take him out, and the rest of them scatter."

Sam looked unconvinced. "And what if the opportunity to take that shot doesn't arise."

"James is concerned that too much is resting on Worsley being separated sufficiently from his demon." Paula said, "It may not happen."

Dougal answered, "Then we shouldn't rely solely on that action. We are looking for ways to infiltrate the estate undetected. If we could manage that and find proof that Joan is at the bottom of that well, we can get the police to raid it. If Worsley has the local police reluctant to act, Colonel Bill could figure out how to do that with forces outside the county."

Sam shook her head but didn't argue further. "Fine. But if we're doing this, we need a hell of a lot more than hope."

The discussion continued, but no definable, concrete plans arose.

As the clock ticked toward 2:30, Paula stood, tying her scarf back in place.

Dougal embraced her, "Remember, take the District Line from Kensington High Street. It's only four stops before St James Park. The rendezvous with Sue is at the Marlborough Gate toilets. After the switch, their eyes will be back on you."

Paula smiled, "I know Doogie, I know. I'll be careful." She gave him a peck on the cheek and moved towards the door.

Mark stepped closer, "Take care of yourself. Stay watchful."

"I always do," Paula said, smiling faintly.

Sam hugged her tightly, her voice low. "You've got this."

"She's got guts," Dougal said, watching her go.

"You can say that again!"

Sam said, "Well what happens now? We don't seem a lot further forward. Too many ifs and buts."

"Where has Miss Optimism gone?"

Dougal interrupted the banter. "We've got some things to work on. Let's concentrate on that. I have some things that need my attention with my boss, one of which is a more drastic back-up plan if things go badly wrong. I won't be travelling back to Cornwall until the day after tomorrow, so if you want to go earlier, you'll have to make your own way."

"We could take another day off in London tomorrow and go back with Dougal on Friday." Mark ventured.

Sam replied, "Paula is travelling back tomorrow by train. I don't like to think of her there all alone, but I suppose James will be there for her and she has her studies. Okay, we'll take some off time and go back with Dougal."

"Right, that's settled then." Dougal said, "I'll be off now and pick you up Friday morning."

Mark smiled, relishing the thought of free time with Sam tomorrow.

Chapter 42
Web of Deception

Clitheroe, Lancashire – 18 April, 10:20 AM

Fiona poured herself a glass of red wine and settled into the armchair by the window of her modest hotel room. The relentless rain battered against the glass, but she barely noticed. Her thoughts were consumed by the events of the previous night and the satisfaction of a mission well-executed. Tomorrow, she would leave this dreary place, spend a brief day in London, and then return to Cornwall to oversee preparations for Walpurgis Night. For now, though, she basked in the glow of her recent success.

She smiled to herself, swirling the wine in her glass. Initially she'd uncovered two covens and two leaders. *One coven leader had been a waste of her time, but Gloria…* Fiona chuckled softly. *With Gloria, she'd hit the jackpot.*

The previous night had been a masterclass in manipulation. Fiona had chosen the plushest table in the hotel bar, knowing it would provide the perfect setting for her meeting with Gloria. Her target had arrived promptly, a woman in her late forties with sharp features softened only by the lines of amusement and indulgence etched into her face.

Fiona greeted her warmly, exuding charm. "Gloria, so good of you to come. Can I get you a drink?"

Gloria hesitated briefly but nodded. "Why not? A glass of red, please."

They exchanged pleasantries over wine, Fiona deftly steering the conversation toward their shared roles as high priestesses. Gloria, at first, was cautious, but Fiona's practiced smile and charisma gradually captivated her.

"The area here must be wonderful for your coven, the history and Pendle Hill being so close by. The energy of your location must be mesmerising. I wager you have seen so much in your time," Fiona said, her tone admiring. "I can only imagine the power your coven wields in such a location and under such leadership."

Gloria flushed, clearly pleased. "We do well enough. But you told me your Grand Master is none other than Sir Giles Worsley? Now that is a man of real wealth and power."

Fiona allowed a coy smile to spread across her face. "He is truly extraordinary. His collection of rare Grimoires is unparalleled. It's an honour to serve under him."

Gloria leaned in, the wine already loosening her tongue. "I'll bet it is. Our Grand Master's no slouch, though. Simon Radcliffe – ever heard of him?"

"Simon Radcliffe?" Fiona repeated. "The name does ring a bell. Isn't he an industrialist?"

"Yes, and he's brilliant," Gloria said, her voice tinged with pride. "And rich, too. Rumour has it that he may be knighted soon."

Fiona raised her glass in a mock toast. "A knight, a warlock? That is amazing how it parallels my own order. We have so much in common Gloria." Fiona gestured to the barman. "More wine please, bring a whole bottle."

By the time they retired to Fiona's room, Gloria was thoroughly intoxicated and disarmed. Fiona had guided the conversation skilfully, leading Gloria to confirm the existence of Zarathustra's Grimoire.

"I have seen it. It is ancient and written by hand in a primeval language. Simon understands it and has used it in our Sabbats to summon and control powerful demons. He is truly masterful."

Fiona had been unable to find out the location; Gloria was not privy to that information. Radcliffe must keep it under wraps somewhere.

Later, in bed, when Gloria lay half-asleep in her arms, Fiona had hypnotized her into forgetting the entire encounter before bundling her into a taxi and sending her on her way.

That morning, Fiona had placed a call to Sir Giles from her room, eager to share her triumph. His voice crackled over the line, cool and commanding as always.

"You have exceeded yourself, my dear," Giles said after she relayed the details. "This Radcliffe... I know him. A precocious upstart, but no match for me."

"Shall I try and dig further?" Fiona asked. "Find out exactly where the Grimoire is kept?"

"No, leave that to me," Giles replied, his tone dripping with confidence. "Once Walpurgis Night is over, I'll tempt Radcliffe into a private meeting – perhaps with the promise of a substantial investment. Once I've earned his trust, I'll make him reveal the Grimoire's location himself. And then I'll destroy him."

"Your wisdom knows no bounds," Fiona said, admiringly.

"Indeed," Giles said, a faint chuckle escaping him. "My mouth is watering at the prospect. And Fiona – excellent work. You've proven your worth yet again. I have eradicated your recent blunder from my memory."

"Thank you, Giles," Fiona replied, swelling with pride.

"And how is my Circe doing? I hear she has been in London."

"Early signs are very encouraging. Yes, she went to give her notice in Watford hospital and prepare her apartment for a long absence. She was under surveillance, and nothing suspicious has been seen. She is back at Trevaunce now."

"Good!" Giles's voice took on a more deliberate tone. "Now, about Walpurgis Night," he said. "I will be coming down on the 23rd to prepare myself. My rise to Ipsissimus is at hand. This year must be unforgettable. The coven expects splendour, and I intend to deliver. I trust preparations are in hand?"

"Of course," Fiona replied smoothly. "The guest list is already curated, the invitations sent. The outer circle has been instructed to provide the necessary offerings. And for the advance rituals, the Dark Chamber is being readied as we speak."

"Good," Giles said. "I will ensure the invocation of Flauros is immaculate. I want his aura to envelop the entire gathering. They need to feel its power, to taste their insignificance before me. As the climax, I intend to summon Baal."

Fiona gasped, "Baal, the all-powerful King of Hell, Commander of Legions. To summon and control him will be totally awe-inspiring. They'll worship you Giles, as the god you are."

"And the sacrifices?" Giles asked, his tone laced with expectation.

"Handpicked," Fiona replied. "They'll stir fear and awe in equal measure."

"Perfect. When the night ends, they'll have no doubt who wields true power." Giles's voice dropped to a near whisper, dripping with menace. "Excellent. Carry on, Fiona. Failure is not an option."

As the call ended, Fiona felt her mind buzz with anticipation, each detail of the night already crystallizing in her thoughts.

Now, as she sat in her hotel room, the rain continuing its relentless downpour, Fiona allowed herself a moment to bask in her own brilliance. The night with Gloria, the conversation with Giles – it had all gone perfectly. After the Grand Sabbat, Radcliffe would fall, Worsley would claim the Grimoire, and Fiona's role in securing this victory would solidify her standing within the coven.

She raised her glass to her reflection in the window, her lips curling into a satisfied smile. "To my genius," she murmured.

This afternoon, she would leave godforsaken Clitheroe behind. London would be a necessary brief respite, but her mind was already on Trevaunce Manor and the grand spectacle of Walpurgis Night. There was so much to prepare, but for now, Fiona allowed herself to revel in the glow of her success.

Chapter 43
An Unexpected Encounter

*B*odmin Moor – 20 April, 9:15 AM
Dougal lay flat on the damp grass atop Hebdon Tor, his binoculars trained on Trevaunce Manor below. The sprawling estate was deceptively serene under the morning sun, but Dougal knew better. The perimeter was a fortress: thick fences reinforced with sensors, patrolling guards, and a surveillance network that left no corner unwatched. His jaw clenched as frustration bubbled within him. Several days of reconnaissance had yielded no viable entry point.

Mark, Sam, and Arthur were equally exasperated, their hopes dwindling. A sniper's bullet might be their only solution, but Dougal wasn't ready to concede defeat. *There must be a way in.*

Paula's recent updates hadn't provided much clarity. She reported that Abdul spent a lot of time either in the cellar or near the ancient stone circle, his movements enigmatic. Dougal had observed him making strange gestures there, but their meaning eluded him. He pushed the thoughts aside. For now, his focus was on the fence.

Slipping his binoculars into his pack, he descended the Tor, determined to search the perimeter again. He moved cautiously, his eyes scanning for patrols as he traced the fence line clockwise.

After a couple of miles trudging over uneven terrain, Dougal spotted a shallow brook. The narrow water channel went under the fence, but entry that way was denied by a roll of razor wire. He knelt by the bed of the narrow brook, studying the obstacle closely. If he could remove the wire, he might be able to crawl under the fence. He reached into his pack and donned the Kevlar gloves. He gripped the wire and tugged as hard as he could. It would not budge.

He marked the spot on his map, making a mental note to return later. Turning back, he decided to retrace his steps. Venturing further along the fence would mean pushing his luck, and the last thing he needed was an encounter with one of Worsley's patrols.

Thirty minutes later, the faint growl of an engine behind him broke the stillness. Dougal froze, his senses on high alert. Peering through his binoculars, he spotted an open ATV about two miles out, heading straight for him. Two men sat inside it, both armed.

"Damn it," he muttered, breaking into a jog. He followed the trail parallel to the fence, knowing it would intersect with the path to the Polzen Fogou, maybe his one chance of escape. The gorse bushes and jagged stones on that trail would be impossible for the ATV to navigate.

The vehicle gained on him, and the shouts of the men reached his ears.

"Stop! You there, stop!"

"Cut him off!"

"I've got him in my sights – head right!"

Dougal ignored them, pushing himself harder. The first bullet whizzed past his ear, the gunshot echoing microseconds later. He ducked instinctively, adrenaline surging as he zigzagged along the trail.

Reaching the Fogou path, he ran crouched up the narrow, twisted trail, the cover of the rocks and gorse bushes concealing him from their view. The ATV skidded to a halt, and Dougal heard the men dismount. They were shouting to each other, the sharp tones of frustration evident.

"You idiot! You dropped the radio!"

"Me? It's your fault for driving like a lunatic!"

Dougal didn't wait to hear more. He sprinted the final stretch to the fogou, hearing more gunshots as the men caught sight of him. He descended the steps and slipped into the dark passage. He pressed his back against the wall, his breathing ragged as he listened for the inevitable pursuit.

The voices of the men drew closer.

"What is this place?" one of them asked.

"Dunno. There's a sign down there."

"He must be hiding inside."

"We can't even call for backup now, thanks to you!"

Dougal suppressed a grim smile, steadying his nerves for the fight ahead. He could hear them reloading their weapons.

"You go in, Joe and check. I'll keep watch out here, in case he's not in there."

"You'd better be ready if I call for help."

"Just go."

Dougal located the concealed passage Mark had mentioned and crouched deeper into the shadows within, as Joe entered the fogou, a torch in one hand and a Glock in the other. The beam of light danced across the walls, illuminating the rough stone.

"You'd better show yourself, mate. I've got a gun and a strong desire to use it."

Outside, Wayne heard Joe's words. There was no reply.

Joe shuffled forward carefully. His torch illuminated the passage. There was a small grill at the end, but it looked far too small for anyone to get through. "There's no one here, Wayne," he called.

"Are you sure?"

"I can't see anyone, maybe he didn't come in here."

"You'd better come out then"

Joe turned back and then his torchlight revealed the side passage.

Dougal struck like lightning. Leaping from his hiding spot, he tackled Joe, the gun discharging with a deafening crack as they grappled. The confined space amplified the struggle, the sound of grunts and shuffling feet echoing off the stone walls.

"Wayne!" Joe yelled. "Get in here!"

Wayne was already running down the steps when he heard the gunshot. He burst into the fogou, his own torchlight illuminating the scuffle. He raised his weapon, aiming at the two men locked together. In fear of his life, Dougal reacted swiftly, twisting Joe into the line of fire. Wayne's shot rang out, the bullet hitting Joe squarely in the back of the head.

"No!" Wayne cried, his voice breaking. "Joe!"

Dougal didn't hesitate. Using the moment of shock, he disappeared into the concealed passage.

Wayne nervously approached Joe's body. *Where did he go?*

Suddenly the stranger came at him, seemingly emerging from a solid wall.

He never knew what hit him, as Dougal disarmed him with brutal efficiency.

Dougal pressed Wayne's own gun against his temple. "You've killed your friend, and you would have killed me. I should end you right here."

"No! Please!" Wayne begged, his voice trembling. "Let me go. I won't say anything."

Dougal barked, "Then give me information. Are the fence cameras operating?"

"No, not yet. They are tested a couple of days a week at varying times, but they will be turned on fully two or three days before the big event at the end of the month."

"How many security people are there?"

"It's just a skeleton crew normally, but a couple of days before, during and after the big event, there could be about thirty of us."

"How many shifts are there? What system do you work?"

"Generally, we work a three-shift system of eight hours, early morning starting at six am, afternoon until 10 pm, and the night shift. We work in six groups of four when at maximum strength."

"Thank you." Dougal's tone turned icy. "Here's what's going to happen. I'm keeping this gun, and your prints are all over it. If the police find Joe, they'll trace the bullet straight to you. Now, you're going to leave, and never come back. Disappear. Because if you ever show your face again, I'll finish what you started. Got it?"

"Yes!

"So go back to whatever hole you crawled out of and lay low."

"Who are you?"

"That is no concern of yours, but know this, our reach is long, very, very long." Dougal said with as much menace as he could muster. "Now scoot!" He pointed. "That way!"

The man set off skirting the fogou mound and headed across the gorse-ridden, rugged terrain in the opposite direction from the Manor. Dougal shouted after him. "Run. And don't stop."

Dougal finally breathed a sigh of relief. That could have gone a whole lot worse. He was confident he wouldn't be seeing Wayne again. He pondered disposing of Joe's body but decided to leave it where it was. With Worsley's goons scaring everyone off the moor near the Manor, it was unlikely that the fogou would receive a visit anytime soon and if it did the local police would have to deal with it.

He decided he needed to move the ATV. He went back in the fogou and searched Joe's body for a key. Nothing. He took a knife and Joe's security pass. He knew Wayne didn't have the key because he had searched him. Keeping Wayne's gun, he made his way back towards the fence.

Dougal located the ATV by the entrance to the fogou path, the key still in the ignition. He drove it about four miles, abandoning it near the fence to avoid suspicion. He wiped his fingerprints from everywhere they might have landed and then made the long trek back to the others. His mind raced with possibilities. This wasn't just a victory – it was a crack in Worsley's impenetrable façade. He grinned, though his muscles still ached, and his nerves still thrummed. He had learned a good deal about the security arrangements and gained a security pass, though he wasn't sure yet how he could use it. "Let's see how you like this turn of events, Worsley."

Chapter 44

Threads of Desperation

Bodmin Moor – 22 April, 10:30 AM

Mark pulled his jacket tighter as the chill wind swept across the moor. Carn Hwytha loomed ahead, a jagged silhouette against the overcast sky. The name, meaning "Windy Crag" in Cornish, felt apt as gusts bit into their exposed faces. Sam, a couple of paces ahead, seemed undeterred, her determined stride contrasting with Mark's more reluctant pace.

"You know," Mark called out, his voice carried away by the wind, "we could have picked a nicer day for this."

Sam stopped and turned. "And miss out on the authentic Cornish experience? Come on, where's your sense of adventure?"

"It's currently buried under layers of hypothermia and mud. Besides, I thought we were supposed to be keeping a low profile, not gallivanting up tors in plain sight."

"Relax. The only thing watching us out here are sheep and the odd pony. And maybe Dougal's paranoia."

"That's not paranoia – it's experience," Mark countered. "After what happened to him two days ago, I'm starting to think he's the only one who'll make it out of this mess alive."

Sam nodded, her tone softening. "He was lucky. If those guards had been even a little more competent…"

"Lucky and trained," Mark interrupted. "If it had been either of us, we wouldn't have made it."

The trail steepened, and both fell silent, concentrating on their footing. The climb was taxing, the rocky path slick from recent rain. Mark broke the silence as they neared the top.

"Remind me again why we're doing this?"

"Because I refuse to stay in a place called Carn View without seeing the crag it's named after," Sam replied.

Mark chuckled despite himself. "Well, let's hope the fog doesn't roll in. I'd rather not end up as one of those stories they tell about tourists who wander off and vanish into the moor."

"Ever the optimist. Remember when we got lost in the Dismal Swamp back in college? Yet another occasion you got us lost."

Mark groaned. "How could I forget? We spent the night fighting off mosquitoes the size of helicopters and praying we wouldn't stumble onto a nest of water moccasins."

"Sleeping rough hadn't been in my plans especially in an area full of wild animals! Lucky it was early summer and warm."

"I remember you being paranoid about the Black Bears attacking us. You made me come and stand sentry when you needed a pee."

"And you were so sure you knew the way out," Sam teased.

"I did know the way," Mark protested. "The ranger just happened to confirm it for me."

"A pity he hadn't shown up ten hours earlier!"

They reached the summit, clambering up the highest rock, despite the wind howling around them. Sam gazed out over the rugged expanse of Bodmin Moor, her expression softening. "It's beautiful in a harsh kind of way, isn't it?"

Mark nodded, his breath visible in the cold air. "Well, it would be if the drizzle wasn't obscuring it! We'd better head back before it turns into a full-blown storm."

"Yay! Windy Carn. We made it."

Trevaunce Manor – 11:20 AM

Fiona's heels sounded against the polished floor as she exited the library, a rare smile gracing her lips. Preparations for Walpurgis Night were progressing smoothly, and Circe – her prize student – was exceeding expectations. Fiona allowed herself a moment of satisfaction. *She truly is as special as Lilith claimed.*

The thought was a welcome distraction from the irritation of yesterday's events. Two security guards had vanished without a trace, their ATV abandoned in a remote part of the moor near the fence. Abdul had dismissed it as desertion, but Fiona wasn't so sure. Why leave the ATV miles from anywhere? She had seen fear break lesser minds before, but something about this incident felt... wrong.

"I no longer have any confidence in Abdul," she muttered under her breath, her smile fading. She had already taken precautions, advancing the arrival of additional security and ordering the activation of the fence cameras. If she could replace Abdul, she would, but she had no one else with his prowess. She could not afford another slip-up – not with Giles coming down tomorrow, earlier than usual. He must be preparing himself for something particularly special for Walpurgis Night.

Paula sat cross-legged on her bed, a pad in hand as she scribbled notes. James's ghostly form leaned against the wall, his arms crossed.

"Fiona's impressed with you That's good. It means she continues to trust you."

"She does," Paula replied. "She even praised me for my assignments – though she made a big show of pointing out the mistakes."

"That was intentional," James said. "She's asserting her dominance. But don't let it bother you. It's part of the game."

Paula glanced up. "She thinks I could make Neophyte in three months. Apparently, that's unheard of."

"It is," James admitted. "It took me almost that long, and I hold the record. But you've got an advantage – I'm teaching you."

Paula smiled. "If all goes well on Walpurgis Night, I won't need to finish the training."

"Don't count on that. Worsley's not going to let you walk away without a fight."

"He can't stop me if he's dead."

"Speaking of fights," James said, "did Fiona mention anything about Dougal's little adventure?"

Paula shook her head. "No, but she did mention increasing the security."

"Anything else?"

"She mentioned that she had some preparations to make for the advance rituals whatever they are."

"They will be rituals carried out one or two days in advance of the Sabbat to facilitate whatever Worsley is planning. He is likely to invite a select few of his inner circle to witness them."

"Would they be some of the people in the coven that attended the last esbat?"

"Oh no, these will be far more important. His inner circle would comprise close associates, business magnates, medical consultants, knights of the realm, all members of his order and adepts of some sort but at a level considerably lower than Worsley. He will have given his preferred list to Fiona to send out the invitations."

"Where will these rituals be carried out?"

"Probably in the aptly named Ritual Room in the North Wing, or maybe the Dark Chamber in the cellar."

Paula shivered as memories of Joan resurfaced. She went back to her studies

Bodmin Moor – 11:40 AM

The rain started as Mark and Sam descended Carn Hwytha. At first, it was a light drizzle, but by the time they reached the trailhead, it had turned into a steady downpour. They quickened their pace, their laughter cutting through the gloom as they recounted old stories.

"This reminds me of the time you tried to start a fire with wet wood," Sam teased.

Mark grinned. "I was trying to keep us alive! Besides, it worked – eventually."

"After two hours and a whole bottle of lighter fluid."

They reached their lodgings at Carn View, soaked but in good spirits. Dougal met them at the door, his expression serious.

"Enjoy your walk?" he asked.

"Windy, wet, and freezing," Mark replied. "The full Cornish experience."

Dougal smiled. "Good. We're all going to need to be sharp. Paula's intel suggests something big is happening at the manor."

Sam's smile faded. "What? You mean something other than the Great Sabbat?"

Dougal's eyes darkened. "Unsure. Possibly gatherings before Walpurgis Night. Worsley is coming down tomorrow. Paula will provide further information when she gets anything. I've already noticed that the fence cameras are now operating full time, which makes it more difficult for me to patrol. I'll need to find a back way up to Hebdon Tor that's out of sight from the cameras. Whatever, we need to ensure we're ready for any opportunity that may arise."

Sam and Mark looked at one another resignedly as their mood became downcast.

Carn View – 22 April, 6:30 PM

Rain pattered against the windows, a persistent background noise as Dougal, Mark, and Sam gathered around the small wooden table. Arthur Parker sat opposite them, his hands gripping the edges of the chair. His face was lined with exhaustion, but his eyes burned with impatience.

Dougal leaned back, his expression as cool as ever. "We've confirmed what we suspected. Security around Trevaunce Manor has increased significantly. Cameras have been activated on the perimeter, and patrols have been increased significantly, since my… encounter."

Arthur's jaw tightened. "The encounter where two guards vanished, you mean."

"Correct. They won't be coming back."

"You're lucky they didn't kill you," Arthur snapped. "If they had, we wouldn't be sitting here discussing it."

"Luck had little to do with it," Dougal replied calmly. "Planning, training, and a bit of improvisation – those are what kept me alive."

Arthur snapped. "This isn't a game, Dougal. We're hanging by a thread, and you're testing its strength."

Dougal met Arthur's gaze without flinching. "And every move I make is calculated to keep that thread from snapping. I don't take unnecessary risks."

Sam cleared her throat, trying to ease the tension. "Arthur, we all know the risks. Dougal's right – his actions bought us valuable intel. We wouldn't have known about the cameras or the security arrangements otherwise."

Mark nodded in agreement. "But it's not just the security we need to worry about. Paula's reports suggest something is happening at the manor before the Sabbat. Worsley's not just waiting for Walpurgis Night – he's planning something prior to that."

Arthur's fingers tapped against the chair, his voice sharp. "And what exactly do we know about these 'events'? Anything concrete, or just more speculation?"

Dougal leaned forward, his voice low and precise. "Based on Paula's observations, Worsley's conducting preparatory rituals. James thinks that he is planning rites to strengthen his prowess for the main event. These will likely take place in the Manor, rather than the Stone Circle. Either in the space called the Dark Chamber or in the chamber known as the Ritual Room. These aren't minor ceremonies – they will have an audience of members of Worsley's order, his inner circle. They will be ceremonies to make the Sabbat even more potent."

Arthur shook his head; frustration etched into his features. "Guessing doesn't help us. We need access, a way to get in."

Dougal grimaced. "Security is very tight. The place seems impassable for now. Maybe surveying how the people accessing the gates for the additional rituals will expose some weaknesses that we can exploit."

Sam placed a hand on Arthur's arm, her voice softer. "We're all frustrated, Arthur. But Dougal's right – this isn't easy. Worsley's no fool. He's built that place to be impenetrable."

Arthur exhaled. "It's just… Joan gave everything to uncover the truth, and now she's gone. I can't let that be for nothing."

"We won't," Mark said firmly. "But rushing in without a plan will only get us killed."

Dougal spread a map of the estate across the table, pointing to key locations. "These are the areas Paula has identified as hotspots. The Dark Chamber is here, beneath the east wing. The stone circle which we know will be the site of the Sabbat, is on the north side, on the moor about half a mile beyond the gardens on that side. The ritual room is in the North Wing on the first floor. Guards are patrolling the exterior of the house and the route to the stone circle every 20 minutes."

"And what about Paula?" Arthur asked. "How is she doing?"

Sam glanced at Dougal, then back to Arthur. "She's holding up, but it's obviously taking a toll. She's noticed heightened tension among the staff – everyone appears on edge. She's getting on well with Fiona who been praising her work."

Arthur's lips thinned. "She remains in danger."

"She knows that and is aware of the risks." Dougal said. "And she's our only chance of finding out what's happening before the Sabbat."

Arthur's voice rose. "Our best chance of killing Worsley is to get inside."

Dougal's gaze hardened. "I agree but we can't risk discovery. We need to find out if there are any parts of the grounds which are not patrolled. Maybe Paula or James can find out. Then we can create an infiltration plan and maybe lay low and await our chance."

Mark interjected. "There must be more we can do. Sitting here while Paula's risking everything – it doesn't feel right."

Dougal's reply was sharp. "You think I like waiting? You think I don't want to act? This isn't about what feels right – it's about what works."

Sam held up a hand, her voice steady. "Enough. We're all on edge, but fighting among ourselves won't help. Let's focus on what we can control."

Dougal tapped the map again. "Maybe the traffic going in for these additional rituals will distract the guards enough for one of us to sneak in using the security pass I took during my skirmish."

Arthur frowned. "What security pass?"

Sam explained, "Dougal took it from the body in the Fogou."

"That is our way in," Arthur cried.

"Yes, but only one of us can use the card. So, who should it be?" Sam posed. "That is the question."

Dougal answered. "If the person chosen fails then that chance is blown. We must also think of back-up plans. One of the plans is for me to shoot Worsley with a sniper's rifle from 2 miles away. Only I can do that, which disqualifies me from using the pass. That leaves Mark and Arthur."

"What about me?" Sam cried, "I can do it."

Mark cried, "Realistically, it must be a man, in case of an altercation. We are stronger. It must be me!"

"No, it must be me! It must be me to avenge Joan." Arthur insisted.

Dougal looked grave. "Before we make that decision, we need to gather what information we can from James and Paula. The date of the prior ritual and the areas free from patrol if any. I suggest we end the meeting now until we know more."

Mark sighed, leaning back in his chair. "This is like playing chess with a blindfold on."

"And Worsley's the one controlling the board," Arthur added bitterly.

Sam leaned forward, her voice filled with quiet determination. "Then we need to change the game."

Dougal's face softened, a rare flicker of approval crossing his face. "That's the spirit. We'll figure it out."

Chapter 45

Fractured Plans

Trevaunce Manor – 24 April, 10:30 AM

Paula sat cross-legged on the edge of her bed, her phone in hand as she typed out a message to Doogie. The room was quiet, save for the faint hum of activity from the hallways beyond. Although Fiona had visited her again last night, she was becoming increasingly preoccupied with preparations for Walpurgis Night, leaving Paula with more freedom to observe and gather information. Her morning sessions with Fiona were shorter and less intense, though no less dangerous.

James's translucent figure stood by the window. "It's risky sharing everything you know," he said. "Fiona's not a fool, and if she catches on… "

"I know the stakes, James. But they need this information. Worsley arrived last night. The Rite of Veil Severance is happening at midnight on the 28th. That may give them a chance to get inside."

She hit 'send' and sighed. "If Worsley succeeds in summoning one of the most powerful demons in Hell, who knows what might happen."

"He's playing with forces even he can barely control. But you're right – if they can get inside the gate, the woodland by the well is their best shot to camp out to avoid detection. No patrols, no cameras, only the occasional sweep near the fence. I'm not sure what they can do, though, even if successful."

"Let's hope Doogie and the others can pull something off."

Carn View – 11:00 AM

The atmosphere was heavy as Dougal read Paula's message aloud. The tension that had settled over them in recent days was momentarily lifted by the prospect of actionable information.

"Well," Mark said, leaning back in his chair, "at least we've got something concrete now. The woodland – it's our shelter if we get in."

Sam nodded, though her expression was troubled. "Yes, but security may be tighter now that Worsley is in residence. Also, four days isn't much time to prepare. We'll need to work something out fast."

Dougal, however, wasn't listening, he was making notes. He finished and, rising abruptly, went to the cupboard under the stairs, to add the paper to the box containing their critical tools and notes. He pulled the box out.

The moment he lifted it, his stomach dropped. Something was wrong. The box was too light. "No," he muttered, yanking off the lid. "Damn, I knew it! The stupid idiot."

"What is it?" Sam asked, her voice sharp.

Dougal's face was grim as he held up the box. "The gun and the security pass – they're gone."

"What do you mean, gone?"

"Arthur," Dougal said, his voice tight with anger. "He must have taken them while we were out yesterday. I trusted him too much."

Sam's face paled. "Arthur? But… why would he – "

"Because he's grieving, and grief makes people reckless," Dougal snapped, slamming the box onto the table. "You saw how impatient he was at our last meeting; he wants to accelerate matters. If he's caught, if he's interrogated – he knows everything. This isn't just about him anymore."

"This is a disaster," Mark muttered. "If Worsley's people find him first…"

"Then the game's up," Dougal finished grimly. "We must find him – asap."

"How?" Sam asked, her voice trembling. "He could be anywhere."

Dougal exhaled slowly, forcing himself to think. "The locals. He might have talked to someone, leaving a trail. I'll check the pub and ask around."

"We'll come with you, you'll cover more ground with the three of us."

Dougal hesitated but nodded. "Fine. But we need to be careful. We will be increasing the risk of being exposed. If Worsley's team is looking for him too, we can't draw attention."

The Prince of Wales, Nansebyn – 12:05 PM

At the pub Mark and Sam were at a corner table, their lunch ordered as they engaged an elderly couple seated nearby.

"He's a friend of ours," Mark explained, showing them a picture of Arthur on his phone. "He's been under a lot of stress and might've wandered into town."

The woman shook her head apologetically. "I'm sorry, love. Haven't seen him."

The man frowned. "Come to think of it, I saw someone like that up near the old church yesterday evening. But he didn't stop to talk."

Mark's heart leapt. "Thank you. That helps."

At the bar, Dougal was having less luck. He avoided the landlord, remembering Arthur saying that he might be a coven member, but everyone else he approached either claimed not to know him or they hadn't seen him.

Mark and Sam's lunch arrived as they gestured to Dougal with a shake of the head.

◄◄◄ ►►►

Ned Jago watched them. They were searching for Parker. He decided to call the Manor and let them know something was amiss.

Trevaunce Manor – 2:30 PM

Paula paced her room as James floated beside her. She had relayed the situation to him, and now they were waiting.

"I don't understand why Arthur would do this," Paula said, her voice tight. "He knows how dangerous Worsley is."

"He's driven to avenge Joan." James replied. "He's unable to think straight. You had better pray he doesn't get caught."

Paula stopped and faced him. "Can you find him? On the astral plane?"

James nodded. "I can try. But if he's close to Trevaunce Manor, it won't be easy. I don't want to be detected by Worsley or Abdul. Also, the pull for me to move up through the spheres is getting much stronger and more difficult to resist."

"Please, James," Paula said softly. "He's not just putting himself in danger – he's putting all of us at risk."

James's gaze softened. "I'll do what I can. But Paula… if I find him, it might already be too late."

Paula closed her eyes, her hands clenching into fists. "We can't let that happen."

Carn View – 4:00 PM

Dougal returned to the cottage, his expression grim. "The locals know something – they just won't talk. If Arthur's anywhere near the manor, he's gone dark. I went to his house but there's no sign of life there. He's not been staying there to avoid Worsley's heavies."

Mark leaned forward. "So, what do we do now?"

Dougal sat heavily in a chair, his gaze distant. "We keep searching. And we pray we're not too late."

Trevaunce Manor – 4:00 PM

The heavy oak doors of the library closed behind Fiona as she entered. Worsley stood by the grand stone fireplace, the flames casting flickering shadows over his sharp features. He held a glass of brandy in one hand, his expression unreadable but his eyes cold and calculating.

Fiona crossed the room, her heels clicking softly against the polished floor. "Ned Jago at the Prince of Wales has reported that there have been three persons making inquiries about Arthur Parker. Two of them were Americans."

Worsley turned, a faint sneer tugging at the corner of his mouth. "Americans, you say?" He swirled the brandy in his glass thoughtfully. "That can only mean one thing – Mark and Sam Benedict."

Fiona nodded. "It does seem likely. We were worried that they might be up to something, but if it is them and they are here in Cornwall, they must be planning something."

"Of course it's them, and if they are asking after Parker, they may know about Joan Summers. Persistent little pests, aren't they?" Worsley mused, his tone laced with disdain. "And reckless, too. They've walked right into our net."

"Reckless or desperate. Either way, they've overstepped. There was another man with them. What do you propose we do?"

Worsley downed the rest of his brandy in one smooth motion and set the glass down on the mantle. He turned to face her fully, his eyes alight with dark intent. "We bring them in. I want them here in the dungeon tomorrow. They will rue the day they came after me. See to it."

Fiona raised an eyebrow. "That may be risky. People may see something."

"Not if it's done correctly," Worsley replied. "Make sure Abdul ensures their extraction is swift and silent. Once we have them in the dungeon, they'll have plenty of time to lament their condition."

"Abdul's recent history does not inspire confidence."

"Agreed, but he is adept at unearthing the truth. We'll soon know what they've uncovered, who they've spoken to, and what they plan to do next. Torture is a pleasure for him,"

Fiona's smile turned colder. "And when they've outlived their usefulness, we kill them?"

"That can wait until Walpurgis night" Worsley said, his voice dropping to a menacing whisper. "The Sabbat on Walpurgis Night requires a sacrifice of a unique nature. Mrs. Benedict will make a fitting offering before joining her husband in hell."

Fiona's brows furrowed slightly. "What about her brother-in-law?"

"I want him to witness everything, make him suffer, before I consign him to hell also."

"We must make sure they last until then. Abdul's methods can be… extreme. Look what he did to Joan."

"Then make sure he does not overdo it. Their suffering must be controlled, prolonged, and deliberate. I want them to serve their final purpose."

"Very well. I'll inform Abdul and have the necessary preparations made. How do you wish to handle the third unknown person and Parker?"

Worsley waved a dismissive hand. "Ah yes, the man of mystery who is presumably helping them. When we get him, we kill him. As for Parker, let him run. If he's foolish enough to show his face near the manor, he'll be dealt with accordingly. For now, the Benedicts must be our priority."

Fiona stepped closer, her voice lowering. "What about Circe? She'll be aware something is happening when they're brought in."

"I don't see her as a threat at present; she is not connected to them, and she is showing great promise under your tutelage. Keep her close, keep her engaged. Her reaction to their capture will be a test of her loyalty."

Fiona nodded, her smile returning. "Consider it done. By tomorrow, they'll be in the dungeon, and the game will be ours to play."

Worsley turned back to the fire, his voice a low murmur. "Walpurgis Night will surpass anything I have ever done. My journey to Ipsissimus will be close to complete."

Chapter 46

Inside the Devil's Lair

Nansebyn, 25 April – 2:15 PM

The spring afternoon in Nansebyn was unusually quiet and a little chilly. Mark and Sam walked side by side, their footsteps echoing faintly on the road as they returned from a late lunch at the Miners' Diner. Despite their best efforts to maintain a light-hearted conversation, their frustration was palpable.

"This whole thing feels like chasing smoke," Mark said, shoving his hands into his jacket pockets. "Arthur's vanished, Dougal's out on the moor trying to avoid cameras, and James hasn't found anything on the astral plane."

Sam sighed, her brow furrowed. "I know. But we can't just give up. If Arthur's out there, we must find him. He might still… "

Her words were cut off by the sudden roar of an engine. A black van sped past them, its tires screeching as it came to a halt just ahead. The doors burst open, and three heavyset men leaped out, their movements rapid and predatory.

"Run, Sam!" Mark shouted, instinctively grabbing her arm.

But it was too late. One of the men had already reached her, yanking her back with terrifying force. Sam screamed, kicking and clawing at her captor, her nails raking across his face.

"Let me go, you brute!" she yelled, twisting in his grip.

Mark turned to help her, only to be met by another man charging at him. He ducked the initial swing and countered with a solid punch to the attacker's jaw, sending him stumbling backward. For a moment, Mark thought he had the upper hand, but the third man tackled him from the side, driving him into the ground. The impact knocked the wind out of him, leaving him gasping and disoriented.

Sam's cries grew more frantic as she was dragged toward the van. She managed to land a kick to her assailant's shin, but he barely flinched, shoving her inside with brute force. Mark struggled to get up, but before he could, the man standing over him produced a handgun. The cold metal of the barrel pressed against Mark's temple.

"Stay down," the man growled, his voice low and menacing.

Mark glared up at him, defiance flickering in his eyes. "Go to hell."

The man grinned and pistol-whipped him across the side of his head. Pain exploded in Mark's skull, and the world spun as he was hoisted up and thrown into the van like a ragdoll. He landed hard on the metal floor beside Sam, who was still struggling against her restraints.

The engine of the van snarled to life, jolting them into motion. The metal floor vibrated beneath them, each bump in the road sending a jarring shock through the frame of the vehicle. It smelled of oil, damp earth, and fear.

One of the kidnappers sat directly opposite, his legs braced, a handgun resting on his thigh. He said nothing – just watched them. His eyes were flat and cold, offering no hint of conscience. His silence was more unsettling than any threat.

Mark groaned, lifting a trembling hand to the side of his head. Blood streaked his fingers. The cut was shallow but angry. "Are you okay?" he asked, turning to Sam, his voice unsteady.

Sam nodded, but barely. Her breathing was shallow, her body rigid. "I… I think so," she whispered, voice cracking. "Jesus, Mark. What is this? Who are they?"

Mark leaned back, exhaling through clenched teeth. "Worsley," he said. "It has to be. He's finally making his move."

Sam's eyes were wide, her expression caught somewhere between shock and disbelief. She stared at their captor. "Where are you taking us?" Her voice was louder than she intended – too loud. It echoed in the metal shell of the van.

The man didn't blink. Nothing. Zilch.

"Please," she said, more softly now, a tremor slipping through. "Just tell us. What is this?"

Silence.

Mark tested the zip ties digging into his wrists. Pain flared, sharp and immediate. "Trevaunce Manor," he said with grim certainty. "That's where he'll be."

Sam shook her head, her jaw tight as tears welled but didn't fall. "He wants to finish what he started. Or worse."

Mark looked at her, steadying his voice. "We'll get through this."

Sam swallowed, nodding once, though her hands were clenched tight in her lap. "We have to."

The van hit a bump, throwing them both slightly off balance. Sam winced as her shoulder collided with the metal wall. "Do you think Dougal will figure out we're missing?"

"He will," Mark said, his voice steady. "And when he does, he'll make Worsley regret ever laying a hand on us."

The guard shifted slightly, his grip tightening on the gun as if in response to the mention of Worsley's name.

Mark caught the subtle movement and narrowed his eyes. "What's the matter? Nervous your boss won't be happy if we show up a little worse for wear?"

Still, the man said nothing.

"We need to stay calm. If we panic, they win."

"Calm. Right. Just another day in paradise." Sam muttered with a bravado that she didn't feel.

The van slowed. Mark and Sam exchanged a glance, their faces a mixture of fear and determination. "We must be coming to the manor gates," said Mark. The van came to a halt. They could hear muffled voices before the van moved again.

As the van came to a stop once more, the rear doors were flung open, revealing two more armed men waiting outside. The guard inside gestured with his gun. "Out. Now."

Mark and Sam hesitated, but the guard's patience wore thin. He grabbed Mark by the collar and yanked him to his feet, shoving him toward the exit. Sam followed, her movements stiff but defiant.

The towering silhouette of the manor loomed above them, its darkened windows like unblinking eyes watching their approach. The cold breeze slapped their faces, as they were marched toward the manor's entrance. Mark's gaze flicked to the guards around them, calculating, searching for any weakness. But for now, resistance was impossible.

As they were led through the grand doors of Trevaunce Manor, Mark glanced at Sam and whispered, "This isn't over."

Her eyes met his, "Not by a long shot."

Carn View – 5:15 PM

Dougal walked into the barn, his boots leaving muddy tracks on the worn slat floor. The emptiness of the place struck him immediately – Mark and Sam were gone. He checked the kitchen and the bedrooms, hoping for a note or any clue to their whereabouts, their belongings were still there, but the house was silent and still.

He pulled out his phone, his mind racing. Had Worsley got them? Or were they just out on a walk?

Fingers trembling slightly, Dougal grabbed his laptop from the bedroom and opened the tracking software linked to their phones. The screen loaded slowly, the seconds dragging like hours. When the location finally appeared, his worst fears were confirmed.

"They're in Trevaunce Manor," he muttered, his voice hollow. He gathered his thoughts. He listed immediate actions in his head. *Tell Paula and the Colonel.*

A wave of frustration washed over him. First Arthur, now Mark and Sam. What could go wrong next? Were they on their way here to get him? He quickly typed out a message to Paula: *Mark and Sam have been taken. They are in the Manor.*

Dougal sat back for a moment. There was no time to waste. He needed to get out of the property as soon as possible. He systematically surveyed the barn and grabbed whatever materials might provide any incriminating information. As he loaded everything in the Jeep, he called his boss and explained the situation in terse sentences. "I'm leaving now," he said finally.

After hanging up, Dougal was already planning his next move. His stash of equipment on Hebdon Tor was well concealed and monitored by a remote camera. That could be left until his return. As he climbed into the Jeep, his phone buzzed with a reply from Paula: *They are here. James saw them in the cellar dungeon. What now?*

Dougal hesitated, the elements of the situation pushing down on him. He texted back: *Stay where you are. Stay calm. Treat as if nothing has happened.*

Going to London to meet with the Colonel and grab extra equipment. Be back soon.

Trevaunce Manor – 6:10 PM

Paula sat in her room, her hands clenched into fists. Her mind raced, replaying Dougal's message over and over. Mark and Sam are here. In the cellar dungeon.

James's presence beside her did little to calm her nerves. The ghostly figure hovered near the window, his expression grim. "You need to keep your composure," he said. "If Fiona or Worsley suspect anything, this will spiral out of control totally."

"Easier said than done," Paula whispered, her voice shaking. "They've got your wife and brother. How am I supposed to act normal?"

James stepped closer, his translucent form flickering faintly. "Because your resilience runs deeper than you think. You've come this far. I, we all believe in you."

Paula blinked back tears, forcing herself to breathe. "I don't see how this ends well, James. Everything we've worked for is falling apart."

"Not yet," James replied. "But you're the key now. Keep your eyes open. Stay close to Fiona. If they make a mistake, we'll need to tell Dougal."

Paula nodded, though her heart felt like it was being crushed.

The Cellar Dungeon – 7:30 PM

Mark and Sam sat slumped, side-by-side, against the cold, damp stone wall of the dungeon, they were each shackled with leg irons and a chain connected to cast iron rings set into the wall. Fortunately, their chains were sufficiently long for them to comfort one another with a hug.

"Could be worse," Mark murmured, his voice strained. "At least we're not naked."

Sam gave a weak chuckle despite the situation. "Not yet. Give them time."

Their attempt at humour faltered as the dungeon gate creaked open, the sound echoing ominously in the confined space. Abdul entered first, his expression as impenetrable as ever. Two guards flanked him, their faces hard and cold. Behind them came Worsley and Fiona, the former exuding arrogant, sadistic energy.

Worsley's lips twisted into a cruel smile. "Ah, Mr. Benedict and the Widow Benedict. What a pleasure to have you as our guests."

"The pleasure's all yours, you monster!" spat Sam, her voice dripping with venom.

Worsley chuckled, shaking his head. "Do you really think your petty schemes could deceive me? You are pathetic, both of you. And now, you will suffer most horribly."

Mark leaned forward as far as his restraints would allow, his eyes blazing. "Do your worst. You won't break us, you pompous bastard."

Fiona smiled but said nothing, standing a step behind Worsley with her arms crossed.

Worsley's smile grew colder. "Oh, I will do my worst. Tonight, you will be visited by the most depraved entities, summoned by my faithful Abdul under Fiona's guidance. They will tear at your sanity, reduce you to trembling shells of your former selves. And yet, you will survive this night and the next three after that. Only on Walpurgis Night will I finally grant you release – by offering your lives to the infernal."

"You're a coward," Mark growled, his voice low but full of venom. "A pathetic excuse for a man. But know this – I'm going to kill you."

Worsley's expression darkened, though his smile remained. "Such audacity. But you're mistaken, Mr. Benedict. You will not kill me. By the end of this, you will beg for death. And before that, you will tell Abdul the name and whereabouts of the man helping you."

"You'll get nothing from us, you beast!" Sam shouted defiantly.

Worsley chuckled, turning to Fiona. "They have such spirit. It will be all the more satisfying to watch it crumble."

Fiona nodded slightly but said nothing, her cold gaze lingering on Mark and Sam. Worsley gave a mocking bow before turning and leaving the dungeon, Fiona following silently. Abdul and the guards checked their chains thoroughly, before exiting and locking the dungeon door. Abdul's malevolent gaze was upon them, menacing. "Until later." He turned and left them.

Unseen, James descended into the dungeon, his spectral form tense with fury. His heart ached at the sight of Mark and Sam shackled and helpless, but his presence had to remain undetected, and he could not afford the risk of Worsley detecting him.

"I won't let this happen," James murmured to himself.

Moving quickly, he began inscribing protective runes in a semicircle round their positions that should prevent anything reaching them. Though invisible to mortal eyes, the marks shimmered faintly with energy, forming a barrier against any of the infernal creatures that Abdul intended to summon. As he worked, James whispered incantations, his voice steady despite the turmoil inside him.

When he finished, he stepped back, his gaze fixed on Mark and Sam. "You're not alone," he whispered. "Not while I'm here."

Chapter 47
Night Terrors

Trevaunce Manor – 26 April, 1:30 AM

Mark and Sam lay on the cold dungeon floor, their legs shackled to the rings on the wall. Two flaming torches on the stone walls provided a dim sinister light. Earlier, they had been given meagre rations of bread and cheese and a bottle of water each. Mark had suggested that they eat something but Sam, dreading the unknown horrors that lay ahead, had no appetite.

"Why hasn't it started yet?" Sam asked.

"It has." Mark said icily. "The surroundings, the waiting, the dreaded anticipation is all part of the torture process. It won't be long before Abdul's unearthly horrors appear."

"I almost wish it would start. I can't stand this delay much more."

"Be strong Sam, it will soon."

Moments later, Sam shivered. "Mark, it's freezing."

Mark's breath fogged the air as he felt the sinister chill creep down his spine. "It's starting!"

They scrambled to their feet, their chains clinking against the stone wall. Mark put his arm round her waist, gripping her tightly as the air grew colder still. The flickering torchlight dimmed, and shadows began to stretch and move of their own accord. Sam pressed closer to Mark, her hand gripping his.

"I'm here, I'm with you" Mark whispered. "Stay strong."

An arctic wind began to form and howl as it increased but, strangely, it wasn't lashing at them. It was as if they were in the eye of a storm. The shadows were writhing around breaking into small impish faces. Sam was trembling. Mark gave her a reassuring squeeze.

The whirling storm suddenly ceased, and an unnatural ice-cold stillness settled on the dungeon. The contrast with the raging winds before was eerie and unsettling, the atmosphere ominous.

Seconds ticked by and then they heard a squelching sound; something unseen outside the dungeon was approaching. A stench of decay began to fill their jail. The wet sucking sound got nearer, and then they saw it, a terrible amorphous, amoeba-like blob was approaching the dungeon gate. Sam gasped and reeled, forcing Mark to hold her up. The thing was massive. A cold perspiration broke out on Mark's face as the horror stopped outside the gate. Then it oozed towards them as it flowed through the bars, leaving a slimy luminescent trail in its wake.

It reeked of corruption and putrefaction, its rippling form radiating waves of hellish balefulness. Its pale olive, clammy skin was covered with pustules and sores that oozed foul smelling liquid. Mark gagged and Sam stifled a scream as it got nearer. Mark began chanting the Lord's Prayer and Sam joined him. "Our Father who art in heaven… "

The immense, slimy slug halted and screamed in defiant rage, before edging forward closer and closer. They both knew horror like never before, trembling in fear of their very souls. "Continue the prayer," cried Mark. They continued their chant, but though the monstrosity flinched and raged, it continued its slow progress towards them. Suddenly about 6 feet from them it halted, twisting and screaming in fury. It ranted and raged in frustration for a few seconds more before fading and dematerialising before their eyes.

Sam collapsed to her knees, sobbing. "What was that?" she managed to choke out.

Mark knelt beside her, his face pale and drenched with sweat. "I don't know," he said, his voice hollow. "But we survived it."

A menacing silence reigned once again, and the dungeon began to lose its frosty chill. Sam was weeping softly, and Mark was visibly shaken. They stood and hugged each other.

"What stopped it reaching us?"

"Saying the Lord's Prayer? That slimy thing did not like that. I have never been so terrified in my life."

"Me neither, I agree the praying undoubtedly slowed it down, but it still came forward. Something else stopped it."

"Thank God!"

A few minutes later, the dungeon air chilled again, the frost on the stone walls thickening until it looked like a thin coating of ice. Sam shivered violently, her breath visible in the dim torchlight. The oppressive stillness was shattered by a clicking sound – sharp, rhythmic, and unnervingly close. It echoed from the shadows, bouncing off the walls and amplifying into a chorus of sinister taps.

Mark's grip on Sam's hand tightened. "Stay close," he muttered. His eyes darted around the room, searching for movement, but the clicking came from everywhere at once.

Then it began to take shape.

The shadows near the centre of the dungeon floor twisted and writhed, pulling together like strands of dark silk. Legs emerged first – long, jagged, and impossibly thin. The creature rose, its body bloated and glistening with an oily sheen. Mark sucked in a sharp breath as the spider-like entity revealed itself fully, standing nearly six feet tall, its mandibles clicking in a grotesque rhythm.

Sam stifled a scream, her knees buckling as the creature scuttled toward them with terrifying speed before stopping abruptly. Its eight glowing red eyes fixed on them, unblinking and malevolent.

"What… what is that?" Sam whispered, her voice shaking.

Mark swallowed hard, his pulse pounding in his ears. "It doesn't matter. Just stay behind me."

In the corner of the dungeon, James watched with mounting dread. The spider's arrival radiated an aura of malevolence that sent ripples through the invisible barrier he had painstakingly created. The glowing runes etched into the floor flickered faintly, struggling against the harsh energy emanating from the creature.

"It's testing the boundary," James muttered to himself, his spectral form shimmering faintly as he focused his energy. The barrier trembled under the spider's probing, its legs tapping against the invisible wall with maddening precision.

James extended his hands, his translucent fingers glowing faintly as he reinforced the sigils. "Not today, you bastard," he growled under his breath. Sweat beaded on his astral brow as the effort of maintaining the barrier took its toll.

The spider hissed, its mandibles clicking rapidly as it lunged at the invisible barrier. Mark and Sam recoiled instinctively as the impact sent visible ripples through the air. The glowing runes on the walls flared brightly for a moment before dimming again, the strain evident.

Sam clutched Mark's arm, her voice trembling. "It's going to get through!"

"Not if I can help it," Mark said, though his voice betrayed his fear. He instinctively shifted in front of Sam, his muscles tense as though he could somehow stop the monstrous creature with sheer willpower.

The spider lunged again, its long legs scraping against the invisible wall, each strike creating an ear-splitting screech. Black ichor dripped from its mandibles, sizzling as it hit the stone floor. The torches in the room flickered wildly, the shadows stretching and contorting as if alive.

James redoubled his efforts, his voice a low murmur as he chanted incantations to strengthen the barrier. The spider shrieked in frustration, its body convulsing as it pushed harder against the invisible boundary. The runes dimmed further, flickering dangerously as cracks began to spiderweb through the barrier.

"It's so strong, could it be a Saiitii?" James whispered to himself, his hands trembling as he poured every ounce of energy he had, into holding the line. "Come on… just hold…"

The spider reared back, its legs twitching erratically before it let out a piercing screech. It lunged with all its weight, slamming into the barrier with a force that shook the entire dungeon. The runes flared one last time, then dimmed almost to the point of extinction.

Mark's breath caught as the creature loomed closer, its massive body pressing against the barrier. "This is it," he muttered, his voice tight, his terror great. "This is how it ends."

The creature stopped. It hissed and reared back again, but the barrier, though faint, held firm. James let out a relieved sigh, his form shimmering as he leaned against the wall. "It's holding… just barely."

The monstrous spider screeched in fury, its legs slamming repeatedly against the invisible wall. It convulsed violently, black smoke seeping from its joints and mandibles. The smoke coiled and writhed before dissipating into the air, taking the spider's grotesque form with it.

As the creature vanished, the room fell deathly silent, save for the ragged breathing of Mark and Sam.

Mark and Sam collapsed to the ground, their bodies trembling uncontrollably. Sam was crying, her tears mixing with the sweat on her face. Mark sat beside her, his chest heaving as he tried to steady his breathing.

"What… what the hell was that?" Sam managed to choke out between sobs.

Mark shook his head. "I don't know. But whatever it was… it's gone now."

"I don't think I can take any more of this."

"Hopefully there will be no more this night."

As Sam continued weeping uncontrollably, Mark held her trying to comfort her. "Let it all out Sam. No matter what, we'll overcome this." His own confidence was shattered; he was unsure whether he could last another night.

⋘ ⋙

In the corner, James's form flickered weakly as he surveyed the room. The runes were nearly extinguished; the barrier stretched to its limits. "This won't hold again," he muttered to himself. "Not against a Saiitii or even worse. I need to find another way?"

He turned to look at Mark and Sam, his expression pained. "Hold on. Just hold on."

⋘ ⋙

An hour later, the iron door creaked open, and Abdul entered, flanked by two guards. His dark eyes glittered with malice as he approached them, his movements slow and deliberate.

"Well," he said, his guttural voice dripping with disdain. "You survived. Impressive. But how long can you hold out, I wonder?"

Mark glared at him, his defiance belying his true despair. "Longer than you think. You'll get nothing from us."

Abdul crouched in front of him, a cruel smile spreading across his face. "Oh, I think you'll find my methods quite persuasive. Now, let's start with the basics. What were you planning to do and who else is helping you?"

Sam spat at him, her voice shaking with rage. "Go to hell."

Abdul wiped his face with a cloth, his leer never wavering. "Such attitude. But let's see how much of it remains after your next night of terror."

He stood, turning to leave. "Enjoy the rest of the morning. Tonight, I'll ensure the entities are… less merciful."

Trevaunce Manor – 9:10 AM

Worsley and Fiona were sitting in the drawing room, their expressions grim but composed.

"They didn't break," Fiona said, sipping her coffee. "Not yet."

"They will," Worsley replied, his tone confident. "No one can endure what Abdul has planned without losing their sanity. They may not talk, but they'll be broken by Walpurgis Night."

"Their defiance is admirable, but it's fragile. I saw it in their eyes – they're hanging by a thread. But Abdul is behaving irresponsibly again. After the first entity failed, he sent them a Saiitii manifestation – one of the most dangerous creatures. Fortunately, they somehow managed to survive."

"What! The fool! I need them alive for the Sabbat, the Saiitii could have, should have killed them. That they endured that is nothing short of miraculous. What was he thinking? Send Abdul to me now. He needs to know in the most severe terms that I want them broken not dead. If he fails me, he will die himself."

"I will fetch him immediately."

Something is not right. Worsley mused. *How are they not broken or dead? They could not have survived a Saiitii without divine help or the protection of another powerful warlock. This needed further examination.*

Chapter 48

A Reprieve

Trevaunce Manor – 26 April, 9:15 AM

Worsley sat motionless, his fury barely contained beneath a thin veneer of control. The mention of the Saiitii manifestation still reverberated in his mind. He had expected Abdul to apply measured cruelty, something to gradually erode their spirits – not unleash an entity capable of annihilating them. He took a slow breath. *They survived.* That was the most troubling part. How?

The sharp rap of heels against the marble floor signalled Fiona's return. Behind her, Abdul entered, his head bowed, his demeanour subdued but not entirely submissive. Worsley noted the defiance lingering in Abdul's posture, in the way his hands were clenched at his sides.

Fiona stepped aside, folding her arms as she watched the impending storm unfold.

"Abdul," Worsley's voice was deceptively calm, yet ice-cold. "Tell me, what exactly possessed you to send a Saiitii manifestation after our prisoners?"

Abdul hesitated for a fraction of a second – long enough. Worsley seized the pause and stood, his movements slow and deliberate, yet radiating deadly intent.

"They needed to be broken," Abdul finally replied, his voice edged with frustration. "They resisted the first entity. I acted to crush them before they became an even greater problem."

Worsley's hand shot out before the last word had left Abdul's lips. A crushing force of invisible energy slammed into Abdul's chest, sending him sprawling to his knees. His breath left him in a strangled gasp, pain flaring across his entire body.

"I do not need them crushed, you imbecile," Worsley snarled, stepping forward, his aura pressing down like a vice. "I need them alive. Weakened, compliant, but alive!"

Abdul gritted his teeth, his body convulsing under the invisible agony Worsley had inflicted upon him. It felt as if his bones were being twisted from the inside out.

Worsley bent down slightly, his voice, a whisper now, laced with venom. "If that thing had killed them, it would have ruined my plans. You are replaceable, Abdul. You serve only as long as you are useful."

The pain intensified. Abdul's fingers clawed at the stone floor, his breath coming in ragged gasps. Fiona watched, her expression impassive.

"I – I will not fail you again," Abdul choked out.

Worsley held his gaze a moment longer, then released the hold. Abdul collapsed fully onto the floor, trembling, his body drenched in sweat.

"No," Worsley barked. "You won't. Now leave my sight!"

He turned back to Fiona, after Abdul shuffled out. "He's too impulsive. We cannot trust him to handle the prisoners any longer. If we didn't need him for Walpurgis Night, I'd get rid of him. You should start looking for a replacement."

Fiona nodded. "Then what's your plan, Giles?"

"They will be moved from the dungeon. Place them in the Northern Wing – one of the guest rooms. Something isolated. Bug the room. I want to hear everything they say to each other."

Fiona tilted her head. "No more torture?"

"Not by conventional means," Worsley replied smoothly. "We must understand how they survived the Saiitii. That was no ordinary luck. Someone – or something – protected them. I will find out how."

"And how do you intend to do that, my lord?"

"Hypnosis. One at a time. Separated. They will tell me everything."

"What if they resist?"

"They won't be able to." Worsley's eyes gleamed with dark amusement. "I will also add an imprint to give them dreams that will prevent them sleeping peacefully. They will be unravelled from the inside out."

"Perfect." Fiona sighed. "You are wise, my lord. And after that?"

"Nothing changes." Worsley's voice was final. "They die on Walpurgis Night."

Trevaunce Manor – 10:30 AM

Abdul was still seething with resentment as he marched Mark and Sam down the long, dimly lit hallway of the Northern Wing toward their new quarters. His body still ached from Worsley's punishment, but his anger burned hotter than the pain.

Mark and Sam shuffled along, still visibly shaken from the horrors they had endured. Sleep had been a distant dream.

"This is your new home," Abdul said curtly, unlocking the door.

They stepped inside. The room was grand but unsettling, decorated in dark wood panelling with deep crimson curtains that blocked most of the sunlight. One king size bed sat against the wall, and a large, ornate mirror faced them from the far end of the room. Another door led to a bathroom with a shower.

Abdul stepped back toward the threshold. "Don't bother trying anything. This room is sealed. You aren't leaving unless Sir Giles allows it. You'll have to share the bed."

With a final glare, he slammed the door shut and locked it.

For a moment, Mark and Sam stood in silence. Then Mark exhaled. "Well. At least it's an upgrade from the dungeon."

Sam let out a dry chuckle, belying the anguish she was feeling, "I mean, we have a bed to share. Feels positively luxurious."

Mark walked over to the window and opened the curtains brightening the room. He pressed against the frame. Nothing. Not even the smallest draft. "Sealed tight," he muttered.

Sam tried the door. "Prison with fancy furniture," she muttered. "Perfect."

Mark raised a finger to his lips and beckoned her to him. He placed his arms round her and whispered softly in her ear. "Say nothing incriminating. Especially don't mention Paula, James or Dougal."

Mark flopped onto the bed. "Think they've bugged the place?"

Sam looked around. "Definitely. Hidden cameras too probably."

Mark grinned. "Well, then. Maybe we should entertain them with a dramatic monologue."

Sam rolled her eyes, but her lips twitched. "I'm drained. At least we have a bathroom. I'm taking a shower, cameras or not."

Despite their attempts at lightheartedness, fear and despair still clung to them both. They had survived the horrors of the past night, but what awaited them now?

Paula sat on the edge of her bed, her heart pounding as James paced before her, his spectral form flickering uneasily.

"We are all in danger," James murmured, his face tight with frustration "even though Worsley has had them moved to the Northern Wing. At least they are reprieved from another night in that dungeon and thank God for that, I barely held the barrier last night. Mark and Sam could not have survived another onslaught in that hellish place. Worsley is suspicious now. He knows that they couldn't have survived an assault by a Saiitii. He'll assume that they must have had outside help."

"So, what happens now?"

James paused, his expression darkening. "Worsley will hypnotise and interrogate them. They won't be able to resist."

"Oh God."

James nodded grimly. "You are only safe because Fiona and Worsley don't know about you yet. But if Mark and Sam say something under hypnosis, even by accident… "

Paula gripped the sheets tightly. "Then I'm as good as dead."

James knelt before her, his eyes intense. "Listen to me. Whatever happens, don't let them suspect you. Keep playing your role. Keep Fiona's trust."

Paula nodded slowly, her mind racing. She had come too far. There was no turning back now. "We had better pray that they don't mention my name then. There seems to be no fallback plan.

"Then we will have to rely on Dougal to save you all."

"I should text him."

"Yes and tell him what has happened and to assume his cover is blown, though I suspect he's already made that assumption."

Northwood, Northwest London – 26 April, 1:30 PM

Dougal stood in the dimly lit space, double-checking his gear before departure. The small, rented lock-up had served as his temporary base, since going off-grid, but now it was time to move. The Colonel had provided him with an untraceable Land Rover Defender, ideal for off-road manoeuvring on Bodmin Moor. His face was a mask of grim determination as he scanned the last message from Paula. Mark and Sam had been moved into the house. Worsley must be preparing to break them.

He had expected it. There was no realistic way they would hold out against the full force of Worsley's will. Worsley had dark powers at his disposal, and Abdul's cruelty was a force in itself.

Dougal clenched his jaw, shoving the phone into his pocket. Paula was also in extreme danger. He couldn't help them now. Their only hope was that Worsley would keep them alive until Walpurgis Night. as he suspected he would. Using them as ritual sacrifices or other diabolical ceremonies would appeal to that evil monster.

That means I have four days. Four days to prepare for the kill. Four days to avenge Nick, James and Joan. Four days to protect Paula. Four days to save Mark and Sam. A sniper's bullet is too good for Worsley, but there may be no alternative.

The Colonel's precautions were already in place. The office in Northwood was shut down, and Turner's team had scattered to avoid fallout. If Worsley's people came looking, they would find nothing. In the meantime, Turner was working on a new extraction plan that he and Dougal had discussed for Walpurgis Night.

Dougal's personal preparations were more drastic. His old stash of supplies was still buried on Hebdon Tor, concealed in a place he was certain remained undisturbed. The hidden surveillance camera had been monitoring the area, and the footage had revealed nothing but wind and wild terrain. But the battery would die soon. He'd better be there before it failed. He was well prepared for sleeping rough on the inhospitable moor, with five days of field rations and bivouac cover.

He zipped up the rest of his gear and loaded it into the land rover. He shut up his storage facility and then drove off into the grey afternoon air.

Bodmin – 26 April, 3:30 PM

Arthur Parker paced the small flat where he was hiding, his nerves on edge. Dougal had been trying to contact him since yesterday, but Arthur had ignored the texts.

He wasn't proud of it, but he knew that if Dougal figured out what he was planning, he'd try to stop him. And Arthur couldn't allow that.

They weren't moving fast enough. Now Mark and Sam had been taken and were probably in the dungeon – just like Joan was.

He shut his eyes, suppressing the painful memory. Joan had deserved better. And if no one else was going to deliver justice, then he had to.

Arthur had spent the last day watching the entrance to Trevaunce Manor, looking for any weaknesses in the security. There were none. The place was locked down tighter than ever. But then, an opportunity had fallen into his lap.

One of the locals, Bert Tanner, had been contracted to deliver groceries to the manor for some grand event on the 28th. Arthur had known Bert for years and slipping him £50 had been enough to secure a spot as his 'assistant'.

He had no illusions about his survival. It was highly likely that he wasn't coming back from this.

Find Joan's body. Kill Abdul. Kill Worsley. Kill Fiona.

That was the plan. And if he failed, he'd die trying. Arthur exhaled slowly, staring out the window at the gathering clouds. This must work.

Chapter 49
Breaking Point

Trevaunce Manor – 27April, 10:30 AM

The air inside the Ritual Room was thick with the scent of smouldering incense. The walls, adorned with arcane symbols, pulsed faintly in the dim candlelight, giving the impression that they were alive, breathing with dark energy. The stone altar, draped in black silk, loomed at the centre of the room, a focal point of sinister intent. Above it, the ominous mural of the winged entity seemed to shift as if observing the proceedings.

Mark knelt before the altar, his wrists bound behind his back, his body rigid with defiance. His eyes burned with determination despite the heavy exhaustion settling over him. Worsley stood before him, his crimson-embroidered robes exuding an air of absolute authority. He looked around him approvingly. The atmosphere was perfect for what was about to transpire. Fiona had done well preparing the Ritual Room.

Fiona watched from the side, her arms crossed as she observed Worsley's methods. This was a different kind of breaking. No physical torture – only the relentless power of hypnosis and dark magic.

Worsley's eyes were compelling, seeming to grow larger the more Mark struggled to avoid their gaze, but he could not. Worsley stepped closer, his voice smooth, laced with hidden coercion.

"Tell me, Mr. Benedict… why are you here?"

Mark clenched his jaw, fighting against the pull of Worsley's words. He could feel something slithering into his mind, something cold and insidious. His thoughts blurred. His vision swam.

"I – " He tried to resist, tried to lock down his mind, but Worsley was inside. His will was too strong.

"Where do you and your companions operate from?" Worsley's voice was relentless, calm yet absolute.

Mark tried to hold back, but the words spilled from his lips involuntarily. "Carn View… outside Nansebyn."

Fiona's eyes narrowed, noting the detail. Worsley barely reacted – he already knew Mark couldn't resist.

"Who else works with you?"

Mark gritted his teeth, sweat beading on his forehead. No. Don't say it. Don't!

"…Dougal Finlayson."

"And who does he work for?

"… Colonel Turner of Vigilant Alert Security.

Fiona exhaled softly. *That is useful.*

Worsley tilted his head, his voice remaining calm, rhythmic. "And what of Arthur Parker?"

Mark blinked rapidly, his breathing growing shallower. His head throbbed as though something was being torn from him forcibly. "He – he was looking into Joan's death… He was supposed to help us, but he disappeared."

A flicker of satisfaction crossed Worsley's face. "And what became of my missing security guards?"

Mark's jaw trembled. His head felt heavy, as if it were filled with fog.

"They tried to kill Dougal but one of your guards shot and killed the other by accident. Dougal disarmed the remaining one and, after questioning him, finally let him go to leave Cornwall for good."

Fiona and Worsley exchanged a glance. That was an unexpected confession.

"What information did the guard give him?"

"Your security routines and shift system."

"Where is the dead guard?"

"Hidden in the fogou."

Worsley crouched before him, his piercing gaze holding Mark in an unbreakable grip. "And what was your goal?"

Mark shook his head, desperate to stop speaking, but the words came out like a confession at the gallows. "To infiltrate Trevaunce Manor… to kill you."

Worsley's smile was cold, knowing. "Of course."

Worsley continued, his voice a measured blade. "How did you resist the Saiitii?"

"I don't understand what you mean."

"The entity. The second manifestation Abdul sent you last night." Worsley's eyes gleamed with curiosity. "Most men lose their minds in its presence. You… you are still here."

Mark swallowed hard. "I don't know. We prayed aloud."

Worsley's expression darkened slightly, his head tilting as if weighing the truth in Mark's words. "Prayer?" He scoffed softly. "Or did something – someone – intervene?"

Mark clenched his jaw but said nothing. He wouldn't give Worsley the satisfaction of knowing his doubts, his fragmented memories of that night. Had it been faith, or something else?

Mark's body shuddered violently as Worsley leaned in and whispered something too low for anyone else to hear. Mark's pupils dilated, his expression contorting with visible distress.

The imprint was complete. The nightmares would come.

Worsley cried out, "Abdul, take him back to his room and bring me the other one."

A couple of minutes later Sam was brought into the room.

The process repeated itself. Sam was no stronger than Mark in the face of Worsley's hypnosis. Her ordeal mirrored his – the relentless pull of his voice, the soft insidious invasion of her mind. She tried to fight it, tried to hold onto her own thoughts, but Worsley peeled them away with surgical precision.

Every answer Mark had given, Sam confirmed. Carn View. Dougal Finlayson. Dougal's organisation, Arthur Parker. The missing security guards. The intent to murder Worsley. And like Mark, she had no idea how they had survived the Saiitii manifestation.

When it was over, Worsley left her with the same imprint – a mark in her subconscious that would plague her with nightmares, depriving her of rest, weakening her spirit further. By the time she was returned to their room, both were broken – if not in body, then in mind.

The Drawing Room – 11:30 AM

Fiona poured them both a glass of deep red wine as she listened to Sir Giles relay what he had uncovered. The fire crackled in the ornate study, its warmth barely cutting through the chill that always seemed to cling to Worsley's presence.

"So, we now know where they were operating from," she said, swirling the wine in her glass. "Carn View. Shall I have it searched?"

"Yes," Worsley replied. "Leave no trace. If there is any remaining evidence, digest and destroy it."

Fiona inclined her head. "And what about Finlayson? He's clearly more capable than we assumed."

"He won't let us find him, but when he tries to break in, we will get him then."

Fiona took a slow sip of her wine. "The body of the security guard in the fougou? And the one who ran?"

Worsley sighed, as if tired of dealing with lesser matters. "Remove it. Get rid of it. Let nothing tie it back to us. Leave the runaway for now. We'll handle that after the Sabbat."

She nodded. "Understood."

Worsley stood, his robes whispering against the floor as he moved to the window. Daylight stretched beyond the manor, the moors grey and brooding. "They won't last much longer, the nightmares will eat at them tonight, leave them raw, vulnerable. Another two nights and they will be completely compliant."

Fiona's smile was smug. "Then they will be ready for Walpurgis Night. But what about tomorrow night? Six of the Inner Circle have said they will attend."

"Ah yes. The Ritual of Veil Severance. Let our prisoners watch that too, restrained of course. Yes, witnessing that ritual will further their suffering. Make it so Fiona, make it so."

Mark and Sam's Room – 11:10 AM

The room was silent when the guards left. Mark and Sam sat opposite each other at the small table, neither speaking for a long time.

Mark rubbed his eyes, his head still throbbing from the ordeal. "It's in my head, Sam," he murmured, his voice hoarse. "It's… something is still inside me."

Sam shivered, wrapping her arms around herself. "I know. I feel it too."

She looked at Mark, eyes hollow, exhausted. "He now knows everything."

Mark swallowed hard, guilt heavy in his chest. "We gave them it all."

"And Carn View. It's compromised."

"I think Dougal will have already handled that."

Silence stretched between them, thick with defeat.

"I don't know how much longer we can hold on," Sam whispered.

Mark forced himself to reach for her hand, squeezing it. "We will. We must."

Paula sat stiffly on her bed, her hands gripping the covers so tightly that her knuckles turned white. James stood beside her, his translucent form unsteady as his emotions warred within him.

"They survived," James murmured. "But they're no longer whole."

Paula felt sick. Fiona and Worsley had broken them down.

She hugged herself, trying to suppress the icy fear creeping into her bones. If Worsley had asked about her… She shook the thought away.

"They didn't mention me. Worsley and Fiona can't know. They'd be here already if they did."

James exhaled, his ghostly form tense. "But how much longer until they do?"

Paula had no answer.

Chapter 50

The Rite of Veil Severance

Nansebyn – 28 April, 8:45 PM

Arthur Parker stood at the car park entrance of the Miner's Diner, waiting for Bert Tanner to arrive. He tugged his green bobble hat lower over his forehead and adjusted the Plymouth Argyle football scarf wound snugly around his neck.

A disguise – of sorts. A poor one, but enough to divert casual scrutiny. He was under no illusions that the manor's security was lax, but he was banking on familiarity dulling their senses. Bert had been making deliveries to Trevaunce Manor for a long time. His face was known. And Arthur – tonight, Arthur was just another anonymous worker, a man in a green coverall moving crates in and out, blending into the background.

He inhaled deeply, forcing his nerves to steady. The gun weighed heavy in his baggy trousers, and for a moment, he fretted over the chilling possibility of a pat-down. If security decided to check him, if they so much as touched him, it would be over before it had even begun.

Headlights rounded the bend, and a moment later, Bert's van pulled up beside him. The window rolled down, and Bert, a burly man with a friendly face, nodded.

Arthur climbed in.

Without preamble, Bert tossed a folded green coverall into his lap. "Put that on," he muttered.

Arthur complied, wriggling into the rough material. As he zipped it up, Bert shot him a sidelong glance. "Tonight, you're Steve – my new assistant. You keep your mouth shut, your head down, and when we're done unloading, you're on your own. Understand?"

Arthur exhaled slowly, summoning a confidence he didn't feel. "Sure."

"Good." Bert put the van into gear. "Because once we pass those gates, there'll be no turning back."

Arthur knew Bert was being uncharacteristically brusque because he was nervous. He was at risk too.

Trevaunce Manor – 9:10 PM

The gates loomed ahead, the iron glinting under the floodlights. As the van slowed, Arthur braced himself, keeping his expression neutral. A guard was already stepping forward holding a clipboard.

To Arthur's immense relief, the gates began to open before Bert even stopped.

The guard waved them through. "They're expecting you at the house, Bert."

Bert gave a casual nod. "Thanks Charlie, appreciate it."

Arthur didn't dare breathe as they rolled forward. No checks. No questions. Just as he'd hoped.

The manor's ominous facade emerged from the darkness, its upper windows ablaze with light. The gravel crunched under the tires as Bert headed for the delivery area, just past the main entrance.

They came to a stop. The refrigerated interior of the van hissed softly as the doors were unlatched.

A surly-looking brute emerged from the shadows, dressed in livery, but with a pistol incongruously holstered at his waist. Arthur took an instant dislike to him.

"Steve," Bert said, "you take these two crates. Abdul will show you where to go."

Arthur's blood turned into ice. *Abdul.* The same man who had tortured and killed Joan. Arthur's grip tightened around the handles of the plastic crates. His heart pounded so hard he was sure the others could hear it. Every muscle in his body screamed to drop the crates, pull the gun, and end it right there – but he forced himself to stay still. Not yet. There were others that deserved his vengeance too. *Not yet.*

Instead, he nodded stiffly and followed Abdul through the lit, manicured gardens, past the ornate fountain, and into a side entrance of the manor. Bert followed behind, carrying two more crates.

They entered a long corridor, the air inside stiflingly warm, scented with a mix of spices. Abdul led them into a pantry, where two foreign looking girls – silent, submissive – hurried to empty the crates.

Arthur barely heard Bert's one way banter with Abdul, too focused on controlling the rage simmering beneath his skin.

"Four more after this. Come on Steve." Arthur followed Bert under the watchful gaze of Abdul, and they returned a minute later with two more crates each. They waited while these were emptied and then slotted the empty crates together to carry them back.

"Enjoy the party tonight Abdul" shouted Bert as he left.

"Cheerful blighter, isn't he?" Arthur said sarcastically, seething inside.

"Always the same, never says much and never smiles." Bert replied. "Now be ready."

Abdul watched them go as Bert drove round the turning circle, back past the house, curving left onto the main drive and out of sight. Bert slowed and said "Now!" Arthur opened the door, jumped out of the slow-moving vehicle and melted into the woods.

The van door swung shut under its own momentum as Bert drove on to the gate which was already opening for him to leave. He waved at Charlie as he went through.

Arthur moved stealthily, deeper into the woods. *He was in. First hurdle over!*

Hebdon Tor – 10:15 PM

Dougal lay prone on the grassy knoll, just below the Tor's jagged peak, his sniper rifle resting on its tripod. His night vision scope cast the manor in ghostly green light, every movement in the grounds sharp and distinct. The night was mercifully dry.

He adjusted his position, watching the house. In the last ten minutes, half a dozen cars had arrived, seen only by their headlights carving paths through the gloom. Dougal narrowed his eyes, mentally noting the volume of guests, they were completely hidden from view by the woodland obscuring the main entrance to the house. But this wasn't some casual gathering. This was the rite Paula had been expecting. He let out a slow breath, steadied his heartbeat.

Paula's last message had confirmed that Mark and Sam were alive – but barely. He assumed that Worsley needed them for his evil purposes on Walpurgis Night. He had to cling onto that hope.

The original plan had been a stealth infiltration, but Arthur had screwed that up. However, there was still the back-up plan that he had discussed with the Colonel when he was in London. Hopefully that was being set up right now. For now, Dougal had one goal. *Wait for the 30th.* Worsley would assuredly be in the stone circle then, and Dougal would have a clear shot.

Until that moment, all he could do was watch… and wait.

Trevaunce Manor, 28 April, 11:40 PM

Mark and Sam lay awake on the bed in their room, afraid to sleep. The previous night had been a relentless torment – nightmares filled with monstrous slugs and giant, skittering spiders. They had held each other but screamed as they repeatedly awakened and then were unable to resist the urge to sleep again. The cycle continued until dawn broke. They had been shattered and sweat drenched before dragging themselves to the bathroom to clean up.

Despite their extreme fatigue they had been too fearful to sleep much even in daylight. They had been brought food on a tray, but their appetite was non-existent, and it was left untouched.

The door opened revealing the odious Abdul and two guards. "You are wanted in the Dark Chamber."

The two guards secured their hands behind their back with plastic ties and then shoved them to the door. They shuffled along the hall and down the stairs in a daze. Eventually they passed the dungeon and stood on the threshold of the Dark Chamber, the heavy iron gate was already open.

The Dark Chamber – 11:45 PM

Mark and Sam were dragged into the Dark Chamber by the two guards who seemed nervous. The air inside was thick and oppressive, laden with the acrid scent of burning incense and something metallic – blood, perhaps. Flickering black candles, lining a pentagram, cast jagged shadows across the room, making the already eerie carvings on the walls seem to twist and writhe.

The chamber was arranged like a stage for the macabre. A massive obsidian mirror dominated one side of the room, its surface rippling like liquid darkness. Blood-red runes glowed faintly on the stone floor, inside the pentagram that seemed to pulse with an unnatural energy. At its centre, knelt a young, quivering and naked initiate, her face pale with terror.

Six robed figures stood in a semicircle around the pentagram, members of Worsley's inner circle. Their faces were obscured by deep hoods, but their postures strangely radiated both reverence and unease. At the far end of the chamber was Sir Giles Worsley, clad in High Priest robes of deep crimson and black and to one side stood Fiona in a shimmering green gown.

Worsley turned slowly as the prisoners were brought forward, his piercing eyes locking onto Mark and Sam. His lips curved into a cold smile. "Welcome," he said, his voice low and commanding. "You are privileged indeed. Few outsiders ever witness the power that will unfold here tonight."

Worsley gestured, and the guards shoved Mark and Sam roughly to their knees not far from the edge of one side of the pentagram. Fiona took a position standing beside them while Abdul ensured their bindings were secure.

The robed figures began to chant in a low, ancient tongue, their voices weaving a sinister harmony that slowly filled the chamber.

"Tonight," Worsley began, his authoritative voice cutting through the chanting like a blade, "we weaken and sever the veil that separates our realm from the infernal. Tonight, we invite the powers beyond to flow through us, to anoint us as their chosen."

Worsley raised his hands, his voice calm but carrying a weight of absolute authority. His words flowed in an ancient, guttural tongue, a language that predated human civilization.

The gathered coven members bowed their heads, continuing their chanting. The candles' flames flickered violently, casting monstrous shadows that danced along the walls, distorting reality itself.

The great obsidian mirror behind Worsley rippled, as if something on the other side was pushing against its surface. The temperature in the room plummeted, mist curling at the floor like icy fingers creeping toward the living.

The initiate whimpered, her gaze locked on the mirror.

Worsley stepped forward, his fingers brushing against her cheek in a mockery of gentleness. "Fear is a gift, child," he murmured, his tone soft yet commanding. "It prepares the soul for the crossing."

The girl swallowed hard, but she did not move. Her terror was absolute, her body rigid beneath Worsley's touch.

The chanting grew louder. The air vibrated. The mirror bulged outward, the glass warping as a viscous black mist began to seep through the cracks forming along its surface.

Mark's entire body tensed. Something was coming.

The mist coalesced into a writhing, semi-corporeal entity, its form half-seen, shifting, terrible to behold. It loomed behind Worsley, its outline crackling with unearthly energy, its countless red eyes burning with malice.

A tremor ran through the chamber. The mirror fractured further, its cracks resembling jagged veins of darkness.

"The veil weakens. The gateway opens."

Mark's eyes darted around the room. The six figures continued chanting but remained motionless, their focus entirely on Worsley. The guards shifted uncomfortably, sweat forming on their brows despite the cold. One swallowed hard, his grip on Sam's arm tightening in what felt more like desperation than control.

The oppressive energy in the room was almost unbearable, squeezing Mark's chest like a vice. But beneath that, he felt something else – a strange awareness of his own abilities. It was faint, but enough to focus on.

His gaze fixed on one of the candles near the edge of the pentagram no more than six feet from him. It was a small target, but the ritual's energy seemed to magnify his reach. He closed his eyes, willing his invisible arm to stretch toward it. The flame flickered, and the candle quivered very faintly. It was no good. He was too weakened by his torment.

The half-formed creature moved ominously towards the girl. The initiate screamed.

"Behold," Worsley intoned, his voice filled with triumph. "The veil is severed!"

Mark tried again. He summoned every ounce of strength, his imagined arm reaching to the candle. His vision blurred from exhaustion, but his will remained unbroken.

The flame of the candle spluttered out.

For an instant, the chamber froze

The writhing mist recoiled. The red-eyed entity let out a piercing shriek, its form fluctuating wildly. The mirror cracked apart, shards falling to the floor in a deafening crash.

A powerful force erupted outward, sending several cultists staggering back. An icy wind raged and howled upsetting candles, urns and incense burners. The initiate collapsed to the floor, shaking violently, her hands clutching her head as though in pain.

The ritual had been derailed.

Worsley whirled around, his furious gaze locking onto Fiona. "What just happened?"

Fiona's expression was tight, controlled, but the sharpness in her eyes betrayed a flicker of uncertainty. "Something interfered," she admitted. "But I do not know what."

For the first time, Worsley's composure cracked. His ritual had failed. Never had he experienced failure. *And he did not yet know why.*

The assembled cultists murmured uneasily as Worsley turned his gaze to the still-quivering initiate. He stepped toward her, kneeling as he brushed her damp hair away from her face.

"You have served well," he said, his voice measured, steady, but far from pleased. "You shall be rewarded."

Fiona approached, draping a dark silk cloth around the trembling girl's bare shoulders. "Come, child," she purred, her tone unsettlingly soothing. "Tonight, you will feast with us – your new family." The girl, still in a daze, nodded weakly. She allowed Fiona to help her stand, her movements weak and fragile as she was led out.

The robed figures bowed reverently to Worsley and filed out of the chamber.

Mark and Sam were dragged to their feet. Worsley approached them, his cold smile returning. "You may not understand now, but soon, you will. What you've witnessed tonight is only a taste of far greater things to come."

Mark and Sam remained motionless, their hearts pounding. Mark knew that he had disrupted the ritual, but at what cost? Worsley gestured and Abdul led them out.

As Worsley turned away, his expression darkened further. His mind was already working, piecing together the threads of what had just happened. The Veil had not been severed. The gateway had not been opened. Something had prevented it.

His gaze flicked across the chamber, landing briefly on the departing Mark and Sam. He sensed no outward sign of interference, yet something deep inside him stirred with suspicion.

His lips curled into a faint, knowing smile. "No matter," he murmured, barely audible.

There was still Walpurgis Night. That would be the true reckoning.

Back in their room, Mark and Sam collapsed onto their bed, drained beyond measure. Every muscle in Mark's body ached, his limbs heavy with exhaustion, but his mind was racing, frantic, alive with what had just transpired.

He had done it. He had snuffed out the candle. He had ruined the ritual.

And yet, he couldn't tell her. Couldn't say a word. The walls had ears, and if Worsley or Fiona even suspected – it would be the end of them both.

His gaze flickered toward Sam. She lay still, her body curled in on itself, her breaths shallow and uneven. Then he saw it – the distant, tormented look in her face, the barely perceptible twitch of her fingers. She was there again, trapped in that hellish place of nightmares, beyond his help. He held her tightly trying to awaken her, but she was beyond the point of no return.

His heart clenched. *God, I wish I could help her.*

Mark fought against the leaden weight of his own exhaustion, straining to stay awake, to watch over her. But the darkness tugged at him, insidious and relentless. His limbs numbed, his thoughts blurred, and despite his fight, his eyelids fell shut.

The nightmares were waiting.

James hovered near the foot of the bed, as he watched Mark and Sam. They were twisting restlessly in their sleep, their breathing ragged, their minds held hostage by nightmares not of their own making. Beads of sweat glistened on their foreheads; their brows furrowed in terror even as their eyes remained shut.

James clenched his spectral fists. He had seen enough. Whatever Worsley and Abdul had done to them, it was malicious and malevolent – their spirits were breaking. He could not allow that.

Taking a step closer, he stretched his hands over them, his voice a soundless murmur, reciting words of protection and relief. His fingers traced invisible runes in the air, long forgotten symbols of old magic. A soft glow emanated from his fingertips – pale blue, faint but unwavering. "Let the shadows release their grip," he whispered. "Let the horrors remain beyond the veil."

The oppressive atmosphere in the room shifted. The air, thick and heavy with unseen malice, eased ever so slightly. The cold that had clung to their bodies like a second skin receded, replaced by a gentle warmth that pulsed outward from where James stood.

Sam's breathing slowed first. The deep creases in her brow softened. Mark let out a shaky breath, the tension in his limbs releasing by degrees. James could still sense the nightmares, lingering just beyond reach, but they no longer had the same iron grip over their minds.

It was not a cure, nor was it a permanent fix – but it was something.

James exhaled, his form flickering unsteadily. This effort cost him. The more he intervened, the more Worsley might sense something amiss. He had to be careful. It was vital that he remained anonymous until after May Day Eve. But seeing the slight calm return to Mark and Sam's features, even for just a short reprieve, made the risk worthwhile.

He watched them for a moment longer before retreating, his presence still lingering like a silent guardian in the dark. Tomorrow, they would wake, still trapped in their nightmare of reality. But for tonight, at least, he had given them a little peace.

Chapter 51
Preparing for Battle

Trevaunce Manor – 29 April, 9:05 AM.

Sam stirred, her body aching, her mind sluggish as she fought the pull of sleep. A familiar wave of dread curled around her chest, but something felt… different. The nightmares that had tormented her the first night, had still been there, lurking on the edge of her subconscious – but they had not consumed her.

She blinked groggily, then sat up with a start, panic flaring in her chest. *What happened?* Why did the nightmares not come in full force?

As her vision cleared, she saw Mark standing beside the bed, his finger raised to his lips, a silent warning. Do not speak.

Her heart pounded.

Slowly, he handed her a small, crumpled piece of paper. Her fingers trembled as she unfolded it, eyes scanning the hastily scribbled note:

Slept relatively well. Minimal nightmares.

Someone or something intervened. Could James have helped us?

I ruined the ritual last night. Snuffed out the candle using my gift.

Say nothing that mentions names.

Our conversation must convey exhaustion and despair.

Sam inhaled deeply, forcing her expression into one of hopeless fatigue. Her mind raced with possibilities. James? Could his lingering presence somehow have eased their suffering? And Mark… *he had done something to upset the ritual?* She glanced at him, but he had already taken the note back.

Her lips barely moved as she whispered, "Another day in hell." Then, louder, she groaned, stretching. "I can't take much more of this. I am totally drained."

Mark nodded, playing along. "Likewise," he muttered. "I can't think straight. I can barely concentrate."

He turned and strode into the bathroom. The sound of water running filled the silence as he wet the paper, scrunched it up tightly, and then flushed it down the toilet.

When he returned, he sat on the edge of his bed, keeping his voice even. "My dreams were terrifying… but not quite as bad as the night before. Either we're getting used to them… or Worsley decided to be a little more merciful."

Sam let out a dry, bitter laugh. "I doubt that. Merciful isn't in his nature."

Mark sighed, "So, what now?"

Sam glanced down at her rumpled, stained clothing, wrinkling her nose. "Well, I've been wearing these for two days straight, and I'm sick of feeling disgusting. I'm taking a shower, changing, and then I'm resting. Whatever Worsley throws at us tonight, I want to be ready."

"Good idea."

Their charade may not have been perfect, but if they were being listened to, nothing in their conversation could arouse suspicion.

But beneath the forced exhaustion and carefully chosen words, something had shifted. For the first time since their imprisonment, they felt the faintest flicker of control. And that, however small, was enough.

The grand Drawing Room of Trevaunce Manor was silent except for the occasional crackle of the fireplace. Sir Giles Worsley stood with his hands resting on the marble mantelpiece, his expression unreadable, his thoughts a tempest beneath the surface.

Behind him, Fiona sat poised on the velvet chaise, her back straight, hands delicately folded in her lap. She watched him carefully, sensing the burden of his displeasure, though she dared not name it.

"You are troubled, Giles," she murmured, her tone soft, reverent.

Worsley did not respond immediately. His fingers tapped against the mantel, slow, deliberate beats of contained fury.

"The veil was not severed," he said at last, "weakened but not severed." His voice calm – too calm.

Fiona lowered her gaze, her stomach tightening at the quiet menace in his tone.

"It is unheard of," he continued, straightening at last. "Everything was in place. The alignment was perfect. The energy was gathered, the sacrifice was ready. And yet… something held it back."

Fiona inhaled deeply, her hands clasping together a little tighter. "Do you believe it was… an outside force?"

He nodded stiffly. "Benedict's brother. The woman. They have coped easier than they should have." His fingers tapped absently against the mantel. "They screamed before. Last night, they did not."

Worsley turned to face her then, "There is no doubt," he said, his voice dropping to a whisper. "Something is interfering. Someone."

Fiona shivered at the certainty in his tone. "The Americans?" she ventured.

His lips curled in something that resembled a smile, but there was no humour in it. "They are resilient, but not capable of this. Not alone." He began pacing again, measured strides, the movement precise, as though every step was a calculated act of control. "But they are protected. Something shields them, keeps them from breaking."

"Could it be Abdul? Revenge for his punishment?

"He would not dare!"

Fiona bowed her head in reverence. "Then we must find out who, my Lord."

Worsley stopped pacing, his eyes narrowing as he regarded her. He reached out and touched her chin, tilting her face upward, forcing her to look at him.

"We will," he murmured, his fingers light but possessive against her skin. "But we must be patient."

"Yes," she whispered.

He let her go, turning his attention back to the fire. "The initiate of last night is now irrelevant," he stated. "Mrs. Benedict will take her place at the Sabbat."

"A fitting tribute," she said softly.

"And her brother-in-law will watch," Worsley added. He exhaled slowly, savouring the thought, the weight of his power reasserting itself. "He will see what happens to those who defy me."

Fiona nodded, utterly devoted, basking in the certainty of his words. "And the nightmares?" she asked cautiously.

Worsley's expression hardened. "No more nightmares." His voice was final. "They were meant to weaken them, to crack their minds before the Sabbat." His smile returned, slow and serpentine. "But now, I would rather they know. I want them to be fully aware. I want them to suffer every moment of what is to come."

"You are wise, my Lord," she said, lowering her head.

Worsley turned to her once more, stepping closer, his presence consuming. He cupped her cheek, his touch cold despite the warmth of the fire.

"And you, my devoted one, are loyal," he whispered.

Fiona closed her eyes, drinking in his power, her voice barely audible. "Always."

Worsley withdrew, stepping away as if already finished with the conversation. His mind had moved on, already orchestrating the next steps in his unshakable plan.

Fiona remained still for a moment, her breath uneven. "You will need to remove the imprint. Shall I inform Abdul?"

Worsley gave a slight nod. "Yes. Get him to bring them to the ritual room."

Fiona exited.

Behind her, Worsley looked back at the fireplace, but his eyes were unseeing.

"I will not be denied my transition to Ipsissimus," he murmured to himself.

The flames crackled in response, as if the very essence of Trevaunce Manor acknowledged his claim.

Hebdon Tor – 29 April, 11:30 AM

Dougal lay flat against the uneven ground, the damp chill of the moor seeping through his clothes, but he barely noticed. His rifle scope remained trained on Trevaunce Manor.

Nothing had stirred since dawn, but the previous night had been different. Half a dozen cars had arrived before midnight, their unseen occupants slipping into the manor's shadowed depths, vanishing into whatever hidden ritual took place below the earth. Dougal had watched and waited, wondering what was happening inside. Four hours later, the same cars had left.

He had spoken to Colonel Bill Turner that morning, the extraction plan was a go. Six ex-special forces operatives, hardened men who had long since left the service but not the battlefield, had been hired. They were already on their way to Cornwall, operating under strict radio silence. Their objective was clear: breach the manor gates tomorrow night on Dougal's signal, secure the area, and extract Mark, Sam, and Paula.

Once the extraction was complete, time allowing, they would move to recover Joan Summers' body and if that was achieved, it would be undeniable proof of Worsley's crimes.

Tomorrow night, the mercenaries would be in position, waiting for Dougal's go-ahead.

He tightened his grip on his rifle. If he got his shot, he'd take it. And if he missed?

Then he'd bring the whole bloody house down!

Trevaunce Manor – 29 April, 1:30 PM

Arthur Parker crouched beneath the branches of an old oak, his body still stiff and aching from a sleepless, chilly night. The thick carpet of damp leaves beneath him had done little to soften the ground, but he hadn't cared. He wasn't there for comfort.

Earlier, as the first pale light of dawn broke through the trees, he had crept through the woods, his breath slow, measured, controlled.

And then he'd found it. The well sat in a tiny clearing, its ancient stones weathered, moss-covered, damp with morning mist. A heavy iron cover rested over it, rusted but firmly in place. Arthur placed his hands against it, his fingers scrabbling for leverage, but the weight was too great for him alone.

His throat tightened. For a long time, he simply stood there, staring at it. Joan was down there. Alone. Forgotten. His fingers curled into fists as grief threatened to consume him. He had failed her. He knelt then, pressing his forehead against the cold, unyielding stone, and let himself mourn. He whispered her name, promised vengeance, sworn that he would make them all pay.

Now, hours later, Arthur remained hidden in the undergrowth, his mind fixed on tomorrow night. The revelry at the stone circle would give him his chance. Worsley and his followers would be lost in their own twisted ecstasy, consumed by their depraved rites.

And he would be waiting. Tomorrow, he would shed blood for Joan. Even if it meant his own.

Mark and Sam were sitting on the edge of their beds, exhaustion evident in their slouched postures. The room felt eerily quiet after their return from Worsley's second hypnosis session.

Sam broke the silence, "It's strange. I still feel like something's missing. Like... a space where the nightmares used to be."

"I know what you mean. It's not relief. Just... emptiness."

"Worsley didn't do it out of kindness. He's shifting tactics. But why? What's the point in taking them away now?"

Mark replied grimly "Because he wants us aware, Sam. Aware, and completely sane when whatever he has planned happens on Walpurgis Night."

Sam exhaled shakily, "He's saving us for something. And it won't be anything good."

Paula was seated on the windowsill of her room, arms wrapped around her knees, staring out at the darkening moor. She looked up at James. "Tomorrow night is going to be bad, isn't it?" she said softly.

"You already know the answer."

"Fiona told me I'll be her handmaiden at the Sabbat. She said I should consider it an 'honour'." She said bitterly.

"And you think she's telling you everything?"

Paula shook her head and whispered softly, "No."

"If Worsley wants you as a handmaiden, it means you'll be close to the altar. That's where it happens, Paula."

"I know," Paula said shakily, "the sacrifice. And I think I know who it'll be." Turning to him, dread seeping into her voice, she murmured, "Sam."

James spectral form flickered. "They need someone significant. Someone important enough to make the offering worthy. Sam would fit that role in

Worsley's eyes. She's an American, a fighter and my wife, was my wife. That makes her fitting, prized – to their twisted beliefs, at least."

"Then we have to stop it. I'll be close to the altar. I must stop it whatever the cost."

James words appeared in her head, "I was hoping you'd say that."

A silence fell between them, not of hopelessness, but of resolve. Whatever happens on Walpurgis Night, they will not let Sam die without a fight.

Chapter 52

Walpurgis Night – The Final Battle

Hebdon Tor – 30 April, 10:30 PM

Dougal lay motionless in the undergrowth, his sniper rifle resting steady on its tripod. The stone circle below had been alive with activity since dawn. He had spent the entire day watching it, his trained eye noting every precise movement, every unnatural ritual conducted by Abdul and the others.

The bonfire had been built, towering and dry, ready to ignite at a moment's notice. Torches lined the trail from the house, also ready to be lit. Then there was the new addition – a single stake, driven deep and standing six-foot above the ground a few feet from the altar.

Dougal's grip tightened on the rifle. He didn't need to guess what it was for.

The extraction team was in position. They had been for over an hour. A final radio check had confirmed they were ready to storm the main gate at his signal. Everything was in place. Now, he just had to wait. The moment would come soon enough.

Trevaunce Manor – 11:20 PM

Mark and Sam stood stiffly by the edge of their beds, clad in the coarse brown robes they had been given earlier. Neither spoke, but fear showed on their faces.

Mark exhaled slowly, then, with a quiet mix of hesitation and desperation, he pulled Sam into an embrace. She tensed for only a second before returning the hug, holding him tightly, as if bracing for an impact that neither could see but both could feel.

He drew back, his hands trembling slightly, and searched her eyes. "Sam," he said, his voice barely above a whisper, "I love you. I have always loved you."

Sam drew a breath, she knew; in her heart she had always known. Her eyes glistened. "I love you too, Mark," she whispered.

Their lips met, and for a moment, everything else fell away – the fear, the uncertainty, the dread of what lay ahead. It was just them, in that moment.

Then the door burst open. Abdul entered first, his cold, cruel smile stretching across his face, followed by a silent, heavy-set guard.

The moment shattered. Mark's hands were wrenched behind his back, a plastic tie biting into his wrists.

He forced himself to keep his voice steady, looking at Sam as she was similarly bound. "Don't worry, Sam," he said, forcing a confidence he didn't feel. "We've already overcome so much. Just one more step."

Abdul laughed softly. "And what a step that is," he said, his voice dripping with malice. "A final one into hell!"

Mark clenched his jaw as they were led down the dimly lit hallway, their fate no longer their own.

The Drawing Room buzzed with conversation, the murmur of cultists clad in black robes, filling the air. Their excitement was almost tangible, a fevered anticipation that made the candle flames flicker as though the air itself trembled.

At the centre of it all stood Fiona, resplendent in her High Priestess attire. The dark, flowing gown, embroidered with silver symbols of power, gave her an ethereal, almost regal presence. But it was the crown-like circlet resting atop her cascading dark hair that truly marked her for what she was tonight – the voice of Worsley's will, his chosen vessel.

Beside her, Paula stood stiffly, the green velvet of her robe doing little to hide the unease coiling in her stomach. The scent of burning incense and candle wax felt cloying, heavy, making it harder to breathe.

Fiona turned to her, her dark eyes alight with certainty. "There is nothing to fear, Circe," she murmured. She reached out, brushing a stray lock of Paula's hair from her face in an oddly maternal gesture. "A wondrous night awaits."

Paula swallowed hard, nodding, though the bile rising in her throat told her otherwise. Nothing about this night would be wondrous.

Arthur Parker took deep, steady breaths, his body pressed low against the damp earth. The moment he had waited for was upon him. Every nerve in his body hummed with tension as he crouched at the very edge of the woods, mere feet from the pathway leading to the stone circle.

The path was lit by flaming torches, burning high against the darkened sky. They had been lit just seconds ago, their eerie, wavering glow creating sinister shadows. The soft murmur of voices carried through the crisp night air as Worsley's disciples assembled outside in one of the gardens preparing for their procession into the night.

Arthur pulled himself further into the shadows, melting into the trees. Now, of all times, he could not afford to be discovered.

The gathered devotees passed him in silent reverence, their black robes blending into the night, save for the occasional glint of silver embroidery catching the torchlight.

At the head of the procession strode Abdul, his expression severe, his presence forceful. The torchlight reflected off the intricate golden stitching of his dark ceremonial robe, the symbols upon it shifting and writhing like living things. He walked with purpose and control, leading the faithful into the waiting night.

Behind him, the main body followed in hushed anticipation, their faces unreadable beneath their hoods. The flames lighting the path, a river of fire weaving its way towards their destination.

And then, a few feet behind them, came Fiona.

She moved with slow, deliberate grace, her silver-embroidered gown flowing around her like a liquid shadow. The torchlight caught upon the delicate diadem that crowned her brow, giving her an ethereal, almost divine presence.

Beside her walked another woman, presumably Paula, her green robe standing out among the black, her movements stiff with barely concealed tension. She did not belong among them, and she knew it. Yet, she moved forward, her face carefully composed, every muscle in her body trained to mask the unease curling in her stomach.

Just behind them, two figures walked under close guard. Mark and Sam.

Their wrists were bound behind them hindering their ability to tread normally. Two of Abdul's enforcers flanked them on either side, watchful, alert, ready. Mark held his head high, his expression set in quiet defiance, but

Sam's fear showed, a tremor running through her as they stepped onto the path that led to the stone circle.

Arthur sighed. *Soon! Very soon!*

The path wound through the moor, a narrow trail of compacted earth. The torches flickered as the procession made its way deeper into the wild heathland, the light dancing against the surrounding stone formations. The further they walked, the stronger the energy in the air became. It was tangible, oppressive, a force insistent against their skin.

The occasional distant hoot of an owl punctuated the silence, but otherwise, the night was still. Too still.

Paula felt her pulse quicken, her instincts screaming at her to turn and run, but she held firmly. She could not falter now, Sam needed her.

Mark exhaled sharply, shifting his bound hands slightly. He caught Sam's eye for a brief second – a fleeting, wordless moment of solidarity.

"Keep walking," one of the guards muttered, nudging Mark forward.

Fiona's cold voice carried over the procession, her tone laced with ceremonial reverence. "Tonight, the veil is thin," she intoned, her voice smooth, unshaken. "Tonight, we stand upon the threshold of power."

The cultists murmured in agreement, their voices weaving together in low, rhythmic tones, a chant beginning to take form as they continued up the gently rising trail.

In the distance a faint eerie glow announced their destination. They reached the crest of the path, and a luminous green halo emerged.

The ancient stone circle was revealed, illuminated by the halo and the torches lining the outer edges. The vast bonfire near the centre had yet to be lit, but its carefully arranged wood and kindling stood ready to roar to life.

The procession entered the circle. The low murmurs of incantations began to ripple through the gathering, a chant that rose and fell with hypnotic rhythm.

A thick, cruel energy filled the air, something old and hungry stirring just beyond the veil of the physical world.

At the forefront of the gathering, Abdul stood poised. He raised a hand, and the chanting fell into silence.

With slow, deliberate steps, Fiona advanced, the moonlight catching the delicate crown upon her brow. Her face was serene, yet her eyes glowed with a zealot's devotion, drinking in the energy of the night, the power of the moment.

Beside her, Paula moved carefully. She could feel the weight of the gazes upon her, expectant, reverent, waiting. She was supposed to revel in this, to embrace the path Fiona had set before her – but her every instinct screamed danger. Yet, she again forced herself to conceal her disquiet, her expression composed. She had come too far to break now.

Behind them, Mark and Sam were forced to their knees, their hands still bound behind them. The guards flanking them remained motionless, their faces impassive, but the tension in their stance was undeniable. Even they were not immune to the growing dread in the air.

Worsley had yet to arrive. The moment stretched, the silence now a living thing, heavy and expectant.

Then Abdul lifted a ceremonial torch, stepping forward. His deep, throaty voice cut through the stillness. "Let the fire be kindled. Let the veil be torn. Let the darkness come forth."

With a flourish, he cast the flame onto the waiting bonfire.

For a heartbeat, there was nothing – just the soft crackle of kindling catching light, a faint wisp of smoke curling into the night. Then, the fire exploded to life.

A towering pillar of flame roared skyward, illuminating the expressions of awe, fear, and devotion reflected in the cultists' eyes. Shadows danced wildly across the standing stones, twisting and contorting as though something unseen lurked within them.

The chanting resumed, now louder, more fevered. The Sabbat had begun.

Up on Hebdon Tor, Dougal adjusted his position, rotating between his night vision binoculars, regular ones and the naked eye, now that the roaring bonfire cast an unnatural glow across the stone circle.

He had already located Mark, Sam, and Paula. Physically, they seemed unharmed, but their wary glances and body language betrayed their growing dread. Dougal's grip tightened on his rifle.

Still, Worsley had not arrived.

A heavy sense of expectation filled the air. The moment was close.

Arthur crouched low behind the stone cairn, just outside the circle, his breath shallow. He had followed the procession from Trevaunce Manor, though he had been forced to take a rougher route, skirting the torches and cutting across the treacherous, uneven moorland.

The effort had been worth it. From his position, he had a clear view of the gathering. The hooded assembly formed a ring of shadowed figures, their faces illuminated in flickering bursts as the flames danced in the wind.

At the centre of the circle, the altar stood ready, its obsidian surface reflecting the firelight like a dark mirror. The tall stake, driven deep into the ground near the altar, remained empty – for now.

Arthur tensed, fingers tightening around his concealed pistol. He had seen Mark and Sam, and who he assumed was Paula standing beside Fiona. He had located Abdul, but his main target had yet to arrive. Arthur's pulse raced. Everything hinged on Worsley's arrival.

A sudden shift in the energy rippled through the air. The figures stirred, their chanting dying away, replaced by hushed reverence. Something was coming.

Then, the flames of the bonfire wavered, the heat distorting the air above it. A deep, unnatural silence settled over the circle. And then he appeared.

At first, it was only an aura, a pulsing distortion in the air, as though the very fabric of reality bent to accommodate his arrival. Then, with an eerie slowness, a shape emerged within the fire itself – a figure draped in flowing crimson robes, his face hidden beneath a gold embroidered black hood, drifting towards the altar.

Sir Giles Worsley materialized upon the altar, standing motionless, his arms outstretched. His form seemed to hover for an instant, before he took a deliberate step forward, planting himself firmly before his gathered disciples.

The cultists gasped, their voices rising in awed devotion. A chant broke out, whispered at first, then it grew louder.

"Hail Lord! Master of the Veil! Keeper of the Path! He who commands the Watchers!"

Worsley pulled back his hood, revealing his face, his eyes burning with something beyond human comprehension.

A slow smile curled across his lips as he took in the sight before him – his faithful, their eyes wide with adoration, their bodies trembling with anticipation. They hung on his every movement, every breath, the sheer force of his presence holding them in rapture. This was power. Not the kind wielded by kings or ministers, but something greater, something ancient and absolute. They had come seeking purpose, enlightenment, and he had given it to them. And now, they were his.

The chant swelled, reverberating through the cold night air, each voice a thread in the grand tapestry of devotion that he had so meticulously woven over the years. They believed, utterly and without question, that they stood on the precipice of revelation, that tonight they would witness the opening of the threshold, the tearing of the veil between this world and the next. And they were right.

Worsley inhaled deeply, savouring the charged energy that crackled through the air. The convergence was near; he could feel it, could taste the thinning of the barriers between realms. He had spent years preparing for this moment, unearthing lost rites, gathering the chosen, readying the sacred altar upon which the offering would be made. He had sacrificed much – oh, so much – to bring about this night.

His hands lifted as if to grasp the very fabric of the unseen forces that churned around them. A shiver ran through the assembly, their bodies swaying as if caught in the pull of an unseen tide. They were ready. They would do whatever he commanded.

And soon, so would Baal.

His voice deepened, reverberating with the weight of prophecy. "The veil is thin. The time is upon us. Let the offering be brought forth."

⋘ ⋙

Arthur gritted his teeth, muscles coiled, poised to strike.

⋘ ⋙

On Hebdon Tor, Dougal exhaled slowly, finger hovering over the trigger.

⋘ ⋙

Mark and Sam stared ahead, their eyes widening in horror.

The crackling fire cast towering shadows upon the standing stones, illuminating the sea of black-robed figures gathered in a perfect ring. Their whispered chants wove through the night, their voices growing stronger as the moment of sacrifice drew near.

Sir Giles Worsley descended gradually from the altar, his crimson robes fluid behind him. Mark and Sam struggled fiercely as Abdul and the guards dragged them forward, but resistance was useless.

Mark was hauled to the stake, his wrist ties were cut free before his arms were yanked backward and tied, the rough rope biting into his wrists. His breath came in sharp bursts as he strained against his bindings, but the knots were too tight, too precise.

Sam kicked and thrashed, her screams piercing the chanting, but the cultists did not waver. Her wrist ties were severed and Abdul's brutal hands ripped away her robe, exposing her bared flesh to the night air. She was lifted onto the altar, her arms and legs pinned down by tight leather straps.

Paula stood frozen, her heart hammering as she watched.

Beside her, Fiona leaned in, her voice low, almost reverent. "Tonight, Circe, you will embrace your destiny." She pressed something cold and heavy into Paula's trembling hands. *The sacrificial knife.*

Fiona curled her fingers around Paula's, pushing the dagger firmly into her grasp. "Take your place at the altar," she murmured. "You have been given the greatest honour."

Paula felt the bile rise in her throat. This was the moment she'd been dreading.

Worsley further raised his arms to the sky, his fingers splayed wide, as though grasping for something unseen. His voice deepened, the ancient words rolling from his tongue in a guttural chant that reverberated through the circle, thick with command and reverence.

His disciples followed, their voices swelling in unholy harmony, their fervour manifesting in wild, ecstatic cries. The fire at the centre of the arena flared violently, tongues of flame licking hungrily at the sky as if answering the call. Shadows stretched and writhed, twisting into grotesque shapes, as though something beyond the mortal plane was pressing against the barrier of reality.

The wind surged, unnatural and howling, cutting through the gathered figures like a blade of ice. The very air thickened, oppressive, charged with an unspeakable presence. Overhead, the stars blinked out one by one, swallowed by an encroaching void that spiralled outward from the altar. The night itself seemed to recoil, as if recognizing the approach of something far older, far greater than the world it sought to enter.

Worsley's chant reached its crescendo, his voice rising to a fevered pitch. His eyes burned with unnatural light, his body trembling not with fear, but with ecstasy. He was the conduit. The chosen.

A tremor rolled through the ground, deep and resonant, as if the earth itself protested against the breach being forced upon it. The fire roared higher still, its embers spinning upward into a swirling vortex. Then…

A crack of sound, deafening, shattering the night.

The wind stopped. The flames froze mid-motion. The world seemed to hold its breath.

Then, from the centre of the vortex, a shape began to emerge, vast and terrible. A darkness deeper than the void, wreathed in smouldering light, its form shifting between monstrous and divine. A low, rumbling growl echoed through the space – not heard with ears, but felt in the bones, in the soul.

The air itself recoiled in reverence. *Baal!*

Its grotesque form materialized high above them, terrifying to behold. A monstrous, hulking shape, its skin blackened and cracked like molten rock, its glowing eyes pits of endless craving. Its horns curved upward, above a face that was both horrific and yet somehow godly.

The devotees fell to their knees, their previous confidence shattered into trembling awe. Even Worsley's face was pale, his lips curling into something that teetered between triumph and dread.

He bowed his head and spoke.

"Mighty Baal, we honour thee. Accept this sacrifice, gifted to you in dedication."

Baal's massive gaze swept over the altar, over Sam's helpless form, over the assembled figures below him.

Mark fought harder, his fury igniting something within him, but the ropes held fast. He could feel power coursing through him, raw and unrefined, but it wasn't enough.

Fiona nudged Paula forward. "Do it. Make the offering. Do it Circe, do it!"

Paula shuddered and shook her head defiantly. "No. I will not!"

The ritual faltered.

Fiona's face twisted in fury. She snatched the dagger from Paula's grasp, her eyes wild with fervour. "Then I will!"

She raised the blade high above Sam's chest.

Mark screamed, "I love you, Sam!"

Moments before, Arthur Parker erupted from his hiding place, gun in hand, sprinting towards the altar, stopping behind Abdul. He squeezed the trigger, and the blast was deafening. A spray of crimson burst from Abdul's forehead, his body collapsing instantly.

Simultaneously, on Hebdon Tor, Dougal took the shot before the knife could strike, and Fiona's head snapped backward, her lifeless body thudding to the ground beside the altar.

Arthur continued charging through the chaos, his pistol raised, his face a mask of vengeance. "This is for Joan, you bastard!" he roared, emptying his clip into Worsley's chest.

The bullets never reached him. Each impact vanished into thin air, absorbed by an invisible forcefield that rippled like distorted glass.

Worsley's face contorted with rage. With a snarl, he snapped his hands forward like claws, seizing Arthur by the throat. "You insignificant worm!" Worsley spat, his eyes burning with supernatural fury. "You dare challenge me?"

Arthur gasped, his body convulsing. Blood streamed from his nose, mouth, and eyes, torrents of crimson pouring as his veins blackened under Worsley's grip. His screams grew weaker, his struggles fading – until his limp, bloodied body dropped.

High overhead, Baal raged, his wrath splitting the heavens. The air trembled as his fury mounted, his roars so powerful that the ground quaked beneath them.

Dougal, on Hebdon Tor, took another shot, knowing it was futile.

Worsley felt the bullet absorb into his familiar. A sniper. He sneered. Then, with a breath that reeked of brimstone, he released Flauros.

The demon oozed from Worsley's torso, its twisted, cloaked form emerging like a monstrous parasite. Its glowing green aura flickered wildly, its grotesque, dwarf-like features twisting into a hateful grin as it turned its gaze toward Hebdon Tor. With a snarl, it shot into the sky, accelerating towards the sniper's position.

James moved swiftly. Flauros was gone. Worsley was vulnerable.

Paula had freed Sam, throwing a robe over her. The two of them edged further from the altar, reluctant to leave Mark behind.

Above them, Baal's fury was boundless. His roars ripped through the air, cracking reality itself. No sacrifice had been made, and the god's wrath burned hotter than the fire now raining down from the heavens. Thunderbolts split the sky, the acrid scent of ozone thick in the air. The black-robed acolytes shrieked in terror, their devotion collapsing into blind panic. They fled into the night, knowing their god's vengeance would be swift and merciless.

Worsley turned, in a terrible rage, his eyes locking onto Mark. "You! You and that wretched bitch have ruined everything. Now you die!"

A sudden chill swept through the air.

James revealed himself.

Worsley froze. His face twisted in disbelief. "No," he breathed. "That's impossible. You're dead. Abaddon took you."

James's ghostly form solidified, his expression dark, vengeful. "You supposed I was dead. That was the plan. But you failed, Worsley. You failed."

For the first time, Worsley hesitated. Uncertainty flickered in his eyes.

James advanced, his spectral form pulsing with ethereal energy. "You didn't kill me, Worsley. You only made me stronger. And now you'll answer for everything."

Worsley recoiled, stepping back. "You can't touch me!" he snarled, raising his hands. But his power wavered, his control slipping. The demonic tether that had shielded him was gone.

James sneered. "I don't need to."

"Now, Mark! James says NOW!" Paula screamed.

Mark concentrated on Worsley, pure hatred in his eyes. He turned his mind inward, gathering every ounce of his power, now magnified by the underlying energy of the stone circle. He reached right inside Worsley's skull and squeezed.

Worsley's mouth opened in a silent shriek. His hands clawed at the air, his entire body convulsing. His eyes bulged, blood vessels bursting. A guttural gurgle escaped his lips as his brain was crushed from within.

He crumpled to the ground, lifeless.

Worsley was dead.

James stood over Worsley's body, his expression unreadable. Just a short while longer and then he could leave.

Paula rushed to Mark's side and cut his ropes with the knife. He ran to Sam and held her tight, whispering "We did it! We killed him."

The crack in the earth widened revealing an unholy glow.

Dougal, still poised at Hebdon Tor, froze as Flauros, now untethered from Worsley, turned its attention to him. The demon hurtled toward him at breakneck speed, its dwarf, hooded form wreathed in unholy green fire obscuring any vision of Worsley. There was no way to take a second shot. He grabbed the radio and shouted, "Go, go!"

Dougal, in mortal fear for his soul, braced himself, his pulse roaring in his ears.

Then, suddenly, inexplicably Flauros stopped.

It tilted its hideous head, cackled gleefully, then turned back toward the stone circle.

Something had changed.

Trevaunce Manor – 12:30 AM

The ex-army transport truck thundered along the road, its engine growling as it hurtled toward the gates of Trevaunce Manor. Reinforced bars jutted from its front bumper.

Inside, five mercenaries gripped their weapons, their bodies tensed for impact. "Brace!" shouted the driver.

The truck slammed into the double gates, the metal groaning and squealing as they buckled inward, hinges snapping under the force. The gates shattered open, debris clattering across the gravel driveway.

Immediately, alarms blared through the estate, piercing the night air.

The truck screeched to a halt, and the back burst open. Five figures leapt down in swift succession, each armed with automatic rifles, their movements precise, disciplined.

From the small guardhouse near the manor entrance, a group of armed enforcers rushed out, their expressions flickering between aggression and panic.

One raised a handgun.

A single crack of gunfire split the air. The mercenary's bullet struck home, dropping the guard before he could even squeeze the trigger.

The remaining guards froze, their courage dissolving. One hesitated, then threw his weapon to the ground. The others followed, hands raised in surrender, their faces pale.

A mercenary stepped forward, rifle levelled. "Which way to the stone circle?"

One of the guards swallowed hard. "You won't be able to drive there. Go to the end of the drive – look for the torchlit trail. Follow it on foot."

The mercenary nodded, then barked. "Right – get lost. We don't want to see you here when we come back."

The guards didn't need to be told twice. They turned and bolted out of the shattered gateway and into the darkness.

The squad reloaded, checked their gear, then piled back into the truck. The engine revved once more, and they sped up the driveway.

They skidded to a halt, disembarked and quickly found the torchlit trail winding through the moorland. No words were needed. They fell into formation and took the trail, their movements silent, swift, efficient – a well-trained strike team closing in on their target.

The Stone Circle – 12:30 AM

The crack yawned wider, a profane chasm splitting the earth, vomiting fire and smoke as the Gates of Hell gaped open. The altar crumbled, swallowed by the infernal maw, the bodies of Fiona and Abdul vanishing with it into the searing abyss.

Baal's descent was slow, deliberate, his massive form wreathed in shadow and flame. His bellows of fury shook the night, a raw, primal rage that echoed across the heavens. No blood had been spilled in his honour. His unrequited wrath was boundless, his vengeance absolute. Lightning flared from his outstretched hands, striking the ruins around him, his fury branding the world itself with his displeasure as he sank back to hell.

Paula gasped as Worsley's astral form wrenched free from his lifeless body, his spectral face twisted in triumph. Until he saw the grinning creature that emerged out of the darkness. Flauros! The demon's jagged teeth gleamed as it lunged, eyes brimming with malevolent delight. Worsley twisted in horror, his spectral limbs flailing, his mouth open in a silent, useless plea.

Then, from the depths of the abyss, Abaddon rose. Monstrous. Immutable. Power radiated from his terrible form, a force of pure and unrelenting destiny. Behind him came others – nameless, hideous things with grasping claws and gluttonous eyes, their shrieks a chorus of unending dissonance.

Abaddon extended one colossal claw, and Worsley's wailing soul was seized, his shrieks rising to a frenzied, piercing pitch. Claws sank into him, rending his spirit, tearing away whatever arrogance or power he had once held. He was nothing now. Nothing but terrified, tortured prey for all eternity.

The demons howled in triumph as they dragged him downward, his screams dwindling as the abyss swallowed him whole. The flames surged higher for one final moment – then the pit began to close, the earth slowly sealing itself over the horror, smothering the echoes of Worsley's endless torment.

Paula gasped as James appeared beside her, steady as ever. "He's in hell now," he said, his voice in her head quiet but firm. "Forever tormented by every demon he ever dared to summon."

For a moment, in the glow of the dying embers, a figure lingered – Lilith. Her gaze was unreadable, but there was something knowing in her eyes. "You have done well, Circe," she murmured, her voice soft as the whisper of the departing flames. "Now take your friends and go." Then she was gone.

The silence that followed was immense, resounding in its finality. The ground was whole again, the lifeless body of Worsley and the bloodied corpse of Arthur, the sole grisly reminders of what had passed. But the scars of what had happened here would never fade.

Paula turned, her breath catching as James lingered. No one else could see him. Only her. She swallowed hard. "You're still here," she whispered.

Mark and Sam turned to her, puzzled. "Who are you talking to?" Sam asked.

Paula wet her lips, composing herself. "James," she said softly. "He's still here."

Mark's expression was unreadable, but he nodded slowly. "What's he saying?"

Paula turned back to James, his translucent form shimmering in the fading moonlight. "He wanted to make sure we were safe."

James gave her a small, knowing smile. "You did it, Paula. You saved them all."

Her throat tightened. "So did you."

James smile widened. "They can't hear me, but tell them this… They have succeeded against insurmountable odds. Mark killed Worsley using the power he denied for so long. They all showed incredible courage. I'm proud of all of them."

Paula exhaled and relayed his words. Mark looked up, while Sam wrapped an arm around Paula's shoulders. "Tell him I'm proud of him, too," she murmured, "and I'll always love him."

Mark said. "Thank you, brother. You were instrumental in our success. I miss you terribly."

James inclined his head, his smile tinged with sadness. "It's time, Paula."

She swallowed hard, fighting the lump in her throat. "I don't want you to go."

His ghostly fingers brushed near her arm, though she could not feel the touch. "You don't have to say goodbye," he said gently. "I'll always be with you. Watching."

Paula closed her eyes, inhaling sharply. "He says he'll always be with us," she told the others.

James looked up, the pull of the spheres strengthening. He hesitated for only a moment longer, his gaze sweeping over them one last time. "I'll see you again," he whispered to himself. He began rising, happy in the knowledge that Mark and Sam had found each other. They would be alright.

Paula watched as he began to rise, his form ascending, drawn toward the golden brilliance above. He drifted higher, past the darkness, past the pain, past everything that had ever held him down. As he was embraced by the light, peace unlike anything he had ever known surrounded him. James Benedict was finally free.

The mercenary team advanced cautiously through the ruined grounds, their boots crunching over scorched earth and shattered stone. The night still pulsed with an unnatural energy, the air thick with the remnants of something vast and terrible. The firelight had died, leaving only the ghostly glow of the moon filtering through the dissipating smoke.

None of them spoke. They had witnessed enough. More than enough.

Sergeant Holloway swallowed hard, his grip tightening on his rifle as he scanned the remnants of the arena. His men, hardened troops all, moved with the hesitancy of those who had glimpsed something they did not, and could not understand. The echoes of unearthly rage still rang in their ears, though whatever had uttered them had now fallen silent.

"Jesus Christ," one of the men muttered, his voice barely above a whisper, "what the hell happened here!"

The ground was blackened, the earth still warm beneath their feet. and the air seemed wrong – warped, humming with residual force. There were scattered remnants of robes and ritual paraphernalia, the wearers having long since fled.

In the dim moonlight, Holloway spotted them. Three figures, slouching in the centre of the circle where the altar once stood. Two bodies lay on the ground near them.

His team closed in warily, as though half-expecting the earth to split open beneath them.

"Dougal sent us." Holloway said. "He'll be waiting for you at the house."

He gestured to his men who led them away. He hesitated just a moment longer, his gaze wandering to the dark stain of reality left in the wake of something… , something he didn't want to know. He had been in war zones. He had seen what men were capable of. But this – this had been something else entirely. He left the bodies where they were, and followed the rest of his team, eager to leave this god-forsaken place.

Chapter 53

Aftershock

Paula's Flat, Bushey, London – 1 May, 1:30 PM
Paula woke with a start, her breath catching in her throat. For a moment, she wasn't sure where she was – her mind still trapped in the flickering images of firelight, whispered incantations, and the oppressive presence of something inhuman pressing down on her. Then reality set in. She was in her bed. In Bushey. The faint glow of the early morning sun filtered through the curtains, painting soft, harmless shadows on the walls. She exhaled shakily, pressing a hand to her forehead. It was over. For now.

They had left Mark and Sam at Abingdon Grove in the early hours, the sky hinting at dawn, then driven in near silence back to her temporary flat. Doogie, unwilling to leave her, had unceremoniously claimed the sofa, insisting he wasn't about to let her wake up alone after what they had been through. She had been too exhausted to argue.

Lying there, she let her mind drift back to the events of the night before. The ritual, the danger, the sheer weight of what had almost happened. She felt hollow, drained, yet at the same time, an odd sense of accomplishment settled in her chest. Mark had killed Worsley. Fiona and Abdul were gone, but, except for poor Arthur and Joan, they had made it through. Barely. But what came next? Could she simply return to the old life of Paula Reynolds, act as if she hadn't walked the edge of something dark and terrible? She wasn't sure. She wasn't sure she wanted to.

Her thoughts drifted to James. The connection they had shared was unlike anything she had ever experienced – an intimacy beyond the physical, one bound by energy, thought, and the veil between life and death. He had been her guide, her confidant. Would he still linger, now that this part of their journey was over? The thought of losing him entirely made her chest ache in a way she wasn't ready to confront.

Then there was Nick. She had barely had time to process his death when everything had begun spiralling. Now, in the quiet of her flat, she allowed herself to grieve. He had been avenged – they had all made sure of that – but it didn't bring him back. Nothing would. But maybe, just maybe, knowing that his killers had paid the price was enough to let his spirit rest. Maybe, in time, it would be enough for her too. She imagined Doogie was grieving too. He had felt the loss of his friend as much as she had. The scars would take a long time to heal.

Sighing, she pushed back the duvet, put on her dressing gown and padded towards the kitchen. The scent of instant coffee and toast told her Doogie was already awake.

Dougal sat at the small kitchen table, nursing a mug of coffee and staring absently at the fading scars on his knuckles. He felt like he'd aged ten years in the past few weeks. He had seen action before, had stared down the barrel of a gun more than once in his time, but this? This was different. This wasn't war, or terrorism, or the kind of violence he had trained for. This was something else entirely, something that gnawed at the edges of reality and made a man question everything he thought he knew. He had been within an inch of losing his life in an unspeakable way, but the death of Worsley had halted the demon which had turned back to join the demons casting Worsley's spirit into hell! He had Mark to thank for that.

He had volunteered for this mission the moment he heard Nick's name. A chance to settle old debts, to stand for his friend when he no longer could. And now? Now it was done. The bastards responsible were either dead or wished they were, and justice – such as it was – had been served. But it didn't bring Nick back. It didn't fill the gap his friend had left or erase the ache in his chest knowing they'd never share another drink, another laugh. Avenging him had been necessary, but it wasn't enough. It never would be.

And then there was Paula.

At first, he had just wanted to look out for her because Nick had cared for her. But now? Now it was different. She wasn't just some woman his best mate had loved – she was someone he respected; someone he admired. She was brave. She was strong, but even the toughest needed someone watching their back. And as long as he had breath in his body, he intended to be that person. He wouldn't let her face this alone, not now, not ever.

Hearing soft footsteps, he glanced up to see Paula enter the kitchen, her hair mussed from sleep, her expression unreadable. He gestured towards the kettle. "Tea or coffee?"

She nodded, sliding into the seat across from him. "Could murder a cup of tea."

They sat in silence as he poured hot water over the teabags, the steam curling lazily between them. Finally, Paula spoke. "So, what now?" she asked, wrapping her hands around the mug he placed in front of her.

Doogie shrugged, leaning back in his chair. "Reckon we try and get back to normal. Or at least pretend to."

She snorted a quiet laugh. "Normal. Not sure I even remember what that looks or feels like."

He studied her for a long moment before speaking. "You did good, you know. Last night. All of it."

Paula looked down at her tea, swirling it absently. "Doesn't feel like it."

"Yeah, well. That's how it always is after the adrenaline fades. You start second-guessing everything. But we got through it. Except for poor Arthur, we all got through it. That counts for something."

She met his gaze, something vulnerable flickering in her eyes before she nodded. "Thanks for staying."

"Anytime." He drained the last of his coffee and stood, stretching. "Come on, let's get moving. Sitting around stewing in it won't do either of us any favours."

Paula sighed but stood as well. "Back to normal it is, then."

They both knew it was a lie, but for now, it was one they were willing to tell themselves.

Abingdon Grove, London – 3 May, 10:15 AM

The morning sun spilled through the tall bay windows. The faint hum of city life beyond the glass was a distant, muffled contrast to the harrowing silence that had followed them from Trevaunce Manor.

Mark and Sam sat in the drawing room, each nursing a cup of coffee, though neither had truly tasted it. The rich aroma hung in the air, yet it did little to ease the lingering unease that settled between them like an invisible load.

The battle was over, but peace had not fully arrived.

Sam's fingers idly traced the rim of her cup. Her eyes were heavy, rimmed with exhaustion that sleep had only partly relieved. Her body still ached from days of torment, but the deeper wounds were unseen.

Mark sat across from her, legs crossed, his hand resting against his chin. His gaze was distant, but his body hummed with restrained tension.

Survival. It should have felt like victory, yet neither of them could bring themselves to feel anything other than the quiet, creeping hollowness that came after experiencing hell and the sad demise of Arthur.

They had been spirited away under cover of darkness, whisked away by the mercenary extraction team hours before the first hints of dawn had kissed the moor.

As Trevaunce Manor receded behind them, Mark and Sam held hands in the rear seats of the land rover while Paula sat alongside Dougal who was driving. They were all experiencing the weight of what they had just done.

They had left behind a single note, pinned to the remains of the estate's iron gates – a cold, factual message detailing Joan Summers' final resting place in the well. There was no need for further explanation. The police would arrive, and the truth, or at least a portion of it, would surface.

By dawn on May Day, they had been dropped off at their respective homes.

She had bathed for almost an hour, scrubbing away the grime of Trevaunce, as if she could somehow wash away the past week, erase the horrors that still clawed at the edges of her consciousness.

And then she had slept – deep, dreamless, and mercifully silent.

When she awoke, Mark was there, waiting. They had gone for a meal, finding some small comfort in the simplicity of normalcy – the clinking of glasses, the hum of conversation, the warmth of a meal that didn't taste like ash and fear. A one sad, emotional moment arose when they toasted the memory of Arthur and Joan. *At least they are together now*, Sam had murmured.

As they walked back, hand in hand, the world started to feel real again.

By the time they stepped through the apartment door, Mark had wrapped her in his arms, and she had kissed him – desperately, fiercely, needing to feel something other than numbness.

She had led him to the guest bedroom, unwilling to step into the main bedroom she had shared with James. That night, they found solace in each other, in the quiet understanding that neither needed words to explain what they had been through.

The next day had been a whirlwind of closure and loose ends. They had met with Colonel Turner, expressing their gratitude, settling accounts for the arrangements that had secured their escape.

Then came the visit to James' solicitor. The significance of James' absence had never felt more real than when the solicitor had spoken of his will and his remaining estate. "Until he is officially declared missing, presumed dead," the man had said solemnly, "his will cannot be finalised. However, I can tell you that both of you are the sole beneficiaries and Mr. Benedict made significant financial transfers to Mrs. Benedict before his departure."

Sam had nodded, but the words had barely registered. She didn't care about the money. She cared that James was gone, and that some part of her had lost him long before his death.

Later that evening, she and Mark had found comfort in one another again. This time, it was not about passion or escape, but about belonging, about reminding themselves that they had made it through the dark and into the light.

Now, as they sat waiting in the apartment, the clock ticking softly in the background, they both knew this would be their last gathering before departure. Tickets from Heathrow to Norfolk, Virginia had already been booked for tomorrow.

Dougal and Paula would be here soon, and then – it would be over. For the first time, there were no plans left to make, no battle strategies to form, no more dark forces to outmanoeuvre.

It should have been a relief. But instead, it felt like standing on the edge of the unknown.

Mark glanced at Sam. "Are we really going to be, okay?" he asked quietly.

Sam took a long sip of coffee, then set it down, exhaling slowly. "I think," she said at last, "we just have to keep moving forward."

The doorbell rang.

Mark stood, glancing toward the entrance. "They're here."

Sam nodded, steeling herself. It was time to say goodbye.

Epilogue

Virginia Beach – Five Years Later

The warm, salt-tinged breeze swept through the open kitchen window as Sam stood at the sink, watching her children laugh and chase each other across the wide expanse of their backyard. The late afternoon sunlight shimmered on the waters of Long Creek, which curved lazily around their home on Bay Island, separating them from First Landing State Park beyond.

A light splash caught her attention – a fish jumped by Mark's pride and joy, his 28ft Grady White fishing boat, currently sitting on its lift to the side of the property. He loved that boat, whether he was fishing in Chesapeake Bay or dolphin watching or merely using it for pleasure cruises around Broad Bay with his family and friends. She knew his heart was at peace when he was sailing her.

Sam smiled to herself. Five years. It felt like another lifetime.

Behind her, the soft thud of footsteps announced Mark's arrival. His arms slid effortlessly around her waist, and she leaned into him, the warmth of his embrace as familiar as the setting sun. She turned, lifting her face to his. "How was your day, honey?"

Mark pressed a gentle kiss to her lips, his fingers tracing absent circles against her hip. "You know… same old, same old."

Sam chuckled and turned back to the sink. "Let me fix you a drink."

"A tea will be fine." He peered through the window, his gaze settling on the two bounding figures outside. "How are the kids?"

"Great," she replied, flicking the kettle on. "Playing well together as usual."

Mark watched their son, James, chase after his younger sister, Paula, his protective instincts always evident. Though only four years old, he had taken naturally to the role of big brother and mentor, a bond forged in the unbreakable magic of childhood.

Sam had become pregnant shortly after they had returned to the States, and the arrival of James Benedict Jr., followed two years later by Paula, had filled their lives with light, laughter, and a joy so deep it had driven away the shadows of Trevaunce Manor forever.

Mark had returned to academia, now holding a prestigious Chair at ODU, balancing his intellectual pursuits with his passion for the children and his boat.

Sam, for her part, had chosen a different path — one of quiet contentment, of full-time motherhood, of ensuring that their children never knew the kind of horrors she and Mark had faced.

It was a good life.

After James Benedict Sr. was officially declared deceased, Mark and Sam had married in a small, private ceremony, not out of necessity, but out of the deep love and gratitude that had grown between them.

With James's estate finally settled, Sam had inherited the apartment in Abingdon Grove, but she had never truly felt it belonged to her. Instead, she had gifted it to Paula, who had carved out her own happiness across the Atlantic.

Paula had found her own family with Dougal — Doogie, as she affectionately called him. Now Mr. and Mrs. Finlayson, they had built a new life together, raising their son, Nicholas — Nick, who was nearly two years old.

Paula had sold the Abingdon Grove residence, using the proceeds to purchase a home in Wallingford, nestled along the banks of the River Thames. With Dougal by her side, she had stepped into a new chapter — co-owning a successful Private Investigation firm, thriving in a world where both of their skills, resilience, and sharp intuition could be used.

And soon, she would be here. In just two weeks, Paula and Dougal would be arriving in Virginia Beach, their much-anticipated vacation together finally at hand. Mark had been counting the days, eager to take Dougal out on the open water, to share in the simple joys of fishing, of companionship that did not come with life-and-death stakes.

In the middle of their visit, Mark had booked them all a week at a beach house in Duck, in the Outer Banks of North Carolina, where the four of them would relax, reminisce, and finally lay to rest any lingering ghosts.

Outside, Mark had now joined the children, his deep laughter carrying on the wind as he playfully dodged their attempts to tackle him. Sam leaned against the doorframe, her arms crossed, watching as they ran across the yard, feet pounding against the lush grass. She strolled across and joined them.

Then, in a moment of innocent exuberance, James kicked the ball too hard.

Sam's eyes followed as the ball sailed over the fence, landing with a soft splash and drifting away in the waters of Long Creek.

Paula's face crumbled instantly, her lower lip trembling, on the verge of tears.

James's little hand landed reassuringly on her shoulder, his face calm, almost knowing.

Then, the impossible happened. The ball lifted.

At first, it barely skimmed the surface, a bead of water trailing off as it hovered above the ripples. Then, slowly, steadily, it drifted back over the fence, floating gently to the ground at Paula's feet. Paula clapped her hands and laughed in delight. James turned, his bright eyes locking onto Sam and Mark. He smiled knowingly.

Sam drew a breath. Mark's hand tightened around hers. They said nothing.

There was no fear, no alarm — just a silent understanding, a whisper of something ancient and eternal flowing through the air. Their son had inherited something beyond their world.

And yet, as Sam watched James and Paula return to their game, laughing as though nothing extraordinary had happened, she felt nothing but peace. The past no longer had a hold on them.

They had found their future. And it was beautiful.

⚬⟨⟩⚬

Acknowledgements

As noted in the Foreword, this novel owes its deepest creative debt to the late *Dennis Wheatley*, whose thrilling tales of the occult first lit the fire beneath this work. I dedicate *The Devil's Magus* to his memory – and to the enduring power of dark imagination.

My sincere thanks go to my daughter Sarah, who, despite the relentless demands of raising my grandchildren singlehandedly, found time to review my drafts, sharpen my grammar, and challenge me to deepen character, dialogue, and flow. Her insights, dedication and encouragement were instrumental.

Warm gratitude also to my dear friend Tina, in Hampton, Virginia, for her unwavering support, enthusiastic encouragement and sharp editorial eye. Her observations helped shape the narrative's tone and rhythm.

A special tribute must be paid to my loyal companion, Sam, a black Labrador of extraordinary heart and patience. From the day he arrived as a boisterous puppy in early 2011 to his peaceful passing in March 2024, he never left my side. Our long walks beside the Lynher River, across the wild bones of Bodmin Moor, and along Cornwall's rugged cliffs and beaches brought not only joy and solace, but the perfect moments for story creation.

I extend my appreciation to Amy and the team at White Magic Studios, whose care and professionalism made the publication journey a seamless one. Their experience was evident at every step.

I would also like to acknowledge the vast, mysterious labyrinth that is the internet – where even the darkest lore awaits rediscovery. Various online resources, from digital archives to mythological compendia, proved invaluable in grounding the supernatural with the plausible and enriching the story's imaginative reach.

Lastly – and above all – my heartfelt thanks to Gillian, my wife of many decades, whose tolerance for my long absences (mental, rather than physical) has been nothing short of heroic. As I wandered through ancient rites, infernal visions, and arcane mysteries, she held the real world together with fortitude and grace. Gill, you are – and always will be – the most magical chapter of all.

Marius Creed

June 2025

Disclaimer:

This novel draws upon real-world occult and mystical traditions, including Kabbalah, Thelema, and various esoteric philosophies. However, the rituals, symbols, and doctrines presented herein have been fictionalised, adapted, or reimagined for narrative effect. No part of this work is intended as a guide, endorsement, or accurate depiction of any specific spiritual practice. Rather, these elements serve to enrich the imaginative atmosphere of the story – a place where mystery, metaphor, and myth intertwine.

9 781835 387870